Hands shaking, Mia sprayed the water vigorously, but there was simply not enough flow to combat the hungry fire.

She retreated to the front porch, skin stinging from the poisonous air.

Dallas appeared at the upstairs window. He shouted something to Mia, but she could not understand. The fire was nearly upon her; heat scalded her face and hands, smoke filling her lungs. She backed farther away, praying the fire engine would arrive soon to douse the flames.

Finally, Dallas came out carrying Cora and led Mia away from the burning house.

Mia put her mouth to the woman's cheek, praying for a reassuring puff of air. Panic swirled through her veins as she felt nothing at all. Starting CPR, she pressed her hands to Cora's chest.

"Come on, Cora," she said. "You're not going to leave me now."

Dallas dropped to his knees and performed the rescue breaths at the end of her compression cycles. After a full minute, Dallas checked her pulse.

He shook his head.

Tears trickled down Mia's cheeks as she began the next cycle.

Dana Mentink
and
Liz Shoaf

High-Stakes Investigation

Previously published as *Flood Zone* and *Betrayed Birthright*

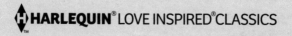

 LOVE INSPIRED BOOKS

Recycling programs for this product may not exist in your area.

ISBN-13: 978-1-335-06128-7

High-Stakes Investigation

Copyright © 2019 by Harlequin Books S.A.

First published as Flood Zone by Harlequin Books in 2014 and Betrayed Birthright by Harlequin Books in 2017.

The publisher acknowledges the copyright holders of the individual works as follows:

Flood Zone
Copyright © 2014 by Dana Mentink

Betrayed Birthright
Copyright © 2017 by Liz Phelps

www.Harlequin.com

Printed in U.S.A.

CONTENTS

Dana Mentink is a national bestselling author. She has been honored to win two Carol Awards, a HOLT Medallion and an RT Reviewers' Choice Best Book Award. She's authored more than thirty novels to date for Love Inspired Suspense and Harlequin Heartwarming. Dana loves feedback from her readers. Contact her at danamentink.com.

FLOOD ZONE

Dana Mentink

Trust in the Lord with all your heart;
do not depend on your own understanding.
Seek his will in all you do,
and he will show you which path to take.
—*Proverbs* 3:5–6

To my Mike, who is always there through the floods.

ONE

Forget meeting tonight. Must speak to you and Dallas now. URGENT.

Mia risked another peek at the cell phone screen as she guided her battered Toyota up the steep mountain grade to Cora's country house just after six in the evening. She'd thought Cora's proposed after-hours meeting at the medical clinic where they both worked was odd in the first place. Now the message to cancel. Stranger still. But Cora had been acting oddly, excusing herself to take phone calls, peeping into file folders squirreled away in her desk for weeks. On this particular day, Cora had left at lunch time. Strange.

Her gaze darted to the rearview mirror. Dallas Black drove his truck behind her. Something about the tall, tousle-headed rebel made her stomach flip, no matter how sternly she chided herself.

Look what the last dark-eyed charmer did to you, Mia.

Stuffing that uncomfortable thought back down into the secret place where she kept all her worries, Mia focused on navigating the winding, wet road, finally pulling onto Cora's graveled drive. Dallas got out, long and lean in jeans and a T-shirt, a couple of months overdue for a haircut. Somehow, the hair spidering across his face suited him, refusing to play nicely.

She knew he'd finished patching Cora's roof only the day before, while on break from teaching Search and Rescue classes. He'd been there every weekend for the past month or two working when the rain let up. While Dallas banged on the roof, Mia and her young daughter, Gracie, helped Cora organize closets. Cora insisted the little group take a long dinner break together every evening during which even Juno, Dallas's German Shepherd, got his share of fragrant stew. What Dallas got out of the deal, besides some pocket change and women chatter, she had no clue. Surely, he didn't need the money that badly. *Maybe he's just a nice guy, Mia. Maybe,* her suspicious heart echoed mockingly. *Yeah, and maybe you were happy to see him every weekend just to admire his roofing skills.* Never mind. They were almost done organizing closets, and then she could put Dallas safely out of her thoughts.

The residence was at the back of a large property, a good acre of shrubland screened it from the road. It was cool, the May rain puddling the already saturated ground. It was to be a bad storm season in Colorado, talk of floods coming. It made her long for Florida's mild climate, but she'd never return there. *Ever.*

Juno hopped out, nose twitching.

"Stay out of the mud, dog," Dallas advised.

Mia joined him.

"Ideas regarding what Cora needs to talk about?" he asked.

"No." Mia shook her head. "She's been secretive

lately, spending extra hours at the clinic. I almost got the feeling she might be lying to me about something."

They looked at Juno who had busied himself snuffling through the underbrush until he froze. Mia thought at first that he'd caught the scent of a bird or groundhog. Then she got it, too. The acrid tang of smoke as she took a few steps toward the house.

Dallas sprinted up the drive with Mia right behind him. They cleared the thickly clustered cottonwood trees in time to hear the whoosh of breaking glass when the lower story window exploded. Mia nearly skidded into him as the shards rained down on the muddy ground.

Her mind struggled to process what was happening. He gripped her arms, and she saw the tiny reflected flames burning in his chocolate irises. "Call for help. Keep Juno out."

Mia's hands shook so badly she could barely manage to hold on to both the phone and Juno's collar. The dog was barking furiously, yanking against her restraining arm in an effort to get to his owner. Nearly eighty pounds of muscle, Juno was determined, and he definitely did not see her as the boss.

Frantically, she dialed the emergency number. Tears started in her eyes as she realized she was not getting a signal. The tall Colorado mountain peaks in the distance interfered. She would have to move and see if she could find another spot that would work. Dragging Juno with one hand, she made her way back toward the car. They'd only gotten about ten feet when Juno broke loose from her grasp and ran straight for the burning house.

"Juno, stop!" she yelled. The smoke was now roiling through the downstairs, and she'd lost sight of Dallas. There was no choice but to keep trying to find a place to make the call. Three times she tried before she got a signal.

"Please help," she rasped. "Cora Graham's house on Stick Pine Road is on fire."

The dispatcher gave her a fifteen minute ETA.

Her heart sank. They could both be dead in fifteen minutes. She stowed the phone in her pocket and ran to the front porch where she remembered there was a hose Cora used to water her patches of brilliant snapdragons. The wood of the old house crackled violently, letting loose with a spark every now and then that burned little holes through the fabric of her jacket. One started to smolder, and she slapped a hand to snuff it out. Flames flashed out the first-floor windows. Juno barked furiously, dashing in helpless fits and starts, unsure how to get to his master.

She cranked the hose and squirted the water at the open front door. *Where are you, Dallas?* Inside, the flames had spread through the sitting room, enveloping the oak furniture in crackling orange and yellow. She climbed up the porch steps, dousing the wood with water and forcing her way into the entry, past the spurts of flame.

She sprayed the water vigorously, but there was simply not enough flow to combat the hungry fire. She retreated to the front porch, skin stinging from the poisonous air.

Dallas appeared at the upstairs window. He shouted something to Mia, but she could not understand. The fire was nearly upon her, heat scalded her face and hands, smoke filling her lungs. She backed farther away, praying the fire engine would arrive soon to douse the flames.

There was no welcoming wail of sirens.

She scanned the upper story and once again caught sight of Dallas. He was batting at the flaming curtains with a blanket. She saw a way she could help. Climbing a few feet up an ivy-covered trellis allowed her to stretch the hose far enough that she could train the water on the burning fabric. Dallas jerked in surprise and then disappeared back inside, returning a moment later with Cora in his arms and stepping onto the roof. Mia's heart lodged in her throat as she watched Dallas walking on the precariously pitched shingles with his precious burden.

His feet skidded, and he fell on his back, somehow stopping his slide before he fell over the edge. Mia jumped off the trellis and cast the hose aside. "Here, lower her down to me."

It was an awkward process, but Dallas managed to ease Cora low enough that Mia could grab her around the waist. Staggering under the weight, she tottered backwards until Dallas jumped down and they both carried Cora away from the burning house. Juno raced behind them to a flat spot of grass where they laid the old woman. Dallas ordered the dog to stay.

Mia brushed sooty hair away from Cora's forehead. Her sparkling blue eyes were closed, her mouth, slack. She put her cheek to Cora's mouth, praying for a reassuring puff of air. Panic swirled through her veins as she felt nothing at all. Starting CPR, she pressed her hands to Cora's chest.

"Come on, Cora," she said. "You're not going to leave me now."

Dallas dropped to his knees and performed the rescue breaths at the end of her compression cycles. After a full minute, Dallas checked her pulse.

He shook his head.

Tears trickled down Mia's cheeks as she began the next cycle. "You haven't finished learning Italian," she said to Cora. "You're only on lesson three, and that's not going to be enough if you want to go to Rome." Another set of compressions and rescue breaths.

This time she didn't allow herself to look at Dallas. Cora was going to live. Shoulders aching she pressed with renewed vigor. "And your nephew is happily married in Seattle. He's not going to want to come and take care of this sprawling old place, isn't that what you always said, Cora?"

Sirens pierced the air and a fire truck appeared through the smoke, rumbling up the grade, followed by an ambulance. Mia did not slow her efforts.

"You wake up right now, do you hear me? I mean it. I told you over and over not to keep those silly scented candles in your bedroom. They did not keep away the mosquitos, no matter what you say. You wake up so I can chew you out properly." Tears dripped from her face and cleared spots of black from Cora's forehead.

The medics ran over, but stopped short when Juno barked at them until Dallas quieted him. They pushed forward, eyeing the big dog suspiciously, and edged Mia out of the way.

"I have to stay with her," she pleaded.

Dallas drew her back, his voice oddly soft. "They've got it, Mia. Let them work."

"But…"

He gently, but firmly, took her arm and moved her several yards distant from the paramedics.

She breathed in and out, forcing herself to stop crying. "I'm okay, I'm okay," she repeated, waving him away when he came close.

Dallas stood there, long muscled arms black with soot, the edges of his hair singed at the tips, looking at her until she couldn't stand it anymore. "What is it? What are you thinking?"

Dallas didn't answer.

"Please tell me." She moved closer, the dark pools of his eyes not giving away anything.

Dallas considered. "I wasn't sure what type of service dog Juno would be. Before I trained him in Search and Rescue, a buddy of mine had a go at making him a drug-sniffing dog, but Juno doesn't obey anyone but me, so he flunked out. Mastered only the first lesson."

"What are you saying?"

He pulled a plastic pill bottle from his pocket. "These were on the bedside table. Do you know what she takes them for?"

Mia took the bottle and held it up to the light from the engines. "It's her blood pressure medication. I pick up her prescriptions myself."

Dallas frowned.

Mia felt the seeds of dread take hold deep down. She put her hands on Dallas's unyielding chest. "Dallas, please tell me what you're thinking."

"The first lesson, the only one that Juno mastered…"

She found she was holding her breath as he finished.

"Was alerting on drugs…like cocaine."

Dallas mentally berated himself for mentioning Juno's behavior at that moment. Mia was already trembling as the shock of what had happened settled in.

Should've waited. How many times had he said that to himself?

This time he did not allow her to pull away when he folded her in a smoky embrace. She was so small, so slight in his arms, and he resisted the urge to run his hands along her shoulders. He thought of all the things he should say, the comforts he could whisper in her ear, but everything fled, driven away by the feel of her. She stiffened suddenly, and he wondered if she'd been hurt in the fire.

"There," Mia gasped, pointing behind the house.

He turned in time to see a woman with a wild tangle of red hair framed by the trees that backed the property. She stood frozen for a moment, eyes wide and face soot-stained and then she bolted into the woods.

"Stop," Dallas called, and he and Juno took off into the trees, Mia stumbling along behind.

"Who was that?" she asked, panting.

He didn't know.

"I thought I saw her outside the clinic one time, talking to Cora, but I'm not sure," Mia said.

A cursory search yielded nothing, though the falling rain and smoke didn't help. After a short time, they left off looking to follow the ambulance to the hospital.

In the waiting room, Mia sat on a hard-backed chair, and Dallas paced as much as the narrow hallway would allow until the doctor delivered his news. "I'm sorry. She didn't make it."

Dallas watched the spirit leak out of Mia as she put her head in her hands. Something cut at him, something deeper than the grief at Cora's death. He swallowed hard and stepped aside with the doctor. "Do you have a cause of death?"

The physician, whose name tag read Dr. Carp, hesitated. "She was dead upon arrival, but we called the police immediately after you told us about the pills. They took possession of them. Autopsy will be later this week." That much Dallas already knew as he and Mia had told their story to a young uniformed cop named Brownley.

The doctor left and Dallas sat next to Mia. He didn't speak. There was nothing to say anyway. Best to wait until she could articulate the thoughts that rolled across her face like wind sweeping through grass. Finally, he took her hand, hoping she would not yank it away. She didn't.

"Cora wanted to tell us something, something important," Mia said, her voice wobbling as she clutched his fingers. "Can you guess anything at all about what it was?"

Dallas shook his head. "No."

"I'm sure Juno was wrong about the pills," she said, a tiny pleading note to her voice. "Those were for her blood pressure. I delivered them to her myself. They couldn't have hurt her. Could they?"

He covered her hand with his palm. "Whatever this is, however it went down, was not your fault."

"That woman… Who was she?" Her brown eyes were haunted. "Dallas…" she whispered. "I'm scared."

He pulled her to her feet then and embraced her because he did not know the words to say. He never did, probably never would. "I'm taking you home."

A short, balding man with a thick, silvered mustache came close. "In a minute. I'm Detective Stiving, Ms. Verde, and I need to ask you some questions."

Dallas felt his gut tighten. Stiving. Perfect.

He and Stiving had been oil and water since Dallas had butted in on a missing-person's case and found a teen lost near Rockglen Creek whom Stiving had insisted was a runaway.

"Kid's a loose cannon," Stiving had insisted. "Drinks and parties like his father."

Runaway or lost, Dallas and Juno found the kid named Farley who'd fallen into a ravine, and the press was there to catch it. Since then, Dallas had gotten a bogus speeding ticket and been stopped twice by Stiving for no particular reason. Not good, but in a small town like Spanish Canyon, Stiving was it.

"Doc says you're making allegations about drugs," Stiving said, holding up the bottle of pills nestled in an evidence bag. "Looking to get some more publicity for yourself?"

"Juno alerted on that pill bottle."

"Juno is a drug-sniffing flunk-out, from what I've heard. I thought his forte was tracking down idiots who get lost in the woods."

Mia wiped her sleeve across her cheeks. "What kind of talk is that for a law enforcement officer?" she said indignantly. "Cora is…was a long-time resident of this town. I should think you'd want to be thorough investigating her death."

His blue eyes narrowed, face blotching with color. "Yes, Ms. Verde, I will. I started by running a check on you. It made for interesting reading. Since you've had such a long and storied history with law enforcement, I guess you'd know that I'll be contacting you for follow up information as soon as I get this to the lab."

Mia went white and then red.

Dallas clenched his jaw. *Don't mouth off to the cops,*

Dallas. "We saw a woman with red hair running away from the house."

Stiving blinked. "Really? Did you recognize her?"

Mia shook her head. "She might have come to the clinic to talk to Cora, but I'm not sure. I only saw her for a moment."

"And you?"

Dallas shrugged.

"Right. Well, we'll investigate that while we're checking into things." The detective's phone rang, and he walked away to answer it and then left abruptly.

Mia put a hand on Dallas's wrist, her fingers ice cold. "I have to go. Tina needs to get home, and I want to read Gracie a story before bed." She looked at her soiled clothes. "It will take some explaining about why I look like this." Her lip trembled. "I'll need to tell Gracie about Cora."

He wondered how a woman with filthy hair, torn clothes and a grief-stained face could look so beautiful, like Whistler's painting of the woman in white he'd seen in his mother's art books decades ago. Would she be so trusting if she knew the truth about what brought him to town? Dallas had been many things in his life, a gang member, a wanderer and a drinker. He'd never been a liar, not until now, with her. It tightened something deep in his gut. He had to remind himself he had good reasons for the subterfuge.

He'd been hired by Antonia, Mia's sister, to keep watch over her due to the prevalence of Mia's ex-husband Hector Sandoval's many enemies. Cora, a friend of Antonia's new husband, was in on the whole thing. An accomplice, he thought ruefully, who'd arranged for Dallas to hang out on her property just as often as the stubborn and ferociously independent Mia did.

He returned to the truck where Juno was sound asleep and waited until Mia got into her car. Following her home, he ran things over in his mind. Cora was obviously disturbed when she messaged both Dallas and Mia. How coincidental was it that her house burned down and she lost her life on the very same night Mia spotted some mystery woman fleeing the scene? Very coincidental, and Dallas Black did not believe in coincidence any more than he believed that Elvis still strolled planet Earth.

He walked Mia to her front door and waited while she stepped into the tiny front room.

Four-year-old Gracie came flying down the hall, short bob of hair bouncing around her, eyes alight with pleasure at the sight of him. They'd encountered each other many times at Cora's house while he was on the roof and she was digging holes around the property. When rain interrupted the roofing, they built card houses together, impressed with their creations until Juno knocked them over with a jerk of his tail.

"Did you come to play?" She took in his appearance and laughed. "You need a shower, Mr. Dallas."

He laughed, too, and Mia tried to draw Gracie away.

"Can he come in for a snack?" the child asked. "I've got Goldfish."

Dallas got down on one knee. "You eat goldfish? Don't the fins get stuck in your teeth?"

She giggled. "They're cracker fish. Juno will like them."

"Juno can't have Goldfish tonight, but we'll come another time."

She frowned. "Okay, but what if I don't have Goldfish then? Mommy eats them sometimes when I'm asleep and she's off her diet."

Mia's face flushed, and Dallas hid a grin.

"Tell you what, Goldfish girl. Next time I come with Juno, I'll bring some Goldfish along. How's that?"

She nodded, finally trotting off into the kitchen.

"You don't have to make good on that promise," Mia whispered as she let Dallas out. "As a matter of fact, I'd rather you didn't promise her things at all. I know you'd never mean to disappoint, but Gracie's been let down in a big way by her father."

"No sweat," he said. Something flickered in her face, something thoughtful. "You're not planning to go to the clinic, right?"

Mia jerked. "How did you know I was thinking about that?"

"Call it a knack. Don't go there by yourself, just in case whatever she was looking into has something to do with the fire."

She stayed silent.

"If you do have to go, I'll go with you."

She offered a courteous smile. "Thanks, Dallas. I appreciate it."

But you'll never allow it. He understood. He recognized the shadows that danced in her eyes for what they were. Fear. A desperate, ponderous weight of fear that she did not want to expose to anyone. Who would? He'd known that, tasted that when he was being beaten within an inch of his life during his gang days. That fear was hideous and bred on itself, multiplying exponentially the longer it was kept in the dark, like a poisonous fungus. He wished he could tell her. There is only one antidote, One who could defeat that fear. Instead, he remained silent until he heard the sound of the lock turning.

Juno and Dallas made one more stop on the way home, purchasing a bone for Juno and a handful of hot peppers for himself. With some help from the store clerk, he also secured five bags of Goldfish crackers, which he stowed in the back of his truck. Who knew Goldfish came in so many flavors? Dallas smiled to himself. Gracie knew, and that was enough.

TWO

The parking lot was empty, quiet, save for the patter of a cold rain and the scuff of Mia's shoes as she made her way to the darkened clinic hours later. She was grateful that Tina offered to stay late. It was almost eight by the time Mia embarked on her mission. She knew she should have called Dallas, but the only thing that scared her more than what had happened to Cora was the thought of losing herself to another man who would betray her and Gracie. She realized her hands were in her pockets, hidden away, a habit she'd developed after she'd stabbed her husband.

The horror lapped at her afresh. Her own hands had lashed out with that knife, powered by terror that Hector would kill her and take Gracie away into his corrupt world. She would never have done it, but she believed, heart and soul, that Hector meant to end her life. After Mia's arrest, she'd endured six months of jail time, knowing Gracie was with Hector, near people both ruthless and greed-driven, the worst being her own husband. After her release, she'd fled with Gracie, unaware that Hector would soon concoct a plot to outwit his enemies that involved kidnapping her sister, Antonia. While her sister fought for her life on a hurricane-ravaged island, Mia hid out like a frightened rabbit.

Sometimes her mind told her it was a dream, a nightmare, but she still remembered the feel of that knife in her hand and how her life had almost ended because she trusted the wrong man in spite of her father's warnings, Antonia's pleadings. In spite of her own troubled intuition.

Never again. Better to go it alone. A quick stop at the clinic. See if by chance Cora had left anything there that might be of help. In and out. Something wheeled along by her feet, and she gasped. Just a leaf, torn loose by the storm.

She bit back a wave of self-disgust at finding herself scuttling along, cringing at every leaf. She was an office clerk at the Spanish Canyon Clinic after all, and Cora was, had been, a volunteer. All perfectly aboveboard. But why had Cora originally insisted they wait until long after closing time to meet?

Her throat ached when she thought of her friend. Had she suffered? Had she known her house was burning around her?

Quickening her pace she sought shelter from the spring rain under the awning, keys ready in her hand, heart beating a little too hard, too erratically. Cora's nightmarish death came on a date that already held terrible memories, her wedding anniversary.

An annual reminder of the worst mistake of her life. But Hector had been so gentle when they'd first met, even professing to be a Christian, until he'd begun to worship another kind of God, the god of money, power and excitement, when he'd gotten involved in the drug trade. It was long over. Hector was jailed on new charges, the divorce finalized two years before, but Hector did not want to accept his losses, so she lived as anonymous a life as she could manage.

With teeth gritted, she wondered—Had Hector found her again?

His reach hadn't extended to Spanish Canyon, Colorado. Not this time.

Wind carried a cold spray of rain onto her face that trickled down the back of her neck. She wished there was someone else around, the janitor, a late working nurse, anyone. They might be parked in the underground garage, she thought hopefully. With a surge of relief she saw the lights on in the back of the building where she and Cora shared a desk.

Jamming her key in the lock, she left the rain behind and headed down the silent corridor to the rear of the building. She did not know what she hoped to accomplish. Maybe it was all just a way to keep busy.

Cora's desk was bare, save for a paperweight rock engraved with the words *Be Still*. An impossible task, it seemed, for the nearly eighty-year-old woman who had recently decided to learn Italian and tour Europe. Her eyes were drawn to her own desk. Shadows must be deceiving. Silhouetted in the lamplight was a vase full of long-stemmed roses. Trancelike, she moved closer and turned on her own work light. Yellow roses, which had once been her favorite. A gilt-edged card.

I'm sorry. I love you and we can be a family again. Hector.

Sweat beaded on her forehead. It was as if he was there, right there, standing in the shadows. Fear turned into hatred for the man who had stripped away her belief in herself.

Hector didn't strip it away. You handed it over, wrapped in a bow.

The floor creaked, and she spun around with a scream.

"I'm sorry," Dr. Elias said with an apologetic smile. "I didn't mean to scare you. I was working late and noticed the florist had been here. Nice roses. Curiosity won out, and I checked the card." He raised an apologetic eyebrow, the fiftysomething face calm and serene. "My wife says I'm incurably nosey, and I hate to admit that she's got me pegged."

Mia forced out a calming breath. "I'm surprised to see you here so late."

"Insomnia. It usually sends me to the computer to play solitaire, but I get tired of beating myself, so I come here sometimes."

"Did you…did you hear about Cora?"

He nodded, mournfully. "Tragic. Cora was an excellent lady and a noble spirit." He shook his head. "Why do the good die before their time?"

It was a question she'd asked many times to a God who'd never given her a straight answer.

Dr. Elias cleared his throat. "Anyway, I'm glad you came so you could get your flowers, but why so late? Insomnia trouble for you also?"

She was about to tell him about the prearranged meeting with Cora, but something stopped her. "I just wanted to clean up Cora's desk."

"Looks clean already." Something in his inflection made her wonder if he'd been looking through Cora's belongings. Ridiculous. Crazy suspicion.

He surveyed the ceiling for a long moment. "It's good, actually, that we have a private moment so we can talk. I feel as though I have treated you well, hired you on in spite of your criminal record."

She winced. "Yes, you have. I appreciate that."

"It was Cora who went to bat for you, you know. She felt passionately that you would be an asset to this clinic. I was reluctant, I'll admit."

Mia started. She hadn't even known Cora when she moved to Spanish Canyon. She'd been following a lead on a job that her sister had dug up. Close to nursing school. Quiet town where nobody knew her.

"So I'm loathe to ask it, Mia, but when were you going to mention the truth about your criminal husband?"

She kept her chin high, even though at five three she barely reached his shoulder. Her phone vibrated in her pocket. "Ex-husband."

He blinked, his smooth complexion bordered by a distinguished head of gray hair that went well with his stature as head of the town's largest general medicine clinic. "I knew he was abusive, you were arrested for stabbing him I realize, but you didn't quite tell me the whole story. The flowers got me curious and I did a little checking. Nosey, just like my wife says. He wasn't just an abusive spouse. He's a Miami drug kingpin with powerful friends." His pale gray eyes locked on hers. "You didn't feel like you should mention that?"

Mention it? She was too busy trying to forget it.

"Is that why you don't use your married name? Sandoval?"

"It's not my name because I'm not married anymore. I haven't been for years. Simple as that."

He looked at the ceiling again while he talked. "Not really so simple. I've tried to support you here, to give you the hours you need to get you through nursing school and help you earn some money to keep food on the table for Gracie."

She didn't like it when he said Gracie's name, for some reason that she could not articulate. Did she feel the swell of distrust when she looked at him because he had the same self-assured manner as Hector? The doctor had been nothing but gracious.

"I would do anything for my own kids, as you know. It hasn't always been easy to afford everything times two, but that's the price of having twins. Jake and Renee are both in private high school now, so I understand wanting the best for your kids. But why lie? Especially to me."

"I never lied. You asked about my ex-husband, and I told you the reason I was sent to jail."

"You neglected to mention your husband is a Miami drug lord. You thought you'd pulled the wool over my eyes, didn't you? Simple country doctor. Easy to do, you figured?"

"No, nothing like that, really," she said.

The phone buzzed again.

Something sparked in his eyes. "Omissions are lies, and I'm afraid I'm going to have to ask you to leave." His brow furrowed. "It pains me to do it, it really does, but I have a professional obligation, no matter what my personal feelings are. My patients have to have absolute trust in me and my staff, and if you're still getting flowers from a drug kingpin, I can't risk having you here."

Mia would not let him see her cry. Head high, she nodded. "I'll be out of here in fifteen minutes." She went to the desk in the corner of the Spanish Canyon Clinic and shoved the picture of Gracie into a bag along with a collection of notepads. Cora's *Learn Italian Today* book was on her desk, under a box of tissue, and she scooped it up as well. She'd never dropped a phone call, never misplaced a file or been anything but pleasant to everyone and even that wasn't enough to overshadow her disastrous marriage.

Blinking to keep the tears at bay, her mind ran wild. No job. How would she finish school? Would it be the end of her dreams to finally give Gracie a stable, normal life? Her phone demanded her attention again and this time she yanked it from her pocket. It was a text from Dallas.

Ok?

Was she?

Dr. Elias still stood there, filling the doorway with his blocky shoulders, a look of indecision on his face. "This husband, Hector. He's tracked you everywhere, hasn't he?"

One of the notepads sliced into her finger giving her a paper cut. She shook off the sting angrily.

"Hector must be jealous." The lamplight etched Dr. Elias in tight shadow. "Have you given him reason?"

She froze. "What?"

"The tough guy with the dog. I've seen him talking to you. Hector can't be happy about this."

Seen Dallas? Something cold trickled through her. Why had Dr. Elias noticed whom she'd been talking to?

He flicked a glance into her bag. "You're not taking any clinic information, are you?"

She burned. "No, Doctor. I would not behave un-ethically, even after I've been wrongly terminated."

A glimmer of a smile lit his face. "I always liked your spunk, Mia Verde Sandoval. Too bad."

Mia grabbed her bag and purse and went to the door, but he barred her path.

He didn't move, just watched her as if he was weighing something in his mind. He reached out a hand to touch her forearm, but she recoiled.

"Hold on. I can see the truth now. You didn't lie to deceive, you lied because you're afraid."

Her breath caught and she shook her head.

"Yes, that's it, isn't it? You're afraid that Hector will find you." He stared closely at her. "No, you're afraid that you can't trust yourself, your choices, your judgments." He took her arm.

The fingers felt cold there against her skin, her own feet rooted to the floor. It was as if he'd stepped inside her, peered into the cold dark place in her heart where she herself dared not go.

"I know what it's like to be lied to. I'm so sorry, Mia," he said, pupils glittering in the dimly lit office. He leaned toward her and lowered his voice to a whisper. "I'm dense, sometimes. I didn't realize. I can help you."

Standing this close she realized how strong he looked. Her fingers clutched her car keys, and she raised them in front of her.

"I want to leave. Now."

He laughed and moved a step closer. She was acutely aware of how empty the clinic was, how dark the outer corridors. "You're a beautiful woman, you know that?"

His gaze flickered up and down her body. "You deserve more. I can help you get your life back."

She pressed back until she bumped into the file cabinets, a metal handle digging into her spine. He put his hands out, kneading her shoulders.

She jerked away from his grasp. "I want to go," she whispered, gripping the keys. "I will scream the place down if you touch me again."

He chuckled. "You came here after hours, almost as if you were looking for me."

The implication was clear. *Who do you think they'll believe?*

She gripped the keys, palms clammy, readying herself to gouge and bite and kick. Unsure.

"You're not seeing things clearly, Mia. You don't know what's right and wrong anymore, do you?" The words were almost a whisper, his mouth curved in a soft smile. "You need help."

Help? Was that what he offered? Her gut told her to run. Should she trust that instinct?

From somewhere far away, she heard herself say, "I want to go. Now."

"Maybe you don't know what you want," he said, eyes glittering.

"Yes, she does," said a low voice. The doctor was jerked back and dumped in an unceremonious pile on the floor. Dallas Black looked down at Elias, his dark eyes blending with the shadows.

She realized Dallas must have been expecting her to act stupidly and visit the clinic and her cheeks burned, but relief overrode any other sensation.

"I was just fired," Mia announced. "And now I'm going to leave."

Dallas didn't move. "Good. Doesn't pay to work for dirtbags."

"Trespassing and assault," Dr. Elias snapped at Dallas, scrambling to his feet. "I will have you arrested."

Dallas ignored the comment completely. "Ready to go?" he said to her.

"Get off my property," Dr. Elias snarled. Gone was the genial smile, any vestiges of warmth, fire blazed in his eyes.

Mia gripped her bag and walked to the door on shaky legs, grateful to have Dallas looking over her shoulder at the doctor. She was desperate to end the situation. Dallas had a complete disregard for rules and she wanted to finish the whole confrontation before anything worse happened.

"You are turning away from someone who wants to help you, Mia," Dr. Elias said, nostrils flared. "And look what you're walking into."

"Goodbye, Dr. Elias," Mia said.

"Don't forget your flowers," he yelled.

"Keep them," she said.

Dallas's truck was parked at the curb, and Juno sat next to it. When he saw her his tail went into overtime, and he whined until she gave him a cursory pat. He licked her face.

"If a man approached my ride, Juno would bark up a storm, but with you he'd hand over the keys," Dallas said. *Smart dog.*

Juno was once an aggressive shelter resident after having been beaten and starved by a cruel owner. Dallas had spent six months tracking down that negligent owner on his own dime, until the man was charged with animal cruelty and subjected to hefty fines. It wasn't enough in Dallas's view.

Mia straightened in spite of Juno's disappointment and gave him a tight smile. "He must know I'm a cat person and he's trying to help me see the light." She paused. "I would have handled the situation, you know. No one will keep me from Gracie."

"No doubt. I'm just glad I was in the neighborhood." In truth he'd been driving around town, too restless to stay home, checking the clinic lot every so often in case Mia showed up like he suspected she'd do. "I'm not sure…" She bit her lip. "I don't know if Dr. Elias was going to hurt me. He said he wanted to help."

Help? That wasn't what Dallas had heard in the good doctor's tone when he put his hands on Mia. "What did your gut tell you?"

"To leave."

"Then you did the right thing." Dallas clamped down on the anger that ticked at his insides. His own instincts told him Dr. Elias was interested in much more than Mia's well-being. He despised the thought of Elias being anywhere near Mia. Or touching her. Or looking in her general direction.

Overprotective, Black.

Overprotective? How could that be when she kept him at arm's length and he wasn't interested in a relationship anyway? Whatever the reason, something about her, her strength perhaps, stayed in his mind like a lingering fragrance.

It made him pretty sure that if she knew the real reason he'd come to Spanish Canyon, to protect her without her consent, she'd let him have it with both barrels, but the roses on her desk indicated there was ample cause for him to keep an eye on her.

He'd met Mia at the wedding of her sister, Antonia, to Hector's brother Reuben Sandoval after the two barely survived a hurricane. Oddly, he'd befriended Antonia three years prior in the wake of a massive earthquake that struck San Francisco where he assisted his brother, Trey, in rescuing Antonia and Sage Harrington, now Trey's wife. At least Antonia and Trey had both found love matches in the midst of disaster. A memory from that wedding stayed sharp in his mind. Mia's face torn with sorrow, or was it guilt, cradling Gracie in her arms. Hemingway said people healed stronger where they were broken. Mia, though she didn't ever discuss her past, was like that, he figured. *Sometimes it takes more strength to ask for help than to go it alone, Mia.*

He snapped out of his reverie when she sighed heavily. "Go ahead and say it. I was dumb to come here, after hours, in light of all that's happened."

He considered. "Yeah."

"I have good reasons for doing things my own way."

"Don't we all." He tried to catch her eye, but she avoided his gaze. "You okay?"

"Yes."

"Sure?"

"I'm perfectly fine," she said with a little too much bravado. He caught the tremble of her lips in spite of the dim light. It made his stomach tighten.

"I'll follow you home again."

"I'm fine. There's no reason."

"It's dark, weather's bad and you were harassed. That's three reasons." He opened the door for her.

She rolled her eyes and started to get into the car

when the bag slipped from her hands. She snatched it up but not before Cora's Italian book plopped out. It fell open, and she saw something stuck inside. Picking it up hastily, she said, "What's this?"

From between the pages she pulled out a four-by-six photo, and Dallas shone his penlight on it.

"We've seen this woman before," she said grimly.

Dallas felt a stir of foreboding flow through his belly. "Running away from Cora's burning house."

THREE

Sleep eluded Mia. Though she felt like throwing herself on the floor and sobbing at the loss of her dear friend, she would not allow Gracie to witness such an outburst. The best thing she could offer now was a heavy dose of mothering in between scouring the want ads and internet sites for employment opportunities. A breakfast of scrambled eggs, toast cut into a heart shape, and a half dozen stories later, and Gracie was content to go into the soggy backyard and hunt for snails. Unless the snails had teeny scuba suits, Mia didn't think she'd have much luck.

She sat on the couch and considered the facts.

The little house they now occupied was rented. Cora had helped her find the place, and though she received a settlement when she divorced Hector, she steadfastly refused to take any child-support money. Dr. Elias was right. Hector Sandoval was involved in the drug trade, and she did not want a single penny of tainted money to find its way to Gracie.

Hector claimed in every letter that he'd repented, but she did not believe him or any other man for that matter. The most important person in her life was

Gracie, and Mia would not fail her. So how could she tell her daughter about Cora? Images of the fire raced through her memory, especially the moment when the red-haired woman had appeared through the smoke. Whoever she was, she had answers. Hopefully, the police chief could help ferret out the truth, though he'd not been able to grant her an audience until the following day. Dallas had advised her to bypass Stiving, and she'd agreed. It was best to talk to the chief. For now, the picture was tucked safely in an envelope in the back of the top desk drawer.

The doorbell rang.

Tina stepped inside, chewing madly on a piece of pink gum with a stack of books under her arm to be perused during Gracie's nap time. Mia greeted her warmly. The stick-thin college sophomore babysat for Mia during the day and took community classes at night. Since Mia's nursing school was off due to a semester break, she'd been logging as many hours at Dr. Elias's clinic as she could and Tina had been invaluable. The two exchanged a quiet talk about Cora's death, news of which had already spread all over the quiet mountain community.

"Have you told her yet?" Tina asked, discarding her gum into a wrapper and snatching a leftover piece of toast.

"No." Mia sighed, eyes misting. "I haven't had the courage."

Tina gave her a hug which almost loosed the flood gates of emotion until Mia stepped back. "I'm glad you could come today. I've got to find another job."

"Yeah? What happened to the gig at the clinic?"

"I was…let go last night."

Tina swallowed the last bit of toast. "Oh, bummer. What are you going to do now?"

"Go into town and beat the bushes if I have to. Anything to make the rent."

"That's the spirit."

Mia nodded. "There's got to be somebody looking for a hard-working gal like me."

"We are women, hear us roar," Tina cried, pumping a fist. "Go get 'em!"

Wishing she could share some of Tina's enthusiasm, she grabbed her bag. After they'd made arrangements for Tina to deliver Gracie to Mia in the late afternoon, she headed for the car.

"Time to hit it," she murmured to herself. "Hear me roar."

Fearing that her roar was more like a pitiful mew at the moment, she headed to town.

After a full day of walking the main streets of Spanish Canyon, Mia had nothing to show for it but sore feet and a rumbling belly. She'd already gobbled her peanut butter and marshmallow fluff sandwich, and at a little past three, her stomach was demanding attention, as it seemed to do no matter what diet she was doing her best to adhere to. Besides, a sign on Sam's Sammies advertised for "help wanted."

I'm a master of the peanut butter and fluff, she reminded herself as she entered and introduced herself to the owner.

Sam Shepherd, a massive man with sprigs of white hair sprouting from the top of his head met her inquiry with enthusiasm. "Sure thing. Why don't you fill out an application?" He pushed over a greasy piece of paper affixed to a clipboard. "Say, I was sure sorry to hear about Cora."

She nodded. "Me, too."

"You know her well?"

Mia only managed a quick yes.

He raised a bristly eyebrow. "Heard talk that it wasn't an accident."

She hadn't noticed Detective Stiving sitting in the corner booth until he spoke up. "Looking more and more like that's the case," he said.

A moment later, Dallas strolled in, surveying the group with quiet amusement and causing Mia to wonder about the timing.

"Well, Sam, seems like business is picking up," Dallas said.

Stiving chewed a pickle spear. "What do you want?"

Dallas arched an eyebrow. "A sandwich. Isn't that why you're here?" He smiled at Sam. "The usual, my good man."

"Vegetarian with extra mustard and no eggplant, heavy on the jalapenos," Sam rattled off.

Dallas slouched into a chair, long legs extended. "Don't let me interrupt."

Mia felt the twin pangs of affection and irritation at seeing Dallas there. She wanted the man out of her life, yet why did something inside her warm up whenever he appeared? Was he keeping tabs on her? The thought both infuriated and tantalized her.

Focus, would you? "I'll just fill this out," she said to Sam, making her way to a chair well away from Dallas.

Stiving followed her. "You might not want to take a new job, just yet."

Something about the gleam in his eye worried her. "Why?"

"Because it seems you're an heiress."

She blinked. "What are you talking about?"

"Just got word that Cora left her house and property to you. Of course, the house is pretty messed up, but the twenty acres of property, well that's worth a nice tidy sum, I'll bet."

Mia realized her mouth was hanging open. "Cora left her property to me?"

"Does that surprise you?"

"Of course it does. I had no idea."

"That right?" He wiped his thick fingers on a paper napkin. Graying chest hair puffed out at the top of his uniform shirt. "No idea at all?"

"None. What are you implying?"

"Cops, you know, look at these things called motives. Inheriting a nice chunk of land is motive."

"For what?" Mia managed to squeak out.

"For murder," he said with a smile.

Dallas moved closer when it seemed as though Mia was unable to marshal a response. "What do you have that points in that direction?"

Stiving leveled a derisive look at him. "Not that it's your business, but the coroner's initial take is that Cora didn't die from the fire."

Mia let out a little cry, her face gone deadly pale.

Dallas tensed. "Cause?"

Stiving stretched against the upholstered booth. "That's as much as I'm going to say right now. You all have a great day. I'll be in touch. Soon."

He left. Dallas realized that Sam had been standing

just behind them holding a sandwich on a plastic plate. "Uh, well, I'm real sorry and all that, Mia, but maybe Stiving is right. With everything going on, it doesn't seem like a good time to have you start working here."

He shoved the plate at Dallas and waddled back to the kitchen.

Dallas dropped money on the counter, no tip, and left the sandwich on the table. By the time he'd finished, Mia had made her way outside, sinking onto a brick planter, oblivious to Juno, who had been watching through the window the whole time, swabbing an eager tongue over her hand.

Dallas sat next to her. Dark clouds overhead promised more rain and dulled the soft brown of her eyes. Or maybe it was the shock that did it. What to say to comfort her in the present situation eluded him, so he went with his gut.

"They don't have any proof. He's trying to rattle you."

The words seemed to startle her. "He thinks she was poisoned with the pills I got for her."

"Speculation and proof are two different things."

"Juno knew there was something in those pills."

"Doesn't mean you put it there."

She pressed shaking hands to her mouth. "I can't believe it. He wants to put me in jail. I can't go to jail, Dallas."

Her voice broke and it killed him. "You won't."

"But my past…isn't lily white."

"Whose is?" He wanted to smooth away the furrow between her brows, the agony in her expression. "It was self-defense before. Totally different. Your ex admits that now."

Her eyes rounded. "Have you been studying my past?"

Smooth, Dallas. Why don't you explain how you know every detail of her life? He went for casual. "Heard it somewhere."

She was too upset to think more about it. "Maybe I should leave here," she whispered. "Go back to Florida."

His pulse accelerated the tiniest bit. He said as gently as he could, "Thought you wanted a fresh start."

"Away from the Sandoval name," she finished. "I do, but my past seems to have followed me here."

And did her husband's past have anything to do with her current situation? He did not see how it could, but it was his job to find out. He'd made a promise. "There was someone else at Cora's house who could have tampered with the pills. We just have to figure out who the woman in the photo is."

Mia chewed her lip. "This is a nightmare."

"We'll fix it."

Her eyes flickered at the pronoun.

We? When had loner Dallas Black begun to think of them as partners? The only partner he'd ever really trusted was the kind covered with fur and with a tendency to slobber. "Look who's just hit town," he said as Gracie broke away from Tina and ran to them, splashing through the puddles on the sidewalk.

"Hi, Mr. Dallas. Hi, Mommy. I'm here," she announced, heading straight for Juno to give him an ear rub. "Tina said we could get ice cream."

Mia recovered herself to give Tina a stern look.

The girl shrugged. "Sorry. I can't say no to those dimples."

"I can," Mia said, her mouth twisting in sadness. "But I won't. I think I could use a scoop, too."

"Mr. Dallas, come on," Gracie said, tugging on his hand. "We can get some for Juno."

Mia's look was enough to discourage him. "I've got to go right now, Gracie. Maybe another time."

Mia's slight nod affirmed he'd made the right choice, so why did his heart tell him otherwise? He moved close to Mia, talking low in her ear and trying not to breathe in a lungful of her shampoo-scented hair. "I've got a friend who works at the police department. I'll go see what I can find out."

She put a hand on his biceps. "I don't want to ask you to do that for me."

"You didn't ask."

He heard her sigh, sad as the sound of a blues song, as she led Gracie away without looking back, her shoulders hunched against the storm-washed sky.

Mia tried to keep Gracie occupied with the ice cream parlor and the park, but all the while her mind was racing. The police thought she'd killed her dearest friend. How could it be happening? And to inherit when Cora had blood relatives to whom she could pass her estate? The only spot of comfort was Dallas, and she had to steel herself against any connection, no matter how much she craved it. Still, she thought she could remember the feel of his hard muscled arm under her fingers—strong, solid, the steady warmth in his eyes.

You've seen eyes like those before, remember, Mia?

Rain began to fall a little after five, and she zipped Gracie's jacket and insisted they return to the car where a nasty surprise awaited her. Her rear tire was flat all the way to the rim.

"Great. I must have driven over a screw or something." With a heavy sigh, she gave her purse to Gracie to hold and got the jack and lug wrench from the trunk. Two gentlemen and a young couple out walking their dog stopped and offered help, but Mia waved with a cheer she did not feel and finished the job herself. The effort took much longer than it should have and it was nearly sundown when she cleansed her grease-stained hands with one of her endless supply of disinfectant wipes and took the road toward home.

Gracie sang "Where Does the Ladybug Live?" as the miles went by and Mia even joined in for a while, but, as darkness fell, her stress returned. No job, no way to pay the rent and now a replacement tire needed to be purchased.

Gritting her teeth, she forced the worry down deep.

"I'm hungry," Gracie announced as they pulled into the garage.

"How can you be hungry when you ate two scoops of ice cream?"

Gracie twisted a strand of hair while she thought about it. "Dunno, but I am."

"Mac and cheese?"

The little girl nodded as she helped Mia unbuckle her car seat straps.

Mia mentally inventoried the pantry cupboard, hard to keep stocked with a voracious babysitter and child. Fortunately, there was one box left of nature's most perfect food. She helped Gracie from the car and hit the button to close the garage door.

Mia noted the interior door was unlocked, probably

because Tina simply could not be induced to lock it. Mia sighed. Oh, to be an innocent eighteen-year-old again. Gracie pulled out her step stool and disappeared into the pantry.

Suddenly, the burdens of the day crashed in on Mia and she felt much older than her twenty-eight years. And why shouldn't she as the ex-wife of a drug runner and now the object of suspicion for her friend's death? *Murder, murder,* the word crawled through her mind. Tears threatened, but she would not allow them, not for a moment. Mothers did not have the luxury of folding up like tents. A shower. A quick five minute shower would wash off the grime from the day.

Hanging her purse on the kitchen hook and plugging in her cell phone to charge, she headed for the bedroom, removing her jacket. Finger poised on the light switch, she froze. A shadow was silhouetted in front of the window, just for a second before it slithered behind the cover of the drapes. Someone was in her bedroom.

Fear rushed hot into her gut, firing her nerves as she ran down the hallway. Behind her she could hear the swish of fabric as the intruder detached from the curtains. Feet thudded across the carpeted floor, her own clattering madly on the wood planked hallway as she raced for the kitchen, sweeping up her purse and grabbing Gracie who was shaking the box of macaroni and singing.

She seized her daughter with such force she heard the breath whoosh out of her, but Mia paid no heed. The man was in the hallway now, only a few feet behind her. Mia burst into the garage, hit the button and dove into the driver's side, shoving Gracie over onto the passenger seat and cranking the ignition.

The interior garage door opened, and the man appeared—thin, white, crew cut. She saw him reach for the button to stop the door from opening. She would be trapped, she and Gracie, at the mercy of this stranger.

No, she thought savagely, flipping the brights on. He flinched, throwing a hand over his eyes. The door was nearly half open now. Only a few more inches and she could get out.

Terror squeezed her insides as she saw him recover and reach for the button again.

Hurry, hurry, she commanded the groaning metal gears.

This time when he reached for the button, he succeeded and the door stopped its upward progress.

He pressed it again and it began to slide down, sealing off their escape.

FOUR

Dallas listened to the rain pounding down on the metal roof of the twenty-nine-foot trailer he rented. It was a gem of a unit as far as he was concerned, far enough away from the other trailer park residents that he enjoyed the illusion of solitude. That and the fact that the river just at the edge of the property had already persuaded many folks to temporarily relocate to another trailer park on higher ground. He wasn't completely familiar with Colorado weather patterns, but he'd give it a good couple of days before he needed to grab his pack and head for another spot.

Dallas sprawled on his back on the narrow bunk, Juno snoring on his mat on the floor. His thoughts wandered back to Mia and the fire. His police contact hadn't been able to tell him much, but he knew that circumstantial evidence could convict a person in the eyes of the law and the community.

Motive and means. Mia had both.

He got to his feet and took up his guitar from the closet. Juno burrowed deeper into his mat as Dallas strummed out a few chords on the instrument that was a gift from his brother, Trey. So, indirectly, was Dallas's damaged spleen and knee, but he did not hold that against his brother anymore. Dallas got into gang life to emulate Trey, but no one had forced him.

He'd gone in willingly and come out so damaged he would never realize his dream of being a Marine like their father.

He tried to remember his sixteen-year-old self, armed and patrolling the ten-block territory as a sentinel of sorts, a lookout for Uncle, the older leader of the gang who pedaled dope, which kept the wheels rolling. He'd admired Uncle, feared him even, yet watched him hand out new shoes and Fourth of July fireworks to the kids who couldn't afford either. They were the same kids who would be members one day, looking for that combination of belonging and protection that Uncle provided. Sixteen years old, carrying a gun, drinking and protecting a hoodlum's drug business. He cringed at the memory. What an idiot. What a coward.

How many trailers had he stayed in over the years? How many apartments or cabins had he called home until people got to know him a little too well and he felt that restless urge to move on? Was he still looking for that place to belong?

Or was it more cowardice? Probably, God forgive him. It was safer not to get to know people and to prevent them from knowing him. Safe…with a helping of sin mixed in. His grandfather's favorite baseball player, Mickey Mantle, said gangs were where cowards went to hide. Maybe they sometimes went to trailer parks, too. He fought the rising tide of self-recrimination with a muttered prayer.

The clock reminded him he hadn't eaten dinner. The fridge didn't offer much so he grabbed a rainbow of hot peppers and an onion. Armed with a perfectly balanced knife, he allowed himself to be soothed by the precision of the slices as they fell away onto the cutting board.

Juno surged to his feet, ears cocked.

Company.

So late? And in the throes of a pounding rain? He put down the knife and sidled to the window, peering through the blinds. Nothing. No cars visible, but then his windows faced the tree-lined creek so he wouldn't see one anyway. Juno was standing in front of the door, staring with laser-like precision, ears swiveling, as if he could see beyond the metal if he just worked hard enough at it. With hearing four times greater than a human's, Juno was not often wrong about what he heard.

Dallas tried to peer through the blinds again, but the angle was wrong. Still no one knocked. Juno maintained his ferocious intensity, which told Dallas someone was out there. The slightest sound or scent telegraphed to a dog just as strongly as a stiff-knuckled rap on the door.

Okay. Let's play. Dallas gripped the door handle. Juno's whiskers quivered, body trembling, sensing a game in the offing. Juno, like every great SAR dog, had an intense play drive that never wound down.

Dallas did a slow count to three and yanked the handle.

Wind barreled in along with a gust of rain, and Juno charged down the metal stairs onto the wooden porch. He turned in circles looking for something that wasn't there.

Dallas kept his fists ready and gave the dog the moment he needed to get his bearings. Moisture-laden air confused Juno's senses, but not for long.

The dog shoved his head in the gap under the trailer and began to bark for all he was worth, tail whirling.

A woman's scream cut through the storm.

"Sit," Dallas yelled to Juno, who complied with a reluctant whine.

"Whoever you are under the trailer, come out."

No answer.

"If you don't come out, the dog is coming in."

Now there was movement, a raspy breathing, a set of slender fingers wrapping around the edge of the trailer, the impression of a face.

"He'll bite me."

Dallas called Juno to him and held the dog by the collar, more to assure the woman than out of fear that Juno would disobey. Juno didn't bite people. He was more interested in getting them to throw a ball for him to fetch. "Come out."

She emerged, soggy and mud streaked, her hair plastered in coils against her face. Red hair.

"You were there at the fire."

She didn't answer, trembling in the falling rain.

"Come inside. We'll talk."

She didn't move. "Are you a friend of Cora's?"

"Are you?" He could see the thoughts racing through her mind as she chewed her lip without answering. "All I can tell you is I won't hurt you."

"How do I know I can trust you?" she said through chattering teeth.

"Guess you can't. You came here to find me and here I am. If you want to talk, we do it inside. Don't want the dog to catch cold."

After another long look at Juno, the woman ran up the steps.

He tossed her a towel, which she wrapped around her shoulders before she sank onto the kitchen chair. Juno did his thing, sniffing her muddy shoes and the hem of her sodden linen pants.

Dallas studied her while he heated water in the microwave and flung in a tea bag which had come with the trailer. Some sort of fruity herbal stuff. Her clothes had been nice at one point, ruined now. A light jacket was not up to the task of keeping her dry from the pummeling rain. No purse.

"Who are you?" he asked as he handed her the tea.

She clutched it between her shaking hands, her knuckles white.

"Susan." She swallowed. "I was going to meet Cora, and I saw the house burning. I tried to get inside to help her."

Nice story. "Why were you meeting her?"

"She was…looking into something for me." She locked eyes on his, hers a pale gray. "Is she all right?"

Dallas considered. Time to find out if Susan really was a friend to Cora. "Dead." He gauged her reaction.

The woman did not move, as if the words were lost in the steam from the mug she held to her lips. "Dead."

"So why were you going to see her?"

She gazed into the tea. "How did the fire start?"

"Maybe I should be asking you that."

She jerked. "You think I set it?"

"So far I've seen you running away from a fire and sneaking outside my trailer. Puts your character in question."

A glimmer of a smile lifted her lips, but there was something under the trailing wet hair, behind the gaunt lines of her mouth that revealed a hardness he hadn't seen at first. "So you're wondering if you can trust me?" she said.

"Not wondering. I'm not going to trust you, not until you give me the truth."

"You're a hard man."

He sat opposite her. "I've got peppers to sauté. What are you here for?"

She held his eyes with hers, a slight lift to her chin. "Justice."

"Not easy to find."

"I know. But I'm going to have it. I'm going to get back what belongs to me." The last words came out as a hiss.

"What were you doing at Cora's?"

"Meeting her there. She was trying to help me unmask a villain, so to speak."

"Who?"

"It's private."

He rapped a hand on the table. "We're wasting time. Cora was likely murdered and you were there at the scene."

"If I was going to kill someone, or burn a house in this town," she said, after drinking deeply of the tea, "that's not the one I would have picked. And by the way, you were there, too, at the scene. Did you have something to do with Cora's death?"

Dallas resisted the urge to raise his voice. "If you thought I did, a quick phone call to the police would take care of it. You came here for another reason."

"I wanted to know about Cora, and I'm not asking the police for personal reasons."

Very personal, judging from the flicker of emotion that pinched the corners of her mouth. Impasse.

They'd gotten there, he could tell. Whatever her motives, he wasn't going to pry them out of her. Women didn't work that way, he'd learned. Instead he sat back in the chair and waited.

Mia's mouth went dry as the garage door stopped with a groan, halfway up. The man hopped off the step and ran to the car. He was coming to drag her out. The old car had no automatic locks so she slammed the button down and realized in a hot wave of panic that he was not headed to her side, but Gracie's.

"Lock the door, Gracie," Mia shouted.

Gracie sat frozen, staring at her mother.

Mia dove across her and hammered the lock, the back door, as well. The man banged his palms against the glass.

Gracie screamed. "Stop, stop!"

Mia nearly screamed too until the man stepped away suddenly. He picked up a metal bucket and swung it hard at the passenger window with a deafening crash until the glass was etched through with cracks.

"Get down onto the floor," Mia yelled to Gracie, "and cover your head with your hands."

She yanked the car into Reverse. After one quick breath, she stomped on the gas. The car shot backwards into the garage door. There was a terrible moment when the roof met the unyielding mass and she thought she had made a fatal error. Groaning metal, the sound of breaking glass and then quite without warning the car punched through, shearing the garage door into a crumpled mess, exploding onto the rain-slicked driveway.

Mia was oblivious to the damage. Only two facts remained, her car was still functioning and they were free from the garage. She reversed down the slope, cranked the car into Drive and sped off down the road, putting as much distance between the man and Gracie as she possibly could. One mile, two, her stomach remained in a tight knot, fingers clenched around the steering wheel.

She forced several breaths in and out before she could coax her voice into action. "Gracie Louise, are you hurt?"

Gracie's tiny voice floated up from the floor. "Scary."

"You're right," she said, relief making her voice thick. "But it's okay now. You can climb back on the seat. Be careful of the glass."

Gracie emerged like a hare having narrowly escaped the fox. Her lips were parted, eyes wide and wet. "Mommy, that was a bad man."

Mia gave a shaky laugh and took her daughter's hand. "Yes, he was."

"Why was he in our house?"

She swallowed. "I don't know, but we'll go someplace safe until we find out, okay?"

"Where?"

The million dollar question. The nearest hotel was an hour away, and they didn't have the money to stay in one for long anyway. Rain splattered through the side window that had broken when it impacted the garage door. She felt the bitter tide of anger rise as she contemplated her own helplessness. Mia risked a quick stop, engine running, to move Gracie to the backseat and buckle her into her booster. She kissed her and caressed her daughter's plump cheeks. "I'm going to figure out something, okay?"

Gracie nodded, shaking the box of macaroni she still clung to. "But I'm hungry."

Mia smiled as she climbed back into the driver's seat, but worry soon overwhelmed her. She didn't even have a cell phone to call the police. The storm intensified as she drove along, rattling the sides of the car. If she could call her sister for advice…

Your sister who is busy with her new husband and her new life. They were tight now, together again after all the anguish Mia had caused, but still there remained in the shadows between them, a heavy weight of guilt. It stemmed from the fact that her sister had been right about Hector when Mia refused to hear a bad word about him, a feeling that burgeoned during her time in jail with all its horrors. Because of Hector, Antonia was almost killed and there was nobody to blame for bringing him into their lives but Mia. No, she would not call Antonia.

"Why not call Hector?" her derisive thoughts chided her. He was sitting around in prison with nothing much to do and a reach that seemed to exceed the metal walls that caged him. She could grovel even more and throw herself on Dr. Elias's mercy. Was there any pride left to salvage? Self-pity gave way to a hot flood of determination.

Stand on your own two feet, for once in your life.

Mile after mile gave her no clarity, no better sense of what to do. Only the instinct to keep going, to get away from whoever had violated their home, kept her pressing the car forward. She'd made up her mind to stop at the next town she came to and call the police when she realized where she was, at the entrance to the trailer park where Dallas lived. She'd given him a lift there once when his truck had engine trouble.

She saw the silhouette of his vehicle, and she pulled her car next to it, motor still running.

"Where are we?" Gracie said, unbuckling her strap.

"Nowhere, I was just stopping to rest my eyes for a minute." What was she doing? She would not go to Dallas for help, the man who already seemed to have a strange influence over her pulse. An image of long-stemmed yellow roses floated into her mind. It was followed by a vision of Hector, the man whom she'd loved desperately, blindly, the husband who lied to her from the first kiss and right on until his arrest for drug dealing and later for the attempted abduction of her sister. *Fool, fool, fool.* Tears brimmed, captive in her eyes.

She swallowed hard. "Put your seat belt back on, we're not stopping here."

"But there's Juno," Gracie gabbled, shoving open the door and hopping out.

"Get back in the car right now, Gracie Louise," Mia said, noting the spill of light from Dallas's door as he emerged onto the trailer steps, peering into the darkness.

"Hi, Dallas," Gracie called. "Can you make me some mac and cheese?"

Mia sighed. God could not lead her to another dark-haired man who would prove her a fool again. If that was His plan, Mia was going to make one of her own. Jaw tense, she stepped out of the car and went to retrieve her daughter.

FIVE

"Sorry to bother you," Mia said, forcing a light tone, as Dallas bent to talk to Gracie, Juno dancing on eager paws beside him.

"Someone broke into our house," Gracie said. "I think it was the Boogeyman. He wanted this." She thrust the box of mac and cheese up in the rain.

Dallas's face was a picture of confusion. "Huh?" he finally managed.

Mia squished up to him, feet sinking into the grass. "We had a break-in. We're going to the next town to call the cops."

It was hard to read his expression through the sheeting rain. "Come inside."

Gracie hooted her approval and headed for the trailer.

"No," Mia said too quickly. "I mean, we don't want to involve you. I can handle it." She wished her teeth had not begun to chatter madly at that moment.

"You can handle it inside, out of the rain."

"I appreciate the offer."

"Inside then." And that was that. Dallas turned his back and ushered Gracie and Juno up the steps, politely holding the door for Mia, his muscled forearm gleaming wetly. And what was a woman on the edge of desperation supposed to do about that?

Just a phone call. A quick stop to rest and then out. She squelched up the trailer steps and inside, stopping abruptly in the doorway until he came up behind and pushed her gently through.

"I'll leave puddles."

His gaze flickered around the tidy interior. "You won't be the first one." He sighed. "Gone."

"Who?"

"The redhead from the fire. Name's Susan. She came here."

Mia gasped. "What did she want? Who is she?"

He shrugged. "Not the chatty type. Only got that she was meeting Cora and she has some big trust issues. She was sitting at the table when I heard you pull up. She must have snuck out." He leveled a look at Juno. "Aren't you supposed to alert me to people sneaking around, dog?"

Juno shook water from his thick coat and hurled himself on the floor to offer his belly to Gracie for scratching.

Mia giggled.

Dallas did not, but she thought there was a slight quirk on his lips. Mia made one more trip into the rain to fetch the bag of spare clothes she kept in the car. In a few moments, Gracie was wearing faded jeans and a T-shirt, one size too small but dry.

"Can you make this?" Gracie said, shaking the box of macaroni at Dallas.

"What is it?"

The child blinked. "It's mac and cheese. Don'tcha eat that?"

"No," Dallas said.

"Well, what do you eat?" she demanded.

"Spicy food that makes you sweat. But I can probably manage mac and cheese."

"No need," Mia said.

Dallas pointed to the tiny bathroom. "There's a sweatshirt hanging on a hook in there. It's ugly, but dry."

"We're not staying."

"I got that. Go put on something dry anyway. I don't think I can enjoy eating this mac stuff while you're dripping all over the floor." He turned to Gracie. "How do you cook it? The label's blurry from the rain."

"Dump the stuff in bubbling water," Gracie sang out as Mia headed to the bathroom.

"Don't get too close to Juno," she warned Gracie. "He'll get mad if you pester him."

Dallas quirked an eyebrow. "He's never mad at kids, but I'll watch them anyway."

Mia walked into the bathroom and leaned her head against the door. *Safe. You're safe for the moment, and so is Gracie.* She wanted to whisper a prayer, but something hardened the words in her throat. *You got yourself out of that jam, Mia, and you can handle whatever comes next. All by yourself.*

She squeezed the water out of her hair and slicked it down straight as best she could. Rolling up her sodden shirt, she pulled on the soft gray sweatshirt that went down past her knees. It felt warm against her skin.

She emerged to find Dallas in deep discussion with

Gracie as she stared at the pile of jigsaw puzzle pieces set out on a piece of plywood that served as a table.

"I don't know what it's going to be," Dallas said.

Gracie blinked. "But what's the picture on the box?"

"A mouse chewed the box, so I put the pieces in a plastic bag. Can't remember what the picture is."

She touched a piece with one soft fingertip. "You haven't gotten many pieces together."

He nodded, staring ruefully at the corner where a half dozen pieces were connected. "I move a lot. Gotta put it away each time."

"How long have you been working on it?" Mia asked.

He squinted. "Going on twelve years now."

She wasn't sure whether to gasp or laugh. "Really?"

"Well, I think it's going to be a dog puzzle," Gracie said.

"Could be. My mother gave it to me for my fifteenth birthday. She can't remember what the picture was, either." He sniffed. "Is mac and cheese supposed to smell like that?"

They looked at the pot which was bubbling madly on the stove. Mia grabbed a potholder and took it off the heat. There were bits of packaging swirling through the noodles and grainy orange tinted water. "Uh-oh. You dumped in the cheese envelope."

"The what?"

"I forgot to tell him," Gracie wailed. "You're not 'posed to put the cheese envelope in the water."

Mia put the mess into the sink. "I'm afraid it's ruined."

Dallas sighed. "I should have paid better attention

while I was dumping. Who puts cheese in an envelope anyway?"

Gracie sat forlornly next to Juno. "Awww, rats."

"Hang on," Dallas said, wrenching open the cupboard. "I just remembered something." He held a bag
of Goldfish triumphantly in the air. "How about some
of these?"

Gracie cheered, and Mia had to laugh as he handed
Gracie the crackers with all the solemnity of a profes-
sor awarding a diploma. "Just don't feed too many to
the dog," he said.

After a moment of hesitation, he said to Mia, "I'm
making tofu and peppers. Share them with me?" She
had not shared a private meal with a man since her disastrous marriage. Sweat popped out on her forehead.

"Oh, I couldn't."

"There's no meat, but I've got plenty." His black
eyes fastened on her.

Mia was a committed carnivore, but how could she
say no to the man whose sweatshirt she was wearing
and who had massacred a box of mac and cheese in an
effort to feed her child?

"Yes," she said humbly. "That would be very nice."

"Here's a phone to call the cops. Then you can tell
me about what happened."

She sank down at the table. "You're not going to
believe me."

"Try…" His words trailed off as he scanned the
kitchen counter.

"What's wrong?"

"Before she took off, Susan helped herself."

"To your dinner?"

"No," he said, voice low and deep. "To my knife."

* * *

Dallas kept the words low so Gracie wouldn't hear, but he needn't have worried. She was deep in conversation with Juno about the merits of some or other Goldfish flavor over the rest.

He selected another knife from the block and began slicing peppers, while Mia phoned the police. There was no way to avoid listening in and that was fine since he was itching to know the details of what sent Mia and Gracie out into the night. To him.

Was she really there in his trailer, rolling her damp hair into a ponytail? He nearly nicked his finger trying to take a sideways glance at her.

Mia explained the break-in to the dispatcher and gave Dallas's cell number as a contact before hanging up.

"They'll send a unit when they can, but the levee is failing just north of town." She laughed, a bitter sound. "They may need to evacuate my neighborhood anyway. It's true what they say, when it rains, it pours."

He dumped the peppers into sizzling olive oil and applied himself to neatly cubing the silken tofu. "It's not a coincidence. Guy was looking for something, maybe."

"Or looking to…" Her voice trailed away.

He stirred the pan with a wooden spoon. "I think he was searching and you surprised him. You said you had a flat. My guess is he made that happen to buy some time so he could search."

"For what? Why?" Her lips parted in exasperation, dark eyes flashing. He found his own mouth had gone dry.

"Could it be connected to the fire?" Mia pressed her

hands to her forehead. "I don't even know what Cora was looking into. She didn't give me the slightest clue."

"Yes, she did," he said, sliding a plate in front of her.

Mia gasped. "The photo. It's in a file drawer. I have to go back and get it."

"In the morning. Sleep here. Juno and I will find an empty unit, and you can have this one."

"No, we couldn't displace you."

He sat on a chair across from her. "You're tired, and Gracie needs a safe place to sleep."

He could see the struggle unfold across her face in magnificent waves. "Mia, I'm not pressuring you to do anything. I'm just offering a safe place to sleep until morning. That's all."

She bit her lip.

He took her hand, the delicate fingers cool in his own. "Let's pray." He closed his eyes and thanked the Lord for keeping Gracie and Mia safe and for the provision of food and shelter. When he straightened, he thought he could see a million thoughts, a cascading river of emotions rolling through her eyes.

"I wouldn't guess you to be the kind to pray."

"Yeah? Because I'm a troublemaker?"

"No, no, of course not." She laughed. "Well, maybe a little."

"Troublemakers need God more than most." He picked up his fork and started to eat.

She did the same. "Wow, hot." She panted, reaching for a glass of water.

"Sorry." He handed her a piece of bread. "Water doesn't really help much. I've done a lot of backpacking. Spicy adds flavor to camping food." He considered the contents of the fridge. "I have some eggs. I'll scramble you some."

He started to rise, but she stopped him with a touch on his arm that seemed to ignite an odd flicker of nerves all the way up to his shoulder.

"This is fine." She swallowed. "Hector...loved spicy food, too, I just haven't had it in a while. Thank you for cooking it for me."

He should have gone with the eggs. "Do you worry about what he'll do when he's out?"

She swallowed and wiped her mouth with a paper napkin. "He already knows too much about my life, even from prison."

And Hector's enemies did, too. He had squirreled away money, so the rumor went, a hefty sum extorted or swindled from his competitors, including the ferocious Garza family. Garza wanted it back and he'd sent out feelers to discover if Mia knew the whereabouts of the jackpot. Could be the guy who broke into her house wasn't searching for the photo, but the money.

A friendly DEA agent had alerted Reuben and Antonia to Garza's interest. And Antonia had hired Dallas to keep tabs on Mia. Dallas was good at watching people, finding the lost—fighting—if necessary, and skirting rules when they did not serve. He had no home, no ties. He was the perfect man for the job.

And Mia would despise him when she found out. He speared another slice of pepper.

For now, he would allow himself to savor the relative closeness between them, a feeling he had not experienced in a very long time. It was a shame that staring was bad manners, because all he really wanted to do was sit motionless and drink her in.

Her gaze was soft as she watched Gracie play with Juno, feeding him way more Goldfish than any dog should consume. When a gust of rain hammered on the metal roof with such force that it boomed through the trailer, Gracie ran to her mother's arms.

"It's okay, baby," Mia crooned. "Just the rain."

"Where's the bad man?"

Mia exchanged a quick look with Dallas.

"Bad man isn't going to come here," Dallas said.

"Why?"

"Because Juno is big and scary, and so am I."

Gracie smiled and hopped in his lap. He was so startled he didn't know what to do, sitting there as if he had a live grenade on his knees. Should he stand up? Give her a pat? Instead he sat rigid, hands raised, like a complete dork.

She grabbed him around the neck and pasted a cheesy kiss on his cheek. "I'm glad we came here."

So am I, his heart supplied, much to the surprise of his mind, but he was still relieved when she vacated his lap.

He saw to the details as best he could, thinking his mother would have played the job of host much better than he. Extra blankets for Mia and Gracie, heater turned on to a low hum to ward off the chill. Couple of clean towels in case anybody needed showering. Was there something else? Antacids, to cure any hot pepper damage. And magazines? *Wilderness Survival.* Did women like that sort of thing? He stood awkwardly in the doorway.

"Keep my phone here." He pulled out a spare he always had handy and programmed his cell into the one he gave Mia. "Call if you need anything. Use the laptop if you want. You can sign on as a guest."

Gracie crimped her lips. "What if the bad man comes while you're gone?" she whispered.

He considered telling her about the trailer he would sleep in across the way which gave him a direct line of sight that he intended to monitor on a regular basis. There were other things he could share, but he did not. "You want Juno to stay with you?"

"Yes." Gracie nodded, hopping from foot to foot. "Juno will watch me sleep."

"Actually, he'll sleep, too."

Mia shot him a look that indicated he probably should have kept that fact to himself. How was someone supposed to know what to divulge to a kid and what not to? Was there some kind of instruction manual?

"Juno will sleep, but he hears things that you can't."

"Like bad men?"

Dallas nodded.

"If he hears me, how will he know I'm not bad?"

"He just knows."

"Like God?"

Dallas took in the little bow of a mouth, the sweet innocence in that sober gaze and something moved inside him. "Yes, Gracie. God made dogs smart that way."

"My daddy's bad," Gracie whispered, so low he almost didn't hear it.

He heard Mia gasp, her lips pressed together. He swallowed and sent up a little prayer that he wouldn't say something stupid and took a knee. "Your daddy made mistakes. If he's sorry, God will help him be a good man again."

"God can do that?" she said, eyebrow raised.

"Yes, He can."

"How do you know?"

Dallas blew out a breath. "Because I was a bad man, and God helped me to be good again." Gracie gave him a long, serious look, then hugged him.

Mia wrapped her arms around herself. Had he made things better? Or worse? He could not tell from the expression on her face. Without another word that might tip the balance to one side or the other, he let himself out into the rain.

SIX

The night droned on. Rain hammered down and thoughts thundered through Mia's mind, three words pinching uncomfortably at her heart.

My daddy's bad.

Hector had done terrible things. He was bad, in some ways, but he had nearly died trying to save her sister from the trap he'd set for her on the island. He'd gone to prison, professing he would come out a better man. They had no future together, nothing that should stir her toward forgiveness. She would never love him again. The rage and hatred inside her would stay forever, she feared, blackening and staining her whole life. If Hector was bad, unforgivable, unredeemable, what did that mean for the child he had fathered? Or the wife who'd made so many mistakes herself?

And what of Dallas? She knew only a small bit about his troubled youth, but without question she was also certain Dallas Black was a good man. Then again, she'd thought Hector was, too.

Mia felt the soft rise and fall of Gracie's breathing, her back curled against Mia's stomach on the narrow bunk bed. How small she was, this little girl who looked to Mia to show her who God was, a god of forgiveness. It was something Mia could say with her mouth, but not embrace in her soul.

If he's sorry, God will help him be a good man again.

She wondered afresh about the strange and straightforward Dallas Black. The troublemaker with a certainty about himself and God that she could no longer deny attracted her. She itched to soothe her restlessness with movement. Careful not to wake Gracie, Mia crept from the bed, earning an intense look from Juno who was stationed on the floor.

He stared at her, pupils two glimmers in the dimness. Dogs were strange to her, galumphing creatures who made messes and were prone to biting. The big lumbering animal scared her a bit, but he undeniably enchanted Gracie for some reason. Slobbery tongue, muddy paws, sharp teeth.

And a friend, to a child who had no others.

She crouched down next to the animal. "Thank you, Juno," she whispered.

The dog swiveled his ears, considering, and then laid his head back on his paws and assumed his watchful rest.

She clicked on the small light above the kitchen table and powered up Dallas's laptop, navigating to her inbox. While the computer booted up, she peered out the blinds into the unceasing rain. Across the way, a dim yellow light gleamed from the window of Dallas's trailer. It made her feel better to know he was there and at the same time grateful there was a safe distance between them.

The previous day played back in her mind like a bad

movie. Cora gone and so was her job. Dr. Elias's face flashed in her memory. Had she misread the whole situation? Had he really been offering help? Trust your instincts, Dallas told her. But she trusted nothing about herself anymore, especially where men were concerned.

Pulling her attention back to the laptop, she opened her inbox. A message from her sister.

How are you? Hurricane cleanup continues here. Reuben is confident that he can start replanting the orchard soon. The man lives, eats and breathes oranges. How did I get fixed up with a guy who loves oranges more than me?

Mia smiled. Reuben loved his orchard, but they both knew that the man was desperately in love with Antonia. She felt the pang of envy. Hector had loved her, too, in his own way, but he'd loved power and money more.

I hear there is flooding in your area. Come to visit us in Florida. Aside from the odd hurricane, we've got perfect weather. We'll put you to work, but you'll be above water. I'd feel better if I could keep my eyes on you.

Antonia knew that Hector tracked Mia everywhere. And Hector's enemies? The people he'd cheated and double-crossed? Did they track her everywhere, too? A shiver rippled up her spine and she read the remainder of the message.

I know you don't want me to do the protective big sister thing. I'll try to be good, I promise. Reuben wants you here, too. He misses Gracie, and he wants to see her climb a tree. Waiting for your reply. A

Mia's fingers stiffened over the keyboard. See Gracie climb a tree? How did her sister know Gracie had managed to clamber up the old cottonwood tree in the backyard of their rented house a few days prior? The child was bursting with pride, even though Dallas had to get a ladder to fetch her down, and reported the accomplishment to everyone who crossed their path in the small town. Was Antonia having someone spy on her? Teeth gritted, she forced out several measured breaths.

She was turning into a nutcase. Reuben's life was trees. Of course he'd want to see Gracie climb one. She read the email again. The tree-climbing reference was purely coincidental, and her paranoia was turning her against the one person she knew was completely on her side. Hitting Reply, she contemplated how to put into words all that had happened the past two days.

Cora is dead. I am under suspicion for the murder. An intruder broke into our house. I'm staying in Dallas's trailer. I'm scared, worried, alone.

She perused the words that would send her sister into a panic. The sister who had been right all along. The woman who deserved above everyone else to enjoy the start of a marriage to the man she'd loved and lost and found again.

Backspace. Delete.

Blinking back tears she typed instead:

Gracie's growing like mad. She checks her teeth every day to see if they are loose, so desperate to use the special tooth box you sent. So busy here with work and school. Will write soon. Love you and Reuben. M

The inbox was cluttered with ads and offers from every company she'd ordered from recently using a credit card with her maiden name. It was a very tiny victory, but she took comfort in the fact that she had been able to provide the bare bones necessities with her very own hard-earned cash. Thanks to a second-hand store in town, she'd even managed a plastic wading pool that had gotten them through the hot months. It was light-years from the expensive toys and top-of-the-line clothes Gracie had when she was a baby in Hector's home, but it was bought with honest money. Gracie didn't seem to realize they were living perilously close to the poverty line. Not yet, anyway.

Clearing out the junk brought her to the last email. Her heart hammered. It could not be. The sender's name, *c.graham,* did not change no matter how hard she blinked. Cora Graham had sent her an email at four-thirty on the day she'd died, shortly after she'd sent the text summoning them to her house.

Panic squeezed Mia's stomach, and for a moment, she was too terrified to click open the email. Finally, with fingers gone cold, she did.

Find P. Finnigan. He knows the truth. I can't...

The message ended abruptly. Mia's heart pounded. Cora had sent the message when? As the smoke overcame her? As the poison paralyzed her body and she realized she could not escape?

Sobs wrenched through Mia. She clapped a hand over her mouth to keep from waking Gracie and staggered to the porch, stepping outside, grateful that the rain had momentarily slowed to a trickle. Sucking in deep breaths, she tried to rein in her stampeding emotions. It should not have surprised her to hear Dallas's door open. In a moment, he was next to her, peering into her face.

"Tell me," he said softly.

She couldn't answer over the grief that welled up inside.

With arms both strong and gentle, he pulled her close, not offering any more words, but the warmth and solace of his body pressed to hers.

With her head tucked under his chin, he let the mist dance lightly against his face, finding himself oddly relaxed with her in his arms. It was as if she molded naturally into his embrace, a perfect fit with a man who never fit in anywhere. He pressed his cheek against her hair and wondered if there was something he should be saying.

He went with silence. She would tell him what made her cry, or not. He would do everything in his power to help. That was all there was to it. So instead he relished the feel of her there, until the mist turned to drizzle and he guided her back into the trailer.

She wiped her face and sat at the kitchen table. He slid in across from her.

"I'm sorry," she said. "I slipped into hysteria there for a minute."

"No sweat."

"It was because of this." She turned the laptop to face him. "It's from Cora."

He read it. "Do you know a P. Finnigan?"

She shook her head, eyes huge in the near darkness. "Should we tell the police?"

"Yes. When you meet with them tomorrow. I'll work on it."

"How?"

"Let me worry about it. Get some sleep."

She offered an exasperated look. "Easy for you to say. You don't seem to need any sleep. Were you keeping watch on us all this time?"

I haven't been able to take my eyes off you since the day I met you, his fickle heart supplied. Fortunately, his mouth was still in charge. "Don't need much sleep."

"Or much furniture?"

He shrugged.

"Or a TV?"

"Too noisy." He won a smile with that one.

She rested her chin on her hand. "What do you need?"

The question surprised him. "Simple stuff. Backpack. Hot shower. Dog kibble."

That got a giggle that faded rapidly. "I mean, you move around all the time, like you're looking for something. What is it?"

How did he get himself into this sticky conversation? The silence stretched into awkward so he broke down and told her. "Ever hear that verse from Proverbs? Starts with 'trust in the Lord' and ends with 'Seek his will in all you do, and he will show you which path to take?'"

She nodded solemnly.

"Well, I tried to take my own path plenty of times, and it got me in jail and beaten badly and deep into gang life." He watched carefully to see if she would recoil. Most women did when he got around to his sorry life history. Those brown eyes stayed riveted to his face.

"Why a gang?"

"My dad died when I was a teen, and I went nuts. Joined a gang, figured it made me a man, cool, like my brother."

"But he got out, didn't he?"

"Yeah. He's smarter than me. Military straightened him out. He tried to get me out, too, but I'm hard-headed. Took the beating to do that. I woke up hand-cuffed to the bed, and the first thing I thought of was, had I killed someone?"

She stayed quiet.

"I hadn't. God spared me from that, but I could have." His voice hitched a little. "Oh, how easily I could have done it."

"You wanted to go into the military, didn't you? Your brother told me, I think." Her voice was soft and soothing, like water over river stones.

He sighed. "My whole life I wanted to be a Marine like my father. My choices ruined that for me. They don't take people with damaged legs and gang histories." It still hurt to say it, but somehow, telling it to her, it was more of a dull ache than a ripping pain.

"I'm sorry."

"I'm not. Oh, I wish I could have done it some other way, but destroying my life brought me to the edge of ruin and that's where I finally found God. From then on, I figured I'd let Him show me where to go and I guess He brought me here for a while."

"Until it's time to go again?"

"Dunno. He'll thump me on the head when He wants

me to put down some roots." He paused. "What about you? What do you need?"

She laughed, but there was no joy in the sound. "I need a place to call home, where I can put down roots so deep Gracie and I will never be uprooted again, but I'm never going to get that."

"No?"

"No, because Hector will never leave us alone, and everywhere we go his bad choices follow us." She closed her eyes for a moment and breathed out a sigh. "No, our bad choices. I've..." She swallowed. "I've been to jail, too, and now it looks as if I might be going there again." Her face paled. "What have we done to Gracie? Two people who were supposed to love and protect her? What have we done?"

Tears sparkled there in her eyes, but she would not let them fall. *Good girl, Mia.*

He took her hands and squeezed hard. "Gracie is happy and loved. Even I can tell that, and kids are like space aliens to me."

Small smile.

"Not one person on this Earth has no regrets."

Juno thrashed in his sleep.

"Except dogs."

"That's probably true." He fell into the warmth of those eyes. "I'll help you find a place to put down roots." Dumb. The moment he said it she pulled away. Way to go, Dallas Foot-in-Mouth Black.

Her tone became careful, formal. "Thank you, but I'm going to take care of us. That's a lesson I learned the hard way. I can only count on myself."

Wrong lesson. No bigger disappointment than one-self. "Sure. I didn't mean anything by it." He looked outside. "Sun's almost up. I'll follow you into town so you can talk to the cops."

He headed for the door, not at a run but close to it. "There are some eggs, like I said, and maybe cheese somewhere. Will Gracie eat that?"

She nodded, face still tight. "Yes, thank you. I'll replace it all when I can."

He let her have that, if it was what she needed to feel in control.

"Good night, Mia."

Two hours later he followed her bashed up car toward town. Ominous signs of disaster preparation were visible as they drove along the main street. Shop owners were filling burlap bags with sand to be piled along the embankment that would optimistically stem the flood. Mia decided to stop and retrieve the photo before meeting with the police chief, so they drove along rain-drenched streets toward the lower lying valley where she rented a home. His gut tightened as a dark-colored SUV trailed behind them along the main drag and onto the narrow two-lane road. Not cause for alarm, per se, but he thought it just might be the same SUV he'd noticed parked on the side of the road several miles back. Colorado plates. Might be a rental.

Dallas slowed and so did the SUV. Not good. Keeping a distance. Nothing to be done to lose the guy at this point. Besides, in one of his stay-up-all-night reading frenzies, hadn't he read some sage advice from a Chinese general in 400 BC about keeping your friends close and your enemies closer?

"All right," he whispered, earning an interested look from Juno in the passenger seat. He maintained a steady pace, and the car dropped back just enough to preserve the gap between them.

He braked hard when Mia stopped abruptly. In a moment, he understood. The road dipped down, following the slope of the valley, only now the asphalt had disappeared under several feet of water. The surface was muddy and rippled, speckled with leaves and broken branches. She got out, hands on hips turning to give him an exasperated look that almost made him smile.

He joined her, noting that the SUV had pulled over a half mile behind them.

"Can your truck make it across?"

"Might, but I'm not going to risk anyone's safety. There's a bridge back a ways. We'll double back."

She groaned. "That will take us another half hour."

"Better late than drowned."

She looked as though she didn't appreciate his pearls of wisdom, but she acquiesced.

Juno sniffed disinterestedly at the water, stopping a moment to eye the car behind them on the road.

A look of fear flashed across her face. "Who is that?"

"Dunno, but I'll find out in a minute. Let's head for the bridge."

Mia gave the SUV a second look. He knew she wanted to ask more questions, but instead she got behind the wheel and turned around. Dallas fell in behind her and by the time they were rolling, the SUV had disappeared. Not for long. As he predicted, it picked them up again some five miles in, once again hanging back just enough.

The bridge was of sturdy steel construction, spanning the river that was normally well below its concrete piers. Now the water lapped considerably above that mark, but not enough to leave the structure impassable.

Yet.

Dallas decided it was time to get a better handle on the situation.

Mia drove over the bridge, and when she was safely across, he followed suit. A couple of feet in, he stomped on the brakes, bringing his vehicle to a dead stop.

"Time to come clean," he muttered, looking into the rearview as the SUV made the approach to the bridge. He stopped abruptly, too.

If their shadow was there for purely innocent reasons, he'd wait patiently, figuring there was some obstruction, maybe even honk after a bit, or try to pass. Certainly he'd get out of the car to investigate why Dallas was stopped, blocking the road.

Instead, the driver backed rapidly off the bridge, did a jerky three-point turn and took off in the other direction.

Dallas almost smiled for the second time that morning. He rolled down the window and called to Mia who had stopped and stuck her head out the window to question him.

"Go on. I'll be there soon."

Her eyes widened, quarter-size. "What are you doing?"

"Just making friends," he called out the window.

SEVEN

Dallas let the SUV outdistance him until it sped around a sharp bend in the shrub-lined road. He slowed and turned up a rough stretch which was probably more a trail than a road, but a way Dallas and Juno had explored many times in their backpacking travels. He stopped for only a moment to call a friend and give him the plate number.

"You know I got things to do 'sides hack info for you, right?" Farley said.

Dallas laughed. "Gonna help me or not?"

Farley snorted. "If you and Fido hadn't saved my life, I'd be in the bottom of a ravine with vultures using my bones for toothpicks."

"Vultures don't have teeth. Staying sober?"

"Yeah, man. Prayed myself through the last real bad stretch."

Dallas had prayed right along with him. And picked Farley up when he hadn't made it through, cleaned him up, filled him with coffee and nearly hog-tied the kid to get him to a meeting. "Gotta win, every day."

"I know, Mother, I know. Stop nagging and let me get to work."

"While you're at it, can you see if there's a P. Finnigan living in the area?"

"All right. See ya." Farley clicked off.

Dallas pushed the truck along, rocks pinging into the bottom, irritating Juno who barked just once.

"Half a mile more." Dallas squeezed the truck by a narrow section of path, branches scraping the sides, until he'd looped back out to the main road. A recent rock slide took out a bend of the highway, leaving the section blocked with a mess of boulders and only one lane passable. It was marked with cones and caution signs. Handy. He rolled down the window and listened to learn if he'd guessed correctly.

The sound of the SUV's approach told him he had. He edged past the rockfall and pulled the truck across the road. SUV guy would pass the blockage, encounter the truck and have to stop and back, which would slow him down enough for Dallas to get a good look. Risky, but with Mia's situation worsening by the minute, he needed some intel. Keep your enemies close…

The SUV was taking an unhurried pace. Dallas got out of the truck and he and Juno took a position behind a pile of rocks. Juno gave him the "you're probably crazy but I'm happy to participate in your insanity" look. They waited less than five minutes.

The SUV made the turn, stopped so fast the tires skidded a few inches. Dallas crouched low, peering over a granite lip of rock to identify the driver. To his surprise, the man shoved open the door and got out. Dallas took a picture with his cell phone.

Not much to him, but strength had nothing to do with size. Fair skin, buzz-cut hair. Tight skinny jeans and a shiny jacket that was probably fashionable somewhere in the world where Dallas hoped he never found himself.

The guy looked slowly around, hands loose at his sides. "We gonna talk?" he called out, voice higher pitched than Dallas guessed.

Dallas climbed out from behind the rock, and Juno scampered over to the man. He gave him a careful circling before he settled on sniffing his sneakers. "You're following Mia. Why? Who are you?"

The kid had to be no more than twenty. "Archie. How do you know I'm not following you?"

Dallas considered. "I'm not worth following. Did you break into her house?"

Archie crouched slowly and offered an outstretched hand to Juno. "I love dogs. Miss mine. He's some sort of lab and husky mix. Chews my shoes when I don't walk him enough and leaves them on the bed for me to find."

Dallas waited, watching to make sure Archie didn't reach for any kind of weapon in his ridiculous excuse for a jacket. "I asked you a question."

"My boss sent me here. I do what I'm told."

"Who's your boss?"

Archie straightened. "Guy who wants his property back."

Dallas's pulse sped up a fraction. "Do you work for Hector?"

Archie laughed. "Good one. I like to be on the winning team." He checked his watch. "You're a roadblock, in more ways than one. You need to step aside."

"Not if you're after Mia."

"She has something that belongs to my boss. He

wants it back. No need for any pain. Just a simple negotiation."

"She doesn't have anything, and if you hurt her, it will be the last thing you ever do." He had not raised his voice, but the intensity made Juno return to his side and sit, rigid with expectation.

"All right," Archie said, pulling out a switchblade and flicking it open. "This is as good a place to kill you as any, but I don't want to hurt the dog. Tell him not to attack."

Juno wasn't an attack dog. In fact, he was the perfect Search and Rescue dog because he was passionately interested in people, but they also had a bond that surpassed owner and worker.

"All right," Dallas said calmly. "I'll send him to fetch and then you and I can get down to business. May I?" He gestured to a stick on the ground a few feet away and Archie nodded.

Dallas bent over to get the stick and while he was at it, grabbed a palm full of gravel loosed from the earlier slide.

"Okay, Juno. Ready to fetch?"

Juno shot to his feet as Dallas tossed the stick into the trees and then turned to fire the handful of gravel at Archie who instinctively raised an arm to cover his face. It was enough. Dallas aimed for Archie's arm and threw himself on top of the man, bringing him to the ground.

Juno returned and danced in crazy circles around the two, barking at a deafening volume.

Dallas used all his strength to slam Archie's knife hand into the ground, but the kid held fast. He dealt Dallas a blow with his free fist that got him in the back of the head, sending stars shooting across his vision. A flash of fire across his forearm rocked Dallas back as Archie rolled away. Dallas scrambled to his feet, a line of red dripping from the wound on his arm.

Archie was already standing, eyeing the dog who continued to bark, uncertain, taking darting hops toward Archie and Dallas. "What happened to fetch?"

"He fetches people, not sticks, and he's not an attack dog, so don't hurt him."

"No," Archie said. "I guess I won't. Nice moves. Heard you were in a gang back in the day."

Dallas did not react to Archie's knowledge. Kid had done some research. "Not anymore."

"You can never get out of that world."

"Yes, you can. I did."

"You're gonna be in my face if I let you leave."

"If you're after Mia, then you're right. I will."

"Why? You into her or something?"

"Just a friend."

Archie gave him a look. "Uh-huh. Sure." He straightened. "Short on time, so I'm gonna end it here, but I'll take care of the dog for you."

"Appreciate that." Dallas went into a ready stance, learned not in a karate studio or a self-defense class, but from adrenaline-fueled fights with other lost young men bent on self-destruction. To defend their brotherhood, what had been his brotherhood, his family, or so he'd fooled himself into believing. All for Uncle, for the territory. He did not want to fight, but if it would free Mia, then he would do it. Juno whined, big torso heaving with confusion. A finder, not a fighter. Dallas wished he had spent his life doing the same.

Self-recrimination later, he told himself. There was

no effective way to defend against a knife attack and he had the scars to prove it. Only one alternative that wouldn't get him killed and he took it. When Archie lunged forward, Dallas jerked aside and aimed a crushing kick at Archie's knee.

Archie's grunt of pain told Dallas he'd hit the target. He stumbled and Dallas aimed another kick at the knife hand which sent the switchblade spiraling into the bushes as Archie fell stomach-first onto the wet ground.

Dallas immediately knelt on his back, knee between the shoulder blades, shushing the furiously barking Juno.

Dallas's heart was pounding, the pulse hammering so loudly in his ears he did not at first hear the chug of a heavy vehicle approaching from the other side of the rock slide.

"Someone's coming. Moving fast," Archie puffed. "What are you gonna do? You don't move your truck, whoever that is could slam right into it and go over the cliff."

He was right, but the second he released Archie, the guy would bolt or find his switchblade and have another go at Dallas. The pop of gravel sounded louder now.

No choice. He couldn't risk causing an accident.

He leaned closer to Archie. "Stay away from Mia."

Archie answered with a laugh. Dallas released his hold and ran to the truck, cranked the engine as Juno leapt in and got the truck out of the way with a screech of tires. He made it just far enough to pull off onto the narrow shoulder when Archie flashed by in his SUV, snapping off a salute to Dallas. A moment more passed before an emergency vehicle swept by, no sirens going, but lights flashing.

They, too, had to take the roundabout way to Mia's neighborhood since the main road was underwater. The driver gave Dallas a wave, thanking him for pulling off the road.

He settled in behind, trying not to crowd the responders. Should he worry more that the situation ahead had turned into an emergency? Or that he'd let Archie, the guy with a switchblade, get that much closer to Mia and Gracie?

Hands gripping the wheel, Mia answered Gracie's myriad questions mechanically, not realizing what she was agreeing to.

"I can have ice cream for breakfast? Super duper," Gracie said. "You never let me have that before. Not even Tina lets me have ice cream for breakfast, only cookies."

Mia blinked. "What? No of course you can't have ice cream for breakfast. I was thinking about something else, and Tina should not give you cookies for breakfast, either."

In truth, she was trying to squash down the concern that washed through her belly. Dallas had taken off after a stranger to do what? Confront him? Follow the car? She hit the brakes as a roadblock appeared. A police volunteer in an orange vest approached her open window.

"What is it? What's going on?"

"Levee failed. Town's flooded. We're evacuating now."

"But I've got to get to my house. I need to…" Retrieve a picture of a woman who was at the scene of a murder? That seemed too fantastic a tale to drop on the harried-looking volunteer who was already wet to the skin, though it had stopped raining. "I have to get something. It's important."

"Sorry, ma'am. It's not safe to drive in. You can see from the road there, where everyone is gathered. No farther than that."

She dutifully pulled the car off the road, turned off the engine and helped Gracie out. They skirted giant puddles and slogged through patches of grass until they came to a gathering of a half dozen people wearing emergency vests who were peering at clipboards along with the volunteer firefighters. It was a sort of makeshift emergency center with a pop-up canopy to keep off the rain. With Gracie bundled close, Mia drew to the edge of the bluff, gazing down at what had been her home.

The house she rented was one of only a half dozen, scattered in between with thickly clustered trees. Now the quiet, country road was a river, water lapping the middle of the doorways. At first she couldn't locate her house, until she saw the weathervane turning lazily in the breeze.

Gracie pulled at her mother's hand. "Where's our house?"

Mia breathed out a long sigh. She had not yet even managed to tell Gracie the hard truth about Cora, but there was no way to shield her child from this. "The levee couldn't hold all the water. It spilled over and flooded our house."

They stood for a moment in silence.

"When will the water go away?"

Great question, and she'd give her eye teeth to know the answer. "I'm not sure."

And when the water did recede, what would be left behind? Sodden clothes, ruined furniture acquired a bit at a time on her meager salary. And the rocking chair, oh that precious wooden chair snatched up at a garage sale when she shouldn't have spent the money. How many hours had she spent in that chair after Gracie went to sleep, studying her nursing coursework, dreaming about the future she imagined she was providing for her daughter.

A lump formed in her throat.

"Where are we gonna sleep, Mommy?"

The question danced away, unanswered on the wind. They watched an inflatable Zodiac boat, guided by two firefighters, as it approached the bluff carrying an elderly couple swaddled in life jackets, their sparse white hair pasted in wet clumps to their foreheads. She searched the area for Dallas. What had happened to him?

Mia felt a hand on her shoulder.

She turned to find Dr. Elias wearing an orange vest over a long-sleeved denim shirt and jeans. Her mind was still dealing with the shock of seeing her whole life submerged and she wasn't sure what feeling floated to the top at the sight of her former employer.

"I'm sorry," he said, eyes somber. "The Army Corps of Engineers couldn't save the levee. They tried their best."

Mia nodded. "I'm sure they did."

"Hiya, Dr. Elias," Gracie said.

He smiled and knelt in front of her. "Well, hello there. I'm glad to see you."

"Our house is all watery now."

"Don't worry, honey. We'll find you a place to live."

Mia took Gracie's hand. "The doctor is here to help people who are hurt. Let him do his job now."

Dr. Elias straightened and put an arm around Mia's shoulders. "Really, I can help you find a place."

She didn't move, torn between shock and uncertainty. Was this the man whom she'd thought meant to harm her only days before? There was no longer a clear answer to any issue crowding her mind and heart.

Where would they go? She had maybe twenty dollars in her purse and a credit card on which she'd already charged a semester's tuition. "Why would you want to do that after you fired me?"

He sighed. "I told you I would help you, even if you couldn't work at the clinic. You lied to protect your child, not to hurt me. I'm sensitive about lying. A foible of mine."

How had the talk become about him?

He squeezed her shoulders. "I can fix you up in…"

A woman approached, dark hair cut into a stylish bob that remained neatly coiffed in spite of the elements. The fragrance of a floral perfume clung to her, odd and out of place at a disaster scene. Green eyes flashed under delicate brows. "Thomas, you're needed at the launch point. They're going out on a rescue for a possible heart attack in progress."

"Of course." He patted Gracie on the head and jogged toward the Zodiac that was being readied to embark on the rescue mission.

The woman gave Mia a tight smile. Her face was carefully made up to show her fortysomething years to full advantage, jewelry small and tasteful. "I'm Catherine Elias, the good doctor's wife."

The slight sarcasm left Mia off balance. "I'm Mia Verde and this is Gracie, my daughter. I work... I worked for your husband until just recently. We met at a party you were kind enough to host for the staff." Mia's eyes were drawn again toward the water. "That was my house down there."

Catherine's face softened, giving her a more youthful look. "I'm sorry. This must be hard for you. No job, no house and a daughter to care for." She seemed to consider for a moment. "I heard Thomas telling you he could help you find a place and I guess..." She shrugged. "Never mind. I'm tired, that's all. Our kids are almost finished with high school, but I remember how difficult it is when they're young. But sweet, too, those little ones." She looked wistfully at Gracie.

"Yes," Mia murmured, uncertain how to respond to the sudden change in mood.

"We have a small cabin up in the mountains here. It's remote, but you are welcome to stay there until you get another place."

"Thank you. That is incredibly kind of you, but we'll find something." Mia was amazed that her tone was calm and controlled. Inside, her gut churned like the gray water splashing against the bluff.

When? Where? And most of all how? She felt like dropping to her knees and praying, but she would not crumble. Not now. Not ever again. She would make a way, where there was none. "Where are the townspeople being evacuated to?"

Catherine pulled her gaze from Gracie. "The college gym just up the hill. It will work for a night or two anyway. You can walk up, or there's a van arriving in a minute to carry people."

"Great." Mia scooped Gracie up. "Mommy always wanted you to go to college. You'll be the first four-year-old attendee ever. We'll just wait with the gang until the van arrives."

Feeling Catherine's eyes following them, she hastened toward the wet neighbors gathered in a forlorn group under a sodden canopy. She texted Tina, relieved when the girl answered back.

College classes canceled. Gone home to folks until flood's past. Kiss Gracie for me and try to stay dry.

"Hiya, Dallas," Gracie called over her shoulder.

Mia whirled, her spirit rising at the sight of Dallas loping toward her with Juno at his heels.

He gave Gracie a tight smile and she immediately crouched to administer an ear rub to Juno. Mud streaked his shirt, and Mia's eyes traveled downward, caught by the circle of bloody gauze tied around his forearm.

Her stomach clenched. "The man in the car."

"I'm okay, but he got away." Dallas seemed to weigh something in his mind before he leaned close and spoke in a low murmur. "He's keeping tabs on you for his boss."

She forced out the question. "Who is his boss? Never mind. It's Hector, isn't it?" Bitterness rose in her throat like a bubbling acid. "He's got people watching my every move. He'll never let us build a life without him."

"I don't think that's it."

Wind slapped her hair into her face. "Who then? Who would bother?"

"People who think Hector passed something on to you."

"Passed what?"

He didn't answer. Instead he showed her the picture on his cell phone. "Recognize him?"

Everything went fuzzy. She inhaled deeply, trying to stem the whirling in her head. "It's the man who broke into my house. I can't understand this. What is happening to my life?"

He embraced her then, and she let him. His arms pressed away the panic, the fear that grew with every passing day. The heat of his skin melted some of the numbing cold that gripped her.

"I'm checking into it. I'll have more answers soon."

"I've been in Spanish Canyon for months. Why would he come here now? What am I going to do?"

His embrace tightened. "Come back to the trailer. I'll keep watch. He won't get close."

Protection. Strength. Safety. And a delicious sliver of fascination. Dallas Black made all those things erupt in her belly. She turned so her lips touched the smooth skin of his jaw. His dark hair cocooned her face against the warm hollow of his neck. How her body craved the comfort of his touch, her soul cried out to have a partner to help her through the flood that she knew was far from over.

But she'd had that perfect union before. A God-blessed marriage, or so she'd thought, until she finally saw Hector for what he was. Now "until death do us part" sounded more like a sentence than a comfort. Never again. Never.

She stepped back, sucking in a breath. "I'm going

to the college. They've got an evacuation shelter set up there."

He frowned. "You want to go sleep on the gym floor where anyone can get at you and Gracie?"

She took Gracie's hand. "We'll be safe there."

"Safe?" His face was incredulous. "This guy Archie was ready to kill me to get to you."

"There are lots of people going. We'll never be alone."

The muscles of his jaw jumped. "Absolutely not."

She stiffened. "We'll be in a group all the time. Never alone. Besides, you don't make decisions for me."

"Somebody should, because you're letting what happened to you with Hector color your judgment."

Cheeks burning, her stomach tightened into an angry ball. "I'm doing what's best for Gracie."

"Are you?" He fisted his hands on his hips, and she saw fresh blood welling through the white gauze when his muscles flexed.

Am I? Suddenly she wondered, but she couldn't reverse course now. Right or wrong she had to call the shots for Gracie. Just her and no one else. "I'll return your phone as soon as I can."

She pulled Gracie along to the van that had just wheezed up the slope, not allowing herself to look back. She knew what was behind her anyway. A disappointed German shepherd.

And one very angry Dallas Black.

EIGHT

"What?" Dallas barked into the phone.

Farley whistled. "Bite my head off, why don't you? Got a burr under your backpack?"

"Sorry. Bad day." Too bad to try to explain to Farley. He molded his tone into something that might pass for civil. "Do you have anything for me?"

"Seven P. Finnigans in the vicinity. Sending you those addresses."

"Thanks."

"And the car was rented to an Archie Gonzales, from Miami."

Miami. Not a surprise. "Okay."

"One more thing, man. Norm, over at the rental car place. I know him, and he's a crusty old codger. He's got trackers on the rentals."

Dallas's nerves quickened. "Illegal, of course,"

"Of course, but he's in favor of slapping a nice hefty fee on the cars if they're taken out of state. Anyway, it was easy to hack into his tracking system."

"Do I want to know how you did that?"

"Probably not."

"What did you find out?"

"Most of his routes were routine, except one I found interesting. Guess who he's been to see recently?"

"Not in the mood for guessing games."

"Dr. Elias."

"That's not news. I think he's been at the clinic shadowing Mia."

"Not the clinic. Archie's been to the doctor's house."

His house? Dallas struggled to put it together and almost missed the finish.

"At 3:13 a.m."

Not the usual time for social calls. "Thanks, Farley. I owe you lunch."

"Yeah, and a vacation in Maui."

"We'll start with lunch."

"All right, cheapskate."

Dallas disconnected. The next call would be to Reuben and Antonia. There was no more room to keep secrets. Mia needed to know everything. He swallowed, picturing her maddeningly stubborn brown eyes, the need for independence burning as bright as the hurt. When she knew, she would hate him.

But at least she'd still be alive.

Dallas's arm throbbed. He strolled as casually as he could through the collection of hastily parked cars on the grassy shoulder of the road, leaving Juno in the truck to catch a nap. He realized he was grinding his teeth when he passed Mia's battered car. If she'd listen to reason…if she'd consider the smart choice.

Like you did? His conscience flipped through the myriad prideful mistakes he'd made. Rival gang members he'd fought, threatened. Store owners he'd intimidated. Petty theft he'd committed to prove himself to his ersatz family. His damaged body would always be a reminder of that disastrous past.

Most of his shame came when he remembered the way he'd coveted the looks he'd gotten from people, the respect he'd imagined in their eyes. Turns out it was not respect, but fear. He'd been too blinded to turn from the smothering blanket of gang life.

In spite of his brother Trey's tough love born of experience.

With no regard for his mother's pleading requests and avalanche of prayers.

It had taken waking up in the hospital with part of his spleen missing and his knee on fire, shaking from alcohol withdrawal and his boyhood dream to become a Marine ruined, for him to fall on his face in front of the Lord. Maybe it was the humiliation of being handcuffed to the hospital bed, knowing he deserved to go to jail for many things, including possession of an illegal firearm and simple assault. Possibly it was the realization that he had shamed his mother, his brother and his father's memory. Undoubtedly, it was God shouting his name.

At rock bottom, there's no more room for pride.

Only God.

Once he'd let go, God had shown him the goodness in people, the desperate love of his family, his own potential to be a man who lifted others, rather than striking them down. Somewhere along the way, he'd found there was goodness inside him, as well.

The fall had hurt, and he wished he could help Mia learn what he had without the dramatic descent. He sighed. *God's job, Dallas. Yours is to keep her safe.* It was a good reminder. No matter what the oddball storm of feelings brewing inside, Mia was his job, his mission. In spite of the pain from Archie's knife, and Mia's ridiculous desire to stay at the college shelter, he moved on through the sea of parked cars.

He saw no sign of Archie's rental, a small mark in their favor.

Sunset was not due for another hour, but the clouds succeeded in sealing the light away behind a wall of gray. Bad sign. The levees were similarly stressed all over Spanish Canyon and the rivers and catchments swollen to capacity. On an up note, the last weather report he'd heard called for only a mild rainfall in the next forty-eight hours. With that weather break, they might be able to stave off any more serious flooding and evacuations.

The flood lent strange odors to the air—the scent of wet stone, sodden foliage and trees uprooted from centuries of packed earth. Mia's house was underwater to the eaves, and so was the picture that might shed some light on Cora's death. He guessed Archie had not been there in Mia's house looking for the photo, but searching for Garza's money. However the meeting between Elias and Archie still puzzled him.

He was about to return to his truck, parked well away from the others when a stealthy movement caught his attention. Trick of the cascading shadows? No, there was another pulse of motion near a well-appointed blue BMW.

He drew back, crouching behind Mia's car to watch as a slight figure stealthily opened the passenger door. Whoever it was wore a hat and a dark windbreaker. Pretty low for someone to take advantage of a disaster situation to rifle through someone's car. But it was true that disasters brought out both the best and worst in people. He was about to demand an explanation, when he realized this wasn't a stranger, not a total stranger anyway.

Easing closer, he could see Susan's profile well enough to be sure it was her, the red-haired woman who'd shown up at his trailer.

And snuck out with your knife, he reminded himself.

Still keeping low between vehicles, he crept nearer.

She sat in the passenger seat of the car, examining the pile of papers in her lap that she'd taken out of the glove box. So intent was she on her mission, she didn't look up until he wrenched open the door.

With a scream she bolted out, spilling the papers on the muddy ground. For a moment, she stood frozen, staring, chest heaving with panic.

"Breaking-and-entering a specialty of yours?"

She let out a gust of air. "The door was open. That's not breaking in."

"Whose car?"

Still no response. Keeping her in his peripheral vision he picked up one of the papers. Catherine Elias. "Why are you interested in Dr. Elias's wife?"

"She's a fake."

"A fake what?"

"She's living a lie, and I'm going to prove it."

"I thought you were interested in finding out who killed Cora."

She nodded, lips tight, eyes flat and hard as wet stones. "That's right."

"Do you think Catherine killed Cora?"

"Leave me alone, Dallas. This doesn't concern you right now."

He took a step toward her. "You're coming with me to the police. No more sneaking around breaking into cars. I'm out of patience with these guessing games."

She shook her head. "I'm not going with you anywhere."

He did not want to force a woman to do anything against her wishes, but this particular woman was dangerous. He took her wrist, the tendons standing out against the skin, pulse slamming violently through her veins. "You need to come with me, Susan."

He'd prepared himself for her to pull away. Instead she surged close, her clawed fingers pinching his biceps, face so close her sour breath bathed his face. "Listen to me," she hissed. "There are dangerous people in this town, people who are not who they appear to be." Her mouth twitched at the corners, and he fought the urge to recoil.

"Like Mrs. Elias?"

She did not seem to hear him. "Dangerous people who will kill Mia Verde and her little girl, just like they killed Cora. If you try to go to the police, or anyone else, they'll just kill her quicker."

His stomach flipped. "Who? Tell me, and I'll help you."

She moved back slightly to search his eyes. "Ah, sweet boy. Are you going to protect me from a killer?"

"If I can."

"I'm not afraid to die," she said, releasing his shoulders. "It's the living part that's scary."

He felt as though he was stuck in a strange horror film. Was she crazy? Was he, for letting go of her wrist?

The sound of voices made them both turn. Susan

quickly returned the papers to the glove box and ducked down, yanking him to a crouch next to her. Through the window they saw Catherine Elias and an orange-vested volunteer consulting a clipboard as they walked toward the car. Catherine pointed to something on the first page and the two stopped to talk.

"Remember," Susan whispered, "if you tell anyone, Mia and Gracie will die. I'll contact you when I can." She sprinted off through the cars and ducked into a screen of trees. He scooted far enough away from Catherine's car that he would not be taken for a stalker, and then walked back to his truck where he sat on the front seat, brooding.

The obvious course of action was to go to the police, but they already suspected Mia of being involved in Cora's death. What would they make of his wild story about some mystery woman poking through Catherine's car?

Her words circled in his gut, cold and heavy. *"Dangerous people who will kill Mia Verde and her little girl, just like they killed Cora."*

Now his head pounded right along with the throbbing in his forearm. He should go home, back to the trailer to think it through, but he didn't want to be that far away from Mia and Gracie with Archie on the loose. If he checked himself in to the college evacuation center, Mia would be furious and possibly try to go find yet another unsuitable place to house herself and Gracie.

Juno poked his nose at Dallas, bringing him back. "What next?" his eyes inquired. The dog was eager to do just about anything Dallas requested except get his nails trimmed. That required several dozen treat bribes and some strong-arming from his owner. "Looks like we sleep in the truck again, boy, but I've got some kibble for you, don't worry."

He opened the door for the dog.

"Don't suppose you've got any notions on how to handle a stubborn woman, do you, Juno?"

Juno huffed out a breath and laid his head on his paws.

"Yeah, that's what I thought," Dallas said, giving his friend a pat.

Mia took the blankets offered to her and found her way to the side of the gym designated for women. She chose two cots together, but at a bit of a distance from the nearby family consisting of a wife and three teenage girls and a few older women who had already set up their makeshift beds. The two older women sat together, hands clasped, praying softly, one with wispy white hair. Perhaps they were sisters. Longing surged through her and she wished Antonia was there.

Gracie stared. "Is that Miss Cora? I want to go see her."

A pain stabbed deep inside. "No, honey. Just looks like her. The hair is the same color."

"Oh." Gracie said, looking up at the ceiling lights. "I don't like it here. Maybe we can go stay with Miss Cora. She prays nice, with songs and everything."

Tears collected in Mia's eyes, and she blinked hard. It hadn't dawned on her until just then that she had never prayed with Gracie, that she'd funneled her own anger into a deluge that kept her daughter far from the

Lord, too. Her choice had bled down to Gracie, staining her with Mia's own sin.

"Gracie, I'm sorry. Do...do you want to pray with me?"

Gracie nodded, grabbing Mia's hands. "Okay. I'll say it. I know how." Gracie thanked God for Mia and Cora and the cheese sandwich and cookies she'd gotten from the volunteer who'd included an extra sweet for the little girl and the blue blanket and Auntie Nia and Uncle BooBen. "And thanks for Dallas 'cuz he says Daddy can be good again and thanks for Juno 'cuz he plays with me. Ayyyyyy men!" The last word came out in such an unexpected volume that the others shot amused glances their way.

Mia raised an eyebrow. "That was a big amen."

"Cora says you should always fill up the amen with joy," Gracie said. "So can we go see her?"

That innocent heart had never confronted death before. Certainly Mia would never have chosen to tell Gracie in the wake of losing every possession to the cruel water that engulfed their house. This time, she did send up a prayer of her own, a halting, awkward, stumbling effort.

Help me tell her.

Help her cope.

Mia forced out the words. "Honey, I have something sad to tell you."

Gracie regarded her soberly, bouncing a bit on the cot beside her.

"Miss Cora died. I'm so sorry. Her house caught on fire and the smoke got inside her lungs." Mia watched in fear as Gracie's brow puckered. "She's in Heaven now."

"Oh." Gracie considered the news as a full fifteen seconds ticked away. "Can we stay at her house until she comes back?"

It was as if her heart shrank smaller and smaller, concentrating the pain until it nearly choked her. "She's not coming back, baby," Mia whispered.

"Never?"

Mia took Gracie's small fingers in her own. "No, honey. Never."

"Mommy, I think that's not right. She's gonna come soon. Can I keep the blanket?" Gracie held up the blue blanket neatly folded at the foot of the cot.

"Yes," Mia said weakly. "The volunteers said you could if you want to."

Gracie wrapped herself up and laid down on the cot, singing softly to herself.

Mia watched her, filled with a river of tenderness that almost overwhelmed her. It would sink in, in time, that Cora was gone. Maybe that was a gift God gave his little children, a gradual realization that was kinder, somehow than the swift bolt of knowledge. Shadows crept along the edges of the gym, and quiet conversations gave way to silence. Mia found she could not sleep, though the cot was not at all uncomfortable.

She tossed and turned on the prickly choices she had made, ignoring Dallas's advice. His words floated back through her memory.

"Ever hear that verse from Proverbs? Starts with 'trust in the Lord' and ends with 'Seek His will in all you do, and He will show you which path to take.'"

She yanked the covers up around her chin. He could afford to believe such things; he had no one depending on him except for a dog. Dallas would not wake up tomorrow to a hungry child with not a single spare pair of socks, no place to live and nowhere to go. That was going to be Mia's scenario in the morning and she'd have to figure out how to deal with it.

A gleam of light crept across the gym floor. Someone entered carrying an enormous pile of towels, heading after a moment of hesitation, toward the locker room. She sighed. At least there was the possibility of a hot shower in the morning. Again she tried to force her body to relax on the cot. This time her wandering attention was caught by whispered conversation as two people talked by the light of a battery-powered lantern.

Giving up the attempt at sleep, she got up in search of a drink of water and caught a sentence of the conversation going on near the doors.

"She's practically a stranger," a familiar voice growled.

"No, she's not," Catherine Elias hissed. "That redheaded wacko is stalking me."

Dr. Elias reached for his wife's hand, but she jerked it away, nearly upsetting the lantern. "She lost her husband. I treated her some time later. She attached herself to me and Peter."

"Peter Finnigan? You never mentioned that."

Peter Finnigan? Mia's heart beat faster at the name from Cora's email. She wanted to ask, to step forward into the lamplight, but she decided to retreat from the private conversation instead. As she did so, she heard Dr. Elias continue.

"I didn't want to upset you, honey."

"What's her fixation with me?"

He sighed. "She wants to be with me, ever since I treated her all those years back. I've tried to keep her away because she's...unhinged."

Unhinged. Mia crept back toward her cot, but not until she heard Mrs. Elias's reply.

"She's dangerous."

Dangerous. They had to be talking about Susan, the woman from the fire, who'd showed up at Dallas's trailer.

She was in such a state of confusion, at first she thought she'd gone to the wrong cot. "Gracie?" she called softy, turning in a quick circle.

Gracie's blanket lay on the floor, but the girl was nowhere to be found. She'd gone to the bathroom. That was it.

Mia made her way quickly to the ladies' room. Empty. Jogging now back out into the main gym, she raced through the rows of cots, peering intently to see if Gracie had mistakenly crawled into the wrong bed.

There she was—at the end of the row, curled into a ball under the blanket. Mia felt the weight of the world rise off her shoulders and she heaved out a gusty sigh.

"You scared me, Gracie," she whispered, laying a hand on the girl's shoulder. "You're in the wrong bed."

The child sat up, blinking dark eyes. The woman on the cot reached out a protective hand. "This is my daughter, Evelyn. Can I help you?"

Shock rippled through Mia. Gracie was gone.

NINE

Gracie's here somewhere. She's not gone. Mia began to run now, around the perimeter of the gym to the men's area, in case her daughter had gotten confused. She rechecked Gracie's cot, snatching up the blue blanket to prove to her hands what her eyes could not accept.

Gracie was not there.

"Gracie?" What started out as a whisper, grew in volume until people began to sit up on their cots.

Dr. Elias and his wife materialized, lantern in hand. "What's wrong?" the doctor asked.

"Gracie's gone."

Catherine scanned the room. "I'm sure she's here somewhere."

Fear clawed at Mia's insides, prickling her in cold waves of goose bumps. "What if she wandered outside?" Down the hill, to the edge of the bluff where there was six feet of floodwater to fall into?

"We'll look right now," Dr. Elias said, heading for the door. "Catherine, keep searching inside." He put a hand on Mia's shoulder. "We'll find her."

At the moment, all her anger at the doctor dissipated in a cloud of hope.

We'll find her.

They ran outside, sprinting along the path to the edge of the bluff, looking down into the swirling, moonlit water. Mia's stomach was twisted into a knot. Would she see her little girl floating there, facedown in the merciless waves? Shaking all over she forced herself to look.

"No sign of her. I'll look downstream," Dr. Elias said, handing her a flashlight. "Would she have gone to the woods back up by the gym?"

"I don't know," Mia answered. "I'll check there." She turned toward the patch of trees, dark silhouettes against the sky. Why would she head out of the gym on her own? Gracie was not afraid of the dark, but she did sleepwalk sometimes. Mia looked for signs that Gracie had passed by, but the ground was littered with bushels of fallen leaves and downed branches. The darkness wasn't helping, either.

"Gracie?" Mia called, her voice tremulous.

She walked under the dripping canopy. Droplets landed on her face like tears. "Gracie?" she called again. There was no answer but the rustle of pine needles, the movement caught by her flashlight the result of debris blowing along the ground. Gracie wasn't here, Mia could feel it.

She had to be inside the gym, she'd fallen asleep somewhere or gone to look for a snack. Mia was beaming the flashlight ahead to find her way out, when a man grabbed her from behind. A hand, smelling of nicotine, covered her mouth, as a strong pair of arms held her in a tight clinch.

"Mrs. Sandoval, listen carefully because I'm not the patient type and I want to go back to Florida. We know

Hector has sent you a stash of money and it belongs to my boss. He wants it back. I've already searched your home and followed you around like a tracking dog, and I'm sick of it so I decided we should have a little meeting. Now, I'm going to move my hand so you can tell me what I want to know. If you scream, I'll hurt you. Understand?"

Blood rushing in her ears, she managed a nod. He peeled away his fingers and she turned to face him. It was the same man who had tried to trap them in her garage. She didn't care. There was only one thing her mind screamed out to know.

"Did you take my daughter?"

Archie's expression was hard to read. "I asked you a question. Answer."

"I don't have any money from Hector, and I don't know where it is."

"Mr. Garza thinks otherwise."

Garza. Powerful. Ruthless. A man who ran the Miami drug trade. "I don't have it. If I did, would I be renting a house here? Driving a secondhand car?"

Archie shrugged. "Not my job to figure you out, just to return the money. Got a tip that you've hidden it somewhere."

"A tip from whom?"

He didn't answer.

"Please," she whispered. "Did you do something to Gracie?"

Flashlights played over the grass outside the gym. Archie stepped back into the shadows. "Think about what's important and what you will lose if you don't give me what I want."

He melted away into the wet trees.

She ran blindly, branches slapping at her face, back toward the gym.

Gracie, Gracie, her heart chanted as she sprinted straight into Dallas, rocking back off his hard chest.

"Gracie's gone. Archie got hold of me."

His fingers dug into her shoulders. "Did he hurt you?"

"No."

His eyes dropped to her hands. "Is it hers?"

"What?" She realized through her fog that she was still holding the blue blanket. "This? Yes, it's Gracie's."

He called Juno and held out the blanket to the dog. "Find."

Juno bounded over the grass, startling those doing the flashlight search.

"Can he smell her?" she whispered.

"He's air scenting, following her smell." They watched the dog jog up to the gym entrance, scratching to be let in.

Dallas eased the doors open and Juno disappeared inside. Mia and Dallas followed her in. The dog followed the scent to the girl's bathroom, but stopped before he made it to the threshold. Juno circled a few times and stood, nose twitching.

Mia pressed shaking fingers to her mouth. "He doesn't know where she is."

"Give him a minute. There are a lot of scents in here. He's an older dog, so he's better at thinking it out and taking his time."

"Are you sure?"

"Trust the dog."

Trust a dog? With her baby's life? She wanted to yell, to scream at the top of her lungs as she watched

Juno make a slow perusal of the room. Most of the occupants were awake now, helping look under cots and in corners, while others stood on the sides of the gym, giving Mia looks of abject pity.

She felt Dallas's hand take her hand and he squeezed hard. She clung to that touch as if it were the only thing that could keep her alive. Maybe it was. If Juno didn't find Gracie… She could not breathe, her ears rang.

She felt the room spinning, and Dallas forced her into a chair. "Deep breaths."

Waves of nausea and panic alternated through her body as she struggled not to black out.

Juno scratched at a darkened door in the back of the gym that Mia had not noticed.

"Stay here," Dallas said. "I'll check it out."

No way. Mia struggled to her feet, shoving down the dizziness by sheer willpower and staggered after him.

The exit opened onto a chilly hallway with metal doors at even intervals. Juno charged into the inky darkness.

Dr. Elias trotted behind them. "All the doors along this corridor are locked except the far exit door, for safety's sake. I saw to it myself."

"And the exit door? Where does it open?"

"Onto the parking lot," Elias said.

Mia ran to the end, ignoring the men. She was about to plunge through.

"Wait," Dallas said. He nodded at Juno who was pacing the corridor in regular arcs, nose quivering.

"You stay with your dog. I'm going to find my kid," Mia snapped.

"We might be wasting time," Dallas said. "Let the dog work, just for a minute longer."

"I don't have a minute," she shrieked. "Gracie might be out there in the water."

"This is why we train rescue dogs, Mia," Dallas barked. "They save time and effort and find a victim faster than a person ever could. You've got to trust the dog. Trust me."

For a long moment she stared at him. Seconds passed into excruciating minutes. Trust. She could not give it to him, not now, not with Gracie's life at stake. She pressed on the panic bar, just as Juno scratched furiously at one of the doors. Dallas opened it.

"So much for locked. It's a door to the stairwell." He held it for Juno who raced away. In a matter of moments, the dog returned, sat rigidly at Dallas's feet and barked exactly two times.

"It leads to the roof, I think," Dr. Elias said, voice low and hushed. "How did she unlock the door? Could a little girl climb three stories all by herself in a darkened stairwell?"

Gracie could. Hope and fear clawed together in her throat and she pushed forward, but Dallas had already plunged through the door, long legs churning up the stairs leaving Mia racing to catch up.

Dallas reminded himself as he ran that Mia did not know Juno like he did. Trust a dog? With his life. If Juno alerted, he'd found Gracie all right. The question was, in what condition? He knew she hadn't unlocked the door that led to the stairwell by herself. Dallas did not allow himself to dwell further on the thought. Three flights at top speed, following the sound of Juno's nails clicking on the concrete until he got too far ahead for them to hear. When they reached the door to the roof, Juno was sitting, nose shoved to the gap under the threshold, tail wagging for all he was worth.

I know, buddy. You found her.

With adrenaline surging his gut, he threw open the door and half fell onto the rooftop, Mia and Elias right behind him.

"Gracie," Mia screamed. "Where are you?"

Juno had already disappeared around a utility enclosure. When they rounded the corner, he was licking the tears off Gracie's face. The girl was sitting in a little ball, sobbing and hiccupping all at the same time.

His own sigh of relief was drowned out by the wail that came from Mia as she threw herself on her daughter, adding her tears to the mix.

Dallas called Juno and gave him a thorough pet and scratch. "Good boy, Juno."

"That's an excellent dog," Dr. Elias said with a winded laugh.

"Yes, he's the best air scenter I've ever worked with."

"And to think he does it all for kibble." Dr. Elias stared at Gracie and Mia.

Dallas caught something in the doctor's tone. "He does it for the joy of the find."

"How do you know he'll come back to you?"

"He's trained that way."

Dr. Elias nodded thoughtfully. "Good investment. You make a nice wage for that kind of work?"

Dallas tried to keep the disgust out of his voice. "We're all volunteer."

He nodded as if he'd just figured out why Dallas wore beat-up jeans and drove a ten-year-old truck. "My son, Jake, always wanted a dog, but we never caved in to that desire. We bought him lacrosse gear instead. Now he's the best on his team."

Dallas figured a lacrosse stick was a pretty poor substitute for a dog, but he refrained from saying so. He waited for a few more moments while Mia held Gracie so tight the girl squirmed for breath.

"Why did you come up here?" Mia said, at last pulling Gracie to arm's length. "You could have fallen. Why did you do such a dangerous thing?"

"It was dark and I was going to find the bathroom. A man told me they were closed and I had to go upstairs. He opened the door for me with a funny stick thing that he stuck in the lock."

"What man?" Dallas said.

Gracie shrugged. "I don't know. It was dark and he had a hat on."

Mia let out an exasperated sigh. "Why didn't you come back to ask me to go to the bathroom with you?"

"You weren't there."

Mia's face whirled through a storm of emotions before she settled on grabbing Gracie again and hugging her close. Over Gracie's shoulder she shot Dallas a look.

Dr. Elias reached for his phone. "I'm glad that's over."

"It's not over," Dallas snapped. "Someone sent Gracie up to the roof on purpose."

"For what purpose? To steal something while we were all busy searching? Mia and Gracie have nothing worth stealing." He looked thoughtfully at Mia. "Do you?"

Mia tightened her grip on Gracie. "No, we don't."

"I don't suppose it's…" He shot a look at Gracie and

lowered his voice. "Someone who is reaching out from prison, for some reason?"

"Why would it be?" Dallas said.

The doctor shrugged. "True, I guess that's letting the past color the present. The door must not have been latched properly. Probably her imagination about the man." He chuckled. "My son was convinced for months that there was a bear living in our attic." He looked at Gracie, bending to look her in the eye. "I'm very happy that you are okay, Miss Gracie. I would be quite sad if anything happened to you." Dr. Elias dialed his cell phone to report that Gracie had been found. "I'll head downstairs and get everyone settled again."

He wiggled his fingers at Gracie and departed.

Dallas knelt next to the child, while Juno rolled over so Gracie could scratch the dog's belly. "Gracie, the man who told you to come up here. Do you think it could have been Dr. Elias?"

"No." She babbled to Juno. "You're a good doggie for finding me. I'm going to get you some Goldfish and we can share my blanket."

"How do you know?" Dallas continued. "How do you know it wasn't Dr. Elias?"

"'Cuz Dr. Elias smells nice."

"And the man who sent you up here didn't?"

"Nope," Gracie said. "He smelled like cigarettes."

Horror filtered past Mia's eyes as she squeezed her daughter closer. "Oh, Gracie."

"I told him cigarettes are bad." Gracie patted her mother's back. "He said to tell you something."

Mia tried to speak, but no sound emerged.

"What did he say?" Dallas used the calm tone he

employed whenever Juno located a traumatized victim, the "everything is going to be absolutely fine now" tone.

"He said he was going to see us again real soon," she said.

TEN

Mia would not stay another second. Heedless of anything but the need to get Gracie out of that awful gym, she waved away the well-meaning urgings from Dr. Elias and Catherine to stay until morning.

"It's dark and the roads are treacherous," Dr. Elias said.

"Not as treacherous as staying here," she snapped.

"Someone phoned the police. They're sending someone, but it's not high on their list since Gracie's been located," Dallas said, grabbing the stuffed animal someone had given Gracie as Mia plopped her on the nearest empty cot to wrap her in a jacket.

"They can come find me if and when they send anyone." She pulled up the zipper. "We're not staying here."

Dallas did not ask where she was going. Honestly, she didn't have the foggiest notion, but Archie would not touch Gracie ever again and if he showed up, he'd wish he hadn't. Fury had replaced the fear. Anger was good, much better than helplessness.

Dr. Elias started to follow her as she led Gracie out the gym doors, but his wife stopped him with a whispered comment and a hand on his arm.

"Do you have my number at least?" the doctor said. "In case you decide you can't go it alone?"

Mia whirled to face him. "Thank you for everything, but that's exactly what I'm going to do."

Dallas followed her out. She hoisted Gracie on her hip and charged toward the makeshift parking lot, stopping short when she peered into the sodden interior of her damaged car. The rain had sheeted through the broken window and the seats were now sopping, bits of glass she had not seen before sparkling on the tattered vinyl.

One more thing. Another small obstacle, but it felt like the last tiny nudge toward complete desperation. She tried to keep her breathing steady as Gracie launched into a round of sleepy questions, rubbing her eyes with a fist. "Where will we sleep? I'm tired."

"Just a minute. Let mommy think." Could she get a ride? Borrow a car? Wait for the police and ask them to take her somewhere, anywhere?

An unusual detail caught her attention through the tension rippling her insides. Gracie's booster, still buckled in the backseat, had been covered up in a plastic garbage bag. She stared for a long moment before she turned around to face Dallas.

"Didn't want it to get wet," he said simply, hands in his jeans pockets. "Would have sealed the window, too, but I only had one bag."

The man had thought about something as menial and foreign to his world as a child's booster seat. "Dallas," she said, but a thickening in her throat kept her mute. She reached out very slowly and pressed her palm to the side of his face. He gazed at her in silence. She searched for signs of pity or disgust in his expression. There was nothing there but compassion and worry. "I am pretty sure that was the nicest thing anybody has done for me in a very long time."

"You deserve nice things, and so does Gracie." He stroked the back of her hand, tentatively, as if it were a bird that might fly away at any moment.

She reached up to press a kiss to his cheek, but his greater height caused it to land just below his jawline. The stubble on his chin tickled her lips. The pulse that revved up in his throat seemed to pass into her body, until her heart matched pace with his. "Thank you," she whispered.

He cleared his throat as she stepped away. "I know you don't want to come back to the trailer. I'll help you find another place in the morning, but we can't right now. It's all there is. It's all I have to offer."

He left the question unspoken. *Will you come with me?*

"Why," she whispered, giving words to the question she hadn't known boiled and bubbled in her broken soul, "is it so hard to do it on my own?"

A beam of moonlight caught his face, highlighting the strong chin, wide cheekbones and a boy-like vulnerability under the tough guy mask. "Maybe because you weren't meant to. No one is."

Mia sagged under the weight of the words and her daughter's limp form. Dallas stepped forward, taking Gracie from her. She fetched the booster and they made a quiet procession back to Dallas's truck.

She squeezed the booster into the backseat of the double cab, and Dallas put her in and secured the buckle.

Juno hopped in next to Gracie whose eyes were at

half-mast, licking her when he thought Dallas was not looking. After what Juno had done, Mia would never discourage him from being near Gracie again.

Dallas opened the passenger door for Mia, his body close to hers, and she pressed herself into his arms. "I don't want this," she said into his chest, dizzy with the nearness of him and the relief that Gracie was safe. "I don't want to…need someone."

"I know," he said as he bent his head and kissed her. Electric warmth circled through her and pushed back a tiny corner of fear as her lips touched his. Breathless, she pulled away. "I should have said it sooner, but thank you for finding my daughter."

Eyes wide, he offered a tentative smile. "Juno found her."

"I'll pay him in Goldfish," she said, her own voice tremulous as she chided herself mentally. "But I don't know how to repay you."

"There's no debt."

The softness in his eyes brought her back to the heady emotion of that kiss. She almost lost herself in the feeling again before she snapped herself back to reality. His kiss was just a physical expression of what they'd just been through. *Don't feel for him. Don't love him.* Deep breaths helped her stop the wild firing of her nerves as he shut the door and went around to the driver's side.

The first ten miles passed in silence until Dallas told her about Susan.

Mia gaped. "Is she crazy? Making it all up?"

"I don't know."

"I heard Catherine say she was basically stalking him. She couldn't get over her husband's death and she became fixated on the doctor after he treated her. They mentioned Finnigan's name, too."

They mulled over the situation for the next half hour. Dallas edged the truck past a monster puddle that nearly swallowed the road. "I don't know who is telling the truth, but maybe this Finnigan is the place to start since his name has come up a few times now."

"Should we tell the police?"

"That's the million dollar question." He shot her a glance, dark eyes unreadable. "Your call." They made the final turn into the trailer park. "But you'd better decide now," he said as Detective Stiving emerged from the police car parked in front of Dallas's unit.

Dallas tried to hide his dismay that it was Stiving and not Chief Holder who greeted them. He lifted the sleeping Gracie from the back and handed her to Mia. Stiving let Mia get Gracie settled inside, Juno flopped down on the floor next to her. He stood on the front porch with Dallas until Mia joined them, a blanket wrapped around her shoulders.

"Folks told me you left the college gym. Said something unpleasant happened. How about filling me in?" Stiving took careful notes about Gracie's disappearance and the encounter with Archie in the woods. Dallas waited to see if she would reveal what Susan said, but she did not, nor did she mention Peter Finnigan's name.

Stiving arched an eyebrow. "So the Archie guy from Miami. He thinks you've got money from your husband squirreled away somewhere?"

Mia nodded wearily.

"Is he right?"

"No," Mia snapped, "as I explained to him. I'm a

single mother with next to nothing in my wallet, no house, a ruined car and only the clothes on my back. I don't even have a change of clothes for Gracie. That's it. And even if I got Hector's money, I'd send it back express mail because I don't want anything to do with my ex-husband, thank you very much." The last few words came out a near shout.

Dallas could not have been more proud. After all she'd been through, she would not be steamrolled.

To Dallas's surprise, Stiving smiled. "Got it. Archie from Miami is a misguided individual. Targeting you for no reason."

Mia let out a squeak. "Does it matter the reason? He sent my child up onto the roof. He could have... hurt her."

"And no one else saw the guy?"

"I did, earlier," Dallas said.

"You don't count," Stiving said without looking at Dallas. "But adding a menacing stranger isn't going to throw me off the trail of who killed Cora."

"Incredible," Mia huffed. "What kind of woman would I be to use my daughter to deflect suspicion from myself?"

"The kind of woman that married a drug dealer and lived in the lap of luxury until hubby went to prison."

Mia's face blanched and she took a step back. "You don't know anything about me."

"I know more than you think. Fire Marshal says the house burned due to a candle fire, so that we have to rule as accidental, but the toxicology reports are what I'm eagerly awaiting. That's going to make for some interesting reading."

"I would never poison anyone, especially Cora," Mia said, arms folded tight across her chest.

"You stabbed a man before. Poison, knife." He shrugged. "Both can be lethal."

Dallas stiffened. "Knock it off. She doesn't deserve that."

Stiving looked close at Mia. "How do you know what she deserves?"

Mia sucked in a breath, then without another word she slammed back inside the trailer, leaving Dallas and Stiving alone on the porch.

"That was low. She's a good mother, the best," Dallas snarled.

"Really? You sound so protective. Good friend?" He quirked an eyebrow. "Or more?"

He burned inside. "None of your business."

"Let's lay it out here, Mr. Black. You and I don't get along."

"No kidding. Because I made you look bad by doing your job for you? Finding the kid when you didn't think it was worth your time?"

The smile vanished. "No, because you're a hotshot who makes trouble in my town. Whatever you think of me, I'm a good cop. Thorough."

"So do your job and investigate. You'll see she's telling the truth."

"Could be, but I think it's more likely that your friend Mia Sandoval murdered Cora and when the lab tests come back and prove that the pills were doctored with poison, I'm going to arrest her. As far as this Archie from Miami thing goes, if he really is threatening her, it's just deserts."

"Just?" Dallas spoke through gritted teeth.

"Sure. She's experiencing the fallout of being married to a mobster. She probably had full knowledge of Hector's activities the whole time."

"You're wrong."

"Maybe, but I'm right about the murder and you'd better believe I'm going to look real carefully at you, too, since you're so tight with Miss Sandoval and everything." He grinned. "Gang boy like you? Arrest record and the whole nine yards? Real stand-up guy."

Dallas bit back his response. It wouldn't help Mia to shoot off his mouth. It probably hadn't helped her that her supposed protector was an enemy of the town's police detective.

"I'll be seeing you around soon," Stiving said as he walked down the steps.

Dallas felt a desperate need to act, to take some small step that would help shed some light. He took a shot. "Do you know a Peter Finnigan?"

Stiving stopped. "Finnigan? Why?"

"Do you know him?"

Eyebrows drawn together, Stiving chewed his lip before answering. "Guy of that name lives about an hour from here in Mountain Grove. Used to live in California until he bought a real nice cabin here in Colorado."

"Know him personally?"

"Read about him." He shook his head. "Witness in a case a colleague of mine worked on in California decades ago. Surprised I remembered it."

"What kind of case?"

"Why do you want to know?"

"Why did it stick in your memory? A case that wasn't even in your state?"

His eyes narrowed to slits. "This colleague talked

it over with me. He thought something smelled funny about the story. Just like something smells funny about this one. So you're not going to tell me why you're interested in Peter Finnigan?"

Dallas remained silent. He was not going to get anything more and he wondered if he'd blown it by bringing Peter's name into the mess. Besides, he needed to check on Mia. Now.

Stiving started up the engine, still smiling, and Dallas tapped on the trailer door before letting himself in. Mia sat at the little table, elbows propped on the surface. He tried to read her expression. Angry? Wounded?

"Sit down and quit staring at me," she said.

Angry. Good. "Stiving has no sense. Ignore him. He did give me a tip on Peter Finnigan in spite of himself. I've got a town name to research."

She drummed fingers on the table. "He truly believes I am a murderer."

"Cops are like that. Don't trust anyone. Don't take it to heart."

"Easy for you to say. He doesn't think you killed Cora." She shot a hasty look at Gracie who slept peacefully. She stared at the little girl, face softening until it was so tender he had to look away.

"Dallas, you…you don't think I would ever put Gracie in danger on purpose, do you?" She turned those luminous eyes on him, and suddenly breathing was difficult.

"No."

"But what if I do it unintentionally? Trying to make a life here has only gotten us in trouble."

"Not your fault."

"I'm not so sure. My number-one priority is to give her a good life, you know?"

He nodded.

"But I look back over my life, and I can't believe some of the things I've done." She looked at her hands. "I stabbed my husband. I actually did that."

"You thought he was going to kill you and take Gracie, didn't you?"

Her sigh was miserable. "But I never imagined I could do such a thing—that I was capable."

It cut at him to see the self-doubt. "You were protecting yourself and your daughter. Don't let guilt twist it around."

She beamed a smile at him that lit up even the farthest corners of the trailer. He could have been sitting in a glorious cathedral and there would be nothing to rival the beauty he experienced at that moment, sitting in a trailer parked on the edge of a flood-threatened town.

"I appreciate your friendship," she said, "I really do, even if I haven't shown it. It's been a long time since I could trust someone."

Trust. The word fell hard on his heart. *But I haven't told you the truth, Mia. Not all of it.* He opened his mouth to let it spill. Tomorrow, everything would change because of the phone call he'd made outside that rain-soaked gym. He remembered the cascade of emotions she'd triggered in him with their kiss that seemed to live inside him long after her mouth was no longer pressed tight to his. Would it all be gone in the morning? Perhaps it was for the best. She needed a friend, not anything more. He would be lucky if she still counted him in that circle after tomorrow.

"What is it?" Mia said, squeezing his fingers. She looked so tired, circles smudging her eyes. He could give her one night of rest, of peace, before her world turned upside down and his did, too.

"Nothing. Get some sleep. We'll talk later."

She laughed softly. "'Oh, I've got miles to go before I sleep.'"

He found himself smiling back. "Robert Frost. You listened in poetry class, too."

"Yes, I did." She pressed the laptop to life. "And I'm going to dig up some dirt on a certain P. Finnigan before I turn in."

He understood. She needed to do something, to manage one small element in a life that was spiraling out of control. "How about if I help?"

She slid over on the bench seat, and he settled next to her, his big shoulder pressed against her soft one, admiring her slender wrists as her fingers danced across the keyboard.

It took them two hours of following cyber bunny trails before they had the pertinent details.

Mia gathered her long hair to the side, eyes darting in thought. "So this Peter Finnigan was a dishwasher at a greasy spoon in Southern California. He's out walking one day and sees a man boating. The boater falls overboard and is caught up by a rip current and shouts for help. Finnigan tries to get to him, but is unable and fearing for his own safety he leaves the water and calls the authorities. By the time they show up, the man is swept away, body never recovered."

Dallas consulted the screen. "The drowned man is Asa Norton, a thirty-year-old small-business owner. He's presumed dead after the appropriate length of time. Survived by his wife—" Dallas leaned closer "—Susan Norton. There's a picture."

Mia crowded close, her cheek nearly touching his. It took everything in his possession not to turn his head and find those lips again. *Knock it off, Black.*

"Does she look familiar?" Mia breathed quicker. "Could that possibly be the red-haired Susan we know?"

"Could be, but it's a bad picture." He leaned away a little, to quiet the pulse rushing in his veins. He read on. "Susan received the ten million dollar insurance settlement for her husband's death." He scrolled down. "Nothing further about it."

Mia chewed her lip. "Something Cora knew about Finnigan troubled her. It has to be a clue as to who killed her, doesn't it?"

Dallas saw the kindling of hope in her eyes as if a light had been turned on inside, somewhere down deep. *Help me keep that hope alive, Lord.* "We'll find out." But would there still be a *we* tomorrow?

They were silent for a moment. Pine needles scuttled quietly along the trailer roof.

"Do you think Peter Finnigan has answers?" she said finally.

"Possibly, but it could also be dangerous to go track him down."

"Dangerous, how?"

"Take your pick. Floodwaters, Archie on the loose and Cora's murderer."

"Could Archie have done it? Poisoned Cora's pills?"

Dallas thought it over. "I don't see why he'd go to trouble. Let's say he suspected you'd left this treasure from Hector with her. He might have searched her house, but he could have done that while she was out. No need to bring attention to himself or the property by causing her death. He's here on Garza's behalf to retrieve Hector's stash, that's his priority."

Mia's breath caught. "But what if he was there searching for all this money he believes I have, and she stumbled across him?"

He saw where she was going. "Cora did not die because of you. Period."

"I wish I could be sure."

"I'll be sure for both of us." He got up from the table, put a hand on her shoulder, trapping some of her silken hair under his palm. Without stopping to think it out, he pressed a kiss to her temple.

She curled a hand up around his neck and held him there. He was certain at the moment, as the nerves tingled through his body, how blessed he was to know Mia Verde Sandoval. But there was a secret between them, a secret that would hurt her. Though it took every bit of will power he possessed, he pulled away. "You've got to get some sleep. Tomorrow will be a bear." *And I want to leave now, while you're still looking at me with that half smile on your lips and eyes that make my heart pound.*

"Okay," she said, a puzzled smile on her face. "Tomorrow has to be better than today."

He wished with everything inside him that it could be, but his brain knew differently.

"Good night, Mia. Sleep well."

He said good-night to Juno, made sure Mia locked the trailer door and settled into the old chair in his own unit, positioned to keep watch, the feel of that kiss still dancing on his lips. It was the last time he'd share a kiss with Mia. He pushed away the sadness and rustled up some grit. *Do the job, Dallas.*

If Archie came, he'd know it.

Protection was all he could give Mia.

And he'd give it with his dying breath.

ELEVEN

Mia awoke to the sound of sneezing sometime after eight o'clock. It took her a few moments of blurry-eyed confusion to figure out it was Gracie who lay in a tight ball on the bed. Juno poked his nose at her, tail wagging.

Mia padded over on bare feet across the sunlit linoleum. "Hey, baby. The rain stopped."

Gracie sniffed. "I gotta sore throat."

Pulling the covers back, she found Gracie pink-cheeked and nose running. "Uh-oh."

"I got germans?"

Mia laughed. "Germs. Yes, I think you're coming down with something." Her forehead felt warm under Mia's palm. She fetched a glass of water and encouraged Gracie to drink it. Fishing through her bedraggled purse, she was thrilled to find the slightly sticky bottle of grape flavored medicine purchased after Gracie's last go around with the "germans." Cora had tended to her through that illness, offering homemade chicken soup and plenty of read-aloud stories. Mia's throat thickened at the thought. In spite of the groans, Mia managed to get Gracie to swallow a dose of the medicine.

"I want my turtle slippers. Can we get 'em?"

"I'm sorry, sweetie. Your slippers are all wet at the house. I'll get you some more soon." Anxiety cramped her stomach as the worries attacked in full force. And how exactly would she get slippers, or Gracie's pajamas, let alone a house? Especially while evading a murder rap and a mobster who'd threatened a return visit?

We'll find Peter Finnigan, and he will have some answers, she told herself firmly.

She grabbed a pair of neatly folded socks that Dallas had left, along with a clean T-shirt. The socks went nearly to Gracie's thighs and they both laughed as she rolled them onto the child's skinny legs. Mia let her mind stray back to the kiss. Why had she allowed herself to be kissed, let alone to respond? She had no clue, other than it was the most amazing kiss she'd experienced in her whole life.

Juno shot to his feet and ran to the door. Mia froze, heart hammering, until there was a quiet knock followed by a familiar voice.

"It's Dallas. I've got some things for you."

Mia found that her spirits ticked up a notch as she went to the door, pulling fingers through her messy hair and straightening the big sweatshirt he'd loaned her before letting him in.

His dark brows rose at the sight of her. "I didn't know that sweatshirt could look so nice."

She blushed.

He held up a brown bag. "Trailer park manager gave me some clothes for you and some that might work for Gracie left over from her granddaughter's last visit. And guess what—" He shook a pink pastry box. "Anybody want doughnuts for breakfast instead of Goldfish?"

Gracie coughed. "Can't. I'm sick."

Dallas shot her a panicked look. "Sick? How sick?"

"Terrible sick," Gracie piped up, adding a cough on the end for good measure.

"Should we take her to the doctor? I'll get my keys." He turned to leave, but Mia grabbed his arm.

"Not that sick. Kids come down with things all the time. It's okay. I gave her some medicine. She'll be okay. I promise." Mia hid a smile at the uncertain look on his face. "Really, it's fine. Kids are tough."

"They are?" His lips quirked. "They're just so… small."

She took the pink box from his hands. "Gracie won't eat them, but I wouldn't want these doughnuts to go to waste."

Soon he'd brewed a pot of coffee and she'd devoured two sugar-glazed doughnuts down to the last crumb. Dallas sipped out of his mug, a look of amusement on his face.

She wiped her sticky fingers. "Don't you eat doughnuts?"

"No sweet tooth."

"You're missing out," she said with a sigh. "Doughnuts are nature's second most perfect food next to mac and cheese. I think they're even on the food pyramid."

"It was worth it to watch you enjoy them." He added in a low voice. "To see you smile."

She returned the grin. "You know, for a tough guy who lives with a dog, you've got a sweet side."

"Don't let it get around."

"Why? Are you afraid you might have girls pounding at your door? Surely there must be some woman who wants a chance to get to know the softer side of Dallas Black."

He flicked a glance out the window before he answered. "I don't usually let them get close."

"Why not?" She shouldn't pry, but for some reason it felt so natural to talk to him and she wanted to understand what made him tick, and why she could not get him out of her mind.

"Don't want to disappoint them, I guess."

"When the mistakes of your past come out?"

He sighed. "Something like that."

"It's funny. You're trying hard to keep moving, and I'm going crazy trying to put down roots."

Yet here they were, sitting in the same banged-up trailer while a storm of trouble whirled around them. She watched the steam from the coffee drift past the waves in his hair. God had sent her a friend in Dallas Black, she realized. A friend when she most desperately needed one. But why did her feelings for him seem like something else?

He fidgeted with his coffee cup. "Mia, listen. I've got to tell you something and it won't wait anymore."

She felt a tremor inside. "Okay. I've had two doughnuts to shore up my spirit, and I don't see how things could get any worse than they were yesterday. Go for it."

Juno barked, and a second later they heard a car approach. Dallas peeked out the blinds.

Archie? The police? Her mind ran wild.

His expression was inexplicably sad as he went to open the door.

Mia blinked incredulously when her sister stepped inside.

"Antonia," she cried, wrapping her older sister in a massive hug. "Why are you here? How did you know where to find me?" She pulled her sister to arm's length. "Is everything okay? Is Reuben all right?"

Antonia chuckled. "I think I should be asking those kinds of questions." She looked over Mia's shoulder at Gracie. "Hey, Gracie girl. How's my niece?"

Gracie waggled her fingers and squealed. "Hiya, Auntie Nia. You're here. Where's Uncle BooBen?"

Gracie was perfectly capable of pronouncing Reuben's name, but her toddler nickname for him had stuck fast and it always made Reuben grin. Antonia kissed her. "I'll tell you in a minute. Let me talk to Mommy first, 'kay?"

"'Kay."

During the exchange, the flutter of unease in Mia's belly grew as she put some of the facts together. Dallas had not been at all surprised to see Antonia arrive. What's more, they seemed to be at ease with each other, as though they'd been in frequent contact.

The three moved away from Gracie. "What's going on?" Mia demanded.

Antonia squared her shoulders and kept her voice quiet. "First off, I'm here because Reuben and I love you and we're worried about you. We know Cora is dead and the police think it's foul play. We also know Archie is in town because Garza believes you've got Hector's jackpot somewhere. Reuben has gone to the prison to talk to Hector and tell him if there is such a prize, he has to fess up, because he's put you and Gracie in danger."

Mia held up a hand. "Antonia, how do you know all this?"

Antonia exchanged a worried look with Dallas. "Because Dallas has kept us informed. We hired him."

She could not believe she had heard correctly. "Hired?"

Dallas sighed. "They asked me to come to Spanish Canyon and keep an eye on you."

It took several tries before she managed a response. "What?"

"There were rumors that Garza's men were looking for something Hector had stashed," Antonia said. "Reuben and I feared they would come after you and Gracie."

The information landed like a bomb in her gut. "That's how you knew about Gracie climbing the tree. Your informant kept you apprised."

Dallas flushed.

"My fault," Antonia said. "I hounded him for details about Gracie. I shouldn't have, but I missed her so much."

Mia folded her arms, trying to steady her pounding pulse. There was more. She could see it in their faces. "What else?"

"Cora was an old friend of Reuben's mother," Antonia continued. "When we heard you were thinking of settling near here to go to school, we contacted her and she offered to help."

Help? Cora? The truth started to worm its way through Mia. "So Cora helped me get a job, find a house to rent. She made sure Dallas had work fixing her roof so he could spy on me. What an amazing network to put together a life for one helpless woman and her kid."

Antonia touched her arm, but she shook it off. "Mia, we knew you wouldn't accept any help because you're stubborn and desperate to prove you don't need anybody. I'm sorry. I didn't want to tell you like this, but that's the truth."

"You knew I wouldn't accept it, but you arranged it all anyway, didn't you? Totally against my wishes." Anger hummed through her veins. "All this, everything I thought I accomplished here, was just charity, set up by people I thought were my friends."

"I'd like to think I am your friend," Dallas said quietly, "no matter how it came to be."

Mia turned her eyes on him. "You don't *hire* friends." Each word fell out of her mouth, cutting like glass. She saw him flinch and she was glad.

Antonia's chin went up, as it had for every head-butting argument they engaged in over the years, from which breakfast cereal to eat to the dire consequence of dating Hector Sandoval. "Listen, Mia. I know you're mad at me and that's okay. I knew that was a price for trying to protect you, but Dallas isn't doing this for pay. As a matter of fact, he refused any compensation at all. He cares about you, like we do."

Cares about you. And lied just like Hector and her sister. She found it hard to breathe. "So, why exactly are you here now, Antonia? Dallas hasn't been feeding you enough information? You had to check up on me personally?"

"Dallas called us after Garza's man showed up at the college. I came to try and convince you to come back to Florida with me, until the thing with Archie is resolved."

"Didn't your informant tell you I'm shortly to be

accused of murder? I don't think I'll be able to leave even if I wanted to."

"We'll get a lawyer if it comes to that. Let's try to get you out while we can. It's safest for Gracie."

Mia exploded. "Don't tell me how to be a mother to Gracie, Antonia," she snarled. "That little girl is the only thing I've done right in my whole life. Please don't imply I've messed that up, too. I can't take it." Dismayed to find tears on her face, she dashed them away.

"I never would," Antonia said, eyes anguished. "Honey, you're a wonderful mother. You just need help right now. That's all."

The emotion on her sister's face, the moisture that shone in her eyes, was too much for Mia. The fire ebbed out of her body, leaving only a dark despair in its place. She sank down on the bench seat. Antonia was right. She could not make a life for herself and Gracie. She did not even realize that her whole world in Spanish Canyon was a setup, neatly arranged for a woman who could not manage on her own.

But Dallas… She could not even look at him. Everything she imagined he'd done for her out of kindness, or, she hardly dared admit it, love? It was a job. She was a job to him.

"I guess I'd better do what you say. I can't trust myself."

Dallas sat across from her. "Mia, you're stronger than anyone I know. What we did… It was only because you have too many powerful people working against you."

"No," she said, her own voice sounding strange and dull in her ears. "You did it because you and Antonia and Reuben all believe I could not manage my life on my own."

"No..." he started, reaching for her hands.

She would not touch him, not look at him. "I said 'All right.'" She fought the thickness in her throat. "You're both right, and I'm not going to argue. When do we leave?"

"I'll get us a flight tonight," Antonia said.

"Tomorrow." Mia glanced toward the bed. "Gracie's sick, and there's something I need to do first."

Antonia quirked an eyebrow. "What? There's talk that the weather might turn bad again. I really think tonight is better."

Dallas stood, hands on his slim hips, eyebrows drawn together.

Mia stared at the pink doughnut box, incredulous that only moments before she'd wondered if her feelings for Dallas could be more than friendly. *They're right. You can't trust yourself.* Dr. Elias's words came back to her.

"...you're afraid that you can't trust yourself, your choices, your judgments." Even her former employer had been able to see her deepest fear that had now been proven true. But she would not walk away, not from the murder of an old woman who had been trying to help her purely out of kindness. She was not a coward, not yet. "I'm going to find Peter Finnigan. He may be able to shed some light on Cora's death."

"No way..." Antonia said.

Mia whacked her hand on the table, startling Juno. "No matter how it came to be, Cora was my friend and Gracie and I loved her. I have to at least try to find out if Finnigan knows something. Please allow me to do that. Will you stay with Gracie?"

Antonia chewed her lip. "Of course, but I don't think…"

"I'll go with Mia," Dallas said.

"You don't need to do that," Mia told him. "Your spy identity has been compromised."

He flinched as her arrow hit the mark. "I'll go."

She didn't argue. If she said no he would follow her anyway. It was his job, after all, she thought bitterly, and he would do it until she and Gracie boarded that plane to Florida the following day.

She knelt next to Gracie and smoothed her hair. "I'll be back soon."

"Mommy, are you mad at Auntie Nia?"

"No, honey. We just had a disagreement. Auntie's going to stay with you while I run an errand. Is that okay?"

"Yes. Will Juno stay?"

Dallas nodded. "I think that's best."

"When you come back are we going to Florida?"

Mia exhaled. "I think so, baby."

"Is that gonna be our home?"

Mia thought there was never such a perfect little face as that of her sweet girl, staring at her expectantly, trusting that no matter what, her mother would provide a home. Was Florida going to be that home? Would any place ever be?

"I'm not sure if we'll stay in Florida."

She sneezed. "Will Juno and Dallas come, too?"

She could not answer above the sudden wave of sadness.

"Hey, Goldfish girl," Dallas said. "You just work on getting better. We'll talk about it later."

"'Kay."

Dallas offered a hand to help Mia get to her feet. She pretended she didn't see. *I'm a job to you, Dallas. Let's keep it that way*, she thought over the grief washing through her body.

Dallas tried to open the door of the truck for Mia but she scooted around and got in herself before he had the chance. What had he expected? She believed he'd betrayed her—and maybe to a woman who so desperately craved independence, he had. He'd crossed many people in his life, disappointed dozens, notably himself, but what he'd done to Mia hurt her worse than any other offense he'd dished out. It had been wrong to deceive her, even though the reasons were right.

I'm sorry, Mia.

The distance between them seemed like miles instead of inches. She stared out the window as his tension grew.

Should he try small talk? Apologize again? Mention the haze of clouds that had started to gather along the sunlit horizon?

Talk about the weather? Stupid, Dallas.

He settled on silence, trying to ignore the leaden feeling in his limbs. He'd hoped in that idiot macho way of his the truth might blow over as the miles went by and he could start again, trying to show her how much she meant to him. Judging from the hard line of her mouth, he'd thought wrong. If only women were as forgiving as dogs.

"Why did you do it?"

He jerked a look at her, startled, praying he would not make it any worse with more idiotic conversation. "To protect you. At least that's what I thought I was trying to do."

"No, I mean why did you do it for nothing? Agree to take the job without pay."

Because to me, it's not a job. "Antonia asked me. I respect her and Reuben."

"You didn't move to a strange town because you respect my sister and brother-in-law."

He shifted, setting the seat springs squeaking. "I never care much where I am. One town is as good as another. Spanish Canyon offered a decent place to teach Search and Rescue classes. Why not?"

She turned gleaming brown eyes on him, skewering him to the seat back. "That's not it. You moved to this town, spent hours working on an old roof and living in a trailer, for no pay, to protect a woman you barely knew. Why did you do that? I think I deserve to hear the truth."

She did, but he knew it meant sharing messy, unformed feelings, incoherent ramblings of his heart that he himself did not understand. He flipped through the memories that had swirled through his mind almost daily since he'd seen her in Florida following the hurricane. "At Antonia and Reuben's wedding. I saw you talking to Gracie before the ceremony."

She waited.

He sighed. "I dunno, something about what you said to her got inside me and stayed there."

"What did I say?"

He tried to repeat the words exactly. "Gracie was little then, just a toddler. Is that what you call that age?"

She nodded.

"Anyway, she asked you where her daddy was and you knelt down, right next to her and told her Daddy was in jail because he made mistakes."

He heard her sniff. "Yes. I remember now."

"And she started to cry so you said, 'We're going to be a family, you and me, and Mommy's going to make it all right.'"

Mia lowered her head. "I haven't made it anywhere near all right."

He went very still, the sound of the tires creating a soothing cadence. *Lord, help me to put words to the feelings, words she can understand.* "You were strong then, and gentle, too, just like you are now. I knew how hard it was going to be, with your past, and starting all over with a daughter and Hector's legacy. I understood because I have wreckage in my past, too." He reached out slowly, praying she would not jerk away from his touch, and covered her hand with his. "I wanted to help you and Gracie have a better shot at making a way for your family. That's why I told Antonia I'd do it."

She looked at their joined hands and one tear splashed onto their twined fingers.

"My whole life has been about where. Where will I go next. This time…" He struggled to find the words. "This time it was about the who, about you and Gracie. I wanted you to have a life." He swallowed hard. "And I guess maybe I wanted to be a part of that in some way."

It was too much. She pulled from him. "I didn't ask you. You invited yourself into our lives and you deceived me."

It cut at his heart. "I'm sorry."

She fished for a tissue in her pocket. "I understand

your motives were sincere. Hector was sincere, too, but he did not trust me with the truth, either."

Her words stung like acid. He'd been put on the same shelf as Hector, a manipulator, a disappointment. Had he permanently severed that delicate strand between them? He could think of nothing to say to repair the break, not one word of comfort to bring the warmth back to her eyes.

The miles droned by in miserable silence until he turned on the weather station just to break the terrible quiet. It was not good news.

"More rain is on the way from an unexpected grouping of storms rolling in. A series of flash-flood warnings and advisories have been issued. Mudslides are already being reported near Mountain Grove and Coal Flats where rainfall on burn areas is causing ground failure. Residents are advised to be ready to evacuate."

Dallas took comfort in the fact that at least the trailer park was high enough to keep Antonia and Gracie safe. For a while.

"We should…"

She shook her head. "I'm going to see Finnigan. If you want to head back, just let me out."

Right. As if he would even consider leaving her on the side of a mountain road. Women. He wisely kept his thoughts to himself and pressed on at as quick a pace as he could manage. The steeper the grade, the more he began to worry about the possibility of mudslides. Slopes already sodden with moisture needed only a tiny push from nature and gravity to loosen tons of debris on the road below.

Finally, they turned off on an uneven path that took

them through acreage so densely crowded with lodge-pole pines that he thought Farley might have ferreted out the wrong address, until they came to the edge of a swollen river with a striking house set beside it. The dark wood tones and forest green roofing material made it appear as if the house was a part of the mountainside behind it.

They got out in time to receive the first drops of rainfall.

"Peter Finnigan has a nice little piece of real estate," Dallas said, perusing the boathouse that perched at the waterline and the modern shingled siding on the house above. "And he doesn't like being too close to the neighbors."

"He must have found something better paying than being a dishwasher." Mia started up the graveled path toward the house. As he followed, Dallas noted a green car parked behind the shrubbery, and the muscles in his stomach tightened. He put a hand on the hood. Still warm.

"Mia," he said.

There was the sudden sound of breaking glass followed by a shout.

Dallas took off for the house at a dead sprint.

TWELVE

Mia was gasping for breath by the time she made it to the house, pulling up next to Dallas who had just about reached the front door when it was flung open. A short, balding man stopped short, mouth wide. His arm was half raised, as if to shield himself from a blow.

"Peter Finnigan?" Dallas said.

The man glared, the fleshy pouches under his eyes bunching. "Who wants to know?"

"We heard a scream," Mia panted, by way of explanation. "Glass breaking."

"There's nothing wrong," he said. "Everything's fine. Go away."

"Not quite, Peter" came a singsong voice.

Mia gaped as Susan stepped up behind Peter. She wore clean clothes, her hair in a neat twist, a placid smile on her lips. Dallas seemed equally at a loss for words until he managed, "Are you hurt?"

Susan laughed. "Such a gentleman." She gave Mia a coy look. "You should keep him."

Mia's cheeks burned. "Susan, what's going on?"

She waved them in with an airy gesture. "Come in, why don't you? I just came to see Peter. We're acquainted. He's the man who tried to save my drowning husband, so he says."

Peter scanned the porch quickly, as if he was assessing the likelihood of an escape. Then he mumbled something, stepped aside and allowed them to enter.

"I'm glad you're here. She's some loony who busted in. When I wouldn't give her what she wanted, she started throwing things. I'm leaving just as soon as I can get her out."

Mia noticed a floral fragrance in the air and there was something familiar in the smell. Peter pulled keys and a wallet from a small bowl. While his back was turned, Mia spotted an old photo on the floor, partially hidden by shards of glass that littered the hardwood floor.

The snapshot was old and grainy, but it showed Peter with a taller man, heavily bearded, standing in a small boat. A third man was seated, holding a net. Peter stood to the left of them, dangling a fish for the camera, grinning.

She saw Susan looking at her. Quickly Mia tucked the picture into her pocket.

"What got smashed?" Mia asked.

Susan waved an impatient hand. "I startled Peter and he dropped his drinking glass. I was asking him what he knew about my husband's death."

He flashed a sullen look. "I dunno what you're talking about. She's crazy, like I said."

Susan sighed. "All right, I'll get the ball rolling. Let's stroll down memory lane. Fifteen years ago, you saw my husband, Asa, drown, didn't you? What a story you told the police about how you tried in vain to save him, battling the waves at your own peril. Made yourself look like a real hero."

Peter folded his arms, then unfolded them and shoved his hands in the pockets of his faded jeans. "You already know what happened, Susan."

"So," Susan said, her tone cheerful as if she was reciting a bit of poetry. "You lied. You and Thomas." She looked at Mia and Dallas. "Dr. Elias, as you know him. To me he'll always be Thomas. Peter arranged with Thomas to make it look like an accidental death. Thomas was hoping to get his hands on the life insurance money. He pays you to keep quiet. That's how you afford this lovely home, isn't it?"

Peter grimaced. "You're nuts, and you're not telling the whole story."

"I probably am nuts. I've had a hard life after all. It took me a long time, years and years, to find Thomas and you. I tracked him down to Spanish Canyon. What a surprise to find out he'd started a whole new life here as a well-respected doctor. And you, too. Cora overheard Thomas threaten me at the clinic after I confronted him. She wanted to go to the police, but I told her they were on his side. She promised to help me find proof to take to the authorities."

"Cora?" Mia gasped. "Susan, tell us what happened."

Peter cut Mia off. "This is nuts. I'm not talking to any of you anymore. Get out, all of you."

Susan's face whitened and filled with hatred. "Thomas killed Cora because he knew she was looking into his past, and the truth was coming out. Now Thomas's going to have to eliminate anyone who can incriminate him and that means you."

"Are you insane? I've never caused him any trouble. I've kept my mouth shut about everything for all these years. He trusts me."

"Not anymore," she said quietly. "Not after he's had to murder again. This time he's going to button up all the loose ends."

Including Susan. Mia shuddered.

"Crazy, but I'm not gonna take the time to sort it out," Peter snapped, turning away. The back of his neck was red.

Mia's mind was still spinning, trying to put it all together. When Peter whirled back around, he held a gun snatched from his pocket.

Dallas stepped in front of Mia. "You don't need to do that, Peter. We're not here to cause trouble for you. We just wanted the truth."

"I'm getting out of this whole business. I was going to leave because of the flooding anyway, so I'll just make it permanent. If any of you tries to come at me, I'll kill you. I don't want to, but I will."

Susan chortled. "You can't get out. You'll never get out."

"Shut up," Peter barked. "Move away from the door."

Dallas and Mia edged aside. Mia took Susan's skinny wrist. "Let him go, Susan." Surprisingly, she did not resist.

"He won't get away," she said softly. "You'll never, ever get away."

Susan allowed Mia to guide her to the corner. When Peter fled out the door and down the path, Dallas ran to the window.

"He's got a boat ready." Dallas was dialing 911 as

he watched. After a minute, he disconnected with an exasperated groan. "No signal."

Peter thundered down to the edge of the dock where a motorboat was moored. He cast off the lines and began to putter out into the swiftly moving water. A duffel bag in the back indicated his departure had been planned out.

Keeping low, Dallas sprinted toward the boathouse. He was going to see if there was another boat.

"Stay in the house," he yelled.

Mia watched as Peter piloted through the rough waters.

She and Susan edged out onto the porch. Mia could not stand it a moment longer.

"You have to tell us everything, Susan. We have to know who killed Cora."

Dallas vanished into the darkened interior of the boathouse, emerging a moment later with hands on hips. There was no other boat. Peter would get away and take his answers with him.

Dallas began to jog back to the dock. Mia started down the steps, leaving Susan behind. Thirty seconds passed. A flash of light and an earsplitting bang shook the boards under their feet. Mia's ears rang. Following Dallas's horrified gaze she realized the explosion had come from the boat.

Peter's duffel bag was burning, along with the interior of the vessel. Peter lay facedown in the water, his shirt on fire.

Susan stared, hands jammed into her pockets.

Dallas finished his sprint to the dock and jumped in the water, arms chopping through the waves. Bits of flaming debris sprinkled down around his head as he pressed on. It was a futile effort. By the time he'd cleaved through the swirling river to the spot where the boat had exploded, Peter's body had been sucked away by the current. The swollen river jerked and pulled at Peter, tumbling him along like a discarded doll. Dallas swam after Peter, and Mia found herself shouting, stomach twisted in fear.

"Dallas, come back. The water's too strong." *You'll drown,* her heart finished for her. She doubted he'd heard over the swirling cacophony, but he must have come to the same conclusion. She watched with her heart hammering at her ribs as he fought the water back toward the bank and Mia grasped his forearms to pull him from the river.

He stood, head bowed, water running from his hair and clothes. His broad shoulders drooped and quite suddenly, she wanted to comfort this man who had betrayed her. She raised her arms to embrace him. *Strength, not emotion, you ninny.*

Instead, she snatched up a towel that lay drying on the wooden rail and draped it around his shoulders. His eyes were shocked, horrified, drawn to the river where Peter Finnigan had just lost his life. In spite of herself, she pressed her hand to his biceps for a moment.

He imprisoned her palm there, his own fingers cold. "I couldn't get him."

She allowed the touch to linger before she pulled away. "No one could."

He heaved in a breath. "I'm guessing there was an explosive device in his duffel bag. It was motion triggered." He paused. "Or someone set it off by cell phone."

Mia glanced into the acres of dark trees and shivered. Were there eyes watching from the shadows? Eyes glowing with satisfaction at the death they had just witnessed? As they moved back toward the house, she realized Susan was still staring out at the burning boat, spinning in helpless circles as it moved downriver.

"I told you, Peter," she whispered.

Dallas left a trail of water along the floor as the three of them searched for a phone with a landline. Nothing. His own cell was now waterlogged thanks to his instinctive plunge into the river and there was no chance of getting a signal anyway. In the course of their hunting, thunderclouds began to roll in along the river canyon, obscuring the mountaintops under a blanket of grey.

"We need to get out of here," Dallas said. "We'll keep trying to call on your cell as we drive."

Mia patted the photo still tucked in her pocket. "Come on, Susan. You can fill us in on the way."

"My car is here," she said. "In the bushes."

"We'll bring you back for it later." Dallas was not about to let the woman slip out of their grasp again. Especially not after what had just happened to Finnigan. He still burned inside with the knowledge that he had not been strong enough or fast enough to pull the man from the monster river. An epic failure and a life lost. Trying to keep watch for any sign of movement from the tree line, they returned to the truck. He fought the urge to bundle both women back into the house and barricade them safely inside, but with floodwater rising all around them, it was not an option. "Let's move a little faster," he said, putting an encouraging palm on Susan's bony shoulders.

Back in the truck with Susan in the backseat, Mia didn't waste a moment.

"How did you know about Peter?"

Susan sighed. "I'm very tired." She leaned her head back on the seat.

"I'm sorry, Susan," Mia snapped. "But we just saw a man murdered back there. You need to start talking."

Dallas felt the tingle in his stomach at the strength in her tone, the fire in her words.

Susan sighed and tears welled up in her eyes. "I killed him."

Mia gasped.

Dallas gripped the wheel as Mia blinked in shock. "Who?" she managed.

"My husband, because I got involved with Thomas. He was a medical student, deep in school loans and credit card debt, but charming, and he seduced me. Made friends with Asa, or pretended to. He knew how unhappy I was in my marriage, but I never dreamed… How could I know Thomas would murder Asa? Actually murder him? I blame myself for Asa's death. I always will for bringing Thomas into our lives."

"You had no idea what kind of man he was?"

"None," she sniffed. "Thomas knew Asa had planned a fishing trip. Asa had a high-stress job running his own business, so fishing was his escape. I think Thomas drugged his bottle of tea so he became unconscious. Peter was waiting nearby, and he made sure Asa tumbled out of his boat and drowned and then he told the story of trying to save Asa so the police wouldn't look into it too closely."

"Dr. Elias did it, why? Out of jealousy? So you two could have a life together?"

Her voice hardened. "Nothing so romantic. Thomas knew Asa had a life insurance policy, and he figured after he killed Asa I would give him the money because we were, um, in love. At least I thought we were. Completely stupid of me, of course. Maybe Thomas figured once I received the payment he could kill me then, too."

What was one more murder for the guy? Dallas thought.

"When the insurance company signed off, I collected the money and ran as far and as fast as I could, but I always knew I'd make Thomas pay." An edge crept into her voice. "Thomas wanted to make a fresh start with a new identity, the good doctor beloved by all, but I found him. And Peter, too."

Dallas hit the brakes as a small pile of rocks showered down onto the road. He guided the truck around it, trying to process Susan's revelation.

"I confronted him, and Cora overheard and started checking into things. She told me she found a photo that she could use against Thomas, but before she could show me, she died. Thomas killed her, I'm sure of it." Dallas saw tears slide down her face. "He got himself a new life. And a pretty new woman."

He remembered finding Susan breaking into the BMW outside the makeshift evacuation center. "It's Catherine Elias, you've been following, isn't it?"

Mia jerked. "The floral perfume fragrance. I thought it was familiar. It's Catherine's. You followed her to Peter's?"

"I've been watching her house. I was curious to see if she knew what kind of man she was married to." Susan laughed. "She's scared of me. Anyway, she brought him the photo of Peter and Thomas. Don't know how she got her hands on it unless she was in on Cora's murder the whole time."

Mia took the photo from her pocket. "Who is the seated man in the boat?"

"Asa." She chewed her lip. "You see? Shows the three were acquainted, though Peter claimed to be a random stranger who saw Asa drowning. The photo proves a connection between them, and the police would connect the dots, I have no doubt."

"And why would Catherine take the photo to Peter? Blackmail? To set him up to be murdered?" Mia wondered aloud.

"Or she's innocent," Dallas said. "Could be she found the photo after Elias took it from Cora and she became suspicious, wanted to check up on her husband."

Mia slid the photo in the visor, staring at it as they drove.

Rain slammed into the windshield. Susan turned her face to the glass and watched the water sheeting along the window. Her eyes drooped. "I'm too tired to talk anymore."

He did not think Mia was even breathing until she heaved a long shaky breath. "It's true. Dr. Elias killed Cora."

"And Asa, and Peter," Dallas said.

"And he'll do the same to me, if he gets hold of me," Susan said.

"But now we have proof." Mia's voice held a tone of wonder. "We can go to the police and expose him. I can have my life back."

The hope shone on her face and his pulse trip hammered. Where would that life take her? Back to Florida? To some other faraway place? Didn't matter. Wherever it was, it wasn't going to include him. He cleared his throat. "Try the police again."

She did, with no better result.

They made it over the top of the mountain and began the descent. Half a mile later, he pulled the truck to a stop behind another truck and an SUV. A gnarled ponderosa pine had clawed free of the earth and fallen, blocking the road in both directions. The road was hemmed in by a steep drop on one side and the mountain on the other.

Dallas got out to talk to the bearded man from the truck just ahead of them. The guy was fetching a chain saw from the covered cab of his vehicle. He introduced himself as Mack.

"Gonna have to chop it up and haul it off as best we can," Mack shouted to Dallas over the roar of the chain saw. "Folks are gonna be packing this road to get out of here if the rain don't stop."

"How much time you figure before they order evacuations?" Dallas called.

"If the storm don't turn ASAP, they'll be evacuating before nightfall. Rivers are full."

Recalling Peter's body whirling away on the swollen river, Dallas fought a pang of horror. He started in, hauling away the branches as the bearded man cleaved them from the trunk. The two from the other stopped vehicle, a father and his strapping teen son, set to work helping also.

"Got some orange cones in my truck," Mack hollered. "Put 'em out on the road so we don't have a pileup."

Dallas nodded and retrieved the markers. He walked past Mia who was still trying to get a signal on her phone. Susan appeared to be sleeping, her forehead pressed against the glass. He had thought she was deranged and he still wondered about her sanity, but he could not deny what she said made sense. Dr. Elias was a killer. And he had to be stopped.

Splashing through puddles, he set the cones down a few yards from the back of his truck to signal oncoming drivers. One more set around the turn in the road would be sufficient, he thought, as he slogged onward. Just in time as a dump truck eased to a stop. He got a glimpse of the driver's face, older, scruff of a beard.

But it was the passenger that made his blood run cold.

Archie Gonzales gave him a startled look as he leapt from the cab.

Dallas was at the passenger door before Archie had shoved it fully open. There was no time for Archie to reach for a weapon. Dallas grabbed him by the collar and slammed him against the side of the truck.

"Funny how you always turn up," Dallas snarled.

The truck driver appeared around the front fender. "What's going on?"

"Private business," Dallas grunted. His tone must have convinced the driver.

"I'm going to help clear the road," he mumbled, ambling away over the muck.

Archie tried to move Dallas's hands away, but he did not loosen his grip. "Wasted effort, man. I'm leaving town. My piece of junk rental got stuck in the mud, and I hitched a ride. Going to the airport."

"Leaving? Why?" It occurred to Dallas that he might have been wrong about what had happened at the river. "Did you arrange to have Peter Finnigan killed?"

"Guy who bought it in the river? No. But I have to say, I didn't see that coming. Nice piece of work. Cell phone trigger?"

"Yeah, and I'm sure you've got a cell phone handy."

"Who doesn't? It wasn't me, though. As I said, I'm out of here."

"Explain," Dallas said, applying pressure to Archie's windpipe.

He squirmed. "I was following you and Mia, like I'm paid to do. Don't know who blew up this Peter guy, but I'm thinking it's probably the doctor. He's the one who looped me in. Or maybe his wife."

Mia ran up in time to overhear, cheeks pink, rain rolling down her long hair. "Dr. Elias contacted you in Miami?"

"He contacted Mr. Garza. Tipped him off that you were in Spanish Canyon, and that's why I got sent here." Archie shot her a look. "What did you do to cross that doctor? He's more ruthless than my boss."

"Oh, no," Mia said. "He knew Cora was going to tell me, warn me about what she'd learned. He must have been tracking her emails."

He shrugged. "Don't care. Not my business. I was sent to find the stash."

Mia let out a cry. "But I don't have any money. How many times can I say it? Hector didn't leave me a thing. How can I convince you?"

"Already done. Seems brother Reuben went to see

Hector and explained that you and tiny tot were in trouble. Hector came clean. His stash was in Miami all along. Mr. Garza has his money, and my job here is done."

Mia shook her head and let out a sigh.

"Not done," Dallas growled. "You led Gracie up to the roof. She could have been hurt. You have to pay for that."

Archie managed a choked laugh. "Lying to a kid isn't against the law. People do it all the time."

"We'll see if the police agree. You broke into Mia's house, too. Better get a lawyer."

Archie struggled under Dallas's grip. "Don't have time for that. This whole county's gonna be underwater and I want to go home."

"Well," Dallas said, anger at the fear Archie had caused Mia still bubbling in his veins, "this just isn't your day."

Rain stung his face as he turned Archie around. "Mia, there's some rope in the back of the truck."

She dashed through the rain back up the road.

A trickle of mud ran down from the mountainside and past Dallas's feet.

"I hate Colorado," Archie spat.

"Should have stayed in Miami." Dallas could not prevent a feeling of satisfaction from sweeping through him. Maybe the cops wouldn't charge Archie with anything, but upsetting his easy escape was a small triumph. At this point, he'd take what he could get. Archie first, Dr. Elias next.

Another wave of muck flowed under the truck and across the road. Dallas looked through the sheeting rain. The mountainside was black, denuded a few years back, he estimated, by a wildfire.

The ground trembled under his feet.

Archie's eyes rolled as he tried to process what was happening.

There wasn't time.

With a roar the mountainside fell away into a river of mud that swept toward the truck.

He thought he detected a scream, Mia's scream, but it was lost in the rumble of movement as the mud carried Archie, Dallas and the truck over the cliff.

THIRTEEN

The river of black engulfed Dallas and Archie, the cacophony swallowing up Mia's scream as she struggled to keep her footing on the trembling road. For a moment, she thought the entire stretch would be sucked up by the massive flow, like a monstrous inverse volcano. There was nowhere to run.

As the movement of the earth slowed, the mighty roar ebbed to a murmur. The flow softened into a trickle and then, eerie silence. Her heart cried out for Dallas. She half stumbled, half crawled, along the edge of the road, wiping the rain from her face. Down below was a sea of mud, coating the steep slope, blanketing the trees, blotting out everything it touched. The upended truck had caught on a trunk, wheels spinning lazily above the black ooze that imprisoned it.

"Dallas," she screamed.

The truck driver and the man with the chain saw raced up.

"Two men are down there," Mia screamed, trying to discern a path she could take to reach them.

"Make that one," the truck driver said, pointing.

A mud-caked figure detached itself from the mess, struggling upright.

The men tied a rope to a tree at the edge of the road and lowered it down. The man grabbed it and hoisted himself up, hand over hand.

Was it Dallas or Archie? Mia found she was holding her breath as the victim fought to pull himself up from the pit. When he was within a few feet of the top, the men reached over and grabbed his arms.

With one synchronized heave, he was pulled over the edge. On hands and knees, he crouched, sucking in a breath. Mia pressed close, unable to force out the question.

"Man," Archie said, wiping a layer of mud from his face. "I really hate this state."

Mia's breath choked off as she ran to the edge again. There was no movement from below, no sign of Dallas.

No, Lord. Please, no.

"I'll try the radio," the truck driver said gently. "We'll call for help."

The other man helped Archie to his feet and moved him away from the slide. Mia stared down into the muck. *Think, Mia.* She spotted the place where Archie had emerged, just behind a stand of three trees that had caught the truck. The thick trunks would have deflected some of the force of the earth flow. If Dallas was there…

"Hey, lady," she heard someone call, as she climbed over the roadbed, clinging to the rope as her feet sank in the mud.

What am I doing? What if I drown in this smothering blanket?

What if she did?

What would she have to show for her life? A perfect daughter, yes, and a heart choked with so much anger, hurt and distrust that it was nearly drowned already. *I've wasted time being afraid. I'm sorry. So sorry.* Her soul offered up the words and it was as if they rose up to the clean, storm-washed air above, even as her body sank into the filth below. A sense of calm ate away at the panic. Mud oozed and sloshed around her, her legs sinking in up to her thighs and then her waist until she was more swimming through it than climbing down. When she came level with the truck, she pulled up the rest of the rope and tied it around herself, transferring her grip from the rope to the sturdy truck fender.

"Dallas," she called. The rain drilled tiny craters into the mud surrounding her. Everything was so monochromatic, a sea of black. She would have to edge around the front of the truck to be able to see beyond. Fingers cold and caked with slippery mud, she groped her way along. A metal shard on the fender nicked her palm.

A few more feet to go, sodden soil sucking against her every inch of the journey, she made her way around the fender.

As she'd suspected, beyond the stand of tightly clustered trees was a space relatively unscathed by the flow. He was not there. Body tingling with despair she scanned frantically.

"Dallas," she yelled again.

A small movement caught her eye. She'd been mistaken. Among the roots of one of the massive trees, she saw him, lying on his side, covered with mud, as black as the shadows that cloaked him.

She scrambled along, fitting between the trees, and made it to his side.

Breathing, let him be breathing. With a shaking hand, she brushed some of the cloying mud from his face.

His eyes blinked open, and it seemed at that exact moment, something inside her opened up, too. She leaned her cheek on his forehead. "Oh, Dallas" was all she could manage.

His eyes widened, the whites brilliant against his mud-streaked face. The breath caught in her throat, and she realized she'd never seen such a truly spectacular sight as those black irises, regarding her soberly, flaming to life as his senses returned. She reached out and stroked his face, running her fingertips along his forehead, his cheeks, again and again, until she began to believe he was really and truly alive.

Was it relief she saw in his eyes? She might have thought it joy, but why would it be so? Her brain reminded her what her heart did not want to acknowledge: she was a job, and she had every right to be angry at this deceiver whose hand she now clung to, their filthy fingers twined together. He had tricked her and withheld the truth from her.

Yet it was definitely not anger she felt, nor anything close to it. And that scared her more than the mudslide. She let go.

His lips moved, but she couldn't detect any sound until she leaned close.

"That was a wild ride," he muttered.

She laughed. It was absurd. Nestled in the mud up to her knees with a man who'd nearly been buried under tons of mountain, rain sheeting down on them both, she could not hold in the relieved giggle that bubbled from her mouth.

"I thought you were dead," she said, biting her lip to steady her frayed nerves.

"So did I, for a while there," he said, struggling to pull himself to a sitting position, letting loose a shower of broken twigs and debris.

"Are you hurt?"

"Dunno yet." Clods of dirt fell away as he moved, the rain washing some of the grime from his face. He stared at her, his gaze so intense it made her look away. "I'm just glad you didn't get sucked down here with me."

"No, I got here under my own steam."

Eyeing the slope he shook his head. "Incredible. Why didn't you wait for help?"

She gave him a casual shrug. The truth was, she did not fully understand why she had done something so rash, for him, when the hurt still echoed inside. "Seemed like the thing to do after only one of you made it out."

He stiffened, as if remembering. "Archie?"

"He climbed up, unharmed, of course."

"Of course." Dallas tried to get to his feet. "We've got to get back up there. Go to the police."

He stood too quickly, staggering backwards. She quickly shoved her shoulder under his. "Slow. I can't carry you out of here, so don't push too hard."

He considered the slope and groaned. "That's a long way back up."

She showed him the rope tied around her waist, ridiculously pleased at the respect on his face.

"Smart thinking to tie the rope."

"I'm not as good at rescue as Juno, but I do my best."

He laughed, winced, and put a hand to his ribs.

"Broken?"

"Probably bruised, but I'll make it."

She unknotted the rope from her body so they could both grab hold. They began the arduous ascent, first climbing around the ruined truck and then struggling up the slope, stopping every few feet to rest, sinking sometimes to their knees, sometimes to their waists in the sticky mud. When he stumbled back, she would grab his arm, holding him steady until he regained his balance. When she slowed, mired down by the cloying mass, he pulled her through the worst of it. Though she did not want his help, she was grateful. Now that the adrenaline from the rescue was depleted, every muscle in her body seemed to resent the effort it took to climb back to the road.

Mack met them halfway down, lowered on another rope fed to him by the truck driver. Mia could have cried in relief when the big man grasped her around the waist and they were hauled to the top by the men, and, to Mia's surprise, Susan.

Susan helped her to sit on the fender of Dallas's truck while Mack went back down the slope to assist Dallas. From somewhere Susan produced a handkerchief and wiped the grit from Mia's face as best she could.

The rain continued to thunder all around them, and now she found herself pleased with the downpour that washed some of the clinging film of mud off her clothes. She felt light and lifted inside, as if she'd somehow left some of her anger at the bottom of the cliff. She was not ready to forgive, not yet, but it did not stop her from enjoying the relief that came from putting down some of her burden. Quietly, she thanked the Lord for blessing her and Dallas with another day of life. How odd to feel thankful. How very strange and foreign.

Dallas was helped over the top, and he walked gingerly over to join her. "Archie's gone," he said morosely. "He got away again."

Mia shook away her strange ponderings, and rubbed at a scrape on her arm. "Good riddance. I never want to see him again. I hope he's right that Mr. Garza is finally satisfied."

"He's got no reason to go after you anymore," Dallas said. "Hector gave him what he wanted."

"Only when he had to."

"Because he heard you were in danger."

She felt shamed. "Yes, I guess so. He loves us, in his own fashion."

"That's one thing he has right." He held her gaze and she found she could not look away. Had the rain become warmer as it fell? The wind melodious as it swept along the road? Had Dallas become even more attractive, filthiness aside? Could be it was all colored by relief, she concluded.

Mack called out from the spot where the tree had fallen.

"I'm going to help clear the road," Dallas said.

"I'll help, too," Mia insisted.

He started to protest and then sighed. "It won't do any good to tell you to wait in the truck, will it?"

"Not one bit," she replied, walking straight to Mack and the truck driver. "Thank you for helping us out of that mess. We're ready to pitch in and clear the road."

Mack chuckled. "And I had you pegged for a city girl."

Mia shot him a sassy smile. "A city girl who's ready to get home to her daughter. Are you going to fire up that chain saw or am I?"

Mack and Dallas exchanged amused looks. In a matter of thirty minutes, Mack sliced off enough of the fallen tree to allow vehicles to squeeze by. Mia, Dallas and the truck driver hauled the branches out of the way while Susan continued to try to get a cell phone signal.

After a shaking of hands all around, Mack and the driver loaded up in his vehicle and the others in Dallas's truck. Mia could not hold back a sigh as she slid onto the passenger seat and Dallas got behind the wheel. The old, cracked vinyl felt like a cloud of comfort compared to the scraping she'd enduring traversing down the cliffside and back up again. It was sheer bliss to be out of the hammering rain. The mud clinging to her skin coated her with an earthy funk.

What she wouldn't give for her favorite lavender lemon bath scrub that Gracie said smelled like candy. She sat up, a current of memory stinging everything inside.

"What?" Dallas said. "Are you hurt?"

"I just thought of something." Mia turned to Susan in the backseat. "You followed Catherine to Peter's house. How long was she there?"

Susan considered. "Only a few minutes. She pounded on the door, but he didn't answer at first. Finally he opened up, they exchanged a few words, and Peter grabbed the photo out of her hand and slammed the door closed. She went around the back and looked through the windows but he refused to let her in. After she left, he came outside and that's when I caught up with him."

"It occurred to me that if Catherine lingered awhile, she also could have put something in Peter's duffel bag while Susan and Peter were inside."

Dallas let out a low whistle. "Is Catherine in on the whole business?"

Mia gave voice to the question that was burning inside her. Peter's duffel bag was already in the boat when they arrived. "Did you see Catherine put anything in Peter's duffel bag?"

"I couldn't see down to the water from where I was in the house," Susan said.

Mia bit back a frustrated sigh.

Was Catherine Elias an unwitting cog in Elias's schemes? Or did she have her own part in Peter Finnigan's death?

Though Dallas had the wipers set at full speed, they hardly kept up with the water sheeting across the glass. His head was pounding a rhythm that matched the throbbing in his ribs. There was no option to drive fast, though he had to fight the urge to ram the gas pedal down. Dr. Elias was a murderer. And his wife, Catherine, might be his partner in crime. Most likely, Elias had taken care of Finnigan, who could prove his guilt. But Mia and Susan could still expose him, and there was the photo tucked under the visor in his truck. The miles passed excruciatingly slowly back to Spanish Canyon.

They headed straight for the police station, against Susan's wishes.

"That detective, Stiving, he won't hear anything bad about the precious Dr. Elias. He's protecting him. Could be the doctor has him on the payroll, even. We can't go to the police here."

"There isn't much choice, Susan," Dallas said. "We'll talk to the chief."

"And you trust him?" she demanded.

"He's given me no reason not to." But Stiving had.

Mia straightened, clutching her phone. "Got a signal. There's a message from Antonia. She got word to evacuate a half hour ago. She packed up Gracie and Juno. They're heading for the airport. She said she'll wait in the parking terminal until we get there." She groaned. "I feel like I should go meet them right now."

"As soon as we report what you…" He broke off as they took the main road into town. The paved surface was covered by inches of water. Shop owners and police officers worked side by side in the rain, filling sandbags. They were fighting a losing battle, as the water was already lapping the sidewalks. Soon it would be spilling through doorways and flooding the businesses all along the block. The police station was obviously evacuating, officers and volunteers carrying boxes and equipment to a waiting van.

Dallas tried to park nearby, but he was waved at by a drenched police volunteer. "Can't stop here. Cantcha' see we're flooding?"

"It's an emergency."

He eyed Dallas and Mia skeptically. "Wet and dirty, but y'all look fine to me. Nobody's getting into the station right now."

Dallas kept his temper with serious effort. "We have to speak to the chief. It's urgent."

"Chief's already gone to our mobile station in Pine Grove. Stiving's out on a call, and every available officer is assisting the fire department. Sorry, can't help you unless you want to drive to Pine Grove and see if they have time for you."

Dallas was about to fire off an angry reply when Mia took his arm. "We'll go to Pine Grove. It's on the way to the airport, anyway."

A pang of grief stabbed at his insides. The airport would be their goodbye, the last time he would ever see her and Gracie. He rolled up the window and drove through the water. Pine Grove and the airport. End of the line. There was no way to stop it. He knew it was better, anyway. Mia and Gracie needed to be safely away from the floods and Dr. Elias. Once they were away, securely settled in Florida, Elias would pay for what he did to Cora, Susan and Finnigan.

Dallas would see to it.

They took the road to Pine Grove, which would provide a higher elevation for the police to regroup. The locals told of floods that had occurred some twenty years before, but nothing like this, and the town was simply not prepared for such a magnitude of disaster.

"Where will you go, Dallas?" Mia said, breaking into his thoughts. "Will you wait until the water recedes and live in the trailers still?"

Why would he? The only thing that meant something was his Search and Rescue classes and he was only filling in for a temporary vacancy. The job would be gone soon, too.

"Dunno. I'll have to ask Juno what he thinks."

Mia smiled and closed her eyes as they drove. She looked very young with her wet hair framing her face, smudged with both dirt and fatigue.

His thoughts wandered. If things had been different and they'd met under other circumstances. Would he have risked a relationship with her? Would she have allowed him past the protective wall she'd built? Might he have stuck around long enough to chip away at it?

Maybe he wouldn't have been brave enough to attempt it. He would have packed up his unfinished puzzle and his uncomplaining dog and left town rather than face his own vulnerability. He would never know if he would have let the most amazing woman he'd ever known walk out of his life because now it was too late. She was flying away, and it felt like she was taking his heart with her. Despair felt as weighty as the oppressive storm.

He almost didn't have time to slam on the brakes. A car he didn't at first recognize, was stopped in the road, doors open, hazard lights on. Juno stood next to the car.

"It's Antonia," Mia cried, leaping from the truck. He was behind her in a flash. Juno raced up to him, electric with some kind of excitement.

Antonia stood in the rain, body shaking, mouth tight with terror. "Oh, Mia. She's gone. She's gone." Tears rolled down her cheeks as Mia gripped her forearms.

"What happened, Antonia?" Mia demanded, voice hard as glass. "Where's Gracie?"

Antonia tried to answer, but no sound came out. Mia's hands tightened, viselike, around her sister's wrists. "Where is my daughter?"

Sucking in a breath, she tried again. "He took her."

"Who?" Mia's words rang with anguish.

"There was a chair overturned in the road. I got out to remove it. When I turned back, a man was there at the passenger-side door. He…he took Gracie and ran up the road. I heard him get into a car and then he was gone." She heaved in a breath. "Juno barked, but I had him leashed in the back and he couldn't get out. I called the police. They're coming."

"No." Mia's hands flew to her mouth. "No, no. This can't be happening."

"He always wins," Susan said, her own eyes round.

"I'm sorry, I'm so sorry," Antonia kept repeating.

"Who?" Dallas said. "Who was the man? Did you recognize him?"

The look she gave him was pure agony. "I know his face because I looked him up online when you told me he fired Mia." She swallowed. "It was Dr. Elias."

FOURTEEN

Mia saw the ground rush up to meet her as her legs failed. Dallas caught her before she hit the asphalt and carried her back into the passenger seat of his truck. She did not feel him lift her, she could not feel anything except a cold river of terror that seemed out to numb her limbs, her mind, her soul. He had Gracie. Dr. Elias had taken her baby.

"Sit for a minute," Dallas's soothing voice urged.

She felt pressure and realized that Antonia was gripping her hand, squeezing hard enough that her sister's nails bit into the tender skin of her palm. She was speaking, and Mia tried to follow. Antonia told the story in halting bursts. "After I called the police, I checked back with the trailer park. They haven't been ordered to evacuate, yet. It was a hoax."

Dallas said. "He probably pretended to be with the fire department. He told you there was an evacuation order so he knew when you'd be passing by."

Antonia nodded, grief stricken. "He must have been watching, parked around the turn in the road, waiting for us. I should have known. I never should have left her in the car alone. Oh, Mia, what have I done?"

It was as if Mia was watching it all from a distance, like a dramatic play unfolding on the stage in front of her. She should comfort her sister. Decide on the next step. Find a current picture on her phone to give to the police. Isn't that what the parents of missing children were supposed to do? The faces on milk cartons materialized in her mind. She'd seen the pictures, the sweet little faces printed there, smiling in moments of innocence while the world fractured into a nightmare for the parents who searched desperately for them.

She should take action. Every moment idle meant Gracie was that much farther away.

But she could do nothing but shake, her body vibrating to the rhythm of the shock which her mind could not grasp. The hands in her lap, the hair hanging across her eyes, did not seem to belong to anyone real. Gracie, her heart, the most precious person on the planet, was in the hands of a murdering madman. And Mia was reduced to a mindless zombie.

How could it be real? She was dreaming, in the grip of a nightmare.

The phone in Mia's purse rang. "You should answer it," Dallas prodded gently.

She could not force her fingers into life, so he removed the cell from the outside pocket of her purse and thumbed it awake.

"Hello?"

"I'm glad I thought to get the numbers off your cell phone when you left it in the office. This is Dallas's number, isn't it? The loser? Mia, your choice in men is terrible. Did we learn nothing from the last criminal you became involved with?"

Dallas stiffened. "Elias? Where's Gracie?"

Mia sucked in a breath and forced her teeth to stop chattering. Dallas put the call on speaker phone and the four of them bent their heads together to listen.

"Don't talk to the police," Elias said. "I don't want them involved."

Calm, collected, as if he was orchestrating every terrible moment. "What have you done with Gracie?" Mia tried to shout. Instead it came out as a pathetic whisper.

"She's with me, as you are aware, I'm sure."

"This isn't going to accomplish anything," Dallas snarled. "It's all over. We know the truth about Asa Norton."

He paused. "The truth is relative. I want the photo. I will contact you soon with the location."

"Please," Mia said, her voice breaking. "Don't hurt Gracie."

His tone was slightly offended. "I don't want to hurt her, Mia. I'm a doctor after all." Elias sounded almost as if he was talking to a patient, discussing treatment options or surgical procedures. "This is strictly a matter of self-preservation. Practical. Keep the police out of it, give me the photo, and there won't be any need for me to use violence. She will be returned, in perfect health. I'll call you back soon."

"No," Mia screamed, grabbing for the phone. "I want my daughter. Give me my daughter!"

There was no answer. Dr. Elias had disconnected.

Panic burgeoned through her senses. *Gracie, Gracie, Gracie.*

Dallas was talking, saying something as a police car pulled in behind them.

"Mia." He pressed his mouth to her ear. "Do you

want to involve the police? I think we should, but I don't know if we can trust Stiving."

The words circled slowly in her mind. *Police. Stiving.*

The police car ground to a halt on the shoulder. Stiving got out and walked over to them. "What's this all about?"

Antonia looked at Mia. She gave a slow nod. What choice did she have, especially after Antonia already called them?

"It's Gracie. She's been abducted." Antonia shook her head. "Aren't you here about my call?"

His gaze narrowed. "No, I'm here for Mia. Who's been abducted?"

Antonia stared at Mia. She felt Dallas's weighty gaze on her, also. They were asking what she wanted to do. Should she trust that this officer could rescue Mia from Dr. Elias? What was the alternative? She didn't even know where to start looking for her daughter. Panic constricted her lungs until she feared she was going to pass out.

"I'm here to arrest you," Stiving finished.

The words sizzled through her addled senses. Arrest her?

"What?" Dallas barked.

"The tests came back like we thought. Cora's blood-pressure medicine capsules were emptied out and filled with cocaine. It caused her to fall into a coma and stopped her heart. Fire Captain says she wasn't alert enough to snuff out the candle on her bedside table which started the fire."

"I didn't do anything to her medicine," Mia heard herself say. "I just picked it up from the pharmacy. Dr.

Elias tampered with it. He must have taken it out of my purse at work while I was in the file room."

Stiving raised his eyebrows. "Pretty crazy scenario. A respected doctor in this town murders an elderly volunteer. With a street drug."

"Cocaine is used in nasal surgery all the time. He had easy access," Susan chimed in.

Stiving shot her a look as if he had not noticed her there until that moment. "And why would he do that, exactly? To gain what?"

"Because he's not the man you think he is," Mia said desperately. "He's a murderer, and Cora was onto him. She—"

Stiving held up a hand. "All right. One thing at a time. You'll have a chance to tell me everything when I get you to jail in Pine Grove."

Dallas slammed a hand on the truck. "Listen. She's telling you the truth. He's got her…"

"Enough," Stiving snapped. "There are only two sets of fingerprints on that poisoned medicine, Mia's and Cora's. If the doctor has access to cocaine at the clinic, then chances are Ms. Sandoval did, too, not to mention the fact that she inherited Cora's property. All of that put together gives me more than enough to arrest her. We're going to jail now and if any of you interferes, you can join Ms. Sandoval."

Stiving was an enemy, Mia knew it then. By the time she convinced him that Gracie had been taken, that Dr. Elias was not the man he seemed, Elias might have killed her. The doctor's words came back to her again.

"You're afraid that you can't trust yourself, your choices, your judgments."

He'd seen right down deep into the core of her, the

real essence of her weakness. He was a master manipulator, and he was still in control, still pulling her strings as if she was a helpless marionette.

Mia could not trust herself, nor her ex-husband, or the police officer who stood there with the satisfied half smile on his face. She could not trust in the life she had built for her child, the possessions she'd accumulated, the schooling she was so determined to complete. It was not even a certainty that the town of Spanish Canyon would still be there tomorrow, threatened as it was by the menacing floodwaters set to swallow it whole. There was nothing on this earth that she could count on.

From somewhere deep down in her soul, came snippets that she had heard long ago when she was a child, maybe not any older than Gracie.

Trust in the Lord with all your heart...
Seek His will in all you do...
He will show you which path to take.

Trust God. Could she do something so simple and ultimately so very difficult?

Trust God.

Standing in front of her were two people who had done exactly that.

Dallas let the Lord rescue him from a minefield of sin and come out the other side a changed man. Antonia gave up years of anger and bitterness and the Lord transformed her life and filled it to the brim with love. It was time to trust Him to show Mia the way. There was a reason He had given her life and kept her living and right now, that reason she believed with every tiny atom inside her, was to save Gracie.

Armed with that desperate knowledge, and a faith

wild and untamed and new, she closed her eyes and surrendered everything to which she had clung so tightly, pride, independence, fear, anger, hurt. *Lord, I trust You. Help me.*

When she opened her eyes she knew. God was there, right there with her as he had been since the beginning. Even when she'd ignored Him. Even when she'd railed at Him and yes, when she'd hated Him. He would be with her through whatever the next few hours brought.

In a flash, she saw the way. There was one person who knew where Dr. Elias had taken her daughter. Only one.

But Stiving would not let her go there, nor would he follow her leads. He would deliver her to jail before he conducted any search for Gracie. If Mia waited, if she let him take her, she would lose her daughter forever.

Please, Lord.

With cold fingers, she slipped the phone in her pocket and stepped out of the car. "All right, I'll go."

"Mia," Antonia cried out. "There has to be another way."

Mia grabbed her in a tight hug. She saw over Antonia's shoulder the naked anguish on Dallas's face. "It's all right," she whispered to her sister. "Tell Stiving everything. Convince him, if you can."

"What?" Antonia mumbled through her tears. "Where…"

"I'm sorry," Mia said to Antonia and Dallas. She locked onto his wondrous black eyes.

Something in her tone must have told him what she was going to do. He shook his head, hand raised to stop her. With all her strength, she shoved her sister backward, causing her to stumble into Stiving, who toppled against his car door and they both went down in the mud.

Mia ran as fast as she ever had in her life, heading for the rain-soaked forest, running toward the only way she could think of to save her child.

Dallas was thunderstruck. Juno barked and raced after Mia, thinking perhaps that it was some sort of game, until Dallas called him back. He stared as Mia raced over the uneven ground, making for the crowded wall of trees. She ran, fleet as a deer, disappearing between the branches.

Dallas helped Antonia and Stiving to their feet, shock and disbelief rocketed through him in waves. Had Mia really just run from the police? How could she think such a rash move would help find Gracie?

But would he not have done the same thing to find his brother?

Or Mia? He swallowed. Yes, he would.

Stiving barreled toward the trees, making it only a few yards, stumbling and slipping, before he must have come to the conclusion that he had no hope of catching up with her. He turned back to the car, rage suffusing his cheeks with red.

Antonia stood in shock, hands pressed to her mouth, staring in the direction her sister had just taken.

"Bad move." Stiving was on the radio now, calling for assistance in apprehending Mia Verde Sandoval.

The radio exchange seemed to snap Antonia from her inertia, and she started in on him before he could get back in the car. "Her daughter's been kidnapped by Dr. Elias. Whether you want to believe it or not, that's what happened. Dispatch will confirm it. I called it in moments before you arrived."

Stiving's lip curled. "I will confirm it, after I bring your sister in."

Dallas offered up everything he knew about Peter Finnigan's death. Susan reluctantly confirmed the facts until Stiving held up his hands. Was it Dallas's imagination, or did he see the slightest sign of belief on Stiving's face?

"All right. I've got enough to look into. I'll send anyone available to help search for the girl, but you have to know that Mia made an idiotic choice running from the police."

"She wouldn't have done it, except that Gracie's life is in danger," Antonia fired back.

"Seems to me she used that bit before, when she took the kid and went on the run after she served her jail time."

"She knows that was a mistake. She wanted to keep Mia away from her father," Dallas said through clenched teeth.

Stiving ignored him, took pictures of Antonia's car and checked it thoroughly before he ordered her to move it off the road. "They just radioed me that they're ordering evacuations of Spanish Canyon. This road will be jammed. I have to go back to town. You three should head to Pine Grove and wait for me there."

"My sister…" Antonia began.

"Your sister is now a fugitive, and she'll be treated as such." He climbed in the front seat. "If you help her in any way, you're aiding and abetting. Remember that." Tires squelched across the road as he did a sharp U-turn and headed back toward Spanish Canyon.

Dallas considered for a moment, trying to corral the thoughts stampeding through his brain. Mia would not hesitate to sacrifice her own life to save Gracie. Right or wrong, she felt she had no other choice than to run. He had to intercept her. Urgency burned like acid through his veins. "Take Susan and go to Pine Grove."

"What am I supposed to do there?" Antonia demanded. The angry quirk to her lips was so like her sister he almost smiled.

"Convince them to look for Gracie. Get to the chief if you can." He shot Susan a look. "And don't let this lady out of your sight."

"Where do you think he took Gracie?" Susan asked.

"I'm not certain."

"Promise me you won't hand me over to Thomas, even if you do find him," she said, staring at Dallas with those oddly haunted eyes. "You are not that kind of man, I think."

"You're right, and I'm hoping you're not the kind of woman who would walk out on a mother and child. We'll need your testimony to bring Elias down once and for all."

She looked away. "I don't know what kind of woman I am anymore. Before I was just angry, but now…"

"It's time for you to decide." He faced her full-on. "You've been hurt and lost your husband. Now there's a little girl involved." He heard Antonia gulp back a sob. "She needs her mommy, and you can help put things right, but not if you run away. Do you understand?"

She cocked her head. "Yes, I do."

"Then stay with Antonia. When we find Mia, we'll need you to back up her story." He reached out and squeezed Susan's forearm. "This time, the doctor is going to pay for what he's done, I promise."

She nodded slowly.

He started for the truck.

"But where are you going?" Antonia cried. "How can you help Mia?"

"It's my job to protect her, remember?" He opened the truck door.

"You're not just doing a job," she said quietly. "It's something much more than that."

He allowed a moment to acknowledge that she was right. Mia was not a job, she never had been. Not to him. "Juno and I are going to find her."

A freshening wind pulled at Antonia's wet hair as the rain continued to fall. "Do you know where she's headed?"

"I have a pretty good idea."

She came close and gripped his hands. "You have to find her. And Gracie."

"I will," he said, a sense of resolve turning all his fears and uncertainties into hard steel in his gut.

I will.

FIFTEEN

Dallas pulled the truck off the road, crunching across the tall grass, making his own trail to a rocky outcropping behind which he parked. He picked up Mia's purse and offered a sniff to Juno. It was probably completely unnecessary. He had always thought that Juno understood much more than the average member of his species. Juno already knew that he was going to look for the small, determined woman who had crashed through the heavy carpet of grass. Perhaps he thought it was one of their many training exercises where he would be sent to discover a prearranged "victim."

"Find," he commanded anyway.

Dallas watched him run, graceful loping strides over the uneven ground, tail wagging with sheer joy at the prospect of engaging in a search. Mia was no doubt heading for Dr. Elias's house to talk to Catherine. It would be feasible to go there and wait for her to turn up, but he did not want to leave her plunging through a heavily wooded area, wanted by the police and not in her right mind with worry about Gracie. She could fall, break an ankle, sustain a concussion. He shut down the worrisome scenarios.

Juno returned after a short while, alerted with his ear piercing bark, and then disappeared again, scrambling up a twisting road which might have once been a logging trail. Dallas hiked onward, the muddy ground clinging to his boots, rain dripping from his hair. The trail crested the top of a wooded hill and drifted back down toward the highway.

Every now and again, Juno would return and bark, a sign that he had tracked Mia and perhaps even found her already and why didn't Dallas get a move on it and pick up the pace, already? Dallas smiled. They'd cross-trained together, Juno and his awkward human, and the dog was fully capable of both tracking and trailing, and air scenting, but Juno always seemed to relish the opportunity to be off leash and following his impeccable nose toward a rescue. Other dogs could do the tracking on leash.

It never ceased to amaze him. With his paltry sense of smell, he could detect nothing but the odor of rain-washed ground and pine. Juno was easily able to discern the scent left behind by the 40,000 skin cells dropped each minute by his human quarry. Not only that, he could pick that scent from a world awash in odors. Dallas had worked with or known canines that detected everything from cadavers, to explosives, to smuggled fruits and vegetables. And now, his chance to find one small amazing woman lost in a sea of giant trees, all depended on Juno's amazing nose.

Dallas kept himself in high gear. In spite of the aching in his ribs and the pounding rain, he increased his clip until he was at a near jog, avoiding patches of slippery pine needles and puddles as best as he was able. She could not be that far ahead, but her pace was impressive, considering she too had survived a mudslide not many hours before.

Time ticked away, sucking up the minutes until sundown. It was edging toward six o'clock. One more hour of daylight. Juno could track at night, they'd spent enough hours training at it, but Dallas was not as surefooted in the dark, and neither was Mia. She had to be cold and terrified. And what about Gracie? Was she frightened? Had he hurt her? Bound her? The thought haunted him.

The way ahead was overgrown, thick underfoot with soggy debris and crowded overhead by tree limbs, weeping icy droplets down on him. And then, without warning, the trail was gone. They found themselves in a forest that showed no signs that it had ever been penetrated by humans for any reason. He listened to the incessant dripping. Wind played with branches and loosed more water down upon them which Juno blasted away with a vigorous body shake.

Juno stopped and nosed around for Mia's scent. With still victims on fair-weather days, the scent rose in a neat cone, emanating from the search target. Today the rain, shifting winds and highly active target, was making the search more difficult. It seemed likely that Mia would stop at some point, perhaps to try and use the GPS on her phone to locate Catherine's house, or simply to rest, to hide.

His heart was pounding and muscles fatigued after the brisk climb. Falling away to his left was a small hollow of firs, clustered close enough together to protect from the rain. She would head there, to regroup.

"Mia," he called. No answer but a quick darting movement from behind the trees. He charged toward it.

Juno stopped him with an impatient bark.

"She's down there," he said as much to himself as the dog, ignoring another louder bark from Juno.

He half ran now, wishing his stiff leg and ribs would work in harmony with the rest of his limbs. He'd spent years, his whole adult life, really, combing through wild corners of the world, quiet forests and ruined buildings, creek beds and mountaintops, searching, searching. Sometimes he and Juno had found the target and he'd celebrated. Sometimes they didn't get there in time and they grieved together. After every mission, the need to search always returned. There would be another someone to find, another search to be taken on, a restlessness that told him he had not yet discovered the person he was destined to find.

"Mia," he shouted again, earning another bark from Juno.

He plunged into the clearing, moving so fast he skidded a good couple of feet before he stopped his forward momentum. The Stellar's Jays in the shrubs shot out with a deafening screech, taking refuge in the branches and squawking their displeasure. The air was heavy with the scent of wet grass and decaying leaves.

He completed a rough circle of the hollow, sinking up to his ankle in water at one point. Mia wasn't there. Bending low, he peered under the taller bushes, searching out any hiding places.

No Mia, nor any sign she had ever been there. Juno stared at him. Recrimination. He'd broken his own rule. Trust the dog. Dallas hadn't.

Early on in his career in search and rescue, a mentor watched him disregard a seemingly impossible positive alert from his dog. That's when Dallas had learned the term "intelligent disobedience."

If you've got a smart dog and you have learned to trust each other, let the dog think for himself. Juno had, and Dallas had disregarded him.

He dropped to a knee in the soggy grass and gave Juno a scratch. "Sorry, boy. I messed up. You're in charge now."

Juno accepted the apology by licking a raindrop off Dallas's chin, before he sprinted back in the other direction. Dallas tried to do the same, stumbling on the uneven earth and slapping aside branches as the slope became steep. He'd lost time with his dumb mistake. He prayed it wasn't too late. As the terrain grew more and more rugged, he had to resort to using his hands to hold on to tree trunks and exposed roots as he hauled himself upward, arriving at the top to find they'd looped back to the road.

Fifty yards ahead a yellow truck was stopped, the passenger door open.

And Mia was just stepping in.

"Mia," he shouted. Juno had almost reached her when she pulled the door closed and the truck rumbled away down the road, leaving Juno and Dallas alone on the rain-soaked highway.

Mia's heart plummeted as she eyed Dallas in the sideview mirror, Juno trotting back over to him as the truck pulled out. He'd come to find her, to help her out of the excruciating mess she'd fallen into. Maybe he'd intended to talk her into going back to the police. Knowing Dallas, he'd more likely determined to help her enact her own desperate plan to find her daughter.

But she could not let him throw his life away on a

fugitive. And that's what she was, she reminded herself incredulously.

She realized the woman at the wheel was speaking to her. "Where'd you come from? Popping out of the woods like that, I thought you were Bigfoot, till I realized you're too small and not hairy enough." She laughed, setting her gray curls bouncing. "Name's Fiona. You?"

She smiled, imagining she must look like a deranged hitchhiker. "My name's Mia. I'm trying to get to the Spanish Villa Estates, on the edge of town. Do you know where that is?"

"'Course. Nice digs up there." She eyed Mia more closely, gaze flicking over her jeans and torn windbreaker. "That where you live?"

"No." Mia tried to stick to the truth as much as possible. "My house flooded. I know someone who lives in Spanish Villa. She said she'd help us find a place."

"Us?"

Mia swallowed hard. "My daughter, Gracie. She's four." She could not stop the tears then, hot and fast they rolled down her face. "I'm sorry. We've had a difficult time."

"It's okay, honey," the driver said, patting her hand and offering her a tissue box. "I got three girls myself. All grown now with kids of their own, but I remember how hard it was. Especially when my husband split town." She offered Mia a thermos. "Hot tea. You drink some now."

Mia protested.

"Your teeth are chattering. Drink the tea. I got plenty more."

Mia poured and sipped. The tea delivered warm comfort through her body and it had the added bonus of keeping her busy. Most of all she desperately did not want Fiona to ask her any more questions about Gracie. She could not trust her emotions.

Just get to Catherine and find out where her husband has taken my child.

Fiona kept up a constant commentary about the flooding and the small trucking company that she owned. Mia checked her phone constantly for any message from Dr. Elias. There wasn't any. He was probably enjoying the thought of the agony he'd created.

"Built it myself from the ground up," Fiona was saying. "Got twelve trucks now, out of Pine Grove. That's where I'm headed. Heard they've got the police moved up there during the flooding."

Mia sipped her tea and stared out the window. What else had Fiona heard?

Fiona sighed. "Awww, man. Looks like we got a roadblock."

Mia stared through the water-speckled windshield. Four cars ahead of them were stopped at a set of blockades straddling the road. A police officer, or perhaps a volunteer, swathed in a yellow slicker was making his way down the line, speaking with each of the drivers.

Her hands went icy around the cup. Were they looking for her? Nerves jumping, she darted a glance at the door handle. She could yank it open and jump down. Run away from the road. Right, and broadcast her presence like a signal flare.

The officer finished with the first two cars and made it to the third. It was almost sunset, and he held a flashlight. To search the vehicles for her? The fugitive wanted for murdering Cora Graham?

Fiona shot her a curious glance. "Drink more tea, honey, you're shaking like mad."

She watched the officer straighten and splash along the road, his boots dislodging sprays of water under the rubber soles. As subtly as she could, Mia reached for the door with one hand, fingers gripping the metal catch.

With the other, she kept the cup at her mouth, hoping to help conceal her face.

Her stomach was a lead weight as the cop waited for Fiona to roll down the window.

"Hello, ladies." He peered at Mia. "Where are you headed?"

Don't tell him about Spanish Villa, she begged silently.

"Pine Grove. Shop's up there."

He nodded. "Road's flooded ahead. Going to redirect you east about ten miles and then you can double back."

Fiona sighed. "I should have listened to the weather reports more closely."

"More rain coming. Just evacuating the lower elevations now, but might need to expand that." He looked closer at Mia. "You all right, miss?"

"Yes, I'm okay. I needed a ride, and Fiona was kind enough to stop for me."

"That right?" He took in the bedraggled hair, the scratches on her face from her plunge through the trees. Was there a dawning of recognition on his face? Would there be a request for an ID next? The roar of her own pulse deafened her.

A slow smile spread over his face. "Great to see people helping each other in times of emergency, isn't it?"

"Yes," she said, her sudden movement spilling some of the tea on her lap. She wiped at it with her sleeve.

"You headed to Pine Grove also?" The officer pinned her to the spot with his hard look. Her breath caught and she could not hide the shaking of her hands.

"I…" Mia started.

Fiona broke in. "I'm taking her to see a friend who's gonna help get her and her little daughter fixed up in a new place." Fiona looked at her watch. "When do you think you'll wave us through? I'd sure like to get this old truck in the barn before nightfall."

The officer gave Mia another long look before he consulted his radio. "All clear," he said and began to wave the drivers on to the detour.

She hardly dared breathe. As they rolled by she kept her gaze fastened out the front window, feeling the officer's eyes on her. How could he not hear the slamming of her heart into her ribs? Guilt had to be written all over her face in vivid ink.

Fiona gave the cop a final wave as she eased the truck by. When they were on the road, a good half mile past the roadblock, Fiona sighed.

"You want to tell me about it?"

Mia started. "No, I just can't. I'm sorry."

"It's all right." Fiona sighed. "I knew whatever it was that happened back there, you were anxious to get away from that guy and his dog."

She'd seen Dallas and Juno. And completely misunderstood. "They weren't…"

Fiona held up a hand. "I don't need to hear about it. You're anxious to get to Spanish Villa and just as eager to avoid the police, but you seem like a nice kid and I've got a soft spot for moms and daughters. Here." Fiona removed a plastic-wrapped sandwich from a bag. "We'll split it."

Mia was going to decline but just then her stomach let out a hollow rumble. Humbly, she accepted the sandwich. "Thank you so much, Fiona. How can I ever repay you?"

"You can tell me I make the best ham-and-pickle sandwich you ever ate."

Mia managed a grin. "I think it might be the only ham-and-pickle sandwich I ever ate."

Fiona laughed. "Close enough. We'll be passing Spanish Villa in about a half hour. Sit back and enjoy these luxurious driving conditions."

And Mia did, eating every scrap of the sandwich and clinging to the knowledge that with every mile, she was that much closer to finding Gracie.

Dallas and Juno endured a miserable hike back to the truck. Dallas kicked himself mentally every rugged step along the way. He'd distrusted Juno and lost his chance to catch Mia. Now he was playing catch-up in a big way.

He called Mia's phone again. No surprise when she did not answer. She didn't want to involve him further. *Involved? Mia I'm more than involved now. I couldn't walk away if I wanted to.*

The thought surprised him. He knew she did not want him in her life, nor Gracie's. And he would never force himself into a situation where he wasn't wanted. All true. But also true was the fact that like it or not, he felt deep down in the place where only truth can survive that he was meant to save Mia Verde Sandoval.

He phoned Antonia. She answered before the first ring had died away.

"Dallas? Did you find out anything?"

The Verde women were strong, determined, practical. It would do no good to sugarcoat, nor would he disrespect her by doing so. In the words of his mother, "Every woman's got a spark, Dallas, and adversity turns it to fire." And oh, how he'd fanned his mother's spark into flame. He'd seen it blazing in her eyes when she'd stumbled upon the gun hidden under the seat of his car. He blinked the memory away.

"I didn't catch up to her." Juno gave him the look. Full confession. "Juno found her but I messed up."

Satisfied, Juno set about licking his paws clean.

"I know where she's going, I'll meet her there. I need Susan to tell me where Catherine lives."

There was muffled conversation as Antonia consulted Susan. "She says it's a street in Spanish Villa." Antonia told him the address.

He set the wipers in motion and started the truck. "Are you both all right?"

"We're at a Red Cross shelter in Pine Grove. The chief is supposedly on his way, says a volunteer." She paused. "I'm hearing radio reports about the flooding. It's really bad—road closures all over and a bridge, the Canyon Creek span, is all but underwater."

Dallas let her talk as he headed off. When she ran down, she said what she most needed to get off her chest.

"I feel helpless. I should be searching since I was the one…"

"Antonia, stop right there. We both know who is at fault here and he's going to pay for that."

She let out a soft breath. "What if you're too late, Dallas?"

"I won't be."

"I'll pray for you."

"That's the best thing I could ask for."

The only thing.

SIXTEEN

Fiona let Mia out on a patch of moonlit road at the entrance to the Spanish Villa housing complex. Mia gripped her hand in thanks. "You've done more for me tonight than you know."

Fiona squeezed back. "Take care of yourself, honey. You're strong. You'll make it through whatever it is that's got you in the crosshairs."

One final squeeze and Mia hopped down, avoiding the mud. The sky was leaden with clouds, but the rain had tapered off to a heavy mist. Though she still felt the grit trapped under her jeans and top, her clothes were more or less dry and her belly was not grumbling, thanks to Fiona's gracious gift of a ham-and-pickle sandwich. Had Dr. Elias given Gracie anything to eat? Fear engulfed her in such a tight clutch she had to stop and fight for breath, steadying her shaking legs by locking her knees. One more check of the phone. Still no message and her battery wouldn't last forever.

Go find out where he's got her, and get your daughter back. She set off.

Enormous houses with red tile roofs and white stucco exteriors perched on well-manicured lots. It was a point in her favor that the houses were spaced far apart and the weather kept residents inside, perhaps packing in case evacuations reached even this higher elevation. She had only been to the doctor's house once, for a clinic party which included all the employees.

Fleeting memories trickled across her recollection of the event. White napkins, delicate cheeses and imported olives, plush carpets and a swimming pool in which Gracie had paddled for hours until her button of a nose was sunburned in spite of the cream. Mia's throat ached with unshed tears until a crazy idea flickered into her consciousness. Was it possible he'd brought Gracie here? Catherine had been at Finnigan's for some reason. If she was just as guilty as her husband, this might be the place they were hiding her.

New resolve flooded her with energy. She practically sprinted to the top of the hill, to the last house at the end of a lonely cul-de-sac. Dr. Elias's house.

Knock on the door? It would give them a chance to lock Gracie away or call the police on her. Heart thundering, she moved closer, trying to piece together some sort of plan. A set of arched windows with fancy iron grillwork decorated the side of the house. Most were dark, but golden light glowed from the farthest one. She moved silently to the edge of the neat stepping-stone walk, keeping to the shadows. Did the doctor have a dog? She didn't think so. Too finicky, too controlling. He wasn't the dog-loving type.

You weren't either, until you met Juno.

And Dallas.

Mia realized that she had changed in a lot of ways since encountering Dallas. She had been too far away to see his face, as she got into the truck and left him on the side of the road, but she could imagine the anger and frustration. It stabbed at her. Why were her feelings a jumbled spaghetti mess whenever she thought of him?

Jaw clenched, she pushed the hair out of her face and shored up her strength. *He shouldn't have followed me. His job is done.* It was all on her now.

Her and God.

She drew level with the window now, fingers on the cold metal grillwork. A quick look. She readied herself to move when a hand went around her mouth, muffling whatever scream she might have managed.

She thrashed against the strong arms holding her, iron bands that kept her fastened against a rock-hard chest.

"Quiet" came the hissed whisper in her ear.

Dallas held her there for a moment, captive against him, and then slowly he turned her around, uncovered her mouth and pulled her into the shadows behind a potted shrub.

She couldn't decipher her own rattling emotions. He looked down at her, moisture beading on his tousled hair, a scratch running the length of his cheek, hands on hips, lips hard with anger. "Mia…" he began, then with a sudden rush he pulled her close and kissed her, palms cradling her head.

The warmth rushed through her in a delicious wave and she kissed him back, forgetting for a moment, everything but the elation that swept through her. A tide of warmth, safety and belonging thundered through her, beating back the desperate fear. When they both ran out of breath, he pulled away and put his forehead to hers.

"Sorry. Shouldn't have done that. You're a pain in the neck to keep track of."

She laughed, a quiet, wobbly chuckle that emerged over the sparks still showering through her. "Where's Juno?"

"He's in the truck because he's not good at quiet. And he's massively upset about it. What did you see inside?"

"I didn't get that far."

He started toward the window.

She grabbed his wrist. "Dallas, I've thrown everything away to find my daughter. You shouldn't. You have a future without us. I don't want you going to jail for me."

The moonlight flecked his eyes with an inner glow. "Noted." He continued to the window and looked inside.

"Didn't you hear me?"

"Yes," he said, still peering into the house. "I heard you, but I'm not obeying. There's a difference."

She huffed, uncertain whether to be angry or pleased.

He moved away from the window. "Catherine's in the back of the house. It looks like there's a living room that opens onto the patio. Let's see if we can get in that way."

"What if Dr. Elias is inside?"

"Unlikely. His car isn't in the garage."

Mia sagged. "I was hoping that he brought Gracie here."

"Don't think so, but we'll find out where. Let's go."

"Dallas," she tried again to stop him. This time she put her palms on his chest, feeling the strong beating of his heart. How could she tell him what it meant that he had come to find her? And that she could not allow him to stay? "This is wrong, breaking into someone's house. If you help me do this, there's no going back."

"No, Mia," he said slowly. "This is right, that I'm here with you now and we're going to get your daughter back."

"It's not worth it for you. I can't repay you in money, or…" She looked at the ground.

He tipped her chin up, his thumb gently tracing the curve of her lower lip. "I know you have a life to build somewhere else. I understand that. This isn't about payment. It's about what's right."

She closed her eyes tight. "Everything's mixed up, Dallas. How can you be sure what's right?"

He waited until she opened her eyes. "You pray and you take your best shot at it."

"I haven't had a good track record figuring out what's right, but…" She faltered. "I've asked His help this time."

Dallas smiled, moonlight illuminating the joy on his face. "Amen to that." He opened his mouth to continue, but instead he pulled her into the shadows. "Security vehicle," he breathed in her ear. "Stay still."

Easy for him to say, she thought, from the circle of his arms. Pressed against his ribs, her chin next to his, her heart was puttering like a motorboat. She was sure it might give out altogether as it ricocheted between comfort at being near him and utter terror about what could be happening to Gracie, to an odd peace that came when she'd given the situation over to God. A mixed up spaghetti jumble to be sure.

When the car passed, she disentangled herself from

Dallas and got to her feet, breathing still hitched and unsteady.

"Ready?" he said, infuriatingly handsome in spite of his sodden condition.

"Are you really sure?"

"Mia," he said, cutting her off. "If you ask me that again, you're going to go wait in the car with Juno."

She was not completely sure if he was joking or not, as he headed off toward the patio.

You kissed her? Again? What part of the plan was that, you dope? The woman was running from the law and terrified for her daughter. He had no business kissing her. He willed his gut to stop quivering like jelly at the residual sensation of her lips pressed to his. He felt like Juno when they first worked together and the dog was more interested in rocketing off after enticing birds than engaging in a search and rescue. Impulse had overridden his good sense. Yet he could not deny the irrational happiness that sprang up in his soul that Mia had invited God in.

Still, had he really kissed her? He had. The electricity still tingled through him.

Focus already, would you?

He pulled his mind back to the present. As soon as Catherine caught sight of them, she would call the police or bolt. Since there was no way he wanted to hurt her, that gave them only a few minutes tops to see if they could convince her to rat out her husband or, if she was an accomplice, to bluff her into thinking she and the good doctor were caught.

Not much of a plan, but he couldn't think of anything better.

They reached the patio just as Catherine Elias stepped out. Dallas and Mia watched from behind a screen of bushes as she turned on the propane gas, and a fire pit sprang to life. She watched it burn in silence. The flames danced high in the darkness.

Mia burst out into the circle of light. "Where's my daughter?"

Catherine screamed, hands pressing a file folder to her chest. "What are you doing here?"

Dallas stepped forward so she could see him, too. "Your husband kidnapped Mia's daughter, Gracie. We're here to find out where he took her. Mia said you have a cabin in the mountains. We need to know where."

Catherine's mouth opened in an *O* of surprise. Or was it anger? He couldn't tell. She took a step toward the house, but one step only, eyes shifting in thought.

"Why would he take her?"

She knew something. Maybe everything. "He wants us to hand over the photo that you took to Peter Finnigan that can incriminate him in Asa Norton's murder."

"Asa Norton? The man who drowned all those years ago?" She cocked her head as if listening to the sound of far off music. "Susan's husband."

"Are you helping him?" Mia fired off.

"Helping? You think I helped my husband kill Asa?"

"No, but he also murdered Cora Graham and Peter Finnigan. You might have pitched in for those."

Catherine's mouth went slack. "This is insane. I'm not a murderer."

Dallas could not be sure it was disbelief or lying. Women confounded him. He had no chance of reading her right, but he pressed on anyway. "You went to see Peter Finnigan, just before he was blown up."

"Blown up? What are you talking about? He was perfectly fine when I left him." She sank down on the brick patio wall, heedless of the moisture. "This can't be true."

"It is true," Mia protested. "You know I'm not lying, don't you?"

She chewed on a thumbnail. "I suspected something was going on when that woman Susan showed up, stalking me. He said he'd treated her for a minor injury after her husband drowned and she became fixated with him."

"But you didn't believe him?" Mia pressed.

"Not really. There have been other women," she said wearily. "I suspected Susan was another one of Thomas's flings and he was trying to cover up. But then things started to happen. Cora died. This thug from Miami showed up. And I found Thomas shredding files. These files taken from the clinic." She waved the folder at them. "There's nothing in them now. They're Cora's. Most were destroyed, but I saved one without him knowing. The photo was in it along with a newspaper clipping about Norton's death."

The pieces were beginning to fall into place, Dallas thought. "You recognized your husband in the picture."

"Yes, that's why I went to see Peter Finnigan. I read the paper's account of how Finnigan supposedly tried to save Susan's husband that day. I can't prove it, but I think Thomas was giving Finnigan money, paying him to stay quiet. I found an envelope of cash one time, addressed to P. Finnigan at his Mountain Grove address. Thomas explained it away, but I always wondered about it."

"Did Peter tell you anything?" Mia asked.

"Nothing. As a matter of fact, he snatched the photo and tossed me out, but I didn't do anything to harm him. And now you say he's dead? Are you sure?"

Dallas nodded. He would never lose the memory of how Finnigan lost his life.

"Why kill Peter?" Catherine mused.

"Both were involved in Asa's death," Dallas said. "Peter must have threatened to tell, so Elias killed him."

"After all these years? Why?"

Mia hugged herself. "Something went wrong."

"Susan's no innocent in all this, you realize," Catherine spat. "She kept quiet about Thomas's involvement all these years instead of going to the police, not to mention the fact that she got millions when Asa died."

"But she can bring Dr. Elias down now." Mia shivered. "So he'll need to kill her, too."

"I didn't want to see it." Catherine looked up at the cloud-washed sky. "I mean, I knew about the other women. I'm not so blind that I couldn't figure that out. I didn't want to believe there was anything else."

"Why didn't you go to the police?" Dallas said. "If you're an innocent in all this?"

She turned haggard eyes on him. "I'm leaving him as soon as I can get my things together. He's a manipulator and covering up whatever he did in the past, but the man is the father of my children. Whatever Thomas has done, they don't deserve to live with his sin. Can you understand that?"

Mia clutched Catherine's hands. "Yes, so you can understand why I need to find my daughter. Please, Catherine, you've got to tell me if you know where he might have gone."

"I don't," she said, detaching herself.

"Where's your cabin?" Dallas watched her mouth tighten.

"He wouldn't abduct a child. He's a lot of things, but he has his own children. He wouldn't hurt Gracie."

"But he did," Mia said. "Your husband called me and told me he had my daughter. You have to face it, just like I had to face the truth about Gracie's father."

"This can't be possible. I would have known I was married to a murderer." Catherine looked away. "What kind of woman wouldn't know?"

"A woman like me," Mia said. "I misjudged my husband, too, Catherine. You feel stupid, vulnerable. And then—" she shot a look at Dallas "—you forgive yourself and you move on."

"I loved him." A tear rolled down Catherine's cheek. "I really did. Maybe I still do."

Mia knelt next to her and took her hand. "Believe me I understand, but your husband has killed and killed again, and now he has my baby." Her voice broke on the last word. Dallas put a hand on her shoulder, trying to squeeze some comfort into her.

"But Thomas is a father himself," Catherine said. "How could he?"

"I think you know deep down that we're right," Dallas said. "That's why you were getting ready to burn this file, isn't it?"

"All the others are shredded. This one only has the clipping left. I… I figured whatever he's been up to, the less evidence the better for my kids."

Mia did not release Catherine's hand. "Even if you can't accept it, would you throw away Gracie's life? A mother couldn't do that to another woman's child."

Her face crumpled. "I'm not a bad person. Really, I'm not."

Dallas sensed they were near to breaking through her defenses. "Then tell her."

Tears cascaded down Catherine's face. "The cabin's near the reservoir, on Sentinel Hill Road."

"Thank you." Mia clutched Catherine in a desperate hug.

"Here," Catherine said, shoving the file folder at Dallas. "Take it. Maybe it will help you prove he's guilty."

Betrayal shone like an exposed wound deep in her eyes.

"I'm sorry," he said.

She waved him away. "I won't be here when you come back. If what you say is true, I'll never come back."

Mia and Dallas left her staring at the fire pit.

SEVENTEEN

Mia was panting hard by the time they made it to Dallas's truck, having had to stop twice to avoid detection by the security people. She still had twigs tangled in her hair from their leafy hiding spots and a new catalogue of scratches. Once Juno was finally convinced to move to the backseat, he could not stop pressing his wet nose to her neck, snuffling her hair until she batted him away.

"Stop, Juno. That tickles."

He responded in doggie fashion by licking her along the hairline which made her laugh.

"I think you blew his mind showing up like this when he was all set to locate you out in the woods."

"Sorry," she said, giving Juno a rub under the chin. "You'll just have to find me some other time." When she'd gotten Juno down to an occasional slurp from the backseat, she called Antonia and put her on speaker phone.

Her big sister alternated between giving her a tongue lashing and expressing heartfelt relief that Mia was now in the company of Dallas and Juno. "I'm still waiting for the chief. Susan's gone to see if she can find a room somewhere for us, but the town is full of evacuees." She huffed. "It's driving me crazy. Every minute I'm thinking about you and Gracie and I want to be doing something to help."

Mia heard her sister start to sniffle. "Don't cry, sis, or I'll start, too. We're going to get her, Antonia, we got some info from Catherine," she explained, giving her sister the location of the doctor's cabin. Saying it aloud spread an eagerness inside that she felt would burst out.

"You can't go. This is too dangerous," Antonia said.

"What choice is there? He's got Gracie, and I'm a fugitive."

"We have to tell the police where you're heading," Antonia insisted.

Mia's head spun. "No, I won't risk it. I can't."

She looked to Dallas.

"You know where we're going, Antonia." He checked the time on the truck's dashboard. "Give us a two-hour head start, then tell them everything."

If we're not back…if we're too late. Suddenly she could not get enough oxygen. There was no outcome possible except that they would find Gracie, unharmed and get her away from Elias. Forcing a breath in, she grated out the words. "Tell whoever will listen, but you and Susan need to stay there where it's safe." She paused.

"Okay," Antonia said.

"I don't know if Susan is trustworthy," Mia said quietly. "She's unstable, and she benefitted from her husband's death financially."

Antonia lowered her voice. "If she was involved in the murder, why would she come back and blame it on Elias?"

"It makes no sense to me, but I wanted to warn you. I can't stand anything happening to you." She scrubbed at a spot of grit on the knee of her jeans. "I wish I could do this by myself and not endanger any more people."

"You've got help now, Mia. You're not alone. Dallas is there, and Reuben's flying here as we speak. He's devastated about Cora and…and Gracie."

Deep breaths. "I'm going to get her back, Antonia." Mia clutched the phone. "I am going to get my daughter back."

"Be careful, sister."

"I'm used to dealing with criminals remember? I used to be married to one." The joke fell flat. She was about to hang up.

"And I wanted to say—" Antonia rushed on "—I'm sorry I didn't tell you about Dallas. Reuben and I…"

"Were trying to protect me." She sighed. "And so was Dallas. I understand." And she did. Though Dallas did not look at her, she knew from his kiss, from his willingness to risk everything, that he was with her because he cared for her. With a stab of anguish, she also knew there could be no future for them. When she found Gracie, she would move back to Florida and be the best possible parent to her child. She would play it safe and humbly accept any help from her sister and brother-in-law. No more striking out on her own. No more independence at all costs.

And Dallas? He would continue to bounce around the country finding the missing, and living the kind of unfettered freedom that was exactly what Mia and Gracie did not need. He found lost souls and returned them home. She would always picture him that way, even when they had separated for the last time.

A branch snapped loose from the trees and cracked into the windshield, shocking her out of her reverie. Find Gracie. That was all that mattered.

"Be careful," Antonia said. "Please, Mia."

She said she would and disconnected.

Dallas kept the truck at a slow speed which maddened her, windshield wipers slapping out their own relaxed rhythm. "Can't we speed up a little?"

"Roads are dangerous right now, and we don't need any cops or security people taking notice of us."

She huffed. "Why do you have to be so…logical?"

He offered a smile which died quickly away.

"What's bothering you? Aside from the insanity which you've gotten yourself into?"

"Finnigan."

"What about him?"

"The way he died. We know Elias killed Asa Norton and Cora. He used drugs in both cases. Neat. No blood. Almost a peaceful way to die. But Finnigan…"

She saw the explosion in her mind's eye, the bright flower of flame that blew away Finnigan's life before the river took his body. "A bomb seems out of place for Dr. Elias?"

"Maybe I'm wrong."

"Could Catherine be lying about everything? Is it possible she killed Peter for some reason and she's trying to hide it by shifting blame to her husband?" The rest remained unspoken. *Could we be driving into a trap right now?*

"That's part of what's bothering me. I don't know if Catherine or Susan can be trusted."

"The only thing I can be certain of is Susan didn't take Gracie and neither did Catherine," Mia said firmly. "And that's all I care about right now, getting my daughter back."

They ran into two detours which cost them time. It was nearing ten o'clock when Dallas finally started the ascent up Sentinel Hill. Posted signs warned of flooded roads ahead.

The more Dallas slowed, the more frenzy whipped inside Mia. At the top of a winding road, he pulled to the side. "Hang on. Gonna climb up those rocks and check things."

He got out, Juno following. Clouds rolled over the moon, leaving only unreliable patches of light that played across the pile of rocks, marbled with shadows and moisture. Juno sat at the bottom, eyes riveted on Dallas's progress as he climbed.

He'd just scrambled to the top when Mia's phone rang. Dr. Elias.

She scrambled to press the button. "Hello?"

"My apologies for making you wait so long, but we developed car trouble on the way."

She fought for calm. "Where?"

"We're at the cabin, top of Sentinel Hill. Roads are flooded so you'll have to be creative. Bring the photo. If you aren't here by midnight, there will be consequences."

Consequences. Mia's nerves turned to trails of ice. "I want to talk to my daughter right now."

There was a sound of movement.

"Mommy?"

"Gracie." Tears rained down Mia's face, her heart rose up and twined itself with those two precious syllables. "Are you okay? Did he hurt you? Mommy's coming."

Dallas climbed down and joined her. With icy fingers, she held the phone between them.

"We're going on a boat 'cuz..."

The phone was yanked away. "Gracie!" Mia screamed.

"Midnight." The phone clicked off. Mia stared. "She sounds okay, like he hasn't hurt her. Yet."

Dallas pressed her shoulders. "She's all right. Hang on to that. Gracie is all right."

Inside she repeated the mantra. Gracie was all right. Until midnight.

Dallas wanted to reach through the phone line and pummel the man. Mia did not resist when he urged her back into the truck. She clutched the cell as if it was somehow still connecting her with Gracie.

"He's desperate for the photo. He won't do anything to her until we deliver it."

She nodded mechanically, like an automaton. He wondered if she would withstand his next bit of news.

"This area is bisected by a river that feeds into a lake. It's all flooded. There's no way I can drive any farther."

Some flicker of life in her eyes. "Where is the cabin?"

"On the other side of that ridge. The place is flooded, and he can't drive out, either. He's going to try to boat out of here. He's probably booked a flight and has his escape all lined up."

Her eyes were dull, breath coming in harsh gasps. "Mia, are you listening?" Was she going into shock? "We need to hike in and probably swim, there's no other option. Let me go ahead, with Juno. You don't have to..."

She fired back to life, fixing him with a look more

ferocious than some of the gang members he'd tangled with. "I'm going." He was smart enough to know any arguing the point would get him nowhere but left behind. Juno had no complaints either, even though the sky was delivering more rain. The dog would prefer monsoons to the backseat of a truck any day of the week. He didn't want Juno in danger any more than he wanted Mia to be, but there was nothing to be done about that either. He threw up a prayer and let out a sigh. "Text Antonia. Tell her to fill the cops in on the doctor's call. Okay?"

Her fingers flew across the keys. "All right, let's go."

He removed a pack from under his seat and shouldered it, handing her a bottle of water. "Drink."

"I'm not thirsty."

"Humor me and drink anyway." He poured some into his cupped palm for Juno, who lapped it up, tail wagging and ready to begin the adventure, and drained a bottle himself. He wouldn't suggest they eat the snacks he'd stowed in the pack, though his stomach was empty. He had a feeling it was going to be all he could do to keep up with her. From a supply in his stash, he handed her a plastic bag for her phone and two more for the photo which she double-bagged and stowed in his pack.

Juno gave an excited whine.

"It's okay, buddy," Dallas said. "This time we already know where to find her."

The question was, how would they handle it when they did? There was no more time to think about it as they started across the sodden grass toward the top of Sentinel Hill.

The ground had been transformed to a marsh by the

relentless rains. Mud sucked at their feet and shins and each step was a struggle, though Juno seemed to have no trouble with it. There was just enough moonlight peering between the clouds to sufficiently light their way. Some half an hour later they made it to the ridge, flopped down on their bellies and scoped out the cabin.

It was what surrounded the neat, wood-sided structure that concerned him most. The lake, which was normally a stone's throw from the cabin, was now engulfing it, clear up to the doorstep. A boat rolled on the rain-speckled surface, tied to the porch support.

Dallas whistled low. "This place will be under water in a matter of hours."

Worse yet, the cabin was on the far shore, a good quarter mile across the lake. He didn't hazard a guess about the depth. Didn't matter. They had no boat and no car. Swimming was the only option.

She read the question in his mind. "I'm a good swimmer."

"A Miami girl? I'd be surprised if you weren't." He emptied the remaining water bottles out of his pack, keeping only the first-aid kit and foil-wrapped food.

She offered the sliver of a smile. "You travel prepared."

"Sometimes it takes a few days to complete a rescue. Conditions are bad more often than not." He felt her watching. "What?"

"I was so mad about how you ended up in my life and just now, I was wondering if God put you here in spite of me, to rescue Gracie."

He reached out a finger and traced the perfect line of her cheek and chin. "Maybe He meant for us to rescue her together."

Moonlight captured the tears gathered in her eyes, jewels that she would not let fall. It made them more precious, somehow, the strength that kept them captive there. Mia was a woman of breathtaking courage, who could not see the best things about herself. If she could see what he saw, only for a moment, it would take her breath away.

"You are an amazing woman, Mia Verde."

She blinked, then blessed him with a smile that would live inside his heart with all the most precious memories he possessed. "Coming from you, I take that as a fine compliment. Thank you, Mr. Dallas Black."

What he wouldn't give to kiss her right then, with the rain covering them in glistening droplets and the moon gilding her hair with a million sparkles. He swallowed hard. "When we get across, try for the east side of the cabin where there's only one window. Okay?"

She nodded, stripped off her jacket and without another word waded into the lake. Juno, who had been busy sniffing, gave him a comical double take.

"Yeah, I know it's a strange time for a swim, but you're up for it aren't you?"

Juno, every bit as silent as Mia, ambled right into the water after her.

EIGHTEEN

Cold. It shivered through her body as she swam into the dark water. Juno paddled ahead, turning once in a while to be sure she was still following along. Dallas kept level at her side. She suspected he could easily outpace her, but he, like Juno, was keeping tabs, ever her faithful guardian.

Her muscles fell into a desperate rhythm. Each stroke, every kick and breath brought her that much closer to Gracie. She would force herself to cross this endless watery barrier between herself and her daughter. Despite her effort, goose bumps prickled her skin. Clearing the water from her eyes, she realized she was still no more than halfway across the expanse. Arms tired, legs leaden and she stopped, treading water.

Dallas was next to her in an instant. "Need a rest?"

She was too winded to respond.

He offered his back. "Hold on. I'll tow you for a while."

Sucking in a breath she shook her head, not wanting to add weight to a man she had already burdened so heavily. "I'm okay." She plunged ahead. More minutes, inching along, the void fighting against her in a strange nocturnal race. There was just the frigid water and her weakened body, battling for each and every stroke. Her heart traveled on ahead, calling Gracie's name into the night.

She remembered Hector and Gracie splashing in the warm Miami waters.

"Blow bubbles, *bebé,* like a little fishy." He'd held Gracie against the foaming sea and laughed at the baby kicks and clumsy wiggles she'd tried. "She's going to be a great swimmer," Hector announced, his face shining with love.

Gracie's soft voice echoed through her memory. *My daddy's a bad man.*

Hector was a man who had done very bad things, but also a man who loved Gracie Louise quite possibly as much as she did. It was a fact she had forgotten, or perhaps, she had not wanted to accept. Maybe someday the Lord could make Hector's path straight, too.

And hers. If she could just get to Gracie. There were so many things she had to tell her, to love her through, comfort her against and lift her over. So many waves to be traversed. *Lord, help me, help me.*

Water broke over her face and she sucked in a mouthful. What if Dr. Elias had hurt her? Or worse? Fatigue and fear started to paralyze her limbs. Her teeth chattered. Wind-driven waves splashed again, sending her into a coughing fit.

His arms twined around her, lifting her head out of the water. "I'll hold you. Rest a minute."

She tried to protest.

"We're in this rescue together, remember?"

"Old habits…"

He kissed the tip of her nose and for a moment, she

thought he might press his lips to hers. Expectation rippled through her body, but then he turned and she clung to his wide shoulders, feeling the muscles moving along his back. Cheek resting against him, she watched the moonlight catch on the surface dappled by the pattering rain. Almost there. What would they find? She pressed her face harder into his back, strong and soothing, a partner in the lowest moment of her life.

Oh Lord, I don't deserve this man who's risking everything to help me. I have been hard-hearted to him and to Hector. Hector was a criminal, yes, and maybe he always would be, but at that moment with the water lapping against them, she prayed he would be redeemed. He was a sinner who could be good with God's help. Just like a small woman in a very big lake whom she now understood was just as much in need of a savior.

"Almost there," Dallas murmured, calling Juno closer as they neared the other side.

"And Lord, thank you for Dallas," she whispered, completing the prayer and giving it to God.

The wall of the cabin facing them had no windows, except a small one cloaked by heavy curtains. They climbed up on what used to be a wraparound porch which was now covered by six inches of water. Juno levered himself out of the water next to them, immediately shaking his sodden coat with such violence both Dallas and Mia threw up their arms for cover.

Dallas peered around the corner, Mia crowding next to him to see.

A motorboat was tied to the porch rail, and a faint band of soft golden light shone from under the drapes in one of the front windows.

"There's a bag and supplies loaded into the boat," he whispered in her ear. "He's ready to get out of here."

The front door was thrown open. Instinctively, Dallas moved Mia behind him.

"Don't be shy," Dr. Elias called. "Come on in."

Mia pictured Gracie inside. What had the monster done to her? She pushed forward but Dallas stopped her.

"If we don't leave with Gracie in a matter of minutes, the police are coming in," Dallas shouted back. "It's all over for you."

"Nice bluff," Elias said. "But it's not going to fly. I've been tracking you with binoculars since you started your swim. Now get in here before I lose my patience."

Mia's heart sank. It was a trap, and there was no choice. What had they expected anyway? To surprise the doctor? Snatch Gracie from under his nose? They splashed along the porch until they reached the door.

Dr. Elias held a small lantern in one hand which added a pool of meager light. He wore jeans and a flannel shirt. His face was marred with stubble and darkened by shadows that added years. He looked nothing like the self-assured doctor, a man respected by the townspeople. He looked, in fact, like a man on the edge of desperation.

He pulled the gun from his pocket. "Inside. Now."

Mia went first, Dallas and Juno following.

It was a small cabin, three rooms, a ratty sofa and an old rocking chair, the only furniture. A fire in the small stone fireplace gave off sooty smoke that burned her throat. "Where's Gracie?" Mia demanded.

"In a minute." Dr. Elias gestured to Dallas. "Put down the pack."

Dallas did so.

"You'd better have the photo I requested."

Mia hurried over, wrenched open the pack and thrust the plastic bag containing the picture. "There. I brought what you asked for, now give me my daughter."

Elias took the bag, flicking a glance inside, while keeping the gun leveled in their direction. "Ancient picture. Old lady was thorough. I wonder where in the world she unearthed it." He tossed it into the flames. "The trouble is, of course, other people could follow the same trail Cora did. Maybe you even made copies before you came."

"We didn't," Dallas said. He wondered if Catherine had, for an extra bit of insurance in case Elias resurfaced in her life someday.

Elias sighed. "In this age of technology, you can't really obliterate anything can you? It's best if I disappear." He shook his head. "Such a waste. I created a good life here, a thriving practice. Raised my kids in Spanish Canyon. I hate to leave it, and them."

"Don't you dare talk to me about your children, after what you did to my child. I want my daughter," Mia shouted. "Where is she?"

Elias laughed. "I have always admired your spunk, Mia Verde Sandoval."

Mia started at a run toward the closed bedroom door which opened abruptly.

"She's here with me," Susan said, stepping over the threshold, holding Gracie's hand.

Mia screamed and ran to Gracie, snatching her from Susan's grasp and sweeping her into a smothering embrace. "Oh, Gracie, my sweet Gracie." Mia cried so hard the tears spilled over onto Gracie's cheeks as Mia planted kiss after kiss on her baby's face.

Gracie looked bewildered, but not physically injured. She wrapped her small arms around her mother and smiled. Dallas's heart tore a bit to see that innocent smile.

"Mommy, you're squishing me," she said. Juno poked a friendly nose at Gracie's leg. "Hiya, Juno."

Mia looked her over. "Are you hurt? Did he hurt you in any way?"

She shook her head. "No, but I want to go home. I don't like it here."

Dallas heaved a sigh. Gracie was safe and his spirit spiraled at the joy of it, but he could not ignore the dread that rose in his stomach as the cost of his error came to light. Somewhere inside, Dallas had known the truth about Susan. Why had he not thought it out before? "You rendezvoused with the doctor when you gave Antonia the slip by pretending to look for a room, I take it."

She nodded. "Easy."

"And you and Dr. Elias killed your husband together, didn't you?"

"That's so heartwarming, like something you'd see on the big screen." Susan was smiling, watching Mia and Gracie as if she was an adoring aunt, not a murderer. "Yes, we plotted to kill Asa together and afterward, I made the biggest mistake of my life. I bolted."

"Leaving me holding the bag," Elias snapped.

"I was young, and I didn't know what I wanted. I apologized for that, Thomas, over and over," Susan said. "I panicked. But I never stopped loving you, not for one moment in all those years."

So it was some twisted form of love that brought her back to Spanish Canyon. The loathing in the doctor's eyes revealed it was purely one-sided. Whatever fondness Dr. Elias had felt for Susan once upon a time, had evaporated when she collected the insurance money and ran.

Elias's nostrils flared. "You should have stopped loving me. You should have gone on and lived your own life and left me to mine. That's what I told you when you came back but you would not listen."

"I couldn't do that. Our love is too deep." A strange guttural noise came from her throat. "Only I came back to find you had married someone else." Her eyes went hard and flat.

"Catherine is a good woman."

"She's a snoop. If she hadn't taken the photo out of Cora's file, things would have been much simpler." Susan considered a moment. "Well, we're all entitled to a mistake now and then."

Elias groaned. "If you'd stayed away, everyone would be better off. You got Cora's suspicions up and filled her head with stories that police were corrupt until she decided to confide in these two."

"And Peter?" Dallas asked. He darted a glance around the dismal room, trying to figure out how to keep Gracie and Mia out of the line of fire. "Did he get scared and threaten to tell?"

"He wouldn't have," Elias said, white-knuckling the gun. "Peter would not have said anything no matter how much these two pried, but you arranged for him to die anyway, didn't you?"

Susan gave him a wide smile, sidling around and putting her hand on his cheek. He flinched away. "It was prudent. When Dallas and Mia are gone, we'll have a clean slate. Peter might have decided to spill the beans someday. That's why we arranged this little kidnapping, remember? To clean up the loose ends, as they say in the TV shows." She laughed.

Dallas bit back a groan. She was the one who had, no doubt, alerted Elias when they'd retrieved the picture from Finnigan's, and who'd called the trailer park to arrange the kidnapping. There had certainly been plenty of time for her to do so while Dallas and Mia dealt with the mudslide.

Water crested the threshold, sending the first gush over the floor. Dallas looked for something he could use as a weapon. He saw nothing within easy reach.

"Floodwater's rising," Elias said. The waves quenched the flames in the fireplace with an angry hiss. "Reservoir's full, and it's dumping into the lake."

Susan's eyes were dreamy, her face soft. "We can go anywhere in the world, Thomas. I've still got plenty of money and we can live the life we were meant to. Finally, after all these years. That's what you want, too, isn't it?"

"Too late to ask me what I want." Elias pointed to a narrow ladder in the corner. "Get up in the attic, Mia. Gracie and your hoodlum friend, too."

"You can't," Mia started.

"The guy with the gun makes the rules," Dr. Elias said, "so that means I can. You get up in that attic and take your chances with the floodwaters, or I can shoot you."

It would not be much of a chance, Dallas knew. Locked in the attic, they would drown. No question about it. Antonia would tell the police what she knew, but by then Elias would be gone. "You're a doctor," Dallas said, edging closer and stepping in front of Mia. "You took an oath to save lives. Didn't that mean anything to you?"

A flicker of emotion rippled across his face. "I was a good doctor. I helped a lot of people, and they loved me in this town. I just made a mistake a long time ago."

Susan stepped back, frowning. "Our love wasn't a mistake."

He ignored her. He gestured with the gun for Mia and Gracie to start up the ladder. The water was now at shin level and climbing fast. Mia took Gracie's hand, fear strong in her eyes as she helped her little girl. "It's okay, honey. I'm right behind you."

"I'm sorry, Mia," Dr. Elias said.

She turned. "But you're going to murder us anyway?" Mia's chin jutted, her voice low so Gracie would not hear.

"As I said, I'm sorry. I really mean that."

Mia gave the doctor her back and continued up to the attic. Dallas figured he had one chance to turn the tide in their favor, but he had to make sure Mia and Gracie were far enough away.

"Up, Juno," he commanded.

Juno scrambled up the ladder with the ease born of hours of training in every possible situation from planes to boats to escalators. The dog sensed no danger, only another adventure awaiting him.

He heard Gracie giggle from up in the attic. "Good job, Juno."

The tear in his heart widened. They could not die. He could not let them drown.

"Now you," Dr. Elias said, swiveling the gun not to Dallas, but to Susan.

Her mouth fell open. "What? What are you saying?"

"I'm saying," Elias said, fury kindling on his face, "that you ruined me, my career, my marriage, everything. Getting involved with you was the worst day in my life and having you show up in Spanish Canyon was the second. You're going to die along with them, Susan. You should have died a long time ago."

Horror dawned in her expression, creeping up to overtake the love that had been there a moment before. "How can you say this to me? You are the only man I've ever loved. I killed Peter Finnigan and got these people here so we could have a future."

"I never even told Peter you were in on Asa's murder. He didn't even know we hatched that little plot together. He did not have to die."

"Well, he's dead, and that can't be changed," she said. "We have to think about the future."

"We have no future. Can't you understand that?" he said, voice like the last peal of a funeral bell. "You will climb the ladder and die with the rest of them."

The color disappeared from her face. "But I love you. We have a whole life ahead of us."

"I had a future and I threw it away for money and because I thought I cared about you. After I killed your husband, you ran. And you know what? I deserved that because it showed me I never really loved you at all."

"That's not true," she protested. "You did. You did love me."

"You were a means to an end, Susan, a shortcut I never should have taken. That's all." The words dropped like bullets.

With a cry, Susan took out a knife, the one she had stolen from Dallas's kitchen, and sprang at Dr. Elias. He deflected her, dealing a blow to the side of her head that made her cry out and fall backward, grabbing the rocking chair for support.

Dallas used the moment of distraction to launch himself at Dr. Elias.

He threw a fist, aiming for the doctor's face, but an incoming gush of water knocked him off target. His punch connected with Elias's temple, but not hard enough to do the job. Elias fired. Dallas felt a sharp trail of fire shoot through his body as he splashed backward into the water.

NINETEEN

The shot exploded through the cabin, and Mia felt as if the bullet bisected her own body. Instinctively, she shoved Gracie farther into the attic, the floor of which had been covered with plywood to provide a surface for storage.

"Dallas," she screamed, grabbing at the barking Juno to prevent him from going back down the ladder. He whined and looked from her toward his fallen master. She strained to see into the dim space. Had Dallas gone under? Had the bullet passed by him?

"He's not dead," Susan snapped. "You shot him through the shoulder. Terrible aim."

Mia's breath squeezed out in panicked bursts. He was not dead. Dallas was still alive. Her thoughts focused on that one paramount fact.

"I'm a doctor, not a sniper. Help him up the ladder, Susan," Elias commanded.

"I won't."

Juno continued to bark.

"Shut that dog up," Elias shouted, "or I'll shoot him, too. I can't think with all that racket."

Mia stroked Juno's head. "It's okay, Juno," she whispered. "Quiet now."

"Don't cry, doggie," Gracie added, petting his trembling flanks with her tiny hands. The lamplight glinted off the gun as Dr. Elias pointed it at Susan.

"Yes, you will get him up that ladder, because if you don't, I will kill you down here, and I don't think you want to be shot, do you?"

She didn't answer.

"Do you?" he demanded, louder. "You've never liked discomfort, Susan. Always enjoyed the nice things, the easy answers. I don't think a bullet hole would suit you."

Susan splashed over to Dallas and took his arm. His groan of pain shot through Mia.

"Gently," she could not stop herself from saying.

"This is crazy," Elias said with a strangled cry. "The whole thing is insane. How did it come to this?"

"You can stop it," Mia called. "You are an excellent doctor and you've helped lots of people. Catherine said you are a good father, too."

"She said that?" His tone grew soft. "Then I didn't totally destroy everything."

Mia felt a spark of hope. "No, you haven't. You could let us go. Then you would be able to see your children, maybe. Still be a father to them."

He paused. "Thank you, Mia, for saying that, but it will be better for them if I disappear. I'm not going to withstand jail. I don't have that kind of strength. I wish things could have been different. I sincerely do."

"But…" She realized he was no longer listening. He moved aside, water splashing nearly to his waist as Susan staggered with Dallas to the ladder and they crowded up together. Mia reached out and eased Dallas as best she could into the attic space where he knelt, one hand on the wood for support, the other clutching his shoulder. Juno licked Dallas and turned in happy circles.

Mia immediately ripped off the bottom hem of her T-shirt and wadded it up, pressing it to the profusely bleeding wound. "Dallas, I'm so sorry. I'm so, so sorry."

He looked up, gave her a tight, forced grin. "Not your fault. Is Gracie okay?"

"I'm okay," Gracie said. "Didja' get shot?" Her eyes were round as quarters in the darkening attic.

"Yeah. Forgot to duck," he said.

"Silly," she answered.

Susan stood at the attic access, staring down at Elias. "You won't get away from me," she hissed. "You will not go anywhere without me."

He laughed. "Watch me." Then he shut the trapdoor. The sound of scraping wood indicated he'd secured it from the outside.

Susan pounded on the hatch, screaming obscenities. "I knew you were a coward, Thomas. Deep down, I always knew it. That's why I went to Cora's house, to be sure you had the guts to follow through."

Mia drew Gracie away and left the woman to her rant. It was more important to figure out how they were going to escape. Dallas was considering the same thing, eyeing the nailed plywood floor.

He ran his hand over the seams. "Try to find a spot where the boards have warped or broken."

Though she didn't want to tear her attention away from Dallas, she did as he indicated.

Gracie crawled into the low spots near the walls.

Splinters drove into Mia's fingers, but she continued to search feverishly.

"I can hear the water," Gracie announced, her ear to a crack between two boards. Dallas and Mia hastened over. Gracie had found a place where one of the boards had splintered away, leaving an inch gap.

"Good work, Gracie." Dallas shoved his fingers into the gap and began pulling on the weakened board, the effort dappling his face with beads of sweat. When he'd lifted the board enough for her to get her hands in, Mia added her strength, yanking on the old wood until it gave way with a crack and a puff of dust.

"Okay," Dallas panted. "Now we can pull up the other boards."

Susan joined in and soon they had cleared enough boards away to create a small hole. Dallas lowered himself into the opening and kicked away the Sheetrock.

"There's the water," Gracie said. "I see it."

The level was only a few feet below the attic floor. Mia shuddered.

Dallas sat at the edge, feet dangling into the opening. "I'm going to swim through the house and make sure there's an exit."

"Dallas…" But he was already done, dropping down into the water after sucking in a deep breath. Juno dove in with him.

Gracie peered into the water. "When's he gonna come back, Mommy?"

Mia wrapped an arm around her girl's shoulders, holding here there to feel the reassuring rise and fall of her breathing. "Soon."

The seconds ticked into minutes.

"Do you think he drowned?" Susan said.

Mia turned on her. "Don't say that. He's doing his best to get us out of here in spite of all the damage you and Dr. Elias have done."

Susan broke into a smile. "You love him, don't you?"

Mia turned away from the crazy woman who had her own twisted version of love. Susan's infatuation had turned into an obsession, and Dr. Elias a possession that she had to acquire.

Love wasn't like that. It was an overwhelming desire to see the other person happy, healthy and thriving. She wanted that for Dallas with all the passion inside her. She wanted him to find a reason to put down roots and allow himself to have the family she knew he would treasure, with a woman who wasn't on the wrong side of the law, mother to a child of a drug lord. He deserved more than that.

Susan would never understand. Love wasn't holding on tightly. It was letting go, even when it hurt.

Dallas surfaced, sucking in a mighty breath of air. Juno popped up next to him.

"We have to get to the front door. I wedged it open. Can you do it?"

"Of course," she said, but his eyes were not on her. He was considering Gracie. He reached out a wet hand for hers, wincing only slightly, voice husky with pain.

"Hey, Goldfish girl."

Gracie giggled and took his hand. "You're wet."

"Yep. And it's time for you to get wet, too. I need you to take a big breath and hold it and we're gonna swim to the door down there. Okay?"

Gracie's mouth tightened. "I'm scared to do that."

"Juno will be there with you. You can hold on to his collar. How would that be?"

"Okay, I guess, but what if my breath won't hold in that long?"

Dallas riveted his eyes to hers. "God made you a strong lady, like your mama. You're gonna be okay and that's a promise. We'll get Goldfish after."

"The pizza-flavored kind?"

He laughed. "Any kind you want."

Gracie nodded. She sat on the edge of the plywood and stuck in her feet. "Cold, cold."

Juno paddled over and rested his paws on her lap, which set her to giggling. Dallas switched on a button that made a red light blink on Juno's collar. "Now you can see him. Ready?"

She nodded.

He turned to Mia and Susan. "Straight down and to the right. Give us a couple of minutes then follow."

He held up an open palm, and Mia grasped it, pulling strength and comfort from those long fingers. Then she helped Gracie over the edge, heart pulsing with fear as she watched the water close over her daughter's head.

I must be getting old. Dallas had been a tough guy, once. Recovered from stabbings, alcohol poisoning and even a snakebite, which had been worse than any of it, but now he felt weakened, the pain in his shoulder swelling with every arm stroke. Or maybe it was the added worry about escorting a tiny child through eight feet of water when her eyes were wide and terrified; panic beginning to set in on her face.

She clung to Juno's collar as he swam. They bobbed

up, skimming the surface just under the ceiling. Gracie pressed her face so it was nearly touching the plaster, sucking in fearful breaths along with some water that set her to coughing. When they reached the far wall, he called over the surging water.

"We're going under now, Gracie. Only for a minute and then we'll be out the door.

"No, no," she said, choking on a mouthful of water. "I don't wanna."

Dallas was not confident that his calm reasoning skills were enough to counter Gracie's growing fears. What would Mia do? She hadn't yet caught up and there wasn't time. In a moment, the gap would be inundated and Gracie would be breathing in water instead of air. No time, Dallas. What are you going to do?

He flashed on how his mother had handled things when Dallas or his brother had come home bleeding or with some sort of contusion. Quick and efficient, before there was too much time for fear to bloom.

He took Gracie around the shoulders. "All right. Deep breath with me. Ready? Go!" Dallas heaved in a breath in exaggerated fashion and Gracie did the same. Then he pulled her underwater and dove for the door.

It was slow going with one good arm and Gracie wiggling in terror, pressing on his bullet wound. Juno managed the dive ahead of them, and Dallas followed in the dog's wake. He could make out nothing but the red blinking light on Juno's collar.

Gracie's movements became more frantic.

Don't breathe in, he wanted to say.

She grabbed at his neck, then started to push away.

Time was up. She would be sucking in water in a matter of seconds.

He tightened his hold on her and made for the door, kicking as hard as he dared.

They surged through and rocketed out the other side. He propelled them both to the surface and nearly brained himself on the roof gutter which was inches from the crown of his head. He grabbed the edge with one hand and held Gracie's head above water with the other.

For the longest moment of his life, she didn't make a sound.

Terror balled in his stomach and shot through his nerves. "Gracie," he shouted, giving her a shake.

Her head came up and she started coughing, vomiting up mouthfuls of water in between anguished cries. It was the sweetest sound he'd ever heard.

"Good girl, Gracie. You did great. The scary stuff is over now."

She cried and clung to his neck. "I don't wanna do that again."

He laughed. "Me, neither. I'm going to put you up on the roof now and go get your mama."

She shook her head. "No, I don't want to."

"I heard you could climb up a tree." He gave her a sideways look. "But maybe I remembered that wrong."

"I can climb a tree," she insisted, indignation stiffening her chin.

"Let's see then. Pretend I'm a tree. Climb up on my shoulders and onto the roof."

She did, setting darts of agony zipping through his wound. She got up on the roof and crouched into a little ball. "It's scary up here. I don't want to stay."

"It will just be for a minute, and then your mommy will come."

Dallas removed the blinking collar light and wrangled Juno out of the water and onto the roof. The dog immediately sat down next to Gracie and licked her all over.

"Be right back." He sank back down in the water, hanging the red light to a nail that stuck out of the doorframe. He felt, rather than saw, the two women kicking their way down. He grabbed an arm, Susan's or Mia's he was not sure and dragged that person toward the door before he did the same for the other, orienting himself using the red light. For the second time he emerged, physically spent, just under the eaves of the submerged cabin. It was all he could do to catch his breath.

"Gracie," Mia cried, scanning frantically, as she broke the surface.

He pointed upward, still gasping.

Craning her neck, she must have caught sight of her daughter. Tears began to stream down her face and she closed the distance between them, and kissed all the pain from his body.

Mia was not sure how they would escape from the rooftop, but she simply could not bring her mind to fret about it much. Gracie was there, safe and sound, her skinny knees tucked under her as she threw pine needles into the water below. Juno kept a watchful eye on her. Susan and Dallas scrambled to the peak of the roof.

"There he is," Susan said.

Mia blinked out of her euphoric trance. "Dr. Elias?"

"Out in the lake," Dallas grunted. "Must have had motor trouble because he's rowing."

"He never was much of a sailor," Susan said with disgust.

Dallas peered into the darkness. "After all this. Can't believe he got away."

Susan continued to watch Dr. Elias make his escape. "We could have been together forever."

Mia noted the revulsion that bubbled in Dallas's eyes. "The police will arrest him," he grumbled. "I'll get my phone."

Susan removed a plastic bag with a phone inside.

"No need," she said, voice soft, fingers pressing the buttons. "I knew he was angry with me so I planned ahead." She sighed. "Of course, I thought he would see reason. I thought I could convince him we were meant to be together."

Mia flashed back to Peter Finnigan. "What do you mean you planned ahead?"

Dallas must have come to the same conclusion because he and Mia both lunged for Susan at the same moment. Too late. With a moonlit smile on her dreamy face, she pressed the last button. There was a deafening blast from out on the lake, and Dr. Elias's boat exploded into a shower of golden sparks.

TWENTY

"What was that?" Gracie said, standing up so quickly she nearly toppled off the roof.

Mia closed her mouth, and Dallas was once again amazed at the strength of mothers to make every circumstance all right for their children. "It was a little explosion. It's not going to hurt us."

He could not comprehend Susan, the woman who had just blown up the man she purported to love, the man for whom she had committed multiple murders. Love and murder. How could they go together? There was not much time to mull it over as two Zodiac boats roared up to the flooded cabin.

Mia waved frantically, and he would have helped if his shoulder hadn't been useless. As it was, he struggled to keep upright against the dizziness.

In a moment, one boat had peeled off toward the burning wreckage. The other was captained by Detective Stiving, who grabbed Antonia's arm and forced her to sit.

"You're going to fall out," he snapped.

Antonia stood again anyway and screamed. "Mia, are you all right? Do you have Gracie?"

Mia was crying so hard she could not choke out a response.

"Yes," Dallas called down. "Mia and Gracie are fine. Susan is here, too. She just blew up Dr. Elias's boat."

Stiving held up a pair of handcuffs. "We're ready for her."

With an elaborate combination of coaxing and lifting, Gracie, Mia, Susan and Juno were loaded into the Zodiac. Stiving wasted no time cuffing Susan. Dallas contemplated his useless arm. "I'm gonna jump," he said. "Too hard to climb down."

Stiving shook his head. "You always were a nutcase."

With that endorsement ringing in his ears, Dallas plunged feet first into the frigid water. When he surfaced, Mia and Antonia dragged him into the boat where he collapsed.

Mia pulled a blanket around him.

He tried to protest. "You need it."

She ignored him and opened Stiving's first-aid kit. Antonia sat with Gracie held tight in her arms, crooning some soft endearments meant for the child's ears only.

Susan sat in silence, staring out toward the ruined boat.

Stiving flicked a glance at Dallas. "Took one in the shoulder, huh? Not so agile as you pretend to be."

"Apparently not." He bit back a groan as Mia pressed a cloth to his shoulder. "And you're not as thick-headed as you pretend to be, Stiving. Did Antonia finally convince you we were telling the truth?"

He grinned. "Nah. Actually I did some research,

called some colleagues and interviewed Catherine Elias. I even discovered that Susan's poor, drowned husband was a demolitions expert and his wife worked for the company. Interesting, don't you think?"

"It explains her prowess in blowing people up."

"So you see, I really am a good cop after all."

"*Good* is a relative term."

Stiving laughed. "Just be quiet and we'll get you to a hospital, Black."

He did remain silent for a while, the pulsing of the engine shuddering through him. Mia adjusted the blanket, fiddled with the bandages, and mopped his face all the way back to the landing spot where Susan was transferred to Stiving's police car. Gracie, bundled to the ears, was loaded into another official vehicle driven by a volunteer who gave Juno a skeptical look.

"Do I have to take him, too? His paws are muddy."

Juno responded with a massive shake that sprayed the volunteer with water from head to boots.

Gracie laughed. "Come on, Juno. Get out of the cold, quick before you catch germans."

Juno leapt into the car and settled himself on the backseat as the dripping volunteer grumbled his way to the driver's door.

"There's a National Guard rescue crew coming, but they'll be another few minutes," Stiving said. "Most direct routes here are flooded." He raised an eyebrow. "You aren't going to bleed out or anything are you? That would create way too much paperwork for me."

"I'll try to spare you that."

Stiving nodded and went to speak to the captain of the other Zodiac, leaving Dallas propped on a plastic tarp, his back to a boulder, Mia kneeling next to him.

She wasn't crying, but her brown eyes were bright, water droplets glittering in her curling strands of hair.

"I can't say the words," she said, taking his hands in hers. "How can I tell you how incredibly thankful I am?"

His heart lurched inside. She was so beautiful, bedraggled, exhausted, bruised and utterly, incomparably beautiful. "We did it together," he managed.

She shook her head. "I've been trying so hard to fashion some sort of life for myself and you know what? I figured out that I already have one."

He stroked the satin of her cheek.

He heard her choke back a sound, the sort of vulnerable tiny peep that a chick might make when confronted with the edge of the nest.

"My whole life," she continued, "is Gracie and…" She stopped, looked away.

Dallas, the man who had never been able to decipher the first thing about women, wondered. Could the tenderness he saw in her face match the love buried deep in his own heart that swelled and undulated like the flood? He took her hand and cleared his throat. Fish or cut bait. Take the chance, or let his heart fly away to Florida. "You and Gracie…" He sucked in a breath and started again. "I hoped that it might be you and Gracie and me."

She jerked, mouth open.

Had he blown it? Scared her right into flight? Misunderstood a woman as he had countless times before? *Do it. Say it,* something deep inside him urged. "Mia, I'm not traditional father material, and you are an amazing mother who doesn't need any help parenting, but all my life I've been waiting for a partner to put down roots with."

She blinked, staring at him.

"You want roots?"

He sighed. *If you're going to bury yourself, might as well go all the way.* "No. I want you. And Gracie. And the life I know we could have together."

Silence.

"I've done bad things, Mia, things I can't sponge away or keep hidden, not from you. You know the good and bad of me and if you feel at all like you could love me, I would like to build a life with you and Gracie." He said it louder than he'd meant to. "I love you."

She gripped his hands. "But I've been to jail."

"Me, too."

"My ex-husband was a drug dealer."

"I know."

"I have control issues and a stubborn daughter and I eat too many sweets and I have terrible handwriting."

"I love you."

Her expression remained frozen somewhere between amusement and something unidentifiable. Fear? Love?

"Dallas, I'm not sure what to say."

"Say we can build a family together as slowly as you need it to happen. I'm not good at following rules, I don't know how to make mac and cheese and I spend most of my time with a dog. But I'm patient. I've got that going for me."

She smiled, lighting a fire in his belly. "Say you love me, too," he choked out.

She leaned closed and stopped, her mouth a tantalizing half inch from his. "I love you, too, Dallas."

Then there was warmth where he was cold, relief for his pain, and the sun triumphing over the floodwaters of his soul as he gathered her close.

Over the crush of joy, he became aware of a high-pitched noise, the squeals and laughter of Antonia and Gracie as they watched the proceedings from the car window. Juno added a robust bark.

He smiled and kissed her again.

Mia turned her face to the sun, relishing the warmth that drove away the last remnants of the storm some two weeks after Gracie's rescue. Spanish Canyon and the entire county was an official disaster area according to the federal government. Efforts were underway for a massive cleanup. Mia was ready to begin her own restoration project.

Dallas looped his good arm around her shoulders and planted a kiss on the top of her head as they stared at the burned wreckage of Cora's house. Gracie poked a stick into the various mudholes she was able to locate with Juno sniffing right along behind. "You sure you want to tackle this?" he said, gesturing to the ruined structure.

She snuggled into his side, careful not to put too much pressure on his shoulder. "I think Cora would have been pleased to see another house built here on the property she loved so much."

"And the matchmaker in her would have appreciated the fact that we're doing this together."

"For our future." Ours. The thought thrilled through her like the spring breeze. If all went well, the house would be built and the beautiful flower beds restored in time for their fall wedding. Closing her eyes, Mia could imagine the details. Gracie with her little basket of flowers, probably followed closely by a four-legged, hairy attendant. Antonia and Reuben would be there to add their heartfelt blessings along with Dallas's friends from the Search and Rescue school where he had signed on to work indefinitely.

"Still," Mia said, an ache in her throat. "I wish Cora was here to see it."

"She'll see it," Dallas said. "And she'll have the best view of all."

"Dallas," she said, turning to face him and marveling once again at the strength and gentleness she saw there. "This place was where I lost my dear friend. I thought I'd never come back."

"And?"

"And now it's the place where I am going to start my life over again. Pain and joy, all in one place."

"Blessings are like that, I think."

She kissed him, pressing him close, her future husband and irreplaceable blessing.

"Hiya," Gracie said, coming over with her muddy stick. "I'm hungry."

Mia laughed. "You're always hungry."

Dallas retrieved a package from the stash in his truck. He handed the pizza-flavored Goldfish crackers to Gracie. "Don't feed too many to Juno," he said, voice stern but eyes twinkling.

"Okay," Gracie agreed.

"And don't fill up before lunch," Dallas said, taking one more item from the truck. He shook the blue box. "We'll go back to the trailer you and your mom rented and I'm going to cook up some mac and cheese. This time, I'm following the directions."

"Hooray," Gracie squealed and Juno barked along with her. "But just in case, can Mommy help?"

Mia and Dallas laughed as Gracie raced off to chase a pair of butterflies.

"I dunno, Mr. Black," Mia teased. "Rebuilding a house is one thing, but tackling mac and cheese?"

"Don't worry," Dallas said, sliding his arms around her again. "Even an old dog can learn new tricks."

"That's what they say." She kissed him. "But I think I'll stick around to help."

His eyes reflected the light as the sun broke through the clouds. "I wouldn't have it any other way."

* * * * *

Liz Shoaf resides in North Carolina on a beautiful fifty-acre farm. She loves writing and adores dog training, and her husband is very tolerant about the amount of time she invests in both her avid interests. Liz also enjoys spending time with family, jogging and singing in the choir at church whenever possible. To find out more about Liz, you can visit and contact her through her website, lizshoaf.com, or email her at phelpsliz1@gmail.com.

Books by Liz Shoaf

Love Inspired Suspense

Betrayed Birthright
Identity: Classified

Visit the Author Profile page at Harlequin.com.

BETRAYED BIRTHRIGHT

Liz Shoaf

For even your brothers and the household of your father, even they have dealt treacherously with you, even they have cried aloud after you do not believe them, although they may say nice things to you.
—*Jeremiah* 12:6

A special note to my dad, Reverend Kermit E. Shoaf,
from your baby girl. You armed me with faith
and courage to face whatever comes my way,
and I thank you for that. I miss you and
can't wait to see you again when my time is at hand.

To my editor, Dina Davis, and her boss
for taking a chance on a newbie. And a special
shout-out to all the various departments at Harlequin
who work so hard to make dreams come true.

ONE

Abigail Mayfield gripped the covers, fear icing the breath in her throat as she strained to hear the noise again. A slight sound had disturbed her sleep. She closed her eyes against the darkness and listened intently. An unnatural silence greeted her. The wind was calm and no tree branches brushed against the side of the house because she'd had them removed after buying the property.

Her eyes blinked open when she heard a small scratching sound. *The stalker is here!* She had moved all the way across the country for nothing. She struggled to breathe and goose bumps pimpled her arms until a cold, wet nose nudged her neck.

In slow increments, Abby forced herself to relax and silently thanked her grandmother for helping her find a trained protection dog before she moved to Texas.

"Bates," she whispered, "did you hear that noise, boy?"

The seventy-pound, playful but dead-serious-about-his-job, black-and-tan Belgian Malinois grabbed her blanket with his teeth and tugged it off the bed. That was answer enough.

As quietly as possible, she slid out of bed, grabbed

her cell phone off the nightstand, along with the Glock 19 pistol her grandmother had given her last year for Christmas. She might appear to be a harmless Tinker Bell—and had been called that on occasion—but appearances were deceiving. While growing up, her grandmother made sure she knew how to handle a gun.

"God, I need a little help here," she whispered as they moved toward the bedroom door. The dog glued to her side bolstered her confidence. Bates would attack an assailant, but his main job was to protect her; at least, that's what the trainer had said during the handler classes.

Tinkling glass hit the kitchen tile floor and left no doubt that someone was breaking and entering. At the top of the stairs, Abby took a deep, steadying breath. She buried her fear—the way Daddy had taught her—dialed 911 with one hand and held the pistol loosely at her side with the other. She had the advantage at the top of the stairs. If someone tried to come up, she'd fire a warning shot.

"Nine-one-one. Is this an emergency?"

Having turned the volume down before leaving the bedroom, Abby held the phone close to her ear. "This is Abby Mayfield. Someone is breaking into my house," she whispered.

"Ma'am, leave your phone on and keep it with you. We can track you through your cell if circumstances change, but for now, give me your address."

Abby swallowed hard. She knew what that meant. They could track her if the assailant removed her from the house. "My address is 135 Grove Street, Blessing, Texas."

"Stay hidden if you can. We'll have a squad car there as soon as possible."

Abby didn't respond because the sound of soft footsteps climbing the wooden stairs reached her ears. This scenario was the reason she'd removed all the carpet and installed wood and tile floors. She raised the Glock and Bates released a low, snarling growl. Bless his heart. The sweet animal she knew and loved sounded as if he wanted to rip someone's throat out, and he probably would if it came down to it.

The footsteps stopped and Abby sensed the menace and hatred floating up the stairs in a thick wave of dark emotion. Whoever it was meant her harm. But why? Who disliked her that much? The police in North Carolina had asked her that question and she still had no answer.

A siren wailed in the distance. Quick footsteps raced back down the stairs and out the kitchen door. Her legs wobbled. Abby plopped onto the top step and blew out a relieved breath. Her dog licked her face and she hugged him close. "Thanks for the help, Bates. I know you'd probably be happier as a police dog, but I sure am glad you're with me."

The trembling in her body started small, but gained momentum as the police cruiser swerving into her driveway illuminated the front of her house.

Noah Galloway pried his eyelids open and squinted at his wristwatch—it was 3:15 a.m.—when his cell phone belted out "God Bless America," his call tune for dispatch. He came fully alert within seconds. "Galloway."

"Sheriff. We have a B and E in progress at 135 Grove Street. Nine-one-one transferred the call."

Night calls were rare. B and Es, even more so in their small town. Grabbing his jeans, he dressed with one hand and held the phone to his ear. "You on your way over?"

"Yes, sir. I'm in my car right now. I'll be there in three minutes. Don't you worry none. I'll take care of Dylan while you're on duty."

He thanked Peggy Sue—his dispatch officer and dedicated babysitter—shoved his gun into his holster, threw on a jacket and raced down the hall. Stepping quietly into his son's room, he reassured himself that Dylan was safely tucked in bed and left the door cracked on his way out.

Peggy Sue was climbing the steps to the front porch as he opened the door.

"Isn't that the address for the church's new choir director?" It was a small town, and as sheriff, he made it his business to keep tabs on everything going on.

"Yes, sir. I can't imagine anyone breaking into a choir director's home. It's blasphemous, is what I think."

Noah ignored the small talk. "Is Cooper on his way?"

"Yep, I called Coop first. Y'all should arrive there about the same time."

Before hopping into his car, he glanced back at Peggy Sue, an older woman who had taken him and Dylan under her wing when they moved to town.

She grinned. "Don't worry. I'll hold down the fort."

Noah gave a curt nod and ducked his head as he folded his long frame into the squad car. He estimated he'd arrive at the scene within five minutes. Grove Street was located on the outskirts of town, where quite a few older homes had been built during the town's more prosperous days.

His jaw clenched when he turned a street corner. Coop had flipped on his siren, and red and blue lights were streaming through the neighborhood. *Nothing like alerting the perpetrator to our presence.* Taking a deep breath for patience, he exited his patrol car just as his young, energetic deputy flung his car door open and presented himself as a target.

Noah motioned Cooper to the back of his squad car and reminded himself that his deputy was new at the job. The eagerness shining out of Cooper's eyes reminded Noah of himself many years ago, before disillusionment set in.

Before he had a chance to put his plans into motion, a woman came careening down the front porch steps. He gauged her to be about five foot three, a little over a hundred pounds with long, soft-looking blond hair. Her eyes were rounded and her mouth formed a grim line. Dressed in pajamas decorated with big pink hearts, she yelled while pointing toward the side of the house.

"He fled through the kitchen door when he heard your sirens. You'll have to hurry if you want to catch him." Her breath came out in short gasps.

Noah nodded at his deputy. "Go ahead, Coop."

"Yes, sir." Coop gave a crisp salute.

He doubted the perpetrator was still in the area— the only reason Noah allowed Cooper to go after him. Keeping a close eye on the dog that had accompanied the woman outside—and the pistol that looked much too comfortable in her hand for his peace of mind—

Noah made a closer assessment of the woman shivering in front of him. He estimated her to be in her midtwenties and her eyes were dark brown. Peering deep into those eyes, he recognized courage overlapping the fear.

He shook off those fanciful thoughts. Though he'd heard the church had hired a new choir director, they'd never met. "Sheriff Galloway, ma'am. Maybe we should take this inside. The perpetrator has likely fled, but we don't know that for sure."

She glanced around, as if coming out of shock. The neighbors' lights had started blinking on and he knew people would soon be in the street demanding to know what was happening.

"Where are my manners? Yes. Please come in."

Thinking she might be a little shaky from the ordeal, Noah placed his hand on her elbow but immediately released her when the dog gave a low warning growl. The animal's posture and demeanor indicated intensive training. This wasn't just a pet. The animal looked like a Belgian Malinois, a dog widely used by both the military and police. It sported a short, light brown coat and black covered its face. *And why does a church choir director need a trained attack dog?*

"Control your dog, ma'am, and please hand me the pistol."

She blushed and he couldn't help but notice that the pink in her cheeks matched the hearts on her pajamas.

"I'm so sorry. Bates is a little protective," she said, but after a moment she straightened her shoulders and looked him in the eye with a glint of determination. "No, I'm not sorry. My dog did his job tonight. He protected me."

His second impression of the woman reminded him

of a soft Southern belle with some feistiness thrown in. Interesting combination. Noah glanced between the woman and the animal. "I take it he's trained. Give him the release command and he'll back off."

The petite woman faced her dog. "Time to be nice, Bates, baby. Sheriff Galloway is a friend."

His incredulity at her choice of command must have shown on his face when she turned around. Hands propped on her tiny waist, she lifted her chin a notch. "What?"

He swallowed an appalled retort. "Nothing." He would have used a more common "off" or "back" command, but that was her business.

He glanced at the front door. "We should go inside. Let me make sure the house is clear."

She dutifully handed him her weapon. "I have a concealed-carry permit." She sounded as if she was just waiting for him to ask to see it. When he stayed silent, she gave him a sweet, tentative smile, and his protective instincts flared to life.

"And there's no need to check the house. Bates would alert me if even a mouse dared to invade his territory."

"That may be true, but I still need to check the point of entry."

The dog had disappeared, but met them when they stepped into the house and moved to the kitchen through which she claimed the assailant had fled. Based on the broken glass pane, it was obvious how the intruder had entered the premises. The ground outside was dry and there were only slight impressions of shoes on the grass. Not enough for a print.

"That windowpane will have to be replaced and you need a dead bolt on this door."

"I'll take care of it tomorrow."

The window would be repaired before he left, but for the moment, he nodded and she led the way to the living room. Outside, the house reflected a Victorian style, and this room was decorated in the same theme. Shelves filled with picture frames lined one wall. They contained photos of children of all ages. A beautiful black, antique-looking baby grand piano was showcased in the room.

As she sat down on a love seat, she smiled and stared, a fond look on her face, at the photographs. "Those are past and present students. I teach piano lessons in my spare time. I'm also the choir director at the local—the only—church in Blessing."

He sat on the couch across from her and stifled his protective urges. He knew nothing about this woman. She had moved to Blessing eight months ago, but he hadn't been to church since his wife died two years earlier.

"Ma'am, describe the break-in. Anything you can remember." She looked so innocent sitting there, her feet tucked under her and her shoulder-length hair slightly mussed. But he knew looks could be deceiving. He'd learned that during his five-year tenure with the FBI before moving back to Blessing to run for sheriff.

"I haven't introduced myself. My name is Abby Mayfield."

Surprisingly, she was very detailed in her account of events. Almost as if she she'd done this before. Suspicious now, he asked the normal questions, but his gut screamed that there was much more to Abby Mayfield than met the eye.

"Do you keep valuables in the house? Anything that might tempt a burglar?" Statistics showed that most thieves broke into empty homes when people were out of town. Not when they were asleep in bed. The perpetrator had a bigger chance of getting caught if people were in the house.

Fiddling with a string on the bottom of her pajama top, she bit her lip, as if debating how much to tell. Noah leaned forward, placing his elbows on his thighs. "Ms. Mayfield—Abby—I can't help you if you don't come clean with me."

Her chin notched up and he was momentarily pulled into the deep pools of her dark brown eyes. He pulled back, refusing to go there. He had responsibilities now. A motherless, six-year-old son. Ms. Mayfield might appear as harmless as a newly unfurled flower, but he reminded himself again that looks could be deceiving.

The dog settled at her feet, placing himself solidly between the two of them. She leaned down and rubbed his head.

"I guess I have to trust someone and you look dependable enough."

He kept his expression all business when she lifted her eyes, as if she was assessing his trustworthiness.

Releasing a sigh, she sat up straight. "I moved to Blessing, Texas, eight months ago because there were several incidents where I lived in North Carolina." He didn't miss the slight tremor in her voice. "There were two break-ins at my home, but praise the Lord, I had a high-quality alarm system. There was also—" she placed her hand on the dog's head again, as if for reassurance "—a car that I'm pretty sure tried to run me down, but nothing that could be proven."

Noah made notes on the pad he had pulled out of his shirt pocket. "Did you report the incidents to the local police?"

She nodded. "I sure did. They were very nice and did a thorough investigation. They questioned my co-workers at church, along with all my music students' parents. They found nothing." Her expression turned quizzical. "It's the craziest thing ever. I don't have one enemy that I know of, and it's not as if I own anything valuable. I'm a choir director and piano teacher. I can't imagine anyone wanting to hurt me."

The exasperation in her voice almost made him smile. She was a cute wisp of air.

"During the investigation, did they delve into your family background?"

If anything, she became even more vexed. "There's only me and my grandmother. My parents died in a car accident when I was six. They were both only children. Grammy is the only family I have left. She's still in North Carolina. I'm trying to encourage her to move here, but I'm not sure what to do now. Whoever did those terrible things in North Carolina has apparently followed me to Texas."

She shuddered and Noah had the sudden urge to take this petite woman home with him where he could protect her and keep her safe. Ignoring his thoughts, he scribbled in his notebook.

"Have you received any threatening letters or phone calls?"

"No, nothing."

"Is that why you moved to Blessing? Because of the danger?"

"Yes, and because I didn't want my grandmother to get hurt. She lived three houses down from me. The police didn't even have a lead, and now this mess has followed me here."

"How did you come to pick Blessing?"

For the first time, a full smile bloomed on her face and his heart lurched. He still missed his wife, but it had been two years since ovarian cancer had claimed her life.

"Grammy got really worried after the second break-in. The police were cruising the neighborhood every once in a while, but it didn't stop the intruders. She hoped whoever was after me was local and would leave me alone if I moved across the country. We studied a map of Texas and she decided that Blessing, with a population of 967, would be a good place to move. It would be hard for the person after me to hide in such a small town."

She leaned forward and grinned. "Did you know Blessing was founded in 1903? The leaders of the town changed the original name from *Thank God* to *Blessing* after the United States Postal Service rejected the first name and refused to deliver the mail. Isn't that a hoot?"

Noah noted that Abby had a sweet, bubbly personality.

"Interesting piece of information. I grew up here and never heard that story. I'll have to share it with my son. Is this the first incident that's happened since you arrived in Blessing?"

Her smile slipped away, and he missed the warmth of it, but they had an intruder to catch and catch them he would. He was a tenacious investigator, if the *media* was to be believed. He may have left the FBI to run for sheriff in his hometown, but his instincts ran true. And if he admitted the truth, he was ready to sink his teeth into something more than lost dogs and domestic disputes.

He would do everything in his power to keep Abby Mayfield safe.

TWO

Abby studied Sheriff Galloway. He looked familiar, but she couldn't place him. The break-in had done a number on her. She'd really believed she'd left whoever was trying to harm her behind in North Carolina. She could still hardly believe anyone hated her enough to try to run her down with a car or break into her house.

But what could a small-town Texas sheriff do that the authorities in North Carolina hadn't been able to accomplish? Remnants of a newspaper article floated through her mind, and then it hit her. "You're that famous FBI guy from New York." Her heart beat faster. "You rooted out those mafia guys trying to kill the mayor and saved his life. It was all over the news."

Sheriff Galloway surely stood over six feet and sported short, dark hair. He was a handsome man, in a rugged sort of way, but when those electric-blue eyes focused intently on her, memories of the newscasts filtered through her mind.

"I'm sorry about your wife." It had been reported that his wife passed away, but at least he still had his son. She had lost her precious unborn baby boy after receiving news of her husband's death several years earlier.

He glanced down at his notebook. "Thank you."

For the first time since the whole mess started, Abby felt a stirring of hope. "Do you think you can find out who's doing this to me?"

He raised his head. A steely glint filled his eyes. "I'll do my best."

Abby sensed a fierce determination. Once he'd picked up the trail of an enemy, he would never stop. He seemed trustworthy, but she wouldn't care to be on the bad side of this particular lawman. His hunting instincts shone bright from his eyes. She privately pegged him as a good predator hunting very dangerous parasites.

"One more question."

"Yes?"

"Are there any irate husbands or boyfriends in the picture I need to know about?"

Sadness engulfed her as she thought of John, her dear sweet husband, gone on to be with the Lord. "No. My husband died three years ago and I haven't dated since."

"Any problems with the in-laws?"

"No. They're nice people, but I'm sad to say we kind of drifted apart after John's death."

"Ma'am—"

"Please, call me Abby."

"Abby. Is there anyone you can call to come stay with you for what's left of the night?"

She shook her head. "There are people at the church I attend who would be more than willing to come, but I'll never be able to go back to sleep, and I have Bates. He'll alert me if anyone comes back." She pointed at her Glock where he'd laid it on a side table. "I know how to use that, and I won't hesitate if someone comes after me."

The right side of his mouth kicked up in a slight grin.

"I don't doubt that at all."

Heat warmed her face. "When I was younger, my grandmother taught me to shoot. She was of the opinion that any self-respecting Southern lady should know how to handle a gun. I practice every once in a while to keep my aim good."

"I'm sure that's true, but I can't leave you alone until the broken windowpane is fixed and the house is secure."

He was going to stay here? Abby needed time to assimilate everything that had happened and calm down. She needed some time to herself.

"That's not necessary, I'll be fine."

"I'll wait outside in the squad car until the hardware store opens. I'll make sure someone comes out first thing to fix the glass."

Abby felt bad, thinking of him sitting outside alone in his car, but not enough to ask him to stay inside with her until the sun came up.

She accompanied him to the front door and turned the dead bolt after he left. Rushing to the living room window, which fronted the house, she watched as he conferred with his deputy, who'd been waiting by his car. After a few minutes, the deputy drove away and the sheriff settled inside his car, hunkered down for what was left of the night.

The house quieted and loneliness shrouded her. After a few minutes, she turned toward the kitchen. A strong cup of coffee would lift her spirits.

Crossing the threshold of the warm, homey room, she glanced out the window over the kitchen sink, stared at the cruiser and thought about Sheriff Galloway staying there to protect her. She got a warm, fuzzy feeling until she glanced up and to the left, and spotted something that shouldn't be there. Her smile disappeared and fear sank its vicious teeth into her belly, worked its way to her throat—almost strangling her with its intensity.

Even with the town's limited resources, Noah refused to leave Ms. Mayfield with no protection. He'd handle it off the clock. He lowered the car window and called Peggy Sue. After checking that everything was safe on the home front and confirming his dispatcher could stay the rest of the night with Dylan, Noah stiffened when he spotted Ms. Mayfield running out the front door, waving both hands in his direction.

He left the car door open as he burst out of the vehicle, his Smith & Wesson M&P9 9 mm pistol in hand. The gun felt comfortable, an extension of his arm. He met her at the end of the sidewalk.

"What's wrong?"

The blood had drained from her face, but she took a deep breath and composed herself. He was impressed. She had a lot of courage packed into her small frame.

"There's something inside that shouldn't be there."

Before addressing her concern, he followed procedure. "Are you sure no one is in the house?"

She began to speak, but stopped, her expression uncertain.

Noah glanced at the dog. He was glued to Abby's

side. "Let me clear the house and then you can show me what you found."

She gave a brisk nod.

It didn't take long to check the house and Noah went back outside. "Let's go in."

She followed him into the kitchen, took a deep breath and pointed at a cabinet built into the wall above the counter. "That's a picture of my mom and dad, but I've never seen it before."

Noah grabbed a paper towel, opened the glass-fronted cabinet door and removed the picture, placing it on the kitchen island in the center of the room. He studied the photograph. Her parents were standing on a beach with nothing but ocean behind them, no identifying landmarks to be found. He focused on the couple. Abby's father was a handsome man, her mother pretty and petite, same as her daughter. A smiling child was held in the father's arms. All wore big smiles. Life looked perfect.

"Are you sure you've never seen this before?"

She rubbed her arms. "I'm positive. I've never seen the photograph or the frame. I've seen plenty of pictures of my parents, but none of them were taken on a beach."

The phone on the wall awoke with a high shrill and Abby jumped. Noah held his hand up when she took a step forward. "Let me answer it."

She nodded.

"Sheriff Galloway."

A moment of silence filled the phone line before a strong voice almost shattered his eardrum. "What's a sheriff doing at my granddaughter's house at five thirty in the morning?" The woman didn't give him a chance to answer. "I woke up a little while ago and felt the urge to start praying. You listen, and you listen good. I want to speak to Abby this minute."

If the situation hadn't been so serious, Noah would have grinned at the older woman's audacity. Abby crossed the room and Noah was glad to see her eyes shining with laughter instead of concern.

"Sorry about that. It's my grandmother. I heard her clear across the room."

Noah handed Abby the phone and she started talking. "Grammy? No, ma'am, everything is fine. There's been a break-in, but Sheriff Galloway is here. I'll explain everything in the morning... Yes, Baby Bates did his job well and I have my pistol. I keep it on the nightstand right beside the bed." She sighed. "Yes, I do believe it's connected to what happened in North Carolina. I'll call you tomorrow after we know more, but, Grammy, please be careful."

Noah's ears pricked when Abby turned away from him and lowered her voice. "Grammy! That's not important. Fine, yes, he's good-looking. Now, go back to bed and stop worrying. Everything is fine."

Noah cleared his throat, buried his grin and busied himself by looking at the photo again as she hung up the phone. She swung around and her face had turned that sweet shade of pink he was coming to adore.

"That was my grandmother."

They both knew he was already aware of that and the pink turned a shade darker.

Noah briefly wondered what it would be like to have a grandparent who loved you enough to call at five thirty in the morning to check on you. His grandfather loved him, but the crusty old man wasn't exactly what you'd call cuddly. He almost grinned at the thought, but cleared his throat instead.

"I'll have Deputy Cooper dust the picture frame and the break-in area for prints tomorrow."

Bates moved into position beside Abby. Noah had always wished to be a K-9 handler, but his position in the FBI hadn't warranted it. He'd heard a lot about the Belgian Malinois breed. Alert, ready for action and easy to train.

"Why don't you try to get some sleep? I'll stay the rest of the night in the squad car and keep watch."

She nodded, but then stopped. "I won't be able to sleep. Why don't I get dressed and make us some breakfast?"

Her offer was better than sitting in the patrol car. "Sounds good."

Abby beat a hasty retreat upstairs. She had been more shaken than she had let on. Deep down, the terror still reigned. She couldn't believe this mess had followed her all the way to Texas. She wanted her grandmother, but wouldn't dare move Grammy here until the situation was resolved.

She pulled pants and a sweater from an antique wooden wardrobe, shed her pajamas and dressed. In the bathroom, she glanced in the mirror and groaned. "My hair looks like a rat's nest." Not that it mattered under the circumstances, but Sheriff Galloway was a sharp-looking man. She smiled, thinking about her grandmother's antics. The older woman was forever nudging Abby back into the dating game.

She brushed her teeth and tamed her hair before hurrying back downstairs, only to realize Bates wasn't dogging her heels. Stepping into the kitchen, she saw why. Noah had started the coffee and was rooting around in the refrigerator with Bates glued to his side. The dog was definitely food driven, just like the trainer had said.

"You've stolen my baby boy's affection."

Noah jumped and hit his head on the rack above him. Abby rushed forward. "I'm so sorry. I didn't mean to startle you."

Noah glared at Bates. "Some guard dog you are."

Laughter bubbled up and it felt good. "He does love his food. The trainer told me to keep him on a strict diet, but I slip him a few goodies now and then."

Rubbing his head, Noah straightened and froze when he looked at her.

Her hand reached for her hair. "What? Is my hair sticking out?"

The right side of his mouth kicked up and her heart pattered.

"No, it's just… Never mind."

An awkward silence filled the room and Abby practically ran to the refrigerator. "We can have eggs, toast and coffee if that's okay."

He nodded and took a seat on one of the bar stools.

"How do you like your eggs?"

"I'm not picky. Whatever is easy."

Eventually an easy camaraderie filled the room while she cooked their simple meal. She remembered spending many mornings similar to this one with John. The memory filled her with mixed emotions.

Loading the food on the plates, she placed them on the kitchen island counter, took a seat across from him and bent her head to pray. "Lord, bless this food we're about to eat. Keep us safe and help us solve the mystery surrounding me. Amen."

"Amen." Noah picked up his fork and began eating. "We'll start by making a list of possible suspects."

Abby chewed and swallowed. "But there are no suspects. That's what I keep telling everyone. And I have students coming for piano lessons today."

"We'll work around that."

A terrible thought crossed her mind. "Are my students safe coming here after what happened?"

His jaw turned to granite and those electric-blue eyes hardened. "We'll keep you and your students safe, Ms. Mayfield."

Warmth and a sense of well-being filled her. She believed him. "Thank you, and please call me Abby."

They finished eating their meal in silence. Abby glanced at the photograph still sitting on the opposite end of the kitchen island. Her hand, holding a forkful of scrambled eggs, froze halfway to her mouth.

Noah straightened in his chair and his gaze sharpened. "What is it?"

She didn't want the photo anywhere near her, but she had to be sure. Laying her fork aside, she stood and slowly walked around the island. Chills snaked up her spine as she leaned over and studied the picture of the happy couple holding a laughing child.

Almost a living thing, dread crept into the very core of her being. "The child in the picture? It isn't me."

THREE

The call of the investigative hunt pulsated through Noah's veins. Every instinct screamed this was a major missing piece of the puzzle, but Abby's obvious devastation shook him to the core. His first impulse was to comfort her. He wanted to promise he would make this situation go away, but that wasn't going to happen. They needed answers.

Maybe trying to find solutions to her problems would calm her down. He pulled out a notepad and pen, making it routine. "You're certain you've never seen the photo before?"

Sliding into a chair across from him, she stared at the picture a moment, then jerked her gaze back to his. "I've never seen that picture in my life."

"And the child? You don't recognize the child?"

She slowly shook her head. "No. I'm an only child and I don't have any cousins." Her eyes brightened. "You know what? The boy in that picture looks to be about a year old. I bet this was taken before I was born and my dad is holding a friend's child. Maybe my parents went to the beach with another couple."

Noah's gut told him otherwise, but he needed more

information, so he kept his opinions to himself. "Let's begin by writing down the names of any new people in your life."

"I can't think of anyone who would want to hurt me." Her voice rose in anger and frustration. "I love living in Blessing, and after so many months passing with no more incidents, I was convinced I'd left this mess behind in North Carolina. I was ready to bring Grammy to Blessing, but this dangerous situation has to be resolved first."

Noah lifted a brow. Abby's back straightened and her shoulders squared. The steel had overridden the putty, and the transformation was amazing. Determination lit her eyes. Abby would be a fantastic mother—deep down, he knew she would fiercely protect a child of her own. He pushed that crazy, unprofessional thought aside and returned to the important issue at hand.

"You said you moved to Blessing eight months ago. Besides the permanent residents in town, have any new people entered your life? Choir members, music students?"

She placed her elbows on the table and leaned forward. "I'm fairly new to town, so everyone is new to me, but all of my piano students are from Blessing. The only new people I can think of are two that recently joined the choir, but surely they didn't have anything to do with the break-in."

Noah raised a brow. "Their names?"

"Joanne Ferguson and Walter Fleming. They're both nice people. She's been here about four months and he joined a couple of weeks ago. He's the best tenor I've ever worked with."

Noah almost smiled. Abby was such an innocent.

"So, because he has a great voice, he can't be a bad person?"

Her lips puckered and he choked back a laugh. He hadn't laughed much in a long time. Not since his wife died, and especially not after the threats against his son's life in retaliation for Noah killing Anthony Vitale's father, Big Jack. Both men had been involved in the attempt on the mayor's life in New York, but they were only able to find evidence on the mafia father. Noah had his own reasons for living in Blessing.

"That's not what I said." She popped out the words, then took a deep breath. "I apologize. Please, go on, but we have to hurry. I have students coming."

"Aren't they in school?"

"Yes. Normally I give lessons later in the afternoon, but we have a recital coming up and the principal allowed them to miss a few classes so we can get in some extra practice. There's an advantage to living in a small town."

Abby's enthusiasm was contagious and Noah's spirits lifted. "I'll hurry it along. We should delve into your background," he said. "Your parents died when you were six years old?"

"Yes. They were on vacation in Jackson Hole, Wyoming, and both died in a car crash. The police deemed it an accident. Neither one had any siblings. My dad's parents passed away when he was in his twenties, and Grammy is my only living relative."

"Where were your parents born and raised?"

Exasperation filled her voice. "What does that have to do with the break-in?"

"Humor me."

"Fine. They were born and grew up in Mocksville,

North Carolina. It's a small town located between Charlotte and Winston-Salem."

"Their names?" Her lips puckered again and Noah hid a smile. They'd only known each other a few hours and already he could read some of her expressions. The pucker equaled irritation.

"Lee and Mary Beauchamp."

He dutifully wrote down their names. First, he'd do surface searches on Joanne Ferguson and Walter Fleming. If he had any trouble, he'd connect with a few of his old FBI buddies. As far as her parents were concerned, if they grew up and stayed in North Carolina, it shouldn't be hard to find information. "Okay, this is enough to get me started. I'll have Cooper bring my laptop when he comes to dust for prints so I can get to work on this."

When she didn't respond, Noah glanced up. Her lips were pursed.

"So you meant what you said, you're staying until the glass pane is repaired? You don't have to do that. I'll be perfectly fine here with Bates, and as I said, I am proficient with a gun in a worst-case scenario. Surely whoever broke in won't return in broad daylight."

"Ms. Mayfield, I won't leave until I'm convinced you're safe." His tone left no room for argument.

She gave him a mischievous grin. "Fine, but don't say I didn't warn you. Listening to beginner music students is not for the faint of heart."

If she was trying to get rid of him, it wasn't working. "I'll take my chances."

A car horn blared outside and Noah jumped to his feet, one hand automatically reaching for the gun in his side holster.

"Settle down, cowboy, that's probably Trevor, here for his piano lesson." He glared at her, but her eyes twinkled as she moved toward the foyer.

He bolted in front of her and reached the door first. Her brows rose in question and he cleared his throat, feeling like a rookie. He didn't like the sentiment. "I'll go first and make sure the front yard is clear."

She chuckled and he opened the door and they stepped out. A white SUV sat idling at the curb. Noah recognized Mrs. Johnson's vehicle. Her son, Trevor—with whom Noah was well acquainted—threw open the passenger door and shuffled up the sidewalk with hunched shoulders. His eyes rounded when he spotted Noah standing beside Abby.

Stopping on the bottom step, his head whipped back and forth between the adults.

"You in trouble with the law, Ms. Mayfield?" he asked, his voice filled with something akin to admiration.

Amused, Noah waited to see how Abby would respond. She patted her hair down and released a nervous laugh. "Trevor, you know better than that. Sheriff Galloway just stopped by to check on me."

Trevor moved up the steps, patted her arm and gave Noah a sly grin. "It's okay, Ms. Mayfield, I won't tell anybody the sheriff was at your house first thing in the morning. That is, if you can find it in your heart to let me skip piano lessons today."

Abby's mouth fell open, then snapped shut. "Trevor Johnson, I can't believe you just tried to blackmail me. Sheriff Galloway has a very good reason for being here, and it's none of your business." She pointed a finger at the front door. "Now, march right into the living room and prepare for your lesson."

Trevor's shoulders slumped as he slowly trudged into the house.

Abby's cheeks were pink with frustration and Noah's mouth stretched into a wide grin. "The kid's a terror. A few weeks ago I had him doing community service—picking up trash—for a minor infraction."

She waved a hand through the air and talked fast. "I don't want to know what that boy's been up to. I better get inside before he destroys my house."

Noah laughed out loud and it felt amazing. He gave her a small salute. "I'm sure you can handle it."

The woman disappeared into the house, and Noah scanned the front yard while pulling his smartphone out of his pocket. He typed a text instructing Cooper to bring his laptop to Ms. Mayfield's house and added a note to swing by his house and pick him up a change of clothes, but then he changed his mind and cleared the text. Instead, he told Cooper to come to Ms. Mayfield's and plan to stay for an hour or so. He'd go home, take a shower, make sure things were well on the home front and pick up his laptop. Cooper texted back and said he was on his way.

Noah slid his phone back into his pocket and checked the surrounding area again. He wouldn't have insisted on staying close to Ms. Mayfield if the break-in had been a normal grab and run. His intuition—one that had served him well during his tenure at the FBI—was screaming that trouble had followed her from North Carolina and the situation was more complicated than either of them imagined.

Hearing mangled piano notes filter out the front

door, he opted to stay outside and sat down on the porch swing to await the arrival of his deputy. He pulled his phone out again. He'd check in with his grandfather, Houston, and make sure he was available to take care of Dylan in case Noah found himself tied up longer than expected.

For the first time in a long while, he was excited about work. Moving to Blessing had been the right thing to do, but truth be told, he missed being in the FBI. The big cases. The camaraderie between agents. He missed it all, but Dylan was safe in Blessing, and his son was the most important thing in his life.

Abby waved at Mrs. Johnson as she picked up Trevor after his piano lesson. Going back inside the house, she closed the door and released a deep sigh. Her dog sat on the floor, his eyes tracking every move she made. "Mercy, Bates. That was a long hour. That child is a terror. As much as I'd love to have a house-ful of children, I think I might pass if I thought I'd get one like Trevor."

Bates canted his head to the side and Abby chuckled. "I know. We take what God grants us, and we're to be happy about it, but I'm still going to say a prayer for Mrs. Johnson. She's been blessed with such a… unique child."

Abby glanced around the foyer. She rubbed both arms as the previous night flashed through her mind. She still couldn't believe whoever was after her in North Carolina had followed her to Texas. She hadn't tried to hide or cover her tracks. She and Grammy had hoped it was someone local to North Carolina and the move would get rid of the problem. The worst part of the situation was that Abby couldn't think of a soul who would do something like this to her.

The police in North Carolina had interviewed everyone she knew and come up empty. The entire thing was scary and frustrating. She headed into the kitchen and gave Deputy Cooper a curt nod. He had a pained expression on his face as he took a sip of coffee, no doubt from Trevor's less-than-sterling piano skills, but she didn't feel sorry for him. He had opted to sit out the piano lesson in the relative safety of the kitchen after Noah fled the scene and left his deputy to babysit. The repairman had come, fixed the glass pane and left. She didn't understand why Cooper was still there. As she had learned in North Carolina, the police didn't offer personal bodyguard protection for a mere break-in.

Cooper stuck his nose back into the newspaper in his hands, and she picked up the landline to call her grandmother. She needed to hear a familiar voice.

"Hello."

"Grammy? It's Abby."

"Girl, I've been worried sick. It's about time you called."

Abby closed her eyes as her grandmother's loving voice washed over her. "Sheriff Galloway left his deputy here with me and I had a piano lesson, but everything's fine." The handset was wireless and she stepped into the foyer, lowering her voice. "Grammy, you're not going to believe this. Sheriff Galloway is the FBI agent who saved the life of New York's mayor."

Silence.

"Grammy?"

"I remember reading about him in the newspaper. It was a big deal back then. He cut the head off the mafia beast in New York. They still bring it up in the news periodically. Everyone claims he's an ace investigator, that he never gives up or backs down until he has his man. Wonder how he ended up becoming the sheriff in Blessing?"

Uneasiness scaled down Abby's spine. Grammy made an effort to sound normal, but Abby sensed that something was amiss.

"Grammy, is something wrong? Is everything okay?"

A nervous chuckle filled her ear.

"Of course it is."

Maybe Abby was imagining things. "Well, if anything happens, call me immediately."

"Same with you, sweetie. I better go now. The bridge group is meeting for lunch."

"Okay. And, Grammy?"

"Yes?"

"As soon as this is over, we're moving you to Blessing. My house is large enough for both of us." Her grandmother was fast approaching her mideighties, and Abby had been trying to encourage her to move in with her for several years now. Her grandmother always insisted she needed her own space, but Abby knew the older woman was secretly hoping Abby would start dating and eventually get married and have a house filled with her own family.

"I'm coming to Blessing, but we'll talk about whether I'm moving in with you later."

"Okay. Love you."

"Love you, too."

Feeling better after a shower and change of clothes, and after lining up Grandfather Houston to take care of Dylan in case he was tied up for a few days, Noah knocked on Ms. Mayfield's front door. A warning bark echoed through the house and Noah felt better knowing she had the dog.

But not better enough to leave her alone in the house. He couldn't justify spending city money on personal protection, so he'd called the mayor and taken a week's vacation. Hopefully, Cooper could handle anything that came up at the station.

He didn't examine his motives too closely. Ms. Mayfield was a resident in his jurisdiction and he would do everything in his power to protect her. At least, that's what he told himself.

He grinned when Cooper opened the door with his hand on his holster.

His deputy blew out a deep breath. "I sure am glad to see you, Sheriff."

"Piano lesson that bad, was it?"

His deputy rolled his eyes. "Ms. Mayfield must have a ton of patience."

Itching to get to work, he waved Cooper out the door, onto the front porch. "Listen, I put in for a week's vacation so I can work on Ms. Mayfield's problem. There's more here than a mere break-in. Her life may be in jeopardy. I'm putting you in charge at the station."

Cooper's eyes widened and his chest puffed out. "I won't let you down, sir."

Noah almost chuckled at the eagerness in his deputy's eyes. "I know you'll do your best. Just call me on my cell if something comes up that you can't handle."

Cooper swallowed hard. "Sheriff, I know you think I'm a country bumpkin, and I also know the only reason I got this job is because my daddy is the mayor, but I'm proud to be working alongside someone with your experience. I've already learned a lot from you."

Noah nodded at the gangly twenty-three-year-old staring at him with an earnest expression on his face. "You've come a long way."

Time to get down to business. "You find any prints while dusting?"

Cooper shook his head. "I took Abby's prints for matching, and called in a favor to get the prints run quickly. I ruled out all the smaller prints that would belong to her students—who are all kids—and I didn't find anything else. The intruder must have worn gloves."

The information didn't surprise Noah. From the beginning this case hadn't felt like a routine B and E. "Okay, head back to the station and call if you need me."

"Yes, sir," Cooper said with a big grin on his face.

Noah took a deep breath and opened the door. He had a strong feeling Ms. Mayfield wasn't going to be happy with him dogging her every step.

FOUR

Abby was irritated with Sheriff Galloway for camping out in her home, but deep down, she was also relieved. This whole mess had shaken her more than she cared to admit.

She closed the front door behind her last piano student of the day, turned the dead bolt and grinned as she hurried upstairs to clean up before choir practice. The sheriff had settled himself in the kitchen to work on his laptop, and sound carried well through her historic house. He was probably pulling his hair out by now.

She freshened up in the bathroom and made her way to the kitchen. The sheriff, with Bates lying by his side, glanced up as she sailed through the doorway. "We have just enough time to grab a bite to eat before heading to church." She raised a brow. "I assume you're accompanying me to choir practice?"

Earlier, they'd had a heated discussion about why he needed to hang around, even though secretly she was relieved that he was there while her students were coming and going throughout the afternoon.

He pushed his computer aside and half rose. "What can I do to help?"

Abby opened the refrigerator door. She had to get dinner on the table. They could talk while they were eating. "Not a thing. We're having leftover lasagna. I'll just stick it in the microwave. It won't take but a few minutes to heat."

The doorbell rang as she put the casserole dish into the microwave and stuck several slices of garlic bread in the oven.

The sheriff scrambled out of his chair and moved in front of her as she headed toward the foyer. "I'll answer the door."

She thought he was being a little overprotective, but bit back a retort and allowed him to answer the door. Standing close behind him, with Bates on her heels, a surprise greeted her as Noah opened the front door. An older gentleman with slightly stooped shoulders gave them a wide grin with a perceptive look in his eyes as he glanced back and forth between Abby and Noah. But most astonishing was the child standing next to him. The boy had to be Noah's son. The youngster was a duplicate of his father, and his interested, electric-blue eyes seemed to be taking her measure.

"My name's Dylan, and you're the choir director at church," he blurted out.

Smiling, Abby made her way around Noah and squatted in front of the boy. "Yes, I surely am, but I haven't had the pleasure of meeting you."

The child shot his father a disgruntled look before turning to her. "Gampy said I had to stay with him because you were having some trouble and needed my dad. Gampy said we came here to offer help in your time of need, and we won't turn down a good meal if it's in the offering." The precocious child lifted his chin. "Dad and Gampy can't cook, and we don't go to church, but a lot of my friends take piano lessons from you and I've seen you around school."

Abby grinned and stood. Dylan was certainly a font of information. "That's right. I come and play the piano when the school is having a special event such as the yearly Christmas play." She grinned. "Which will be coming up soon. As soon as my recitals are finished, we'll start working on the play. You'd make a great Joseph. Why don't you try out for the part?"

His grin revealed a missing front tooth. "Maybe I'll do that."

The older man stuck out his hand. "Name's Houston Galloway." He nodded at Noah. "That's my grandson—" he pointed at Dylan "—and this here's my great-grandson."

Abby shook his hand. "It's nice to meet you, Mr. Galloway."

"I'd be happy for you to call me Houston."

Noah's grandfather and son were a delight. "I'd be happy to call you Houston."

Realizing time was running short, Abby motioned them inside. "Come on in. I have to get to choir practice soon, but we were just about to eat. There's enough lasagna for four if you're hungry."

Two sets of eyes lit up, one young and one old.

Houston spoke for the both of them. "We knew Noah was over here and were hoping you would say that. As Dylan said, us guys don't know our way around the kitchen too much."

Abby ignored Noah's soft snort and led everyone in. Evidently his grandfather was taking care of Dylan while Noah was protecting her.

They moved into the house but came to a standstill in the foyer. Bates stood ready and alert, but his eyes were filled with longing as he gazed at the child. Dylan reflected the same expression.

"A dog," he breathed, awe filling his young voice. "What's his name?"

Abby grinned. A dog and a boy. A match made in heaven. "His name is Bates." She glanced at Sheriff Galloway. "It's fine if they play, but you'll have to give permission."

With wide, excited eyes, Dylan begged his father. "Can I, Dad?"

Sheriff Galloway squatted in front of his son and gently placed a hand on his shoulder. "Bates is a trained attack dog. He's a working animal and you'll have to be careful. You can play with him as long as you're in the same room with us. Now, approach him from the side and squat down beside him so he can sniff you. From a dog's perspective, that's the proper way to greet him."

Abby's heart pinged at the tender way Sheriff Galloway—a hardened former FBI agent—treated his son. A pang of loss gripped her. Her own son, had he lived, would now be over three years old. She stowed away the painful memories and watched as Dylan followed his father's advice. Bates sniffed all around the child and licked his face.

They all laughed and the group moved into the kitchen. "Everyone take a seat. I'll have dinner on the table in a jiff." She laid the table with plates, silverware and napkins, then nuked the whole dish of leftover lasagna and pulled the bread out of the oven. Dylan's eyes rounded when she filled his plate.

"We don't eat like this at home. Dad buys those frozen dinners and sticks them in the microwave."

Abby laughed. "Well, you're having a homemade dinner tonight. When I cook, I always make a lot because I love leftovers." She said grace and everybody dug in. If not for the dangerous incidents that kept happening, Abby would almost feel at peace, but one look into Sheriff Galloway's eyes reminded her that her life would be unsettled until they had some answers.

When they finished eating, Abby stood. "Leave the dishes. I'll clean up after choir practice. I'll be late if I don't hurry."

The sheriff stood. "I'll drive you there."

Houston gave her a peck on the cheek and winked at her, his faded blue eyes twinkling. "That was a mighty fine dinner, Ms. Mayfield. Dylan and I are much obliged. We'll head on and get out of your hair."

Abby gave both of them a hug. "It was my pleasure. Y'all come back soon."

She stood at the door and watched as they walked down the sidewalk and climbed into an old truck.

A throat cleared behind her. "I'm sorry they showed up unannounced. My grandfather tends to live by his own rules."

Abby grinned. "They're quite a pair. I enjoyed both of them."

While waiting for Ms. Mayfield to gather her things, Noah processed the information he'd gathered. Both choir members, Joanne Ferguson and Walter Fleming, had checked out on a surface search. If they didn't find some answers soon, he'd give them a second, deeper look.

Pulling his cell phone out of his pocket, Noah decided to give Sheriff Brady in the Mocksville, North Carolina, police department a quick call to follow up on the previous incidents involving Ms. Mayfield. Maybe Brady had discovered something new.

The phone rang twice before it was answered.

"Mocksville Police Department."

"This is Sheriff Noah Galloway. I'd like to speak with your sheriff."

"Yes, sir. I'll connect you to Sheriff Brady."

"Thank you."

A few seconds passed. "Sheriff Brady speaking."

"I'm Sheriff Galloway, calling from Blessing, Texas. There's been an incident here that involves a former Mocksville resident and I'm gathering information."

A long sigh filled his ear. "I assume you're calling about Abigail Mayfield. I'm aware she moved to Texas about eight months ago. Her grandmother calls me frequently."

After hearing Abby talk to her grandmother on the phone, Noah could imagine the older woman demanding answers.

"What happened this time?" Brady interrupted Noah's musings.

Noah filled him in on the B and E. "She has a trained attack dog and we responded quickly. The intruder fled the premises. No one was hurt, but there is an interesting twist. At some point, someone left a photograph of Ms. Mayfield's parents standing in front of the ocean holding a child. She claims the child isn't her. The picture was placed inside a glass-fronted cabinet in her kitchen. I don't know if the intruder left the picture during the break-in, or if it was left at another time. Ms. Mayfield filled me in on the incidents that happened in your jurisdiction and I called to see if anything new has surfaced."

"Nothing solid."

Noah sensed the man holding something back and he was determined to dig it out of him. "I'd appreciate anything you can give me, including your opinion."

"Fine, but be aware this is pure conjecture. I don't have a shred of evidence to back it up."

"Understood."

"It's just interesting that these incidents began after her husband was killed in a car crash several years ago. There were no other cars involved. It happened in the Blue Ridge Mountains and he went over a cliff for no apparent reason. The car was checked thoroughly and Mr. Mayfield was tested for drugs and alcohol. Everything came out clean as a whistle."

"What led you to check on the husband's death?"

"I interviewed everyone connected to Abigail Mayfield and came up empty, so I dug deeper. Turns out Mr. Mayfield had a big life insurance policy and that's why I checked on his death."

Goose bumps pricked Noah's arms. "How much?"

"I'll put it this way. Ms. Mayfield is a wealthy woman by most people's standards. Her husband was insured for half a million tax-free dollars. There was nothing to indicate foul play regarding her husband's death, and I couldn't find one person who had anything bad to say about Ms. Mayfield. The whole thing doesn't make any sense."

"I appreciate the information."

"Let me know what you find out and call if I can help in any way."

Noah slowly tucked his cell phone back in his pocket.

Was Abigail Mayfield the innocent choir director and piano teacher she appeared to be, or did she have a sinister side? One capable of murdering her husband for monetary gain?

With these unsettling thoughts in mind, Noah watched Ms. Mayfield descend the stairs. He followed her out the front door and waited while she locked the house behind them. They climbed into his patrol car and he headed toward Blessing's one and only church. His mind ran a gauntlet of different scenarios. He'd witnessed the underbelly of society during his tenure at the FBI, and nothing would surprise him, but deep down he didn't believe—or want to believe—that Abby was capable of such violence. Her voice brought him out of his musings.

"Okay, I'm a straightforward woman, Sheriff Galloway, and I want you to lay your cards on the table so we can get past whatever's bothering you."

She surprised him with her frankness. "How did you know something was bothering me?"

"Sheriff—"

"Call me Noah."

"Fine. Noah, and if we're going to be spending time together, you can call me Abby. Now, spill."

He grinned. He couldn't help it. Abby might look like a beautiful rose, but the woman had grit and he did want answers. "I just spoke to Sheriff Brady."

Eagerness filled her voice. "Has he found any more information on the occurrences in North Carolina?"

"Not exactly."

"What, exactly, did he say?" Exasperation replaced her enthusiasm.

"He hasn't found any new information on your case, but he did bring your husband's death into question."

"What?" Genuine bewilderment came off her in waves.

Noah didn't think she could fake that. "During the investigation, Sheriff Brady didn't come across one person in your life who came under suspicion. Because of that, he expanded his investigation and discovered your husband had a rather large insurance policy."

Silence filled the car. Noah took his eyes off the road for an instant and glanced at Abby. Her face had turned an alarming shade of red and she looked ready to explode. Easing the car to the side of the road, he brought the vehicle to a stop.

"Are you alright?"

"Am I alright? No, I'm not alright. Are you telling me Sheriff Brady thinks I would murder my husband for such a piddly amount of money? I'll tell you this right now, my husband was a good man, and he was worth a whole lot more than half a million dollars."

Big fat tears rolled down her cheeks and Noah felt like a heel. Abby was either playing on his sympathy or she was telling the truth. He wanted to believe the latter. Her emotions were too raw.

"And I'll tell you another thing that only my grandmother knows. I was pregnant when my husband died." She pulled a Kleenex out of her purse and blew her nose. Her voice wobbled when she spoke again. "I lost the baby not long after he died. I was devastated. I-it was a baby boy. And just so you know, I used part of the money to move to Texas, put some aside to take care of my grandmother as she grows older and gave a substantial amount to a local orphanage in memory of my son."

Noah felt bad for even bringing it up. "Ms. May-field—Abby—I believe you. I'm sorry I brought up such painful memories."

She blew her nose again. "Thank you."

"Truce?"

She gave him a tremulous smile. "Truce. Now, get me to choir practice before I'm late." Her tone was filled with false bravado, but he let it go.

He guided the car back onto the road. "Yes, ma'am."

The church was only five minutes away and Noah canvassed the outer perimeter of the church grounds as Abby hurried up the front steps of the building. A few minutes later he slipped inside, slid into a pew at the back of the church and settled in. He counted twenty people and wondered if Joanne Ferguson and Walter Fleming were in attendance. He really didn't think they were involved, but he'd ask Abby to intro-duce them before everyone left.

His attention was drawn to Abby's elegant hands as they flowed over the keys of the antique baby grand piano. He wondered how a church this small had raised enough money for such a nice piano, and then it hit him. Abby's piano at home was a Steinway and he suspected she had purchased the church's piano with part of the insurance money. He would check out the orphanage donation, but he believed her. His internal antenna had convinced him she was innocent.

He subtly checked out each choir member. They were all smiling and seemed to appreciate the work Abby was doing as their director. His attention zoomed in on a guy seated in the back row. He had a strong, male voice that rose above the others.

The man had to be Walter Fleming. He was tall and distinguished looking. The guy would be right at home working as a banker.

Noah closed his eyes as the old hymns he remembered from childhood washed over him. A peace he hadn't felt in a long time settled in his soul and he breathed deeply.

He really wished—

The music stopped and he opened his eyes as Abby said a closing prayer before the group started to disperse. Several people spoke to him as they left, and he stood when Abby scurried down the aisle—the woman did everything so energetically—with the tall, distinguished man at her side.

"Noah—Sheriff Galloway—I don't believe you've met Walter Fleming." Her words came out in a rush. Subterfuge was not one of Ms. Mayfield's—Abby's—finer points.

"Walter, the sheriff gave me a ride to church, and since you're new in town, I thought you'd like to meet him."

The man had a firm handshake. "Nice to meet you, Walter."

Walter nodded briskly. "You, too, Sheriff." Fleming patted Abby on the shoulder and Noah stiffened as a jolt of jealousy shot through him. It was unwarranted. He'd only known the woman for two days. He contributed the feeling to being her protector. "I'll see you early Sunday morning if you don't mind running my part for me again before the service."

"I'll be happy to. See you then."

Fleming left and Noah raised a brow at Abby.

She huffed out a breath. "I thought you'd want to meet him."

Noah grinned. "I did. Good work. I take it Joanne Ferguson wasn't here?"

"No. And she didn't call or email, either. I hope nothing's wrong."

"Well, let's get you home."

As they were leaving, something struck the old wooden door behind them, mere inches from Abby's head.

Noah knew exactly what the sound meant. He grabbed Abby, twisted her around, threw open the church doors and shoved her back inside the building.

A multitude of emotions crashed through him as he held Abby, wrapped in the safety of his arms, against the back of the closed door. He had a burning desire to protect her. Fear for her well-being roiled through him. She trembled and his emotions intensified.

"It's okay."

She pulled out of his arms, took a deep breath and lifted her chin. He admired a woman who could pull herself together so soon after being shot at.

"Did someone just—"

"Yes. Someone shot at you and they used a silencer. It suggests a professional hit."

Her eyes rounded, but it didn't take long for her to take in the information. Tight fists landed on her hips and her eyes narrowed. "I want to catch the person doing this." Noah moved back when she took a step forward. "I'm tired of being afraid to look over my shoulder. I can use myself as bait and lure whoever is after me out into the open. It's time to set up a sting operation."

It took a moment for her words to penetrate his brain. "Absolutely not. It's too dangerous. There's a good chance we're dealing with a professional killer."

Her shoulders slumped, her face crumbled and his heart melted. Those adorable, soft brown eyes found his. "What am I supposed to do? I can't live like this the rest of my life."

"Let's deal with tonight first. I'll call Cooper. He'll check the grounds of the church and we'll get you home." Her eyes shimmered with unshed tears and it was his undoing. "Trust me to help you, Abby. This is what I do." The corner of his mouth lifted. "I'm very good at my job."

She nodded and he reached for his cell phone. Before he had a chance to call his deputy, he heard the familiar sound of a timer going off. He grabbed Abby, shoved her back out the church doors and down the front steps, and shielded her body with his as they hit the ground.

The explosion in the church covered Abby's scream. The shooter wasn't trying to kill her with a bullet, he'd wanted them back inside the church where all evidence would be destroyed in the fire. A second, fiercer explosion lit the night sky. Someone wanted Abby Mayfield dead and they were willing to blow up a church to make it happen.

FIVE

Abby spit dirt out of her mouth and coughed as she tried to lift her head. Her eyes felt scorched and her throat burned from the smoke. She could barely breathe beneath the heavy weight covering her.

Noah! Is he okay?

Facedown on the ground, she tried to move, but froze when he stirred on top of her. Relief slammed through her when he whispered against her neck, "Don't move. If the shooter is still here, we want him or her to think we're dead."

Her heart slammed against her chest and she whispered a quick prayer. She wasn't ready to die, and Noah had a son to raise. It would be her fault if that sweet young boy was orphaned. "Dear Lord, please, please, please keep us safe until help arrives."

Noah stayed quiet and Abby took short, gasping breaths until a siren wailed in the distance. Within minutes, Cooper's patrol car swerved into the church parking lot and skidded to a stop. Noah's deputy opened the driver's door and took position, using the door as cover, his gun raised through the open window. Abby's fear and tension lessened when soft lips moved against her neck.

"At least Cooper followed proper procedure. There might be hope for my deputy, after all."

Her anxiety lessened, but there was someone who wanted her dead badly enough to blow up a church, and they might still be out there. A shiver of fear racked her body and she hated it. She'd never been afraid of anything and she refused to start now. She had faith that God was in control and Noah would solve the mystery surrounding her. He didn't know it yet, but she was going to help him. Her grandmother had always taught her to face fear head-on.

A passing thought of the beautiful, Steinway baby grand piano that she had donated to the church—now burning to ashes along with the rest of the building—brought forth a blaze of fury.

"Abby, can you get up and run to the car?"

"You bet I can." She swiped the hair out of her eyes. "I'm fine, just shaken."

"Here's what we're going to do. On the count of three, I want you to stand as fast as you can and run to the car. Jump in through the driver's-side door, climb into the back seat and lay down on the floor. I'll be right behind you."

He didn't give her time to think. He counted to three and she scrambled to her feet. He used his body as a protective shield as she stumbled to the car. Once inside, she crawled into the back seat and nose-dived to the floor.

She heard Noah whispering instructions to his deputy.

"Looks like the shooter is gone, but we won't take any chances. You cover me to the tree line. I'm going to check the perimeter of the property. I know the general trajectory of the bullet. The perp was up high, possibly perched in a tree."

Abby squeezed her eyes shut when Cooper gave a shaky response. "Are you sure, Sheriff? I've got a bad feeling about this."

"Cooper, you've been trained for this and you can do it. Stay focused and cover me."

Noah's voice oozed authority, command and encouragement. A true leader. In that moment, Abby's heart—one that had slammed shut after losing her husband and unborn child—opened just the tiniest bit.

She prayed until she heard Noah's voice.

"All clear."

She didn't know how much time had passed, but finally another siren wailed in the distance and Noah spoke again. "I don't think there's going to be much left for the fire truck to save."

Abby closed her eyes against an invasion of disbelief and devastation. *Fire truck*, as in *one*? Blessing's only house of worship was burning to the ground and it was her fault. The building, over a hundred years old, had tremendous historical value. It was irreplaceable.

The back door of the patrol car opened and Noah held out a hand. She grabbed it and allowed him to help her from the floor and out of the vehicle. Both of them coughed and stood in morbid silence, watching as four firemen fought to douse the flames.

God's house was slowly being reduced to a smoldering heap of burning timber. Abby curled her hands at her sides and gritted her teeth. "This is my fault. I led whoever is after me to Blessing and now they've destroyed the church."

Before Noah could offer platitudes, she turned to

him. Soot covered his face, but she didn't see any burns. "You saved my life. Are you okay?"

"Abby, this isn't your fault. We'll find the person responsible."

"Yes, we will, and they're going to go to jail for burning this beautiful building. And my piano."

Cooper joined them. "The fire chief says it's a total loss. I hope the church has insurance." A sad, quiet moment passed as they stood, staring at the burning building.

Abby spoke up first. "I'm now taking an active role in this investigation, so get used to it."

His sudden grin threw her off balance.

"What?"

His smile widened. "Ever since meeting you, I've thought of you as a steel magnolia. A sweet Southern belle with a spine of steel."

The description stunned her for a moment, but then she realized she liked it. She liked it a lot. "You can thank my grandmother for the steel side of my personality. At least you didn't call me Tinker Bell."

"Now that you mention it—"

"Don't even say it."

The next morning, Abby cracked her eyes open and carefully stretched her body to work out the kinks. Before going to bed, she had taken a long, hot shower to get rid of the horrid, smoky stench and relax her muscles. Hitting the hard ground and having a large man slam his body on top of hers had left a few bruises. But she wasn't complaining. Noah had saved her life.

Bates jumped on the bed, sat on his haunches and stared at her. She chuckled at the dog's antics. "Come on, Bates, baby, give Mama a morning snuggle. I sure could use one."

He licked her face and rooted his nose against her neck. She laughed, but after a few minutes pushed the dog away. "Enough. I have to get moving. I have a ton of things to do today."

The familiar interlude put things in perspective.

Abby put the finishing touches on her makeup and wondered if Noah was up. He had insisted on staying in her guest bedroom—she would *never* tell Grammy that a man she wasn't married to had stayed in her house overnight. The doorbell rang, and Bates was already standing at attention in front of the door when she hit the top of the stairs. The dog was alert but not concerned. He always stayed quiet, but she was beginning to understand his body language. The person ringing her doorbell was not an enemy.

Noah sped out of the kitchen just as she reached the foyer. "I asked Cooper to bring me some clothes."

She smiled. "Good morning, Sheriff."

He didn't smile back. Something was wrong. He opened the door and there stood Cooper with a suitcase in hand.

"Got here as soon as I could, Sheriff. Ms. Newsome's cat got stuck in a tree again and I had to get him down. Sam's an ornery old tabby. Bit me on the hand while I was rescuing him."

Noah grabbed the suitcase. "Thanks. Call if you need me."

He was about to shut the door but Abby scooted around him. She frowned at Noah as she passed and then blessed Cooper with a big smile. "Would you like to come in and have a cup of coffee?"

Cooper reacted to the dark look on Noah's face. "No, ma'am. I appreciate it, but I have to get back to the station."

The deputy practically ran off the porch before Abby could say a word. She rounded on Noah. "That was rude."

He ignored her and turned toward the kitchen. "Come on. I got a pot of coffee going."

She followed him, fixed a cup for herself and sat down across from him. They stared at each other. The situation reminded her of two circling dogs. She didn't care for the suspicious look in his eyes. She'd always been a straightforward person, and she leaned on that trait now, even as her heart plummeted.

"Spit it out, Sheriff. I have a right to know what's going on."

Noah wanted to believe Abby Mayfield was exactly who she claimed to be, but during his tenure at the FBI, he'd learned things were seldom as they appeared. He had to separate his emotions from the facts and do his job.

Firming his resolve, he organized his thoughts and maintained a mask of professionalism. "I need more information on your parents' histories. Did they always live in North Carolina, or is it possible they lived elsewhere before you were born? Anything you can remember will help."

Her lips formed a tight line and her eyes narrowed. Noah leaned back in his chair, waiting for the steel part of the steel magnolia to come alive.

"You don't believe me, do you?" Her voice lowered. "I told you the truth. My parents were both only children. They grew up in North Carolina and lived near the Winston-Salem area their entire lives. I grew up in the small town of Mocksville. Grammy is my only living relative and that's it. I'll swear on a stack of Bibles if that's what it takes to convince you."

Anger left her chest heaving, searching for air. Was she telling the truth? He couldn't afford to take her at face value.

"That won't be necessary."

Her hands curled into fists on top of the table and she glared at him. "And to think I was starting to like you."

Noah had never second-guessed himself in the past, and he couldn't understand why he was doing it now. Was he making a mistake by not believing her? Before he had a chance to respond, she stretched out her fingers, relaxed her hands and wiped all emotion from her face, mimicking his behavior. The loss of her smile, even her anger, left him feeling disgruntled.

"I'm sorry, that was inappropriate. I don't know what I was thinking. I assume you came across new information that accounts for your reaction. Please share what you found and I'll do my best to answer any questions you may have."

His throat tightened. He didn't want to upset her, but the information he'd found earlier while doing a search on her parents didn't look good.

"I ran your parents' names through our database." He hesitated. If she was innocent, this new information would bring chaos to her life.

"Yes?"

He cleared his throat. "Based on federal and state

records, your parents' and grandmother's total history begins in 1987."

He watched her closely. Her eyes rounded and he could almost see her brain working through those soft brown eyes, connecting the dots.

"That's the year I was born."

He nodded in agreement. "Before 1987, there's no record of either of your parents or your grandmother. They were easy to find because they were the only Mayfields living in Mocksville, but I'm going to need any information you can lay your hands on."

Her face crumbled. His gut clenched when her eyes filled with moisture, but it didn't surprise him when she straightened her shoulders and blinked away the unshed tears. In a short amount of time, he already knew her well enough to anticipate her responses.

"I'll get you the information you need, Sheriff, but I'm certain there's been a mistake, and I'll prove it."

SIX

Abby was afraid her heart would pound right out of her chest. There had to be a mistake. Faint memories of her parents swirled in her head. Their home had been filled with laughter, and for the short amount of time she had with them, she'd always been at the center of their circle of love. Her dad had claimed Abby was a duplicate of her mother and declared how blessed he was to have two such beautiful women in his life. She recalled a lot of laughter and a ton of love even though she'd been only six years old when they died.

Shadows moved through her mind. There were also a few times she'd overheard her parents in private conversation, her mother crying in her father's arms.

She shoved the memories aside. Noah had to be mistaken. Abby had a sudden, desperate urge to see Grammy. She needed the comfort her grandmother would offer. Someone who believed in her and would stand by her side through this mess.

She'd have to cancel her students' piano lessons for that day. Her thoughts racing, she looked at Noah. He didn't trust her, and right now she wanted to get rid of him so she could think things through.

"If that's all, I have a full day ahead of me. I'll notify you as soon as I gather the information I have on my parents." She heard the frost in her tone, but couldn't help it. She had the sickening feeling Sheriff Galloway's investigation was getting ready to blow her life apart.

He shook his head. "I'm not leaving your side until we find out what's going on."

Abby took a deep breath and steeled her resolve. "I appreciate everything you've done, but I have Bates and I'm proficient with a gun. I want you to leave. If you refuse, I'll call your boss, who I assume to be the mayor, and tell him to ask you to leave."

Her heart was pounding. She really needed time to process the information he'd unearthed and she wanted to speak to her grandmother in private. Grammy was the only one left who could answer questions about her family history and why there was no information about them before 1987.

With a locked jaw, he stood. "Fine."

That's all he said. He gathered his jacket and suitcase on the way out. Abby unplugged the coffeemaker and made several phone calls to her students. Quickly packing a bag, she called Bates to her side and locked the front door behind her. She'd been fortunate to catch a flight to Charlotte at the last minute. It was expensive, but she was anxious to get to Mocksville. She had a burning desire to talk to Grammy. Abby had the sinking feeling her grandmother knew more about her parents than she let on.

She opened the driver's door and threw a carry-on bag onto the back seat, ready to cue Bates to load his lovely self into the car, but spotted something on the seat. The dog released a low growl when Abby tensed, staring at the item in horror. It couldn't be.

She slowly backed away. Her life was spinning out of control and nobody seemed able stop the madness.

Noah sat in his patrol car on the opposite side of the street in front of Abby's house. He refused to leave her vulnerable to whoever was creating havoc in her life. He visualized his wife as Sonya lay dying in a cold, sterile hospital room. He wouldn't allow someone else to die on his watch.

Lost in thought, he almost missed Abby as she opened the front door, pulling a small suitcase. The dog trotted along beside her. Anger ripped through him. She was leaving town, which reinforced his suspicions. Distressed at being proven right, Noah flung the car door open, ready to confront her. Then he saw her slowly back away from the car.

Fear and adrenaline propelled him forward. He instinctively had his weapon in hand, positioned at his side, ready for action. He checked the area around them before approaching. Her eyes were focused intently on the car and she didn't acknowledge him. Bates lifted his head, but allowed Noah to move close.

He touched her arm, trying not to startle her. "Abby, it's Noah. Everything's okay. I need you to tell me what's going on."

Her chin lifted and Noah almost lost it when he caught sight of a tear rolling down her cheek.

"Noah?"

"Yes, it's me. I hadn't left yet and I saw you backing away from your car."

She took a deep breath, steadied her voice and pointed at the car. "I don't understand any of this."

"Tell me what happened."

"Someone left another picture. It's on my car seat. It caught me off guard, but I didn't want to touch anything."

Noah moved close to the car and pulled out a handkerchief. Lifting the photo by a corner, he held it up. This one wasn't framed, and it was a different picture of Abby's parents and the child. The small family stood in the middle of a field—nothing in the background that could reveal their location. Noah got a sick feeling in his stomach. He suspected the couple had only taken pictures that couldn't be traced to a specific location.

"We'll check for prints, but I don't expect to find anything."

Abby nodded. He felt callous, interrogating her after she'd been through more trauma, but he needed answers. "Are you going somewhere, Abby?" He gentled his tone, but her eyes flashed and relief punched him in the chest. Her spunky self was sputtering to life.

"It's really none of your business, since I'm completely innocent in all this," she said. Then added in a dark undertone, "I'll be happy to tell you I'm going for a visit with Grammy."

And why is she hurrying off to North Carolina right after I questioned her about her parents? "I'm coming with you." He wanted answers and Abby was in danger, whether she knew more than she was telling or not. He'd also get a chance to question the grandmother about Abby's parents.

Maybe Abby's truly innocent in all of this and her grandmother holds the answers.

"What? You can't come with me."

He crossed his arms over his chest. "I'm knee-deep in this investigation. You want answers? I'm going to find them."

"What about Blessing? You're the only sheriff. And your son, you can't just leave him."

"Cooper can take care of Blessing, and Grandpa Houston will babysit Dylan."

She threw her hands in the air. "Fine, but Bates and I are getting on that airplane whether you're there or not."

"Abby, listen to me. Someone has made several attempts on your life. You're in danger, and my gut is telling me the pictures and the threats against your life are two separate occurrences."

She stilled. "What do you mean?"

It disturbed him to frighten her, but she had to know the truth. "Think about it. Whoever wants you dead has been forthright in their attempts. Why would they taunt you with pictures of your parents holding an unknown child in their arms? It feels like two separate issues."

"I don't know why any of this is happening." She lifted her chin. "The whole thing is crazy. I don't have an enemy in the world."

"Let me help you, Abby. We'll find the answers."

She nodded and his stomach settled. He didn't want to examine his motives too closely. He had a burning desire to protect her and he wanted answers. That's all he'd allowed himself to think of at the moment.

"Okay." Her quiet answer tugged at his heart, but he ignored it. "I'll call the airline, change my flight and get you a ticket."

* * *

After changing her flight and getting a ticket for Noah, Abby closed her bedroom door behind her and rubbed her temples. She'd fled to her room on the pretext that she'd forgotten to pack something. She just needed a few minutes to herself. It'd be a wonder if she didn't end up with a headache. Bates whined, garnering her attention. His eyes, a startling amber, were focused intently on her.

Her life had been flipped upside down and she didn't know which way to turn. Kneeling, she wrapped her arms around her precious baby boy. The Malinois breed was known for its intelligence and fierce protection abilities, but Abby had discovered a soft side to hers. Bates wanted to be with his people and was the most loving dog she'd ever been around. She needed that affection now, more than ever.

She laughed when he nuzzled her throat. She often wondered if he wanted to feel her heartbeat. Sometimes she woke up at night with his neck draped across hers.

"Oh, Bates, baby, my life is in chaos." With his soft, warm body leaning against her chest, she closed her eyes. "Dear Jesus, please show me the truth and protect me. I don't have any idea what's going on, but I know You surely do."

All the horrible, recent events clouded her mind. She analyzed what Noah had said about there being two separate factors involved. The more she thought about it, the more she became convinced he was right.

She had prayed for God to show her the truth, but did she really want to know? She shook off that negative thought. Of course she did.

Bates followed her downstairs where Noah was waiting by the front door. She tried to hang on to the angst she'd been harboring, but it fled at the sight of him. "I apologize for getting angry earlier. I'm not upset with you. I know it's your job to follow up on all leads and unexplained circumstances. We'll talk to Grammy. She can answer any questions you might have."

His gaze softened and he touched the brim of an imaginary hat. "I appreciate that, ma'am."

Her smile widened. "Why don't you wear a cowboy hat? Everyone else around here does."

"No particular reason. We better get going."

"Right."

Noah grabbed the handle of her small carry-on suitcase and Abby called her companion, "Bates, come on, baby. It's time to go see Grammy."

The once-proud dog slunk into the foyer with his tail tucked between his legs.

Noah's brows raised. "What's wrong with him? And is that a—"

"Bates is afraid to fly, so we got him certified as a service dog so he can stay in the passenger section of the plane with me. He can also go anywhere he pleases as long as he wears his cute little vest."

Noah appeared flummoxed and Abby sighed. She got that reaction from a lot of people.

After loading up in the car, and a quiet hour on the road, they were finally seated in the bulkhead of the plane with Bates shivering at her feet.

"I have to say I'm impressed with your airport savvy."

She grinned. "After my first trip with Bates, I learned to get my confirmation number first, then tell them about the dog. So far, they've always moved us to the exit seats where there's more legroom."

After takeoff, Bates settled down and Abby leaned her head back. "So, tell me, Noah, why do you think there's two different people involved in what's been happening? I agree with you, but I'm interested in hearing your thoughts on the subject."

Sitting in a row to themselves, their small section of the plane felt secluded and cozy to Abby. Like their own private world. A time and place where secrets could be shared. But until her parents' names were cleared, she didn't feel like sharing. She wasn't angry, but matters still didn't sit well between them.

"Think about it. You've had three break-ins, and someone tried to run you down with a car. You were shot at and the church exploded. We barely got out alive. Why would the person, or persons, behind that leave you pictures of your parents with an unknown child? Their intent was indicative of murder. These people aren't playing games. In my opinion, the pictures were left by someone else."

A cold chill iced her body. "But why would someone leave those pictures? It's just cruel."

The tension gathering in her body was producing a headache.

"It's okay, Abby. I promise we'll find out who's trying to harm you and who's leaving the pictures. I won't rest until we dig out the truth."

A chill snaked up her spine. That's what she was afraid of. The truth didn't always set a girl free.

SEVEN

Noah gripped the steering wheel of the rental car with one hand and grabbed his phone off the console when it rang. He cringed when he checked the caller ID. Just the person he didn't want to talk to. Now or ever.

Abby sent him a questioning look as he answered the call. He knew from past, painful experiences, if he didn't pick up, his father would keep pestering him.

"Hello, Dad."

Abby became absorbed in the passing scenery, but he knew she was listening.

"No, I'm not at the office. I'm out of town working on a case... That's none of your business... No, Grandpa Houston is taking care of Dylan."

His father's surly tone and blistering words filled his ear. Years of pent-up anger flooded him, same as it always did when his father called. He didn't need this right now, and he sure didn't want Abby to know about his dysfunctional family.

He lowered his voice. "I don't care how long you've been sober, you're not seeing my son. I have to go." Noah hung up on his father and gently set the phone back down, even though he wanted to put a fist through the windshield.

"You love Dylan very much."

"Yes, I do."

"You want to talk about it?"

"No. Yes. I—"

They had a tail. Noah checked the car's rearview mirror several more times and Abby caught on quick.

"Noah, what is it? What's wrong?"

"Someone is following us in a beige sedan. I spotted it at the airport, but didn't become suspicious until it followed us off the interstate."

She took a deep, steadying breath. Noah disliked scaring her, but she needed to be ready if he had to floor it.

"Maybe they're also headed to Mocksville."

"Let's just say I have a reliable instinct when it comes to these kinds of things, and it's screaming right now. Hold on."

Abby gasped and grabbed her door handle when he took a sharp right onto a side road. Three cars behind them, the sedan must have realized he'd been seen and gave up all pretense of the charade. The larger car sped up and rammed their bumper. Abby stayed quiet, but Bates growled from the back seat.

"Hold on." Wishing he had his patrol car with the big, high-powered V-8 engine, Noah stepped on the gas, but the sedan was faster and quickly closed the gap. At least they were on a country road where traffic was scarce.

"Noah, there's a sharp curve ahead with a steep drop-off on the right side. There's been a lot of wrecks there." Noah appreciated the fact that Abby had a level head and wasn't falling apart. Within moments the curve was in sight.

There was nowhere to go, with a steep embankment on the left and a deep gully on the right. The sedan took his choices away when it sped up and came alongside their car. Noah cut the steering wheel and rammed the vehicle, but the small compact did little damage.

He knew what was coming next. "Abby, hold tight. We're going over the embankment." A second later the sedan slammed into his side of the car and then sped ahead.

He caught part of the plate number right before their vehicle sailed through the air. There was a beat of absolute silence, suspended in time, until the moment of impact.

An airbag exploded in his face along with the sound of metal slamming against hard ground. His seatbelt strained against his chest and he knew the car had balanced on the front end. Half a second later, the back end slammed back to earth, making his teeth rattle.

"Abby! Are you okay?"

She didn't answer and Noah waged a war against his airbag. Barely able to reach his jeans pocket, he struggled to gain hold of his pocketknife. Jabbing a hole in the airbag, he frantically swatted it out of the way. His heart almost stopped when he saw Abby. Her airbag had failed to deploy and she had a nasty gash on her temple. Her eyes were closed and blood ran down the side of her face.

"Abby!" He reached over to check her pulse and a low, menacing growl rose from the back seat. With slow, precise movements, he turned and faced the animal. The dog's lips were peeled back, revealing a mouthful of sharp, canine teeth. He'd never heard such a vicious snarl. The dog was in full protection mode. His heart raced. Abby wasn't conscious and he had to get her to the hospital. Head injuries could be serious.

"Bates, you know me, boy. I have to help Abby. Can you calm down?"

A long, low growl was his response. Bates stood on all fours in the back seat, fur bristling. The dog could rip Noah's throat out in a second flat.

He hadn't prayed in a long time, didn't even know if it would do any good, but it couldn't hurt. He closed his eyes. "God, if You're really up there, Abby needs Your help in a bad way." It wasn't much of a prayer, but then again, Noah didn't expect much of an answer. But maybe He would help Abby.

His eyes still closed, a memory of Abby calling her dog off the first time they met surfaced with gentle clarity. Would it work?

He opened his eyes and met Bates's stare. In a light tone, he murmured, "Bates, baby, you be nice now."

The dog quit growling, canted his head at Noah and then sat back on his haunches.

Noah didn't take the time to examine his prayer too closely, he was too concerned about Abby's condition. Keeping a close eye on the dog, he leaned across the console and laid two fingers against her throat. She was alive! Relief washed over him. It was more than relief, but he didn't take time to analyze those feelings.

Confident that Bates was under control, Noah searched the floorboards for his cell phone. He found it by running his hand under the seat. Fumbling, he almost dropped it when he dialed.

"Nine-one-one. What's your emergency?"

He breathed deeply to steady himself and brought his training into focus. Abby sitting beside him, unconscious, with blood running down her face, was almost his undoing.

"This is Sheriff Noah Galloway visiting from Blessing, Texas. There's been an accident and you need to send an ambulance right away. I don't know the name of the road we're on, so you'll have to track us via GPS on my cell phone."

"I'm setting up the tracking system right now. What's the nature of your injury?"

"I'm fine. Just bruised up. My passenger, Abby Mayfield, is the one who's hurt. Her airbag didn't release. She has a head injury."

"I'm sure you know not to move her."

"Yes, ma'am. There's something else you should know. We were forced off the road by another vehicle. I was able to get a partial plate number—*C* as in *cat*. *A* as in *apple*. And *M* as in *man*. *C-A-M*."

"We've tracked your position. The ambulance and patrol cars are on their way. Stay on the phone until they arrive."

"Yes, ma'am."

Noah jerked when Abby groaned. "N-Noah?"

Bates laid his head on the back of Abby's seat and whined.

Noah leaned across the console and placed his hand against her cheek. "You're okay. Just stay still until the ambulance arrives. Everything's okay."

"Bates? Is he okay?"

The dog raised up over the seat and licked her.

She chuckled and winced at the same time. "My

head hurts." She raised a hand to her temple, but Noah gently stopped her.

"Your airbag didn't work and you banged your head. You're going to have a terrible headache before this is over, but we're okay."

She turned toward him and winced again. "And you? Are you okay?"

"I'm fine. Just a few bruises."

Sirens wailed in the distance and he forced a smile. "Here comes the cavalry."

She grimaced. "What about the car that forced us off the road?"

He wanted to track down and slay whoever had done this to them, but he tamped down his fury and gentled his voice. "You don't need to worry." He couldn't stop his voice from hardening. "I'll find them, and when I do—"

"We'll find them, Noah, but don't let them fill you with hate. God has a way of working these things out."

They'd get worked out alright, but now was not the time to discuss it. He heard the sirens of the ambulance and patrol cars as they stopped on the road at the top of the gully. "Will you be okay if I get out of the car?"

She rallied. "Of course I'll be okay. You know I'm a GRITS girl."

At his raised brows, she explained, "You know, GRITS. Girls raised in the South. I'll show you my T-shirt sometime."

He grinned. The woman had more spunk than most men he knew. "I'd like that."

"Well, then, go. Shoo."

By the time Noah forced his door open, the police and EMTs had made their way down the embankment.

The car was swarming with people and one guy took Noah by the arm. He shook off the man's grip and raced around to Abby's side of the car to make sure she was okay. They had her on her feet by the time he got there. He rushed to her side and glared at the EMT standing next to her.

The guy shrugged his shoulders. "She said she was okay and insisted on getting out before we could check her properly." The man's eyes rounded and he took several steps back when Bates hopped out beside Abby. The dog obviously took his cues from Abby and didn't growl at the guy.

Staying well away from the dog, the EMT addressed Abby. "Ma'am, do you think you can make it up the embankment with help, or do you need a stretcher?"

Noah answered for her, "She'll go up on a stretcher."

She raised a brow but, thankfully, didn't argue.

Abby would have taken issue with Noah's domineering attitude, but her body felt like someone had used it as a punching bag. The EMT had shaken his head when Abby insisted on getting out of the car, but she would know if something was broken. Two of the guys laid out a stretcher and Noah helped her onto it. She smiled and then winced when they strapped her in.

"Are you okay?" Concern clouded Noah's face.

"Don't worry so much. I'll be fine."

A tall distinguished-looking man clad in khakis and a starched white shirt came around the back of the car and hovered over Abby with both hands shoved into his pockets.

"Evening, Ms. Mayfield. Looks like trouble's found you again."

She gave him a sharp look. "Looks like you've been barking up the wrong tree, Sheriff Brady. So you think I had something to do with my husband's death, do you? When I prove you wrong, I'm going to send an article to the *Mocksville Observer* and let the decent, upstanding folks of this county know what kind of a job you've been doing."

Noah stepped between Abby and the sheriff with an extended hand. "Sheriff Galloway. It's nice to meet you, but we should get Abby to the hospital. We can talk there."

"Of course." Brady raised a brow at Abby and that burned her gut. "I'll need to get your statements."

Bates released a low growl. The dog sensed her distress. She reached over and brushed his fur. "It's okay, baby. Everything's fine now."

The EMTs, who had waited for permission from Sheriff Brady, lifted the stretcher at his nod. Bates followed as they moved toward the embankment. Noah called his name, but the animal ignored the summons and stayed glued to her side. Her muscles ached and her head throbbed as the two guys carrying her up the hill muttered back and forth about a dog not being allowed inside the ambulance or hospital.

Noah jogged up beside the stretcher and addressed the EMTs. "The dog goes with her. He's special needs certified and I'll clear it with the hospital when I arrive."

The crash caught up with her and Abby felt tired all of a sudden. "Thanks, Noah."

Her eyelids drooped as they loaded her into the ambulance. Lying prone, she had a good view of the pine trees growing on the steep incline to the left. A flash of gold caught her eye and she squinted. A man moved from behind a tree and trekked farther into the dense forest. She only saw the back of him. He had blond hair and wore jeans and a dark blue jacket. She had to tell Noah—what if the man was the one who had run them off the road?—but when she tried to form the words, her mind clouded with drowsiness and she welcomed the escape.

EIGHT

A big uproar ensued at the hospital over the dog, but Sheriff Brady pulled some strings and Noah was grateful. They sat waiting in the emergency room while the doctor checked Abby. A nurse looked Noah over and gave him a clean bill of health. He'd have a few sore muscles and several large bruises, but that was the extent of his injuries. He paced the floor while Brady sat on a hard plastic chair, coffee cup in hand.

"So, that's the way the wind blows, is it?"

Noah stopped midpace and his mind played catchup. He'd been imagining all the horrible things that could result from a head injury.

"What?"

Brady propped his elbows on his thighs, both hands wrapped around his coffee cup. "You're interested in Ms. Mayfield."

Noah stiffened and faced the sheriff. "That's none of your business."

Brady leaned back in his chair and stretched out his legs, crossing them at the ankles. "From all appearances, Abby Mayfield appears to be a pillar of the community, but someone wants her dead and there has to be a reason."

"You haven't found one yet."

Brady winced at the truth, stood, stretched, and held out a hand. "I apologize for intruding into your personal business."

Noah hesitated, then shook Brady's hand. "Apology accepted."

They both took a seat.

"I ran your name through our database after you called from Texas. I'm impressed with your credentials. That was quite a coup you had, saving the mayor's life in New York."

"Yes, well, there's always a price to be paid. It comes along with the notoriety."

"Yes, well, you have your hands full with Ms. Mayfield." Brady raised his hands in surrender when Noah's face clouded. "Just saying. I take it you haven't met her grandmother? The old lady's a spitfire if I ever saw one."

Before the conversation disintegrated, Abby was wheeled into the waiting room by a nurse, Bates trotting at her side. Noah rushed toward her. Her blond hair had been pulled back into a ponytail and she sported a large bandage on her left temple. "Are you okay? Do you hurt anywhere? What did the doctor say?"

Her lips curved and she tapped her forehead. "I'll live to see another day. No concussion, which is what the doctor was worried about. Just a few bumps and bruises. The painkiller they gave me is kicking in as we speak. God protected us."

Noah didn't know about God, but the tension that

had been holding his body hostage eased off and he found he could breathe again.

Abby turned her attention to Sheriff Brady. "That wasn't very nice, what you just said about my grandmother."

Brady released a long sigh. "I apologize, ma'am."

Abby nodded, as if accepting his apology. "I have something to tell you. When they were loading me into the ambulance, I looked up the hill on the other side of the road and spotted a man in the woods."

Fear sliced a sharp edge through Noah's gut. Abby could have been taken out, right there on the side of the road. He should have been more diligent, but the car that ran them off the road had long disappeared. The driver hadn't had time to circle back, hide the car and trek through the woods. Who was the man in the trees, and how did he get there so fast? The driver had had no way of knowing Noah and Abby would turn on that country side road when they did. The only explanation? Someone besides the sedan had been following them. Abby's eyes widened in fear and he could see they had reached the same conclusion.

"There was someone else following us?" Her voice rose in volume and seeing Brady wince gave Noah a stingy amount of satisfaction.

"She sings a lot," Noah said.

"I can tell."

Abby wagged a finger at them. "I'm sitting right here."

And out comes the steel magnolia, Noah thought, and he was happy to see it make an appearance. He could deal with the feisty side of the woman much more easily than the vulnerable Tinker Bell. He reminded himself never to call her that out loud.

She lifted worry-filled eyes. "Did they—whoever is doing this—follow us from Texas?" She took a deep breath, as if girding herself for what she was about to say. "Or is it more like a group thing, with several people involved? Do you think it's the same people who blew up the church?"

Sheriff Brady stiffened and his own tone rose in volume. "A church was blown up?"

Abby smirked at Brady, and Noah wanted to hug her when she said, "If you'd quit spending all your time trying to prove I did something to my husband for the insurance money, you might learn something."

Time for a referee, Noah thought. "Abby, why don't we calm down and give the sheriff our statements? We can fill him in on everything that's happened."

Abby mumbled under her breath as Noah wheeled her closer to the hard plastic visitor chairs. "Fine, but I'll sic Bates on him if he doesn't behave."

Noah laughed and Brady threw her a sharp look right before his cell phone rang. "Oh, and by the way, my officers are keeping an eye out for a beige sedan with the partial plate number you gave us. Maybe we'll find something. Sorry, I have to take this. It's the station." He moved a few steps away.

Taking a seat, Noah reached over and laid his hand over Abby's. Her skin felt cold to the touch. "We'll find who's doing this. I promise. And Sheriff Brady only wants to help."

Her lips firmed. "I just don't get it. Who is doing this and why? Nothing makes sense anymore."

He removed his hand from hers just as Brady got

off the phone and clipped it back to his belt. Over Abby's shoulder, Noah's eyes met Brady's and he knew the news wasn't good.

He gave Brady a questioning look. "What is it?"

Abby glanced over her shoulder at the sheriff. "Is something wrong?"

"Your statements will have to wait. There's been a break-in at your grandmother's house. A neighbor called dispatch when she spotted your grandmother crawling out the front door and onto the front lawn. She's in an ambulance on her way here."

A gasp filled the room and Abby's voice reached a higher crescendo than ever before. "Grammy's hurt? They broke into her home?" She stopped long enough to fill her lungs. Her voice lowered and her words came out low. "Those people dared to lay hands on my grandmother? I need to draw them out into the open and put an end to this farce once and for all."

He wouldn't allow it! Noah's heart almost jumped out of his chest at the thought of Abby placing herself in harm's way until Sheriff Brady stepped forward.

"Ms. Mayfield, I'm the law in this town, and we will not be using a civilian as bait. If I get wind that you're planning on doing any such thing, I'll put you in jail and keep you there for the duration of this investigation."

Abby scrunched up her face. "I'm going to the ER desk to wait on the ambulance. Everything can be put on hold until I see that Grammy's okay. Did your dispatcher say anything about her condition?"

Brady shook his head and Abby scuttled out of the room.

"It's time you and I have a talk."

Noah bristled at Brady's tone, but he had a good view through the room's plate glass windows of Abby harassing the poor woman at the check-in desk. Bates stood by her side. She shouldn't be out of the wheelchair and moving around like that. It was a blessing she didn't have a concussion.

"Sheriff Galloway?"

Shaking off his worry, he sat down and faced Brady. It didn't take long to bring him up to speed, and the sheriff wasn't happy with the situation.

"Since moving to Texas, Ms. Mayfield's house has been broken into, she's been shot at and a church was blown up?"

"Yep, that about sums it up." Noah ignored the man's sarcastic edge and pulled out his phone. He wasn't above asking for help. Between keeping Abby safe and dodging the attempts on her life, he hadn't had time to follow up on leads. He punched in a secure number and it was answered on the second ring.

"Ridenhour."

"Alex, it's me."

"Well, I'll be a son of a gun. If it isn't the hero of the hour and my old partner." Alex had always enjoyed mimicking Noah's Texas drawl. It used to get on his nerves, but he kind of missed it now.

"Yeah, it's me. Got something I want to run by you."

"What? No 'hello, how's the wife and kids'?"

Noah held on to his patience by a very thin thread. "Hello. How're the wife and kids doing? And you don't deserve the wonderful woman you scammed into walking down the aisle with you." That wasn't really true. Alex was one of the most honest men he knew, and Noah had trusted him with his life on many occasions.

"They're doing great. When are you coming back to the FBI? I figured by now you'd be bored to tears down in Tombouctou, working as sheriff of a small town." Alex's clipped New York accent had returned in full force.

"You know why I'm living in Blessing, and things are working out just fine. Dylan is safe from Anthony Vitale, and that's all that matters." Time to get down to business. "I have a problem and I need your help."

"I'm listening."

"I need information and I need it fast." Noah gave him a condensed version of everything that had happened. "The only new people in Abby's life are a couple of choir members—Joanne Ferguson and Walter Fleming—recently moved to Blessing. I did a surface search and everything appeared to come up clean, but I don't have any other suspects and I don't have the time, or the resources, to do a deep search on my own."

His old partner whistled. "Did I say you were bored in that two-horse town? After what happened with New York's mayor, leave it to you to step right into the middle of another big case."

"It's not a big case. It's one woman with no known enemies, but someone is trying to kill her."

"My gut says different. I'll have Simon see what he can find on the Ferguson woman and Walter Fleming."

"At this point, that's all I have to go on. I'm tracking down other leads, Abby's grandmother being one of them, but the older woman's house was broken into about the same time we were run off the road. There's more than one person involved in this situation and I need answers fast. The attempts on Abby's life are escalating."

"I'll call Simon now."

Simon was the FBI's best computer geek, and if there was anything to be found, the wonder boy would root it out.

"Thanks."

Noah ended the call and faced Brady. The sheriff wouldn't be happy he'd called his buddy in the FBI, but that was tough. He'd do whatever it took to keep Abby safe, whether he trusted her or not, and after meeting Brady, he was more inclined to trust Abby. The sheriff had hit a dead end on the investigation, anyway.

After Nurse Ratchet sternly told Abby to sit down and wait, she crossed her arms and stood in front of the ER doors, watching the ambulances come and go. She rubbed her arms. The reality of the car crash had settled in. She was more angry than afraid for herself, but she wanted her grandmother protected until the terrible people who had tried to kill her and hurt Grammy were caught and locked behind bars.

She tried to hold on to the anger because it was so much easier to deal with than the paralyzing fear she had for her grandmother. Bates whined at her side and she reached down to pet her faithful companion. "It's okay, boy. God is in control and Noah's doing everything he can to find out what's going on."

She tensed when another ambulance careened into the ER parking lot, but controlled herself and waited until they unloaded the patient and rolled the stretcher into the building.

"Grammy!" she cried when the stretcher—guided by the EMTs—raced through the automatic sliding doors. Her grandmother's beautiful silver hair was caked with dried blood and she looked as if she'd aged twenty years since Abby last saw her. With the sheet covering her, the older woman looked as thin as a rail. Tears sprang forth as Abby raced alongside the stretcher even though the nurses told her to get out of the way and let them do their job. They wheeled her grandmother into a cubicle and whipped the curtains closed.

A nurse grabbed Abby's arm. "Ma'am, you have to leave. The doctor will be here soon."

Abby faced the nurse and drew a deep, calming breath. "Please, let me stay with my grandmother until the doctor comes. She's the only family I have left."

The nurse's hard look softened and she gave Abby a curt nod. "Just a few minutes and stay clear of the nurses as they prep the patient for the doctor."

"I promise." The nurse left and Abby carefully worked her way around the busy nurses to the top of the stretcher where her grandmother's head lay. Abby reached out and lightly rubbed a finger across her forehead. Leaning down, she whispered, "Oh, Grammy. I never should have left you. We're moving you to Texas to live with me as soon as you're able." A choked sob escaped and her grandmother's eyelids fluttered.

"Abby? Is that you, sweetheart?" Her words sounded weak and it broke Abby's heart. This was her fault. Guilt consumed her, but she managed a watery smile when those precious brown eyes—so similar to hers— opened to half-mast.

"It's me, Grammy. You're at the hospital and the doctor will be here soon. Everything will be okay."

A spark of spirit lit the older woman's eyes and her voice gained a tiny bit of strength. "Of course it will, girl. God will see to everything." Her grandmother winced in pain and nausea churned in Abby's gut. It was killing her to see the usually strong, vibrant woman lying helpless in bed. This should never have happened. Grammy had always been a rock of strength, and to be brought so low for no good reason…

Churning anger mixed with fear and Abby leaned close. "We'll catch whoever did this to you. That I can promise."

Her grandmother's eyes drifted closed, as if in prayer, then blinked open again. "Come closer, Abby-girl."

Abby leaned down further.

"Don't poke into things. It's too dangerous. And don't trust anyone." Her grandmother's words drifted away and she closed her eyes just as the doctor flung a curtain open and gave Abby a nasty stare.

"Get her out. Now!"

A nurse took her by the arm and gently led her away.

Frozen, she stood there, staring at the closed curtain, her grandmother's words echoing through her mind. What did she mean? *Don't poke into things. It's too dangerous. And don't trust anyone.*

Abby started shaking, and on a subliminal level, she was aware of Bates whining at her side, but she couldn't move. Childhood memories that had seemed insignificant at the time flooded her mind. Times when she'd questioned Grammy about her parents and fraternal grandparents. Her grandmother would always laugh, tell some sweet little story about them and then change the subject. Now, as an adult, Abby recognized how evasive the answers had been.

She had the sinking feeling that Grammy knew a

lot more than she ever admitted. And then there was her grandmother's odd reaction when she found out Noah—a well-known FBI agent recognized for digging until he found the truth—would be investigating Abby's problems.

Grammy had told her not to trust anyone. Did that include Noah?

NINE

Overwhelmed by everything that had happened in such a short period of time, all Abby wanted was to find a place to hide and think things through. Events were spinning out of control and she needed some time to mull over everything. Grammy's last words lay heavy on her heart and greatly troubled her. Without a doubt, her grandmother knew more than she was telling. Much more.

Closing her eyes, she breathed deeply and sent up a quick prayer for guidance, strength and protection. Her nerves calmed at once and she could think rationally. She had to stay by Grammy's side. Her grandmother was the most important person in the world to her. She had to be okay. Abby didn't know what she'd do without the woman who had taken her in and raised her after her parents died when she was so young.

Footsteps trod down the hall and Abby knew without turning that it was Noah. She could feel his presence. Her back to him, she opened her eyes and took another calming breath, but almost choked when she caught sight of a man standing at the end of the hall in front of the exit to the stairwell.

He stood still for a few seconds, staring straight at her. There was an odd look on his face...almost apologetic, and she had the strangest sense of familiarity. As Noah's footsteps came closer behind her, the guy gave a curt nod and turned to flee through the exit door. Her breath caught in her throat when she noticed the stranger's collar-length blond hair. It was him! The man hiding in the woods at the crash site. Her heart pounded so hard in her chest she was afraid it would burst. Who was he? Why was he following her? And, most important of all, why had he allowed her to see his face?

Abby's head pounded from her injury and she swayed on her feet. Two strong arms caught her from behind.

"Abby! What is it? What's wrong?"

As she staggered under the heavy weight of the last few days, that strange sense of the familiarity that the stranger had created made her want to check Grammy's house for leads, but she wanted to do it alone. What if she discovered something she didn't want Noah to see? Something that shed an unfavorable light on her family's name?

She felt herself being lowered to the floor and a worried voice penetrated her haze.

"Abby! Are you okay? What happened?"

Noah! Reality came rushing back and she took a few seconds to pull her thoughts together. Should she tell him about the stranger? She was certain the man fit into this mess somehow—at least, her gut was telling her he did—but the man she saw... Something inside her locked down when Grammy's words of warning surfaced in her brain.

Noah's voice rose in volume as he called for help. He looked down and she felt silly lying prone on the floor.

"I'm fine." She held out a hand. "Help me up."

He gave her an accusing frown. "You almost fainted and then you smiled. What's that about?"

He helped her to her feet but kept a reassuring arm around her waist.

"I couldn't help thinking," she improvised, "when you called the nurse, well, you have a beautiful baritone voice. You should sing in the choir."

He grimaced and she followed suit.

"Well, maybe after we rebuild the church you can join the choir," she added.

He faced her and placed both hands on her shoulders, his probing eyes staring deeply into hers. She could see why he was so good at his job. "Abby, something frightened you. What was it?"

Her heart told her to trust Noah, but she needed time to sort things out. He tucked a strand of hair behind her left ear. He would handle this whole mess if she gave him free reign, but Grammy had taught her to be a strong, self-reliant woman, so she pulled away.

She missed his warmth and the security of his embrace—even if it was just to help her to her feet—but she needed to stand strong. She wasn't stupid, though, and she was an honest, upright person. She'd never lie to him. "Yes, something did frighten me, but I'm okay now, and I need some time to think things through."

His eyes changed. There was a flash of something that closely resembled wariness, but his expression quickly became shuttered. His arctic-blue eyes turned to ice, making Abby wonder if she'd just made a big mistake by withholding information.

"You don't trust me." His voice was tightly controlled, revealing nothing.

She tried to make him understand. "I barely know you. It's not that I don't trust you. I just need to make sure Grammy's okay and think about everything that's happened."

With her eyes, she pleaded for him to understand. He responded by taking her arm and leading her back to the waiting room.

"Come on, we'll sort this out later. Sit down and I'll check the nurse's station, see if there's any word on your grandmother."

On the threshold of the room, Abby effectively stopped him by laying a hand on his arm. "Speaking of trust, Noah, I have to know. Do you believe I had anything to do with my husband's death?"

A moment's hesitation gave Abby her answer and she removed her hand. "You expect me to trust you, but you don't trust me."

He started to say something but clamped his mouth shut. "I'll check on your grandmother."

With a heavy heart, Abby ignored Sheriff Brady, who sent her a suspicious look, and sat in one of the hard plastic seats. She closed her eyes, laid a hand on Bates and prayed for Grammy.

On the way to the nurse's station, Noah took several deep, calming breaths. Something had upset Abby enough to make her come close to fainting, and the woman he knew had a backbone of steel. Definitely not fainting material. His fury simmered as he reached the front desk, but he forced a smile after the woman recoiled and rolled her chair away.

"Sorry I startled you. It's been a long day."

She returned his smile and rolled her chair back toward the desk. "You got that right. It's always crazy in the ER. Can I help you?"

He propped an elbow on the countertop, mimicking a relaxed state while, inside, his gut churned. "I'd like to check on the elderly lady, Althea Beauchamp, brought in recently. I'm here with her granddaughter."

She pecked on her computer. "Oh, yes. The doctor is with her, but he should be out soon. I'll let you know if I hear anything."

"Thanks."

Noah forced his body to relax and entered the waiting room. His anger quickly turned to amusement. Abby and Sheriff Brady sat there, glaring at each other. The steel magnolia was alive and well. The comical sight relieved the tension in his shoulders.

Like a punch to the gut, he realized he wasn't upset at Abby for not sharing information. His irritation stemmed from something much deeper, feelings he wasn't ready to examine too closely. His true anger was caused by the people threatening Abby.

Before Brady and Abby could kill each other with nasty looks, a harried doctor swept into the room. Dressed in green scrubs, he held a chart in one hand and focused on Abby. "Abigail Mayfield?"

Abby scrambled to her feet and Noah moved to her side as she faced the doctor.

"Is my grandmother okay?" Her words came out fast. Fury suffused him and his fists clenched at his sides once again. He wanted to fix this for her, but felt helpless to do so. He hoped with all his heart her grandmother would make it.

Noah was impressed when the doctor slowed his frantic pace and took his time answering.

"Your grandmother is a tough lady, but she's not out of the woods."

Abby opened her mouth, but the doctor held up a hand to stop her from speaking.

"She has multiple bruises and contusions on her body, but my main point of concern is the trauma to her brain. She has a buildup of fluid and I've placed her in an induced coma until we can resolve the problem."

Abby gasped. Noah looked at the doctor. "Anything else we should know?"

The doctor shook his head and Noah thanked him. He left the room as quickly as he'd entered. How did physicians handle this kind of emotional stress every day? He couldn't have done it but admired those who did.

"It's okay, Abby. Everything's going to be okay." He gave her a comforting hug, and her hair felt soft and silky in his hands.

Without warning, she jerked away and wiped her eyes with one angry swipe. "Everything's not okay! Grammy's in the hospital fighting for her life and some fanatical people I don't even know want me dead. The whole world has gone crazy. I'm a choir director and piano teacher—" her fist tapped her thigh in anger "—and I've never hurt anyone. Why is this happening to me?"

Her pain and frustration mimicked his own.

Color suffused her face and those soft brown eyes he'd come to adore turned flinty. "I'll say one thing, if we don't find some answers soon, I'm going to figure out a way to lure whoever is after me out into the open."

His mind immediately rejected the idea of Abby taking any kind of a risk and he hardened his own expression. "Over my dead body."

She gave him a dubious smile and patted his hand. He didn't trust the change in her demeanor for a second.

"I'm sure we'll find answers soon. Now, why don't you just run along and find a hotel room? I'm staying at Grammy's house and I'm sure you could use a good, hot meal."

The small spark in her eyes belied her sugary sweetness. She was trying to get rid of him. But why? Something had happened right before she almost fainted and he wouldn't rest until he found out what she was hiding.

"I don't think so. You're staying glued to my side until this thing is figured out. And you can't stay in a house that has just been broken into. It's a crime scene. We'll both stay at a hotel where it's safe."

She turned and included Brady in their conversation. "Sheriff Brady, I don't believe Sheriff Galloway has jurisdiction in your county, does he?"

Brady shook his head and stood. "He's right. You can't stay at your grandmother's and y'all beat anything I've ever seen." He held out his hand toward Noah. "I have everything I need for the time being on the hit-and-run. I'll keep you informed of any progress on the investigation. Let me know if you need any help on your end." He cast an annoyed glance at Abby. "You'll need it with this one and her grandmother."

Abby gasped and Noah shook the man's hand. Brady left the room.

"I can't believe he just left like that. I never have liked that man."

"He's just doing his job."

She sniffed. "Not very well, if you want my opinion." She changed the subject. "I'm going to check on Grammy and then we'll find a place to stay."

* * *

Abby wanted to weep as she stood by her grandmother's bed. The air was cool and the room was deathly quiet except for the beeps coming from several monitors at the head of the bed. Tubes crisscrossed in every direction.

God, please be with Grammy. Let her live. She's all I have left.

Noah moved to Abby's side. "From what you've told me, your grandmother's a fighter. She'll make it."

"You don't know that."

"If she's anything like her granddaughter, she's strong enough to handle a bump in the road and come out fighting."

Standing beside her, he gave her a sense of rightness. Even though he didn't trust her—and she didn't care to have a relationship with someone in a life-threatening profession—for some strange reason it felt right. Maybe she should tell him about the blond-haired man.

She *would* tell him—maybe—but with Grammy's warning still ringing in her head, she wanted to check her grandmother's house herself, make sure there were no family secrets she didn't want revealed, because she was now convinced there *were* family secrets. She only hoped her family hadn't done anything illegal, which was why she wanted to visit Grammy's house by herself. Her grandmother had several guns. Abby would avail herself of one and Bates would be by her side. She should be safe enough.

But first she had to get rid of Noah.

TEN

There were two motels in Mocksville. Abby stayed quiet as Noah picked the one that fit his requirements for security. She had to admit the place was well lit and the clientele appeared to be of the family variety. She kept her mouth shut while they stood at the front desk and Noah requested rooms at the side of the building facing the street versus the back. But she did become vocal when he requested one room.

"I'm not spending the night with a man I'm not married to! It's not right and my grandmother would have a heart attack."

She assumed Noah would insist, but after rubbing his right temple, he ordered two rooms with an inner connecting door. Well, she'd lock the door between them. She meant what she'd said about not sharing a room, but she also planned on sneaking out after he was asleep.

She had to see what was in Grammy's house. Especially the attic, where old family belongings had been stored. She wanted to do it alone, but she wasn't foolish. She would take every precaution. She'd call a cab and have it drop her off at the house. She'd open the front door and let Bates check the place before she went inside. Then she'd go straight to her grandmother's bedroom and grab the gun hidden in the closet. Abby briefly wondered why her grandmother hadn't retrieved her gun. Maybe the intruders had surprised her and there wasn't time. Or had she known the intruder and allowed them in, not knowing what would happen? So many questions and very few answers. Abby was determined to find the answers tonight, after Noah was asleep.

He stopped in front of room number 122, first floor, facing the street, as requested. "It would have been safer at a hotel with rooms inside versus facing the outside," he grumbled.

Exasperated, Abby shot back, "At least we have two motels in Mocksville. Not so long ago there wasn't even one. We'll be fine here and Bates will be in my room. Trust me, I'll yell if anything happens." He smiled and guilt rode Abby hard. She was about to break an unspoken trust, but she didn't have any choice.

"I'm sure you will, and I enjoyed the local diner. Food was good," he admitted.

Noah preceded her into the room, gave it a once-over and unlocked the adjoining door. He shot her a suspicious look as he stood on the threshold, so she had to convince him he could trust her.

"Don't worry. Now that I think about it, you were right. It wouldn't have been safe staying at Grammy's. Let's get a good night's sleep and start fresh first thing in the morning. I appreciate your stopping at the grocery store. Bates wouldn't have been a happy camper without his dinner."

He hesitated, as if he wanted to say something, but only gave her a curt nod before closing the door.

Abby released the breath she'd been holding, tiptoed to the door and pressed her ear against the painted surface. She couldn't hear a thing, but just in case he could, she turned and faced Bates. "Come on, boy, I know you're hungry. Let's get you fed and then we're hitting the sack," she said in an overloud voice.

She fed and watered Bates, then stomped around the room as if preparing for bed. After thirty minutes, she lay down on the bed, fully clothed, turned off the lights and waited.

Abby Mayfield was up to something. But what? His gut told him it wouldn't take long to find out. She'd given in too easily when he insisted they stay at a hotel, and her little routine about being tired and ready to go to bed didn't ring true.

The only way she could leave without him was in the rental car he'd had delivered to the hospital or in a cab—if they had cabs in this small town. He'd made sure she didn't have access to the spare set of keys to the rental, so a cab was the logical solution. With a quick glance at his room, he kept his duffle bag in hand and eased out the door. Fall had brought a whiff of cool air, but it was warm enough to stay in the rental car where he could keep a watch for any intruders— and Ms. Mayfield herself.

He flung his duffle in the back, slid into the driver's seat and hunkered down to wait.

He passed the next hour thinking about everything that had transpired, but nothing made sense. He called his grandfather. Houston assured him Dylan was fine and asked all kinds of questions about Bates. Noah laughed when his granddad admitted to having to get on one of those stupid computers to find out more about the breed. Houston was from the old school. He and new technology didn't rub along very well. Noah didn't know what to think when his grandfather slyly told him that Dylan was asking a lot of questions about the new choir director in town. Like if she was married. They said goodbye and Noah hung up.

His phone vibrated and he checked caller ID.

"Coop, what's up?"

Cooper's voice quivered with excitement. "Sheriff, I took a notion to follow Walter Fleming and you'll never guess what I saw. I caught him meeting up with Joanne Ferguson. But that's not the best part. They didn't meet in the diner or any place like normal people. They met in the park. At night. As if they didn't want to be seen."

Interesting. There might be nothing to it, but… "Good work, Coop. And you're sure they didn't see you?"

"No, sir. I parked my car and followed on foot, but I didn't get close enough to hear anything. And there's more. Appeared to me like they were fighting. When they left, I followed Walter Fleming home. He went inside for about an hour, then came out the front door with a suitcase in hand. He got in his car and left."

A few threads started connecting and Noah straightened in his seat.

"What time did this happen yesterday?"

"Well, now that I think about it, it wasn't long after you and Ms. Mayfield left."

Noah got the tingly feeling he always got when

things started coming together. It was almost too much to hope for. "Coop, did you keep following him?"

"I sure did. Straight to the airport."

Was it possible Walter Fleming had left his sedan at the Charlotte airport in North Carolina and rented a car in Texas?

"You did a great job. I'll be sure and tell your dad how well you're working out as deputy."

Cooper perked up. "Thanks, Sheriff. I'll keep tailing Joanne Ferguson and let you know if anything unusual happens."

"Sounds like a plan." A taxi pulled in to the parking lot and stopped in front of Abby's door. "Gotta go. Stay in touch."

He ended the call, slid down in his seat and watched Abby stealthily leave her room. She glanced around the parking lot, as if expecting him to jump out and stop her, then hurried to the cab. Before following her into the vehicle, Bates stopped, looked straight at Noah and perked his ears, then jumped in behind her.

Smart dog. Bates had spotted Noah, but didn't alert Abby. Noah decided Bates could play with Dylan anytime he wanted.

He waited until the cab pulled in to the deserted street—small towns closed down early—and followed. He had to ferret out Abby's secrets. Things were beginning to break loose and the call of the hunt soared through his veins.

Abby tried to control her rapid breathing as the cab approached Grammy's house. The closer they came to the neighborhood, the more Abby wondered if she had made a huge mistake by leaving Noah behind. There were people out there who wanted her dead, but she took a deep breath and calmed herself. She had to go through the attic without Noah. If she found anything about her parents that would hurt her grandmother— like family illegal activity—Abby would destroy it. She would protect her grandmother with her dying breath.

Why else would Grammy warn her not to trust anyone? Now that she knew her parents' names were possible aliases, Abby's imagination had run wild, and deep inside she knew something wasn't right.

Hopefully she would find answers in the attic where her grandmother had stored a ton of stuff. Grammy didn't have a safe-deposit box, and this was the only place Abby knew of to search for answers from the past. Bates nudged her hand with his cold nose after she paid the taxi, got the driver's number so she could call him back and stood alone in the darkness, facing the house she'd grown up in from the time she was six.

Once warm and welcoming, the house now looked cold and deserted with yellow police tape strung across the front. The porch light—always left on at night— was dark. Shoring up her courage, Abby ducked under the yellow tape and climbed the front steps. This might be her only chance to find answers and nothing was going to stop her. She removed a hidden key from the top of the door frame. Holding her breath, she unlocked the door. Nothing happened and she started breathing again.

"Okay, Bates, baby, check for bad guys."

The dog shot through the door and she shivered. She jumped when a neighborhood dog howled in the distance. She straightened her shoulders and took a deep breath when Bates came flying back out the front door, giving the all clear.

Hurrying in, she locked the door behind her and turned the dead bolt. Feeling a small measure of relief, she hit the light switch and gasped. The living room— to the right of the small foyer—was in shambles. Furniture was overturned and shattered lamps were scattered across the floor. Visions of her grandmother fighting for her life created a maelstrom of fury Abby had never before experienced.

"Lord, I'm asking You to remove my anger and help me find something that will lead us to the culprits."

Peace didn't steal over her—she was too livid for that—but she did calm down. She wanted this over as soon as possible. She refused to bring Grammy back here when she left the hospital. Abby would take her straight to Texas after this mess was resolved so they could start over.

"Come on, boy, let's see what we can find." After retrieving the gun, Abby felt bolder and pulled down the attic stairs using the attached string. She mounted the steps with Bates right behind her. When she reached the top, she flipped the light switch on the wall next to her and glanced around. Stuff was scattered everywhere. Old furniture covered with sheets. A bunch of boxes taped shut were piled high in one corner, as were all of Abby's baby things, which her grandmother had retrieved from her parents' house after they died.

Her parents. Were they even her parents? No! Abby wouldn't question that. Grammy would have told her something that life altering. Wouldn't she? Full of doubts about her very existence, Abby straightened her shoulders. "Okay, Bates, let's get started. We have to hurry if we want to get back to the motel before Noah wakes up." She moved across the creaky floor and lifted a dusty box off the top of the stack.

Surely there were papers, or something, that would explain the truth about her parentage. Was Grammy even her true grandmother? The mere thought was mind-blowing.

Noah shook his head at the rickety stairs he presumed led to the attic. Abby could have fallen and broken her neck, but this proved the woman had secrets.

Earlier, he had followed her from the motel and parked several houses down while the cabdriver deposited her in front of her grandmother's house. A mixture of admiration and irritation had vied for position as he'd watched her hesitate, then straighten her shoulders and march up the front steps.

The woman was gutsy. He couldn't fault her for not trusting him because he didn't fully trust *her*. There was something building between them that was more than mere attraction, but the woman was trouble. He didn't know if he wanted to deal with that.

He followed Abby's voice up the stairs. She spoke to her dog like he was a person.

There must be something hidden in the attic. Testing each step, he moved slowly up the stairs. He didn't want to scare her, but he did want to find out what she was hiding.

Noah quietly opened the door to the attic and watched as Abby lingered on a few of the treasures she'd unearthed from the boxes. It looked like she had a picture in her hand. He still couldn't believe she'd tried to give him the slip.

She made a small noise when she pulled something from the bottom of a box. She carefully unwrapped the tissue and lifted what looked like a pleated, vellum, silk-embroidered fan in front of her. She flicked her wrist and held the fan close to her face. Noah almost smiled when she spoke to her dog. "Well, Bates, do I look intriguing?"

The dog canted his head and stared at her.

"I'll take that as a yes." She lowered the fan and studied what he assumed were initials in the corner. "A.C. I remember Grammy saying the fan was passed down through Dad's family. I wonder if the *A* stands for Abigail. Maybe I was named after an ancestor. And who is that man who keeps popping up? And why did he allow me to see his face at the hospital?"

It was time to make his presence known. "I'd like the answers to both those questions."

His deep voice echoed from the top of the stairs, and even though he didn't want to scare her, he was almost glad to see her jump. She needed to know anyone could have followed her and broken into the house, just like he had. She could be dead right now if that had happened. From her position on the floor, she glanced over her shoulder and met his gaze. The jig was up, but righteous indignation set in and she went on the offense.

"You're not my keeper and I don't have to tell you anything. I have enough sense to protect myself." Reaching to the floor beside her, she lifted the Glock. "I have Bates and I'm locked and loaded."

Noah took long strides across the wide, wooden planks and sat on the floor beside her. He relieved her of the gun and released a long breath. It was time to be honest with himself. The woman was driving him crazy, and in more ways than one.

He hadn't dated since Sonya had passed away two years ago because that felt as if it would be unfaithful to his dead wife. Then Ms. Abigail—Abby—blew into his life like a hurricane, catching him off guard. Maybe it was time to join the land of the living again. If only he could trust her.

He turned his head and gazed at her soft brown eyes. He had no idea how she felt about him, and that made him edgy. He didn't like feeling unsure about anything. He'd been told he had nerves of steel, but they seemed to have deserted him.

"Noah? Is something wrong?"

"Yes! I'm attracted to you." His face heated and he scrambled to his feet. He couldn't believe he'd just blurted it out like that. He was an idiot. "I can't believe I just said that."

Her eyes softened, and she stood up and faced him. He wanted to fall through the floor when she grinned.

"So that's what's wrong? You're attracted to me?"

"No. I mean yes. I don't know what I mean. Forget I said anything."

She moved close and cupped his cheek with one hand. "It's okay. I'm kinda attracted to you, too."

Before he could stop himself, he pressed his lips softly to hers and she relaxed against his chest. Noah thought of a million reasons he shouldn't be doing this—one being he was supposed to be protecting her—but it felt so right.

After the sweetest kiss, he pulled back and tucked a stray strand of hair behind her ear. "You're the most beautiful, exasperating, kindhearted, troublesome woman I've ever met."

She opened her mouth, probably to take exception to his words, but he placed a finger on her lips.

"Abby, you have to trust me. Your life is in danger and we have to work together. There can be no secrets. If you have information, you have to share."

With no warning, she jerked out of his arms. "You just kissed me to try to butter me up. I don't appreciate that."

Horror filled his mind. "You're wrong. Everything I said is true. I think you're a wonderful person."

He could almost hear her brain going a hundred miles an hour.

"Why don't we agree to table this discussion until later?" She took a deep breath. "And you're right. I do have to trust someone." She picked up the fan. "While going through some old boxes, I came across this fan. When I was a child, I remember Grammy saying it had been passed down through our family." She pointed at the initials. "I'm wondering if the *A* stands for Abigail, maybe a name that's been passed down through the generations. I don't know what the *C* would stand for."

Noah wanted to disagree with her about discussing the kiss later, but he moved on. "I'm more interested in the man at the hospital."

She hesitated, then shrugged. "I'll tell you, but I want your word that if we find something incriminating about my family, anything that would hurt Grammy, you won't tell anyone."

His mouth formed a tight line. "I can't promise you that."

She appeared to mull it over and he breathed a sigh

of relief when she said, "Fine. I'm pretty sure the man I saw at the hospital is the same one I spotted standing in the woods at the car crash."

"Describe what he looked like and his demeanor toward you. Did he appear hostile?"

Bates plopped down beside her and she ran a hand over his soft fur. "No," she said slowly. "He had a wistful expression on his face. It was odd, but I didn't feel threatened."

"Did you get a good enough look at his face to work with a police sketch artist?"

"Yes, I did."

"I'll set that up, and I have some information that might tie into this. Cooper called. He followed Walter Fleming. Fleming left town shortly after we did."

"You think Walter ran us off the road?" She blew out a breath. "I still don't believe one of my choir members is involved in this. What about Joanne Ferguson?"

"Coop is keeping a close eye on her."

Abby excitedly waved the fan in front of her. "The fan. Look at the initials."

He took the fan and squinted at the small print. "You said they were A.C."

Abby bounced on the floor. "Yes! The fan and the license plate you saw before we went over the embankment both have *C*. This could be our first clue."

"That's quite a long shot. Most license plates are random."

She shook her head. "True, but a lot of people have personalized plates. It's worth looking into."

Bates lifted his head, ears pricked. He stood on all fours and whined.

Noah frowned.

"What?" Abby whispered.

"Shh. Give me a second."

He strained to hear what had caused the dog's reaction and heard a faint ticking sound. Noah grabbed Abby's arm and pulled her to her feet. Bates started growling.

"Get out! Now! Go, go, go."

"What is it?" she shouted.

"It's a bomb. Run!"

ELEVEN

Abby froze and Noah pulled her across the planked floor. "Wait! The family pictures. We might need them."

He pushed her toward the stairs. "Go! Follow Bates. I'll grab what I can and be right behind you."

Even with fear tightening her throat and making it hard to breathe, Abby followed Bates down the rickety stairs. In the midst of a possible bomb destroying Grammy's house, it still amazed her that a dog could be trained to climb and descend stairs.

She hit the bottom step and turned, waiting for Noah to come scrambling down behind her. When he didn't appear, she yelled at the top of her lungs. The pictures weren't worth his life. "Noah, leave the boxes. Get down here."

She blew out the breath she'd been holding when he made an appearance at the top of the stairs.

"Get out! I'm coming," he yelled.

She turned to run. Bates flew out the front door. She had one foot over the threshold when an earsplitting explosion rocked her world. As if in a dream, her body lifted into the air before a bone-jarring slam claimed the breath in her lungs.

A thick cloud of smoke followed the boom. Barely conscious, her eyes watered. She coughed and tried to draw air into her lungs. "Bates," she whispered, relieved when a wet tongue licked her face.

"Bates. Find Noah." She fought the darkness closing in. Noah had been right behind her. Did the explosion kill him? She rolled to her side and tried to stand. Bates growled and a voice penetrated the pain and dizziness overtaking her.

"It's okay, boy. Take a big sniff." A hand found her shoulder and gently pushed her back down. "Shh, it'll be okay. I called 911."

Abby fought the smoke-induced tears and stared at the man. "It's you," she breathed. "The man in the woods and at the hospital. Who are you?" She inhaled a lungful of smoke and coughed. Noah! Right now it didn't matter who the guy was, he had to help Noah. "Noah. He's still inside. Please help him." Abby fought as long as she could, but the throbbing in her head won the battle and she reluctantly closed her eyes, giving in to the darkness.

Noah hadn't prayed in years, but he'd sent up a heartfelt one. "God, please get her to safety." As the words had left his mouth, a deafening boom had filled the old house and the stairs gave way. He'd been halfway down and fell to the floor as hot embers burned through his shirt and pierced his skin.

He'd rolled when he hit the floor, taking the brunt of the fall on his left shoulder. Scrambling to his feet, he'd grabbed the box of pictures that had fallen to the floor, and would have made it out if the ceiling hadn't caved. Now, through the roar of the fire, he heard Bates barking and it terrified him. This whole thing could have been planned, with people waiting outside, ready to kill Abby if the fire didn't do its job. But how would anyone guess that Abby would show up at her grandmother's house tonight? It had been a spur-of-the-moment decision.

A falling beam knocked him sideways and landed on his left leg, effectively trapping him in the roaring fire. He tried to push the wood off and pull his leg loose, but it would take the help of another person to free him.

Gritting his teeth as debris and hot embers rained down on him, scorching his skin, he grabbed a chunk of wood that had fallen from the ceiling. It was hot, but he forced the wood under the beam and shoved with all his might. It didn't budge an inch.

Giving up was not an option. Noah had a son to raise and he refused to leave Dylan orphaned. He coughed and took shallow breaths, trying to stay alive long enough to figure a way out of the situation.

Through the dense smoke, he saw movement and called out. There hadn't been time for the fire department to arrive. Maybe a neighbor? Or the people trying to hurt Abby? Locking his jaw, he lifted his midsection and reached back, relieved to find his gun still in the waistband of his jeans. He pointed and cocked the weapon just as a man appeared in the smoke. The crazy guy ignored the gun and rushed over to Noah. Bates belly crawled in behind him, grabbed Noah's pant leg and started pulling.

"Put the gun away. I'm here to help," the man choked out.

Noah didn't have much choice. The stranger took

the piece of wood out of his hand and placed the tip under the beam.

"On the count of three," he yelled.

Noah nodded.

"One, two, three!"

Noah scooted back on his hands, grabbed the box of pictures laying on the floor beside him and crawled to all fours before forcing himself to his feet. His leg burned like fire, but it wasn't broken. He was mobile. Barely.

The person threw his arm around Noah's waist and pulled him forward.

"Go, go, go. The roof's gonna cave."

Noah propelled himself forward. They made it to the front porch, and he thought they were home free until the roof collapsed and a sharp object pierced his temple. Black dots blurred his vision, but the guy kept pulling him forward and lowered him to ground when they were clear of the fire. Taking a deep breath of clean air, Noah tried to get a visual on the man leaning over him. His face was slightly blurred.

"Hey, you're okay, and so is Abby."

Noah had a million questions, the first being how this person knew Abby's name, but a coughing fit halted all inquiries. He had blond hair. Could it be the same man from the crash scene and the hospital?

Noah heard a siren wailing in the distance and the man leaned closer.

"Listen, I know who you are, ex-FBI agent Noah Galloway and I know your history. Abby and her grandmother need to disappear and you can make that happen. Please, I beg you, use your contacts and help her."

The sirens were getting closer.

"I gotta go."

Noah lifted his hand to stop the man, but it fell to his side, weakened by his injuries.

The sound of a soft beep gently woke Abby and her eyes popped open. She was in a hospital. Memories of the explosion at her grandmother's house rushed into her brain. She briefly closed her lids against the pounding in her head.

Noah! Bates!

She tried to move herself into a sitting position, but was gently pushed back down by a woman wearing a nurse's uniform.

"You're in the hospital, but you're okay. A little smoke inhalation and a few bumps and bruises, but no serious injuries." The woman was being nice, but Abby had a searing desire to see Noah and Bates and make sure they were okay.

"I don't care about me. Where are Noah and Bates?"

A whine came from the side of the bed and Abby turned her head. Relieved, she stretched out her arm and touched Bates on the nose. "You okay, boy?"

A throat cleared. Sheriff Brady moved in beside her dog and frowned. "The animal wouldn't allow anyone in the hospital to touch you unless he was by your side. He's created chaos in this building. I almost called animal control."

Fury tore through Abby, but she contained her anger and gritted her teeth. "Where is Noah?"

The sheriff snorted. "You're just like your grandmother. All sweet Southern charm on the outside, the disposition of a wildcat on the inside. I didn't call animal control because the dog likely saved Noah's life. We found teeth marks on his jeans."

He held up a hand when she tried to interrupt. "I know we'll never be best friends, but I'm here to help in any way I can. Noah's fine. Same as you, smoke inhalation, bumps and bruises, a few minor burns and a nasty bruise on his leg. I'm sure he'll be along shortly. He refused treatment until the doctor threatened to stick a needle in him and put him to sleep unless he got checked. I'll warn you, he does have a nasty wound on his temple, but the doc assured him it wasn't a concussion. Y'all were blessed to come out of that mess alive."

He scraped a chair across the floor and sat down next to her bed. "I'm sure you realize I have a ton of questions. We have some major problems on our hands."

Abby whipped her head around when a deep, scratchy voice came from the vicinity of the doorway. "We appreciate all your help, Sheriff, but as soon as Abby is up to it, we're headed to New York. I have contacts there who can hopefully help us find some answers."

At the sight of him, Abby's heart pounded in her chest. Noah had a bandage on his temple, his shirt had small burn holes in it and his jeans were torn. He looked like he'd just been in a war zone. And that's what her life felt like. A war zone.

How had this happened? She was a simple choir director who'd never harmed anyone in her life.

"I need to talk to Abby alone," Noah said to the sheriff.

The sheriff stood. "Fine, I'll need a statement, for all the good it'll do. From what the fire chief concluded after the first walk-through, it was a professional job. I don't think the answers lie in my county."

Noah didn't respond and the sheriff left. Abby stared at Noah, drinking him in. He moved to the side of her bed. He looked like he wanted to touch her, and Abby couldn't decide if she was happy or sad that he didn't.

"That was a close call, Abby. We have to find answers fast."

She swallowed hard, knowing what she had to do. "Noah." Her voice cracked and she tried again. "Noah, you have a son to raise. Whatever's going on is too dangerous. I can't allow you to risk your life. We don't even know who these people are."

He gave her a lopsided grin and it lifted her heart. "I appreciate the sentiment, and I don't plan on leaving Dylan orphaned, but this is what I do."

Her heart fell. Even though he was ready to risk his life to save hers, this was exactly why she should distance herself from that kiss in her grandmother's attic and whatever was happening between them. Determined, she thrust out her chin. She might not be able to convince him to change his mind, but there was one thing she could do.

"If anything happens to you, I'll take care of Dylan. I promise."

He grinned and his electric-blue eyes twinkled. "That won't happen, but Dylan would love having Bates full time."

They both chuckled at his lame attempt at breaking the tension.

He sat in the chair beside the bed and his smile melted away. "Are you up to talking about the explosion? But before we start, I checked on your grandmother. Her condition is stable, but they're still keeping her in an induced coma for the time being."

"I appreciate that, and I do want to discuss anything that will help us understand this mess."

He leaned back in his chair, as if contemplating what to say. "A man, at high risk to himself, ran into that burning house and saved my life. My leg was trapped under a beam and he helped free me. He pulled me out of the house with the front porch roof collapsing on top of us."

Abby's heart beat faster. "He has blond hair."

Noah nodded. "So you saw him?"

"Yes! He was the same man at the crash site and the hospital. He made sure I was okay and I told him you were still in the house."

Noah nodded as if he'd figured as much. "The question is…why was he there in the first place? And who is he? If he's working for the bad guys, it was a perfect time to kill us."

Abby felt the blood rush from her brain and Noah stood when she swayed. "You're not okay. I'm calling the nurse."

She waved a hand in the air. "I'm fine. It's not every day a girl has a close brush with death. Just give me a minute." She took several deep breaths. "So, who do you think he is?"

"I have no clue, but don't worry. We'll find out."

Noah hesitated and Abby jumped all over it. "You're hiding something. What is it?"

"The blond man made a good suggestion. He asked me to hide you and your grandmother. Permanently."

Abby shook her head fiercely. "You can get that right out of your mind, Noah Galloway. I won't rest until the people who hurt my grandmother are behind bars."

Noah shrugged. "I figured that's what you'd say. Okay, then, Coop called. Joanne Ferguson left Blessing. It wouldn't surprise me if she's headed to North Carolina, but we won't be here. Alex Ridenhour, my old partner from the FBI, called. Simon, our resident computer whiz, found out that both Joanne Ferguson and Walter Fleming aren't who they claim to be. They passed a surface search, but Simon dug deeper, and their false identities didn't hold up."

"Do you think Walter Fleming tried to blow us up?"

"Like I said, we'll find out. We're starting to connect the dots. Simon is working on the car tag. He's already eliminated half the list of plates starting with *C-A-M*. It's only a matter of time before we have a name to go with the tag, unless the plates were stolen."

Abby groaned. "It can't ever be easy, can it?" Then she cheered up. "But God never said it was going to be easy, did he?"

Noah ignored the biblical reference. "Let's get you out of here and go track down some bad guys."

TWELVE

A nurse took Abby out of the hospital in a wheelchair and she fussed all the way to the car Noah left idling beside the curb, claiming she had two good legs and could walk perfectly well. Noah bit back a grin when the nurse muttered "Good riddance" under her breath after helping Abby up and into the vehicle.

Noah rounded the hood, slid into the driver's seat and grinned at her. "We look like a couple of refugees." They both chuckled, but he was concerned about her health. "You sure you're up to this? You can always stay with your grandmother. Sheriff Brady posted a guard on her door 24/7. You'd be safe here."

She puckered her lips, a telling sign of irritation. "No. Grammy is being well taken care of, and—" her lips tightened "—I have to see this through. If my grandmother taught me anything, it's to face my fears head-on." Her voice firmed and a dangerous glint entered her eyes. "And when we find the person who hurt her, I have a couple of things I'd like to say to them."

Noah grinned and put the car in Drive. "I just bet you do. We'll swing by the motel, change clothes and grab our bags."

After a quick shower and change of clothes, Noah felt like a human being again. His throat was sore and his body ached, but that was to be expected. He shuddered every time he thought about their brush with death and how close Abby had come to dying.

They'd been in the rental car for thirty minutes. Neither of them had spoken, but it was a relaxed, comfortable silence. His fingers were wrapped loosely around the steering wheel. He quickly glanced at Abby as she stared at the passing scenery out the passenger window, then turned his gaze back to the road. She had dressed in black leggings and a loose top that came to her thighs. She'd pulled her soft-looking blond hair up into a ponytail.

"So, you grew up in Texas?" she asked without turning her head.

The question made him uneasy. He never talked about his past if he could avoid it. His fingers tightened on the steering wheel for a moment before he forced them to relax.

"Yep. I grew up there, went to college and joined the FBI."

Out of the corner of his eye, he saw Abby fiddle with a loose string on the bottom of her sweater. "That's it? Sounds to me as if you left out a lot of stuff. If you don't want to talk about it, that's fine with me."

A new, tense silence filled the car and it irritated him.

"Why did you kiss me in the attic?"

The question came out of left field and his body tensed, but then he blew out a breath and chuckled. "You're one tough cookie, Abby Mayfield."

The tension leaked out of the car and she grinned. "You betcha."

He took a moment, gathering his thoughts. "I kissed you because it felt right, not to get information. And as for my childhood… Well, let's just say my family would never be nominated for a family of the year award."

Abby lifted a questioning brow and he shrugged. He'd kissed the woman, which he figured gave her the right to delve into his dysfunctional past.

"My mom skipped out when I was ten. My old man was sheriff, but he was also a mean drunk."

Her expression softened and she reached across the console to touch his arm. "Noah, I'm sorry. I shouldn't have intruded into your personal life. You don't have to talk about it if you don't want to."

Her offer sounded genuine and he relaxed. "No, I want to tell you." He paused and took a deep breath, preparing to open old wounds. "I don't blame my mother for leaving. My dad was sheriff, but he lived on the shady side of life. He traded favors with people and made deals he shouldn't have."

"Your mother left her child with a drunk father of questionable character?"

Her indignation and protectiveness on his behalf warmed him. Grandpa Houston had raised him, for the most part, but his grandfather wasn't exactly what you'd call soft and fuzzy. Houston had spent Noah's childhood teaching Noah how to be a man. And working on a ranch part-time wasn't conducive to much coddling.

"Not exactly, but when you live in a small town and your old man's the sheriff, let's just say she didn't have a fighting chance of taking me with her."

"Have you stayed in touch with her?"

"When I got older, I tracked her down. She remarried and has two daughters. She deserves to be happy."

"What about now? I was there when your father called, asking to see Dylan."

His grip tightened on the steering wheel and his knuckles turned white. "He claims to be on the wagon, but I've heard that too many times to count. He doesn't deserve to see my son. I don't trust him." He paused. "But there was a silver lining in my childhood."

"What was that?" she asked.

His gave her a genuine smile. "Grandpa Houston. He's a wily old coot."

Abby laughed. "He's a sweet man with a wonderful, deep baritone voice. I think he should join the choir."

A hoarse laugh escaped before Noah could stop it. "I'd like to see that. Grandpa's smart as a whip. I spent the majority of my childhood on his ranch, learning all the ropes. It helped make up for the time spent at home with dear old Pop."

"You grew up a cowboy, joined the FBI and now you're a sheriff. Some people would call you an overachiever."

Bates blew out a sigh from the back seat and they both laughed.

"Turnabout's fair play. I know about your grandmother and your parents. Did you have a good childhood?"

Abby turned introspective. "The loss of my parents was devastating, but Grammy made up for it. I had a wonderful childhood, except…"

"Except?" he prodded.

"I would have loved to have had a brother or sister."

"I know what you mean. I have two half sisters, but I've never met them."

"Maybe it's time you did."

"What?" The thought startled him. After tracking down his mother, he'd thought it best to leave her and her new family in peace. He didn't think she would enjoy having a grown son show up unannounced on her doorstep. She'd probably shaken the Texas dust from her feet and hadn't looked back.

"Maybe it's time you met your sisters. As we've recently learned, life can be short. I'm sure they'd love to have a big brother looking out for them."

It was an intriguing idea. "I just might do that."

His phone buzzed and Abby turned back to gazing out her window, but he knew she was listening to his conversation. She glanced at him when Dylan's name came up.

"Hey, Dylan, what's up, son? Grandpa Houston treating you right?… Chocolate chip cookies?" He smiled. "That's great. I'm with Ms. Mayfield and we're driving to New York… Yep, we're tracking down the people who broke into her house, but you don't need to worry, we'll find them and put them in a nice, cozy cell… Yes, Bates is with us."

Noah cleared his throat and lowered his voice. "We can discuss that when I get back home… Not now, we'll discuss it first." Noah released a big sigh and handed Abby the phone. "He wants to talk to you."

Abby took the phone and grinned. She loved kids and their cute antics. "Hey, Dylan. Did you want to speak to me?"

"Yes, ma'am. Is my dad doing okay?"

"Yes. He's just fine. Why do you ask?"

"Well, sometimes he works too hard and I don't think he has enough fun. When y'all get back, maybe we can go on a picnic or something."

Abby choked back a laugh. The kid was playing matchmaker for his father. It was funny but serious, too. She had to be careful with Dylan because she didn't know if she was ready for a relationship with any man, much less one with a dangerous profession, even though she'd love to have a smart, cheerful child like Dylan brightening up her life.

"That's a good suggestion. We'll discuss it when things settle down."

"I'd like to be in the church Christmas play, and maybe it'd be a good idea if I started taking piano lessons, too."

Dear Lord, have mercy on this sweet child, was the first thing to pop into Abby's mind. She had taught children long enough to know when she was being manipulated, and she also knew how to handle it.

"Now, Dylan, you know I'd love to have you in the Christmas play and as a piano student, but don't you think your father should have a say in this? And you need to ask yourself why you want to take piano lessons. Is it a lifelong dream of yours, something you're willing to give up other after-school activities for?"

Dead silence filled the phone, then he said, "Maybe not the piano lessons, but I definitely want to be in the Christmas play."

"And I'd love to have you, after you discuss it with your father."

"Can I talk to him again?"

"Certainly." Abby handed the phone back to Noah.

He mouthed "Thank you" and took the phone.

Her mind wandered while he finished his call. Her life had been turned upside down, but Noah's soft tones and loving conversation with his son filled her with longing. She was twenty-eight years old and had always wanted a family with two or three children hanging on to her skirts, as her grandmother would say.

Thinking of Grammy brought the ugly reality of her life crashing back in. She glanced at Noah and the soft, sweet look on his face as he spoke with Dylan gave her heart a jolt. So what if he worked in a dangerous environment, her heart argued. Her deceased husband had led the safest life any wife could ask for, yet it had been cut short by a car crash. A dark, unsettling thought crossed her mind as Noah hung up the phone.

"That son of mine is a pistol…" His words trailed off when he caught her expression. "What? What's wrong?"

Abby tried to shake off the ugly thought, but it wouldn't budge. Once there, it took hold and expanded. *God, are You sending me a message?*

"What if…"

"What if what?"

"What if my husband's and parents' deaths weren't accidents? They were all killed in car crashes. Don't you think that's odd? The three people closest to me died in car accidents?"

Noah didn't laugh. She appreciated that he took her conspiracy theory seriously.

"I think," he said slowly, "that we'll stop by my old office in New York before we do anything else. I have lots of connections. If your theory is right, we'll need some help, but it's really a long shot. There's too many years between the accidents. It doesn't make any sense. Why would the perpetrator wait so long between murders? There's no motive that we know of."

She nodded, then remembered something. The boxes of pictures Noah had risked his life for. She cringed at the thought. If he had died during the explosion at her grandmother's house, his blood would have been on her hands. Pushing the morbid thought away, she reached behind her seat, grabbed the box and plopped it across her thighs.

Noah glanced at her lap. She grinned at his raised eyebrows when he spotted Grammy's Glock in the box on top of the pictures. The ambulance attendants had rescued the box on the ground beside Noah after the explosion, and it was given to Abby in the hospital. Thankfully no one had looked inside. "A girl's gotta have protection. And I haven't thanked you for saving both the pictures and Grammy's gun. It's amazing that you were able to get both out of the house after the explosion. I didn't take any pictures with me to Texas because I'd planned to move Grammy as soon as it was safe. I was going to go through everything in her attic at that time."

He didn't say a word and she started digging through the pictures. They brought back a lot of memories. Some sad, but mostly good.

She held up one of the photos. "I begged to go to Disney World for over a year. On Christmas morning, I opened a present and there were the tickets." A tear slid down her cheek. "It was a wonderful trip."

"You don't have to do this right now."

She gripped his strong fingers. "Yes, I do. There

might be a clue buried in these pictures. I haven't thanked you for saving them from the fire."

"You're welcome." He grinned. "You were a cute girl."

"And you, Noah Galloway, are a kind liar. I was a chubby kid, but I do have to say I grew out of it when I was about ten. My baby fat just disappeared."

His lips stretched into a big grin and he chuckled. "I'd love to have a cute, chubby baby daughter that looked just like her mama." His grin was replaced by an expression of horror. "I didn't mean…"

She laughed. She hadn't seen Noah at a loss for words since meeting him. He was so in control all the time, it was a relief to see he was human, after all.

"No worries. I didn't take it as a proposal."

They both laughed and Abby absently picked another picture out of the box. Her amusement died, her heart lurched, and frustration took hold.

"What is it?"

She held the picture up where he could see it. "It's another picture of my parents holding that same baby." She scrutinized the background. "I don't remember ever seeing this one. They appear to be at a fair or carnival of some sort. I can't make out any identifying marks or names."

"Keep it out. We'll take it with us to the FBI and see if Simon can find anything."

Her stomach lurched and nausea followed. She could explain away two pictures, but three? What were her parents doing with the same child in three pictures? Her original explanation was beginning to waver. Would they travel to that many places with another couple and have their pictures taken with the other couple's kid?

Dizziness blurred her vision when Noah asked, "Abby, sweetheart, are you sure you're an only child?"

THIRTEEN

Noah jerked the car off the side of the interstate after glancing at Abby. Her face had turned paper white. He slammed the car into Park and took her hand in his.

"Abby, I'm sorry. I shouldn't have said that."

She rolled her shoulders, as if shrugging off a heavy weight. "I'm okay, and you have nothing to be sorry for, but what if you're right? What if I have a sibling?"

He was coming to admire many things about her, especially her fortitude and strength.

"If what you said is true, my whole life is a lie and my parents were dishonest." She firmed her lips. "They took me to church every Sunday. What if we sat in that pew every week and their lives were full of deception?"

She looked frustrated and upset, and he didn't like that his careless words were the cause. "I'm just being silly. I'm sure there's a good explanation for the pictures."

Her eyes were full of hurt and questions. He was determined to give her the answers she desired, but something else in her expression bothered him.

"Abby, whatever we find out about your parents, you can't let it shake your faith."

She snorted and the small sign of normality lifted his spirits.

"This from a man who doesn't go to church anymore?"

He grinned. "Maybe times are changing," he joked.

She smiled and laid the picture back in the box. "There could be a million reasons why my parents had these pictures made, and as you cops like to say, I shouldn't assume anything without proof."

With things calm now, Noah pulled the rental car back onto the highway. "Absolutely true."

A comfortable silence filled the vehicle as Noah drove, his thoughts processing everything that had happened in such a short period of time. He also considered Abby's suggestion about meeting his half sisters. For so many years, he'd blamed his mother for leaving him, but did she really have a choice? Abby had a way of making him rethink his past and look at it from his mother's perspective.

He pulled in to a paid parking garage and tried to gently shake her awake. She had fallen asleep during the long ride. "We're here." She lifted a hand to fidget with her hair and he chuckled.

"Don't worry, you look fine."

She gave him a disgruntled look and fished a comb and compact out of her purse. She responded to his interested stare. "I refuse to meet your friends looking like something my dog dragged in."

He laughed and peered at her purse. "I always wondered what women toted around in those big pocketbooks."

She sliced him a sharp look. "That's none of your business, Noah Galloway."

He held his hands up in mock surrender, then turned serious. "Listen, Abby, you've been through a lot. I can easily place you in a temporary safe house until this is over. Your grandmother is secure at the hospital in North Carolina. I'd prefer you to be protected, too."

Her jaw firmed resolutely. "I'm staying glued to your side until this mess is over. I want to know who's doing this and why. They've turned my life inside out and I want a word with them before they're hauled off to jail for the rest of their lives."

"And the steel magnolia makes an appearance," he muttered.

"I heard that."

"Okay, then, let's go."

Abby invited Bates out of the car and hooked a leash to his collar. They left the parking garage, emerged onto the street and headed toward the FBI building. "Wow," Abby breathed.

Noah guided her across the street. People gave them a wide berth when they noticed the dog.

"Impressive, isn't it?"

"I'll say. You really worked here? It's so different from Blessing."

He shot her a rueful look. "Like night and day."

Without warning, Abby tugged on his sleeve, pulling him to a stop on the sidewalk. "Noah, you said you moved to Blessing to protect Dylan because of the thing with the mayor. Is Dylan's life still in danger? Were all the bad guys caught and put in jail?"

Once again, her concern for him and his son warmed his heart. He explained the situation, hoping to put her mind at ease. "Jack Vitale—Big Jack—was killed during the investigation. We couldn't get enough evidence against his son, Anthony, to put him behind bars. He made a few threats, which is why I moved back to Blessing, but I believe they're empty threats. The FBI keeps close tabs on him and they'll notify me of any changes."

"That's why you leave Dylan with your grandfather when you're gone."

"Dylan is safe on the ranch. There are plenty of ranch hands milling about at any given time, and all of them would spot a stranger a long way off. Plus, Grandpa Houston knows how to shoot a gun, and he won't hesitate to use it if need be. Come on, let's go inside."

Noah led the way and Abby followed him through the front doors. They had to go through security, and she threw him an endearing, embarrassed glance when she had to empty the contents of her purse into a container for security. He grinned at the amount of stuff she had, but knew better than to comment on the things a woman thought she needed to cart around everywhere. There were several questions and a few snafus about the dog, and then they were on their way.

An elevator took them to the twenty-third floor and they stepped into his comfortable past. The boisterous office was loud and filled with numerous cubicles. People ran to and fro all over the place. Many had phones glued to their ears and several stood in their cubicles, shouting across the room.

It felt like coming home, and he missed it, but Noah had no regrets. Blessing was a great place to raise Dylan, and he was starting to appreciate the peace and quiet more every day versus the hustle and bustle of New York. He was a country boy at heart.

An old friend walked down the aisle, looked up,

grinned and shouted to the room at large. "Look what the cat dragged in. If it isn't Sheriff Galloway, returned to the big city."

The man slapped Noah on the back and a group of men surrounded him, all talking at once. He was aware of Abby standing outside of the close-knit circle. Noah had always gotten along with most of his former coworkers.

Except one.

"And who have we here?"

Noah whipped around and moved to Abby's side. "Back off, Romeo. She's with me."

Noah gave the guy his due. He'd guess most women would consider him good-looking in his starched shirt and pressed jeans. He waggled his brows at Abby and Noah didn't like it.

All the men laughed.

"Stay away from him. He loves all women." Noah tried to make his comment sound humorous, but he didn't quite manage it through his clenched teeth.

Abby smiled and Noah took her hand. There was a round of Ho Hos before he sobered and put a stop to the silly nonsense.

"Abby's having a few problems and we need some help."

Like turning off a light switch, the men went from jovial to solemn in an instant. Every man there offered to help Noah in any way needed and Abby blinked back the moisture in her eyes. They were so nice. It was obvious Noah was well respected and well liked by his peers.

He pulled her through the group toward a large office at the back of the room. Through the glass walls she spotted two men, one seated behind a large desk and the other standing in front of it.

"Good. Just the people we need to see."

Bates picked up on Abby's anxiety and released a low rumble. She rested her hand on his head as they followed Noah. "It's okay, baby. I'm just a tad nervous. No one in their right mind would want to visit an FBI office."

Noah must have overheard her. He shot her a quick grin over his shoulder before the two guys in the office greeted him with enthusiasm. It was interesting to see him in this environment.

With his notoriety in saving the mayor's life, she assumed a small amount of jealousy abounded in the office, too. She hoped she looked okay when Noah turned to introduce her.

"Abby, meet Director Henry Wilson, my old boss, and this crazy guy is my former partner, Alex Ridenhour."

Both men had firm, but non-ego-enhanced handshakes. Abby liked their smiles. "Nice to meet you, gentlemen. This guy beside me is Bates, my best friend and the greatest protection dog in the world."

Director Wilson grinned. "I hear a strong Southern accent, and, please, call me Henry."

"You're right. I was born and bred in North Carolina, south of the Mason–Dixon Line, and you may call me Abby."

Everyone in the room laughed and Noah's eyes lit with amusement. His twinkle of pleasure warmed her entire being.

The ice was broken and Henry got down to business.

"Noah, Alex tells me the two of you have run into a few problems down in Texas."

Noah pulled a third chair in front of Henry's desk and the three of them sat down.

"Yes, sir. I called on Alex and Simon to help out with a few things, but our problems have become complicated and we need resources I don't have available in Texas. I don't have enough information to warrant bringing in the FBI, but—"

Henry interrupted and waved away Noah's concerns. "No problem. Tell me what's going on and how we can help."

Their smiles turned into grimaces as Noah explained their situation.

A frown creased the director's forehead and he turned his attention toward Abby. "You have no idea who may be doing this?"

Everyone stared at her, as if she should have the answers. "I'm sorry, I don't have any idea who's behind any of this, but I plan on finding out, no matter how long it takes or what I have to do." Anger laced her next words. "They hurt my grandmother."

Director Wilson's eyebrows rose at her forcefulness, but she'd had enough. It was time for action.

The director glanced at Noah and grinned. "I can see why you like it down there in Texas."

The men laughed, then went straight to the matter at hand.

"Alex, get Fisher on board. Let's see if we can get a picture of Fleming, Ferguson and the unknown man."

Noah explained. "Abby, Joe Fisher is the best sketch artist the FBI has on staff. If you can describe Joanne, Walter and the unknown man, he'll draw them and we'll run the pictures through our system, see if anything shows up. I'll also work with him on Fleming and our unknown, since I've seen both of them."

Director Wilson gave more orders to Alex. "Get Simon to examine the picture placed at the carnival. Maybe he can dig out a location where the shot was taken, and also see how he's coming with the partial plate number."

Abby nodded at Noah, dug the picture out of her purse and handed it to the director.

Noah cleared his throat and Director Wilson raised a questioning brow in his direction. "Abby insists on being involved in the investigation."

Noah's former boss sighed. "It's your responsibility and your call. You no longer work for the FBI."

Noah gave him a crooked grin. "Thanks. I appreciate the help."

Abby stood when Noah rose. He reached across the desk to shake Wilson's hand. "You have my cell number. I'll take Abby down to Joe's office."

Director Wilson grimaced at Abby. "Please accept my apologies in advance for the state of Joe's office. He's not the neatest person."

She nodded, but before she could follow Noah out of the director's office there was a quick knock and the door was slung wide-open. A young guy—he looked like he belonged in high school with his old sneakers, torn-at-the-knee jeans and ratty sweatshirt—practically ran them down as he rushed into the room. His eyes lit up when he spotted Noah.

"Noah! I heard you were in the building." He straightened his shoulders as he stood in front of them.

"I've been good. I swear it." The kid glanced at Alex, and Abby smiled at his exuberance. "Tell him, Alex."

He jerked his gaze back toward Noah without waiting for Alex to answer. "I have straight As this semester and I haven't broken into any computers except when Director Wilson told me to."

Abby grinned at Noah and he chuckled. "Abby, this is Simon, and I'll explain his role here at the FBI later," he whispered.

To Simon, he said, "That's good to hear. Did you track me down for a reason?"

It was then Simon noticed Abby standing to the side. He flushed an unbecoming red and stammered. "S-sorry, ma'am, I didn't see you there."

Noah took charge. "Simon!"

"Yes. I concentrated on the car and the plate beginning with the letters *C-A-M*. We're running them through the DMV, but I also connected my computer with every major traffic cam, including airport security cameras, to try to track the movement of car itself." In an aside, he said to Abby, "The terrorism threats make it easy for me to find stuff. We have cameras all over the place now."

She kept quiet and he continued, "I had Franny— that's my computer's name—run a cross-reference to see what plates crossed state lines in the last twelve months and where they went."

He beamed and Noah sighed. "And?"

"A beige sedan popped up at the Charlotte airport and on a street in New York, but there's a problem."

"And that is?" Noah asked patiently.

Simon studied the hole in his sneaker. "I got a clear

visual on the letters—*C-A-M*—but it looked like someone smeared mud on the rest of the plate."

Abby's heart sank. Every time they took one step
forward, if felt as if they took two steps back.

FOURTEEN

Abby's disappointment was palpable. Noah waved her forward, indicating she should precede him out of the director's office. He wanted to roar in frustration. He had learned patience during his tenure at the FBI, but had a burning desire to slay all of Abby's dragons and help her get her life back.

He was also dealing with his attraction to her, and he was beginning to have doubts about the wisdom of that. He'd kissed her, but maybe it was time to take a step back. Being in New York had reminded him of his previous life, and the agony he'd lived through as Sonya lay dying in a hospital bed while he stood by, unable to do a thing to help as the insidious cancer ravaged her body.

He didn't think he could go through that again. Loving a woman so much his heart ached, then watching her slowly fade away.

"Abby, it's been a long day. Why don't we grab a bite to eat, find a hotel and get some rest before we connect with Joe?"

She surprised him when she pivoted sharply and faced him, her mouth a grim line. "I'm not tired. Well, maybe a little, but I want answers. I'll work all night if Joe's willing."

Joe would be willing. He practically lived in his office.

Worry and trepidation shone out of her eyes. As much as he wanted to order her to eat and get a good night's sleep, he couldn't find it in his heart to do so.

"If you're sure."

She nodded and he turned toward the elevator. "Come on, then, but prepare yourself. Joe Fisher has his own little hovel that the FBI rented especially for him in the bowels of the building. As a general rule, he doesn't like people—and has very few social skills—hence his private space, but he's the best in the business."

As the elevator descended, Noah tried to erase his last images of Sonya, the day of her death. He thought he'd properly mourned her passing, but with the move to Blessing, and raising his son, Noah now wondered if that was true.

Bates whined during the elevator ride, interrupting his morbid thoughts. Abby placed a calming hand on the dog's head until they stepped off into an underground level of the building. A musty odor assailed his senses as Abby followed him down a plain, narrow hall lit by harsh, florescent lights, a few of which blinked in an annoying fashion.

They stopped in front of a door with peeling paint and Noah knocked twice. No one answered so he called through the door. "Joe, it's Noah. Open the door or I'll break it down."

A gruff voice answered back. "Hold your cotton-pickin' taters."

Abby chuckled. "I take it he's from the South?"

Noah grinned. "You two should get along great."

She poked him in the arm. "You're from Texas."

"True, but I worked in New York long enough to lose some of my roots."

She gave him a saucy grin. "Don't worry, you'll be back to normal before you know it."

The door swung open and a familiar, man of indeterminate age dressed in wrinkled khakis and a rumpled shirt stood in front of them. His hair was mussed and a pair of wire-rimmed glasses were perched on the end of his nose.

"What?"

Noah pushed his way through the door and Abby followed him. The room was a disaster. Papers littered the floor around a wastebasket and old fast-food wrappers and containers were strewed everywhere. The only saving grace was one corner of the room. It had a comfortable-looking couch, two chairs and proper lighting. Noah knew it to be his work area.

"What? No 'hello'? 'How are you, Noah? Glad to see you again'?"

Joe grumped. "I'd have called if I wanted to talk."

Noah motioned Abby forward. "This is Abby Mayfield. We need three sketches done. Already approved by Henry."

Abby held out her hand. "Nice to meet you, Joe."

The man grinned and Noah decided it'd been a while since Joe had been to the dentist for a cleaning. Joe scrutinized Abby. "You from the South?"

"Yes."

"What part?"

"Mocksville, North Carolina."

"Good. Okay, then, let's get started."

Noah shot her a befuddled look. "What is it with you guys? Is there some sort of secret handshake between Southerners?"

Abby grinned and took a seat on the sofa. "If I told you, it wouldn't be a secret, now, would it?"

Joe snorted and Noah made himself comfortable in one of the two chairs. Joe pulled the third chair close to Abby and, with a sketch pad in hand, started firing questions.

They began with Joanne Ferguson. Joe had a litany of queries.

"Wide or narrow nose? Broad, slanted or flat forehead? Eyebrows thick or thin, slanted or straight across? Mouth—large or small? Lips—full or slim? Chin—square and strong or weak? Length, texture and thickness of hair? Hair color? Eye color?"

The list went on forever and Abby started squirming in her seat. Finally, Joe flipped the sketch pad around and Noah heard her gasp.

"It's her! It's Joanne Ferguson. Joe, you're a genius."

Joe preened and Noah grimaced. "Don't give him a big head. He knows he's good."

Sitting up straight in her chair, Abby turned to Noah with renewed energy. "But, Noah, now we have a picture of her. Can't the FBI run her through the system and find out who she is?"

Being a sharp lady, Abby didn't miss the subtle message Noah sent Joe.

"Listen, you two, I'm not some wilting Southern flower who has to have a man's protection. I have Bates, a gun and a brain. I know how to use all three.

Just because I'm a choir director doesn't mean I can't protect myself."

"Steel magnolia with a thin veneer of Southern genteel," Noah muttered to Joe.

"Understood. I'm well acquainted with the type. You've never met my mother."

Abby looked like she wanted to pull her hair out, or maybe his, Noah thought, grimacing.

"What, exactly, aren't y'all telling me?"

Joe leaned back in his chair, crossed his arms over his waist and left the explanations to Noah.

Noah sighed. "It's not that simple. Yes, we'll run the picture through the FBI database and hope for the best, but that doesn't mean we'll find a match. If Ferguson and Fleming are as savvy as I think they are, they likely altered their appearances so they couldn't be identified."

Curiosity lit her eyes. "You mean like plastic surgery?"

Joe jumped in. "That's a possibility, but you can use commercial makeup and prosthetics to change your appearance. For example, you can pad your chin or nose, or change the structure of your face with an elaborate mask. And hair color can easily be changed."

Abby huffed. "The one thing I do know is Joanne Ferguson is a true brunette. I can spot a dye job a mile away. The woman sang in my choir for four months and I never saw discolored roots."

"Listen, Abby, Simon is the best. If there's not an immediate match, we now have computer programs that can add and delete facial changes and come up with possible matches. It's a long shot, but possible."

She took a deep breath. "Fine. Let's get the other two

done and we'll go from there." At about four o'clock in the morning, Joe finished the last sketch.

They had a perfect rendering of Walter Fleming, at least how he appeared now, and Joe had finished the image of the unknown man who'd helped save Abby's and Noah's lives. Joe sat, studying it for a moment. He looked at Abby, then back at the sketch again, a weird look on his face.

"Well, what does he look like?" Her words came out sounding tired and cranky. Noah was feeling those sentiments himself. It had been a long day.

Joe shot Noah one of those secret FBI looks and Abby exploded, "Just show me the picture!"

Wrinkles marred Joe's forehead as he slowly turned the sketch pad around. "In answer to your question, he's a male version of you."

As soon as she caught sight of the drawing, Abby swayed. Noah was at her side in an instant, yelling for Joe to get a glass of water.

Abby ignored Noah's concern and grabbed the sketch pad Joe had thrown in his chair after running to get her some water. "Why didn't I see it sooner? I should have known. I have a brother."

Noah could only imagine what she was feeling. He took the sketch pad from her hands and placed it on the sofa cushion. "Abby, we don't know that for sure. Remember what Joe said about changing one's appearance. Whoever's after you could have planned this to throw you off their scent. In the FBI we call it misdirection."

Her eyes softened at his attempt to console her, but he pulled back, both physically and emotionally. He wasn't ready for this. Her eyes reflected a moment of hurt, but she took a deep breath and said, "Thanks,

Noah. I'm okay. Maybe I'm not so tough, after all. It would never occur to me that someone would go to such lengths to hurt another human being." She paused and pressed a hand against her heart. "Do you think this is a horrible, mean trick, or is there a real possibility I may have a brother out there somewhere?"

"Anything is possible, Abby, but there is one thing I know. I'll do everything in my power to find out the truth. Why don't we grab a bite to eat and get some sleep?"

Joe came rushing into the room with a glass of water in hand. The poor guy looked terrified of a crying woman. Noah had been known to have the same weakness.

Abby stood and gave Joe a big hug, and Noah's gut clenched when her arms went around his old friend. "Thanks for everything, Joe." She brushed a friendly kiss against his cheek and a light blush covered his face. "We'll come and visit when this is over."

"Y'all do that now, and let me know what happens."

"We will," Abby said, and Noah led the way out the door.

The next morning, Noah awoke and stretched the kinks and soreness out of his body before swinging his legs over the side of the bed. Between the car crash and the explosion at Abby's grandmother's house, he had more than a few aches and pains.

The clock on the nightstand read seven thirty. It was much later than he usually slept, but they hadn't gotten to bed until after five o'clock in the morning. They could have gone to bed sooner, but Abby refused to stay in the condo the FBI kept on hand for various uses. She claimed it wasn't proper for them to stay in the same

space, so he'd had to hunt down a hotel that allowed
dogs and had two rooms available in Manhattan during the wee hours of the morning. It aggravated him,
but he also respected her for sticking to her principles.

In his line of work, he didn't come across women
like Abby Mayfield often. She was beautiful, with her
soft blond hair, petite stature and big brown eyes. But
it was her quirky, strong, interesting personality that
drew him in like a magnet. A magnet he was working
hard to disengage from.

He grabbed his cell phone, disconnected it from the
charger and called Abby in the room next door.

"Noah?" she whispered.

"It's time to rise and shine."

"Noah," she said, louder this time. "Someone's rattling the doorknob to my room. It sounds like they're
trying to jimmy the lock."

"Hold tight," he shouted into the phone before
throwing the device onto the bed. A surge of adrenaline shot through him, alleviating all signs of morning
drowsiness as he ran for his door. Flinging it open, he
spotted the back of a man disappearing through the
stairwell door. Abby's door creaked open and he yelled
over his shoulder, "Get back inside and lock the door.
Stay put until I return."

He heard the door slam shut. Knowing she was safe,
he lit out after the man, but by the time he reached the
ground floor, the guy had disappeared. Noah bent over
and placed his hands on his knees, trying to catch his
breath. His mind raced with possibilities. From his
brief glance at the man, he couldn't tell if it was Walter Fleming.

He slapped his thighs in frustration. Who wanted

Abby dead, and more important, why? Nothing made sense. He turned back toward the stairs, and determination and fear for Abby's life hurried his climb up the steps. He took a deep breath and centered himself while approaching her door. He knocked and she threw it wide-open, flying into his arms.

He pulled her arms from around his neck and took a step back. Abby moved away, a confused and embarrassed look on her face.

"Oh, I'm sorry. I thought after that kiss…"

Noah held out a hand in supplication. "Abby…"

She backed away farther. "No problem, I completely understand. Now, did you get a good look at the guy? Did he have a gun?"

Noah wanted to say more, to explain, but maybe it was better this way.

"I'm fine. He got away. I couldn't identify the man."

She gave a jerky nod. "Okay, then. As long as you're safe."

Noah ached to comfort her and remove her fear, but gave a brisk nod instead. "Let's get dressed, grab some breakfast here in the hotel and head back to the FBI office."

Abby pulled her pink robe tightly around her waist. "Yes, okay. I'll be ready in half an hour."

Noah left her room and returned to his own. He closed off his emotions and concentrated on the investigation—what steps they should take next—while showering and dressing for the day. He buried the image of Abby's soft brown eyes widened in fear. He would never have allowed her to stay in a room alone if Bates hadn't been with her. That dog was the only reason he'd gotten any sleep at all.

FIFTEEN

Entering the FBI building, Abby felt a measure of relief and safety. She hadn't realized how tense she'd been until this very moment. She thanked God her grandmother had insisted she buy a protection dog before moving to Texas. Noah was noted in his profession as being the best, but he was only one man.

She squelched her emotions concerning Noah. One minute he was kissing her, and the next minute he was pulling away. His actions had hurt, but she had enough on her plate without worrying about his mixed signals.

She followed him through the hustle and bustle of the FBI room toward the big office at the back. A few greetings were yelled across the room, but he barely acknowledged them. He'd been all business since leaving the hotel. Not that they had a relationship or anything—he'd only kissed her once but, still, they'd been through a lot together.

She wasn't even sure she wanted a close bond with a man in such a dangerous profession. She sighed as she followed him into his former boss's office with Bates trotting at her side. Life used to be a lot simpler. And she thought dealing with church politics was complicated. It was nothing compared to what Noah did every day, putting his life at risk when he went to work.

He had called ahead. Everyone was waiting, crammed into the office. Greetings were short and they got down to business after everyone took a seat.

Noah fired the opening salvo. "Someone tried to break into Abby's hotel room early this morning. I chased them down the stairwell, but lost them. I can't identify the man. As far as I could tell, he doesn't resemble anyone we've dealt with so far. The security cameras were useless—bad lighting in the stairwell and the guy wore a baseball cap. He was smart enough to keep his face turned away from the cameras."

It was depressing how few clues they had, Abby mused.

The door banged open and Simon came rushing in, clutching a file folder in his hand. His rumpled clothes looked suspiciously similar to the ones he had worn the previous day. Abby wondered if any of the FBI agents ever slept as all eyes focused on Simon.

He slouched into the empty chair beside Abby. "Sorry. I was up late studying for an exam."

Abby remembered Noah had said Simon was also attending school. "You have an awful lot on your plate," she whispered.

Simon studied the toe of his scuffed sneaker. "It was this or go to jail."

His annoyed tone tickled Abby. "Good choice."

"Yeah," he said before Director Wilson took firm control of the meeting.

"Simon, what do you have for us?"

Simon straightened in his chair, and Abby thought having him work for the FBI while in college was a good idea. He was experiencing things most young men his age would never see in a lifetime.

"I'm still eliminating license plates that begin with the letters *C-A-M*, specifically searching for a cream or beige sedan. Franny's running Joe's sketches of Joanne Ferguson, Walter Fleming and the unknown guy as we speak. I'll let you know if anything pops."

Abby remembered Franny as the name of Simon's computer and smiled. It was good to forget about Noah's cold shoulder for a while.

"I've been trying to track down information on Abby's parents' backgrounds, but their lives are a total blank until right before she was born in North Carolina. Their Social Security numbers are bogus."

Abby stiffened. Noah had asked Simon to search her parents' backgrounds without talking to her first? That was the reason for going to her grandmother's house in the first place, but how dare he do so without her permission? One of her biggest fears was that they'd find something that would hurt Grammy. Surely they could figure out who was after her without destroying the only family she had left. Noah must have found their Social Security numbers mixed in with the box of pictures they'd saved. She shot Noah a disgruntled look, but he still had that stony-face thing going.

Director Wilson addressed the group. "We need to look at Abby's parents' and husband's deaths."

Nausea churned in her stomach, but she swallowed hard and gritted her teeth. She would get through this. Noah hadn't even glanced at her at the announcement, and it hurt, but she held her head high and addressed the group.

"As I've explained to Noah, my husband died three

years ago in a car crash. There were no other vehicles involved. The police reported it as a terrible accident."

Memories swamped her, the loss of a husband and an unborn child so close together, but she pushed them away. "My parents died in a car crash while vacationing in Jackson Hole, Wyoming. It, too, was deemed an accident. There were no other vehicles involved that time, either."

Describing both accidents at the same time did sound suspicious.

"Why did they choose Jackson Hole for a vacation?" the director asked.

The question threw her off balance. "I don't know. I was only six at the time. They left me with Grammy. She might have some information that will help."

"I understand your grandmother is in a hospital in North Carolina in an induced coma. Is that right?" Director Wilson asked.

"Yes, she is, because whoever these people are, they attacked her and put her there." Abby didn't even try to hide the vehemence in her voice. Every time she thought of her grandmother lying in that sterile hospital bed, it broke her heart.

Alex Ridenhour spoke for the first time that morning. "My team will comb through the reports on her parents' and husband's deaths. We'll also see what we can find out about their trip to Jackson Hole, but it's going to be a cold trail."

A million thoughts swamped Abby's tired, overwhelmed mind, but something kept nagging her. She couldn't quite put her finger on it…then suddenly it became crystal clear.

"Y'all can do whatever you want to, but I'm going to Wyoming."

The room burst into chaotic speech.

"You're a civilian. I won't be held responsible for placing you at risk." This from Noah's former boss, Henry Wilson.

"No way! You shouldn't even be allowed to accompany Noah," Alex Ridenhour added his two cents' worth.

"Absolutely not. I forbid it." The last, and most hurtful, objection came from Noah.

Bates released a low growl and Abby placed a calming hand on his head. He had taken a position on the floor beside her. "That's right, I'm a civilian. Y'all can't tell me where I can go or what I can do. I'll accompany Noah anywhere he goes, and if he doesn't want me tagging along, I'll go by myself. As a teacher, I know how to get people to open up and talk. I expect I'll find out more than any of you. I have Bates and my grandmother's Glock. I can take care of myself."

Noah's glacial mask had fallen away, replaced by a look of horror. Good! She was sick and tired of his stony, closed expression.

"Why, Abby?"

Her anger subsided. She knew he was worried about her, and she appreciated that, but she would stand firm. "I think there are secrets in Jackson Hole. I intend to unearth every one of them. I will not risk my grandmother getting hurt again." She took a deep breath. "And if that means rooting out every dark, nasty family secret, I will."

She realized, in that moment, in order to stop these terrible people, she and Grammy both would have to deal with whatever secrets they uncovered. It was the only way to stay safe and be able to move forward with their lives.

After shedding her reluctance at delving into family secrets, Abby felt free and wanted to get on with it. She stood and looked straight at Noah. "Well, are you coming or not?"

He stood, but talked to the guys before following her out of the room.

"Alex, I'll call if we run into trouble."

"No problem."

"Simon, let me know as soon as you find anything."

"You got it," came his reply.

Abby could only imagine the looks of pity Noah received from his former colleagues, but now that she had decided to open her family's can of worms, she had a burning desire to know the truth. Good or bad.

"Lord, help me," she said softly under her breath, as Noah followed her out the door and through the maze of cubicles.

Noah stole a glance at Abby as she stared out of the plane window while they waited for takeoff. He knew he'd hurt her, but it was for the best, even though it left an empty, hollow place deep inside him.

After leaving the FBI offices, they had gathered their luggage, checked out of the hotel, grabbed a bite to eat and made reservations to fly to Jackson Hole. The last-minute tickets cost a mint, but Noah refused to allow Abby to pay the airfare, even though she tried to insist.

He paid extra for bulkhead seats so Bates would have plenty of room to lie at their feet. Abby had attired the dog with his special vest, but she allowed several kids to pet him as they boarded the plane.

Even though Noah had stepped back from their budding relationship, he wanted and needed to understand exactly what had happened to her husband and parents. In his line of work, he'd seen the most congenial of people turn out to be serial killers.

He stayed quiet while she sent several texts.

"Everything okay?"

She tucked her phone inside her purse. "Yes. I had to check on several of my students. If you'll remember, we have a big recital coming up, along with the Christmas play. That's if we can find a place to have them, since the church is gone."

Her voice wobbled at the end of her sentence and it shattered the thin layer of ice he'd been building around his heart.

They were given instructions to buckle up, and he waited until the plane was fully in the air before shifting sideways in his seat. "Abby, listen to me. The explosion at the church wasn't your fault. We'll track down the culprits and they'll spend the rest of their lives in prison."

"That won't pay for the church," she grumbled, and Noah was glad to see her spirits lift.

"I'm sure the church has insurance."

She turned in her seat and fire lit her eyes. Good. He'd take irritation any day over despondency.

"I wish I'd kept more of the life insurance money. I'd rebuild the church myself. You know how those insurance companies are. They never pay enough to restore things like they were."

"If the money comes up short, I have no doubt you

can raise what's needed. There are a lot of good people in Blessing who will contribute to seeing their church rebuilt, and they won't blame you. From what I've heard, the people of Blessing love their new choir director."

She squirmed in her seat, as if embarrassed. "Well, I love them, too, but you're not going to sweeten me up with pretty words. I'm still upset that you asked Alex to look into the deaths of my husband and parents without talking to me first. Not that I don't think it's a good idea, I want these people caught and I'm willing to lay my life open to make it happen. I just wish you'd had the courtesy to speak to me before you brought it up in front of everyone."

He cleared his throat. "Abby, I'll do whatever it takes to keep you safe, and if that means upsetting you with my methods, then so be it."

"Listen, Noah, I know you mean well, and I appreciate all your help, but I'm at the center of this mess. I don't know what's going on, but I mean to find out. If that means dragging my family's name through the mud, then I'm willing to do that. My grandmother's life is more important than anything."

"Your life is more important than anything, too."

"Well, we should make plans for when we reach Jackson Hole. Like where we should start first."

Noah straightened in his seat and faced forward. "I called the sheriff in Jackson while we were waiting in the airport. We'll rent a car when we land and head straight to his office. He's expecting us. Why don't you close your eyes and get some rest?"

Noah followed his own advice, hoping Abby would do the same, but his mind raced with the information they had and didn't have. Why did Abby's parents decide to take that fateful trip to Jackson Hole, and why did the pictures of an unknown child in their arms keep popping up? Noah was afraid Abby wouldn't be happy with the answers.

SIXTEEN

Abby woke up with a start when the plane's wheels bumped against the landing strip. She checked on Bates. He had been trained to fly, but wasn't happy about it. His ears stood up straight, but he didn't whine. Abby patted his head. "Good boy," she crooned.

Beside her, Noah chuckled. "I've never been thrilled about flying, either."

Abby yawned. "I never would have thought I could sleep after everything that's happened."

Noah stretched his legs out. "I had a few winks myself."

He shifted in his seat and Abby glanced at him. "Is something wrong?"

His eyes bored into hers, as if seeking answers. "Abby, are you sure you're ready to deal with what we might find? The place where your parents died?"

Was she ready? "To be honest, I don't know, but I'm going to dig as hard as I can and ask God for His grace and protection no matter what we discover."

He studied her a moment longer and gave a short nod. "Okay."

The plane landed and people were lined up in the

aisle trying to be the first off. They waited until the last person passed by, then Noah grabbed their carry-on luggage from the overhead bin.

Abby bid the flight attendants goodbye.

Stepping off the small airplane, she took a deep breath of frigid air and smiled for the first time in what seemed like centuries. It was November, and snow covered everything. It looked like a winter wonderland.

Noah grinned. "Beautiful, isn't it?"

"Yes," she breathed. Fog puffed out of her mouth. She pulled her coat tighter around her. "And cold. You've been here before?"

He had both their bags and carried them as if they weighed ounces instead of pounds. "Yep. Couple of years back I came to Jackson on business."

Abby assumed that meant FBI business, but she didn't want to discuss investigations. For just a few minutes, as they walked toward the airport building, she wanted to immerse herself in God's glorious creations. Pine tree boughs hung low due to the weight of the snow, and red cardinals stood out in stark relief. A few flakes swirled around her, and Abby thought Jackson Hole a romantic place. A gush of warm air hit her when they stepped inside the terminal. After retrieving their checked luggage and weapons, they rented a SUV and were on their way.

She continued her moments of peace by staring out the window, when all of a sudden, she saw a huge mountain to their left with skiers racing down the steep slope. "Wow. That's gorgeous."

"Jackson Hole consists of two parts. We're in the town of Jackson, and that mountain you're admiring is Jackson's ski mountain. A few miles to the west is a place called Teton Village. The Teton mountain is the steepest ski slope in the United States. Jackson Hole is also one of the coldest. A bus runs between Jackson and Teton Village every thirty minutes all day, every day, carrying tourists between the two places."

Noah pulled the SUV to the curb in front of the police station and Abby's momentary peace was shattered. She didn't want to deal with the ugly things going on in her life, but she didn't have a choice. She grabbed the door handle and slid out of the car before Noah had a chance to do the gentlemanly thing and help her out. It was better if he didn't touch her, considering the recent past. She was dying to know what had caused him to back off, but now wasn't the time to delve into things probably better left alone.

She wanted answers and she wanted her life back. The only way to make that happen was to face her problems head-on. Grammy would be proud. As if sensing her resolve, Noah moved in front of her and opened the station door. The heat warmed her body, but she was still chilled at the thought of what was to come.

The woman at the front desk called out, "Can I help you?"

Abby felt more comfortable here than at the FBI office. Just like her, these were small-town people. A Christmas tree with children's names hanging in place of ornaments stood lit in one corner. The front desk had been decorated with a strand of greenery.

Noah took the lead. "Sheriff Hoyt is expecting us. Noah Galloway and Abigail Mayfield."

The older woman carried a few extra pounds and was bundled in a heavy Christmas sweater and slacks.

Her eyes crinkled merrily when she spoke. She reminded Abby of a sweet little grandmother.

"Ethan told me you were coming. Y'all are a long way from home." Abby knew the woman was dying to know what they were doing in Jackson Hole. She considered it a credit to Sheriff Hoyt that he hadn't spread their business around the office. Noah took care of the woman's nosiness by raising a brow.

She straightened an already neat stack of papers on her desk. "Yes, well, his office is down the hall, first door on the left."

"Thank you," Noah said, and headed in that direction, but Abby lingered behind. She had a few seeds to sow. Abby read the name tag on the desk—Mrs. Wanda Armstrong—and figured the woman probably knew everything that happened in the town of Jackson, and she was about the right age. Wanda would have been a young woman when Abby's parents came to Jackson all those years ago.

"Mrs. Armstrong—"

"Call me Wanda."

It was a good start. "And please call me Abby."

Wanda stuck out a hand. "Nice to meetcha, Abby."

Abby shook her hand, propped her elbows on the raised front part of the desk and leaned forward, inviting a good gossip. "Sorry about Noah. You know how men are, worried to death somebody will impede their investigations."

Wanda bobbed her head. "I know what you mean. Sometimes it's the small, overlooked details that solve a problem."

Bingo! Abby had her. Noah and Sheriff Hoyt could conduct their investigation the way they saw fit, but

Abby would stir the local gossip pot and hopefully come up with some information.

Abby lowered her voice. "We're here because twenty-two years ago, my parents died in a car crash in Jackson."

Wanda commiserated. "Oh, I'm sorry to hear that. What were their names?"

"Mary and Lee Beauchamp. My last name is Mayfield. I married, but my husband was also the victim of a car crash. My maiden name is Beauchamp."

Wanda clucked. "You poor dear. To lose one's parents and husband, too. Is that why you're in Jackson? To find out more about your parents' deaths?"

Abby didn't want her life story bandied all over town, so she skirted around the truth. "Partly. Some new information has come to light and Sheriff Galloway has reason to believe that their deaths might not have been an accident."

Wanda's hand flew to her heart. "Oh, my."

Abby grabbed a pen and piece of paper sitting on top of the desk and scribbled down her cell number. She passed it to Wanda. "If you know of anyone who might remember my parents being here all those years ago, I sure would appreciate it."

Wanda grabbed the paper, determination lighting her eyes. "I'll start calling around now."

Abby stood straight. Her work here was done. "Thank you so much. I sure do appreciate people like you, kind enough to help a stranger in need."

It was the right thing to say. She hurried down the hall and heard a heavy tread coming toward her. She met Noah halfway.

"What were you doing?" he asked.

She gave him a smug smile. "Just planting a few seeds, Noah, just planting a few seeds."

Noah let it go. He'd been surprised before entering Sheriff Hoyt's office to realize Abby wasn't behind him. She had something up her sleeve, but he'd find out later what she was up to.

Sheriff Hoyt rose from his desk after they knocked and he invited them in.

Hoyt was tall, about six-four, with the weathered face of a rancher. He didn't wear a standard uniform, but was decked out in faded jeans and a Western shirt. From his last visit, several years back, Noah remembered that Hoyt, along with being the town's sheriff, also owned a spread a few miles outside of town. He ran a small herd of cattle, if memory served.

"Noah, good to see you again." He turned to Abby. "And who's this pretty little lady with you?"

Noah also remembered that Hoyt was single, his wife having passed on from a heart attack early in their marriage. Ethan Hoyt was about Noah's age, and jealousy shot straight through Noah, causing his reply to come out short and brisk, even though it was his choice not to pursue Abby. "This is Abigail Mayfield. Abby, meet Ethan Hoyt, sheriff of Jackson."

Hoyt's eyebrows rose at the shortness of Noah's tone, and curiosity crossed his features as he studied Noah and Abby. He held out a hand to Abby. "Nice to meet you, Abigail Mayfield. Everyone take a seat and we'll see how I can help you. Noah didn't tell me your reason for visiting our fair city."

Noah didn't pull any punches. "Someone is trying to kill Abby and we have very few leads." The affable, small-town sheriff disappeared and Hoyt's eyes sharpened. Noah had researched Hoyt the last time he'd dealt with him. The good sheriff had left a job in Chicago as a top detective for a simpler, safer life in Wyoming after he married. He'd decided to stay on after his wife died.

"Tell me more."

It took a while for Noah to fill Hoyt in on everything that had happened in North Carolina and Texas. He added everything the FBI was tracking down. "I'll have Joe send copies of the sketches of Ferguson, Fleming and the unknown man to your office."

Hoyt whistled long and hard. "And you think Abby's parents' deaths are connected?"

Noah leaned back in his chair. "That's what we're here to find out."

Hoyt nodded at Bates and addressed Abby. "Is that a trained protection dog?"

"Yes, but he's also a pet," Abby said. Noah choked back a chuckle. He couldn't wait to see Hoyt's face when Abby used one of her commands.

Hoyt's chair creaked when he followed Noah's lead and leaned back. "My resources are at your disposal. I'll help any way I can. If you run into trouble, call me immediately."

"First, we'll need the accident reports. Alex is going to follow up on that, but I'd like to take a look at them."

Hoyt grimaced and Noah's heart sank.

"We had a fire several years ago. The town had just hired someone to computerize all the records, but they went up in flames. It should have been done years ago, but the county budget is always tight."

Noah sat there, thinking. "Was it arson?"

"It was, but we never caught the arsonist." Hoyt looked at him sharply. "You think there's a connection?"

Noah stood. "I don't know, but it seems awfully convenient. Thanks for your help. I'll be in touch."

Hoyt touched the brim of an imaginary hat. "Ma'am. And I'll be waiting to hear from you, Galloway. Keep me posted."

Noah followed Abby out of the office, his mind racing a mile a minute. Had the fire been set to destroy a specific accident report, or was it coincidental?

Abby pulled away and moved to the front desk when the woman with the big hair they'd met earlier waved her down. Noah followed and was jerked out of his musings when he caught the last part of the conversation.

"What did you say?" he bluntly asked the woman. The name plate on the desk said Wanda Armstrong. "Wanda," he added for good measure.

Wanda gave him a wide smile. "I was just telling Abby that I tracked down where her parents stayed when they visited Jackson all those years ago. It's a bed-and-breakfast just down the street. Old Mrs. Denton has owned the place forever, and she fondly remembers Mary and Lee Beauchamp staying there, but that's not the best part. Mrs. Denton said the nice couple also had the cutest little boy with them."

The information hit Noah like a steam engine but he knew it had to be worse for Abby. The unidentified child in the pictures? Could it be?

One look at Abby's face had Noah thanking Wanda for the information and pulling Abby out the door. She was shell-shocked and her hands were freezing.

He herded Bates into the back seat and prodded Abby into the passenger seat. He turned the ignition on and put the heat on full blast. Her expression reminded him of soldiers coming back from war. The empty, dazed looks in their eyes. It scared him spitless.

"Abby. Look at me."

No response. Noah grabbed both her hands and blew on them. "Abby. Please say something. I need you here with me."

Finally, finally, she turned her head toward him. "The child in the picture…"

"I know. We'll find out what's going on. I promise."

She closed her eyes, as if in prayer, and Noah said a silent one himself. He begged God to help them solve this case before someone else got hurt or, worse, killed. The people after Abby meant business and he was the only one standing between them and her.

Bates whined and shook Abby out of her frozen state. "I'm fine. I'll be okay in just a minute."

She took a deep breath and straightened her shoulders. "It's just that… It was big shock, knowing my parents came to Jackson with a child."

"I know, but, Abby… Look at me." She cut her eyes toward him and relief hit him square in the gut. "I promise we'll find out what's going on and I'll be with you every step of the way."

She nodded briskly and he missed the sweet smiles she used to throw his way, before he decided to protect his heart from any unforeseeable sorrow.

"Thank you, Noah. You've gone well beyond the call of duty."

Duty wasn't what was prodding him to stay at

Abby's side. He ignored that thought and concentrated on the present.

"Can you handle staying at the bed-and-breakfast where your parents stayed so we can scope out the place and talk to Mrs. Denton?"

She jerked her chin up and down. "I am definitely ready to stay at Mrs. Denton's. The sooner we find answers, the sooner we can go home."

Noah buried his desire to wrap his arms around her and protect her from this nightmare. They had to move forward. He put the car in Drive and headed toward the bed-and-breakfast. Within ten minutes, he parked in front of a quaint inn. He grabbed their bags while Abby released Bates from the back seat and attached his leash. They mounted the steps that led to a beautiful wraparound porch.

Abby grabbed the front doorknob. "Wanda said she'd call ahead and let Mrs. Denton know we were coming. Maybe she'll have something we can eat."

Noah felt like a heel. With so much happening, he hadn't even thought about food since lunch. Then the fine hair on his neck pricked, and Bates released a low growl just as Abby swung the door open.

Before he could grab her elbow, removing her from potential harm, she took a step inside and started screaming.

SEVENTEEN

Abby was in shock after she stepped into the bed-and-breakfast and spotted an older woman crumpled on the floor. A small puddle of blood had gathered beneath her head and more was streaming out.

It took a few seconds for her to realize someone had grasped her shoulders and was shaking her. "Noah?"

"I'm here. Abby, you have to stay calm and help me. Call 911. I'll check on the woman."

She took a deep breath and did her best to get control. But after everything that had happened over the last few weeks, she was using her last reserves. "Is it Mrs. Denton?" she whispered.

"Call 911. Tell them to contact Sheriff Hoyt."

No! It couldn't be. "Noah, do you think this has something to do with me?"

His voice firmed and it acted as a catalyst, prodding Abby into action. "Call 911. Now."

Fumbling inside her purse, she dug out her cell phone and punched in the numbers.

"Nine-one-one. How can I help you?"

Abby's words came out in a nervous stream. "We're at Mrs. Denton's bed-and-breakfast. I don't know the name of the establishment, but you have to hurry. We just arrived and there's a lady on the floor with blood seeping from the back of her head. And please notify Sheriff Hoyt."

"Stay on the phone, ma'am. I'm dispatching an ambulance and notifying the closest patrol car. They'll arrive on scene in less than five minutes."

"Thank you," Abby whispered. If Mrs. Denton had been hurt because of her, she didn't know what she'd do. Maybe it would be better to let Noah handle things. Maybe she should go back to North Carolina and stay by Grammy's side.

Abby held the cell phone in a death grip and closed her eyes. *Dear Lord, please show me what to do. I don't want anyone else hurt because of me.* A peace that could only come from above settled on her like gossamer wings, giving comfort and the sure knowledge that she was to see this through, no matter the cost. *Okay, Lord.*

"Abby, she's alive. Open the front door but stay in the house, and guide the ambulance attendants inside as soon as they arrive."

She breathed a short prayer of thanks that the woman lived. The ambulance arrived first, careening down the road and screeching to a halt in the middle of the street. Abby waved both hands above her head and yelled when they piled out of the vehicle. "Here! Over here!"

A man and a woman carrying medical bags ran up the sidewalk and Abby motioned them inside the house. She followed, but stayed out of the way.

"It's old Mrs. Denton, alright," one of them said.

Sheriff Hoyt walked through the door and stood beside Abby. They stayed quiet while the EMTs checked out Mrs. Denton.

While they were doing their business, the older woman regained consciousness and slapped their hands away. "I'm fine. Just let me get my bearings," she groused.

Abby took her first normal breath since arriving at the bed-and-breakfast. *Thank You, Lord.*

Determined to get on her feet, Mrs. Denton allowed the attendants to help her rise and they guided her to a chair. They were checking the back of her head when she happened to look up. She reminded Abby of a sweet little grandma until she opened her mouth.

"Who are you?" she sniped at Noah. She cut her eyes toward the sheriff. "I know who you are."

Abby walked forward and knelt in front of her, taking a cold, blue-veined hand in hers. "I'm Abby May-field and this is Noah Galloway. Wanda was supposed to call and let you know we were coming."

Mrs. Denton grinned. "She did. You're a pretty little thing."

Sheriff Hoyt broke up the conversation. "Mrs. Denton, did you get a look at the intruders?"

A canny gaze swung back to the sheriff. "I would have if they hadn't had their heads covered with ski masks. Half the people who come in here are wearing those things after skiing. I didn't think a thing about it when they walked through the door."

Both attendants stood up. "We'll take her to the hospital, do a few X-rays, but from what I can see, it's not a deep wound. She needs to be checked for a concussion."

Abby hid a grin as Mrs. Denton faced off with the

ambulance attendants. The older woman reminded her of Grammy. "I'm not going to the hospital. That place is for sick people. I just hit my head on the corner of the check-in desk when one of those hoodlums shoved me."

Sheriff Hoyt nodded his head toward the door and the attendants backed off after dressing the wound.

"Call the hospital if you need us, and wake her several times throughout the night to make sure she's okay," the woman said, and they scurried out the door.

Bright, intelligent eyes shone out from a roadmap of wrinkles when Mrs. Denton zeroed in on Abby. "You look just like your mama."

Abby's heart took a giant leap in her chest and she knelt back down in front of the older lady. "What do you know of my mama?"

"Wanda called and told me what was going on. I remember everything about that lovely couple—the Beauchamps—and that cute little boy." She got a faraway look in her eyes. "They only stayed at my place that one time. I always kenned the old sheriff was wrong. That car accident weren't no accident."

Please, dear Lord, give us some answers. Abby picked up the woman's hand again. "Anything you can remember about that time will help."

The woman's eyes cleared and focused on Abby. "That's what those men wanted, you know, the ones who pushed me. They told me to keep my mouth shut about the Beauchamps or they'd come back and finish the job. One of 'em wanted to kill me, but the other one said it would cause too much trouble for them, seeing as how the FBI was already on their tail."

Mrs. Denton peered up at Noah. "You FBI, boy?"

"Used to be, ma'am. I'm a sheriff in Blessing, Texas, now."

She cackled and looked back at Abby. "Boy's got manners. I like him."

Sheriff Hoyt had stayed silent and Abby was grateful. She wanted answers. "Did they say anything else, the men who attacked you?"

"Nope, just told me to keep my mouth shut."

Abby didn't want anything to happen to the dear old lady. "Maybe it's best if you do keep quiet."

Noah shifted on his feet, but Sheriff Hoyt stayed silent.

Mrs. Denton cackled. "Darlin', I done lived long enough for two people. You don't have to worry about me. Only God knows when my time is up."

The older woman licked her lips and Abby turned toward Noah. "Get Mrs. Denton a glass of water, please."

Within a couple of minutes, he presented Mrs. Denton with a full glass. She drank half of it and Abby removed it from her hand.

"Anyways, it was a long time ago now, when your mama and daddy visited my establishment. Can't remember exactly how many years, but it was two weeks before Christmas. What's interesting is, after they got here, a woman brought a boy to them. He was maybe about ten years old or so."

Her eyes filled with sorrow and Abby's stomach clenched.

Abby swallowed the lump in her throat. She had to know everything. "And what about the accident? Why didn't you agree with the old sheriff?"

"Well, the night it happened—the last night of their stay—I couldn't sleep and went down to the kitchen to heat up some milk. I heard a car start up and glanced out the window. It was the Beauchamps' car. The whole thing seemed odd to me, so I went to their room and knocked. No one answered the door and I used my master key to get inside. The room was empty."

Abby gathered her courage and asked the question burning in her gut, "And the child? Do you think he left with them?"

Mrs. Denton shook her head. "That's the thing. That's why the old sheriff didn't put much stock in my theory that the couple was taking off with the boy. I only saw the car drive off, not who was in the car. The woman who brought him could have picked up the child when I wasn't around. The old sheriff ruled it an accident and that was that."

Abby briefly wondered why her parents hadn't brought her with them to Jackson Hole instead of leaving her at Grammy's. The whole thing was very strange.

Abby looked over her shoulder at Noah. "If the accident reports are gone, how will we know if the child was in the car?"

Mrs. Denton answered her question. "The child was nowhere to be seen at the accident site 'cause I asked the old sheriff. He claimed there were only two people in the car, identified as Mr. and Mrs. Beauchamp."

Sheriff Hoyt stepped forward. "Mrs. Denton, since you refuse to go to the hospital, you should get some rest, but you'll need to be checked on throughout the night."

Abby stood and held out a hand. "Let me help you to your bedroom."

The older woman grinned. "You're as nice as your mama."

Abby's heart felt like it was bleeding inside at the thought of her parents and the boy. Who was he? And why did someone drop off the child for them to visit with in Jackson Hole?

As they made their way upstairs, Mrs. Denton told Abby they should make themselves at home. There was food in the kitchen that could be heated, and they could pick any rooms in the place as she had an empty house at the moment.

After settling their hostess, Abby closed the bed-room door quietly and made her way back to the kitchen. Her stomach growled when she caught the scent of fried chicken. As she entered the room, Abby saw that Bates had a dish filled with dog food on the floor and Noah had laid two filled plates on the table. They both sat down. She said grace and they ate in silence. When they finished, Noah placed the dishes in the sink.

"We'll talk tomorrow. We need sleep. I'll wake Mrs. Denton in an hour and check on her."

She agreed. Noah picked two rooms next to each other. Abby entered her room and glanced at the bath-room. She should at least brush her teeth. Instead, after slipping her gun under her pillow, she fell back onto the bed, fully dressed, and crashed.

Abby had no idea what time it was when something disturbed her sleep. She patted the bedcovers and found Bates sitting on his haunches, totally focused on the window. He released a low, intense warning growl. Her heart started beating wildly when he released a second, more lethal growl. Abby followed Bates's line of vision and saw a man with one leg thrown over the inside of the windowsill. She reached for the Glock hidden under her pillow.

"I have a gun and my dog will rip your throat out." She was proud of how strong her words sounded, but in truth, her hands were shaking.

"Please, don't shoot. I'm not here to hurt you. I'm here to help."

Abby didn't trust the soft, pleading voice. She should scream for Noah, but instinct told her to find out what this man wanted. "Help me how? Who are you?"

He slowly climbed into the room and placed both feet on the floor, but froze when Bates snarled.

"It's safer if you don't know anything about me. I'm only here to warn you. You have to go into hiding. Permanently. Don't trust anyone. The people after you, their arms reach far and wide, from local law enforcement to politicians in high positions, and they want you dead."

A chill iced her body, but Abby followed her gut. "They're after you, too, aren't they? Tell me. Maybe I can help."

Silence, then he said, "I made sure they believe I'm dead."

Noah must have heard something because a hard knock shook their connecting door.

"Abby? Are you okay? Open the door. Now!"

The man in the shadows slipped back out the open window. He grabbed a tree branch close to the opening before glancing back at her, but she couldn't make out his face.

"Don't trust him, either," he said before fleeing.

"Abby! Open the door, or I'll break it down."

Abby scooted out of bed and closed the window as the man's words pounded in her head. *Don't trust him, either.* She needed time to think and assess. Throwing on her robe, she stopped and took a deep breath before forcing a yawn and opening the door.

"Where's the fire?" She forced another yawn and wiped her face of emotion.

Noah gave her a hard stare and pushed his way into the room, flipping the light switch on as he passed. He prowled around and stuck his head inside the bathroom. He came back and faced her. "I could have sworn I heard Bates growl."

Abby waved a negligent hand in the air. "Oh, that. Sometimes Bates hears a squirrel or something outside and takes issue with it."

His eyes glittered with mistrust. Abby hated seeing that expression return, but she needed time to think things through.

He turned toward the connecting door. "Yell if something happens. The walls are thin in this old house."

Abby closed the door behind him and leaned against it and shut her eyes. Had she just made the biggest mistake of her life in not confiding in Noah?

EIGHTEEN

Noah awoke the next morning with one thought. Abby was lying.

He had interrogated some of the most sophisticated liars in the criminal world, and he knew Abby Mayfield had lied through her teeth. But about what? And why? Even though he'd stepped back emotionally, he'd been on the verge of fully trusting her, but now she'd blown that out of the water. Was her secret something sinister? Did she know more about her husband's and parents' deaths than she'd revealed? Had someone been in her room last night? Did she sneak them in through the window?

He grabbed his cell phone off the charger on the nightstand when it buzzed. It was six o'clock and he hadn't gotten much sleep the night before.

"What?" he barked.

"And good morning to you, too, Mr. Sunshine." Alex sounded rested and ready for the day. His old partner's enthusiasm soured Noah's mood even more.

"It's early. You got something for me?"

"Is that any way to treat your old partner? Hey!

Maybe I'd like to get out of the big city, too. You need a deputy in Blessing?"

Noah growled into the phone.

"Fine. I have information on the husband's death."

Noah came awake with startling clarity. "Spill."

"I sent Toby snooping."

Toby was a private investigator Alex and Noah had used on occasion when they wanted work done on the down low. In other words, they used him—someone not connected with the FBI—when they wanted to hide something from their superiors.

"Why use Toby?" Noah's gut burned. He didn't know if it was because of Abby's lies, or the fact that Alex calling in Toby meant this thing was big and went high up the food chain of law enforcement. How high was the question.

"The husband's death appears to be clean. It was ruled an accident and Simon didn't come across anything to contradict that, but here's the interesting part. Simon found a sealed file buried deep within the FBI's system on the parents' deaths."

Noah squeezed his eyes shut. Simon was supposed to be reforming, not breaking into sealed FBI files, but at this point, he didn't care. He wanted to know what Simon had found.

"And?"

"There's a police report on the parents' accident in Jackson Hole. It shouldn't even be in the FBI files if it was a mere accident. Simon decided to snoop when we found out about the suspicious fire in Jackson that destroyed all police records."

Noah loosened his hand on the cell phone and took a deep breath. "Cut to the chase, Ridenhour."

"Fine, but you sure know how to take the fun out of everything."

He hurried on before Noah had a chance to blast him. "The report states that Lee Beauchamp lost control of his car and ran off a steep embankment. No other vehicles involved. The key here is that the accident shouldn't have been an FBI case."

Noah's gut burned with acid.

A vision of Abby and him being run off the road played in his mind.

"What about the old sheriff in Jackson? Maybe he'll have some answers. Is Toby tracking him down? I'd love to have a chat with him."

"Well, now, that's a problem. Toby did track him down. The old sheriff died two months after Abby's parents."

Noah pinched the bridge of his nose. "Please don't tell me he was run off the road by another vehicle."

"Nope. Word is, after retiring, the old sheriff enjoyed fishing. He drowned early one morning in a large fishing pond in Jackson Hole. The coroner ruled it a heart attack."

"This just keeps getting better and better," Noah mumbled to himself and closed his eyes. "This whole thing stinks to high heaven."

"Agreed." There was a long moment of silence.

"You know, buddy, you can bow out at any time and scuttle on back to Texas."

Noah didn't say anything and Alex sighed. "I didn't think so. This woman mean that much to you?"

Noah kept quiet. *Did she?*

"I'll send the report to your email. You can access it on your phone."

Noah's grip tightened on the phone. "Thanks."

"No problem." And then Alex was gone.

Noah lay on his back and stared at the old beaded ceiling of his room. He didn't owe Abby anything. They hadn't even known each other that long. He could go back to Blessing and let Alex handle the case. But everything in him rebelled against that idea as he visualized Abby running out of her house in her pink heart pajamas. And the kiss they had shared, the kiss he was trying to forget.

He punched in a number. He needed to touch base with his son. Dylan always lifted his spirits. Noah had been angry with God for a long time for taking his wife, but he did have Dylan, and for that he would be forever grateful.

Abby woke up and shoved Bates out of her face. The dog loved to lick her awake every morning. She had woken several times during the night, and each time her dog had had his throat draped across hers. It was a Malinois trait, or so the breeder said. But after having lived with him, she understood it was a protective maneuver that showed the animal knew she was upset. And she *was* upset.

The previous night flooded her mind. Who was the guy who had visited her room? She hadn't gotten a good look at his face. He appeared to be the same height and build as the man from the crash scene and the hospital. Could it be also be the person who'd saved them during the explosion at Grammy's house?

A lump crawled up her throat. Could he possibly be her brother?

The man had warned her not to trust anyone—not

even Noah—but after praying for what seemed an eternity, Abby felt in her heart that she should tell Noah about her nocturnal visitor. She laughed—and it felt great—when Bates jumped off the bed and ran into the bathroom to drink water out of the toilet. Normally, she wouldn't allow that, but the poor fellow had to be hungry and thirsty. Probably needed to go outside, too.

A sense of relief and rightness flowed through her as she scrambled out of bed and slipped into her robe. She would see to Bates and then tell Noah everything. He might have distanced himself from her, but she would be mature and do the right thing. Bates's paws clicked on the old wooden floor when he heard her get out of bed. Adoring eyes followed her movements as she washed her face, dressed, brushed her teeth and combed her hair.

"Come on, baby boy. Let's get you outside before you have an accident."

She didn't bother with a leash and they hurried down the stairs. Noah was waiting at the bottom with a steaming cup of coffee in one hand. Those electric-blue eyes were stone cold and his jaw was squared, but things would change once she shared everything.

"Morning, Noah. We'll be right back."

He looked at the dog in understanding and gave a brisk nod. "I'll go out with you."

The cold outside air pierced her thin clothes and Abby's breath caught in her throat. Bates did his business and she hurried them back inside. Noah was right behind them and his predatory gaze tracked her as she poured herself a cup of coffee. The warm liquid almost made her purr in appreciation. She placed the coffee on the small table, sat down and looked at Noah.

"Noah, I—"

He held up a hand. "Don't say anything. First, I checked on Mrs. Denton several times throughout the night. Right now, she's sleeping soundly and I want to talk to you before she wakes."

Abby smiled. "Praise the Lord."

Noah grimaced. "Don't praise the Lord just yet."

Bates ignored the humans, munching happily away at the food Noah had put out for him.

Abby was bursting to clear the air. "Noah, I have to tell you—"

"Quiet!" The shouted command took Abby off guard and she waited as he drew in a deep breath.

"Alex Ridenhour called this morning. You know the accident report that burned in the fire here in Jackson?" She nodded. Where was he going with this?

"Simon found a file buried deep within the FBI system. It was on your parents."

A sense of foreboding crept over Abby. "Why would the FBI have a file on my parents' car crash if it was ruled an accident?"

If anything, Noah's jaw squared even more. "Bottom line? There's something bad going on here."

Abby took several deep breaths and centered herself. She could do this. If her parents had been murdered, she had to hold herself together so they could find the truth.

Bates whined and she rubbed his head.

"Please sit down." He was less intimidating when seated.

He sat and she slid into a chair across from him.

"I get the feeling that you're holding something back. If I'm to help you, I need to know everything."

He was right, and she had already come to that conclusion herself. "Last night, I had a visitor."

His lips tightened. "Go on."

"I think it might have been the guy from the crash scene, the one I saw in the hospital and the man who saved us after the explosion at Grammy's."

"You didn't get a good look at him?"

"There was a little light filtering through the window from the streetlamp, but no, I didn't get a clear look."

"You should have called me." His voice sounded grim and guarded.

Abby shrugged. She couldn't even explain it to herself. "Something told me to get as much information as I could. I had my gun trained on him, and Bates would have attacked if I had given the word. Anyway, I didn't get much information. He told me it was safer if I didn't know who he is. He advised me to hide, permanently. He said I shouldn't trust anyone—" she looked at him "—including you. He said the people after me have far-reaching arms, including local law enforcement and high-placed politicians. I asked if they were after him, too. Said that maybe we could help. He told me they, whoever 'they' are, think he's dead."

NINETEEN

Noah ached to trust her with every fiber of his being. And it did help that she'd come clean about the previous night, but her late-night visitor only raised more questions. Avoiding the trust issue that had built a wall between them, he zeroed in on the intruder. "Is that everything he said?"

"That's when you started banging on my door."

"From what he said, it sounds like he faked his own death. If we had a time frame, we could make a list of all high-profile deaths."

She shivered, and Noah felt a surge of protectiveness but pushed it away.

"You think it's really high profile?"

Bates left his food bowl and settled on the floor at Abby's side. Noah was truly impressed with the dog. He appeared to sense Abby's every mood. "From what the guy said—if he's telling the truth and this isn't a smoke screen and a way for whoever is after you to get close to you—then, yes, I'd have to assume the people responsible are high profile. There's also the sealed FBI file to consider. Someone has to be very rich and powerful, with connections in high places to have made that happen. We have to think big."

A myriad of emotions passed over Abby's face—frustration, confusion, anger—and Noah felt helpless to make them disappear. It was not a feeling he was accustomed to.

"That coffee I smell?" Mrs. Denton asked from the doorway before slowly shuffling into the room, breaking the mind-numbing tension.

Both Abby and Noah stood, but he reached their temporary landlady first and took her elbow, guiding her to a chair.

Abby filled a cup with steaming coffee. "Cream or sugar, Mrs. Denton?"

"No, dear, I take mine black and strong."

Abby handed her the cup and sat beside her. Noah wondered how he could even think of mistrusting Abby as she took Mrs. Denton's arthritic hand in her own.

"I bet you're sore this morning. My grandmother has a salve she always used on my scrapes and bruises when I was a kid."

The older lady smiled and her eyes drifted in remembrance. "I've doctored scrapes and bruises a time or two, myself." She refocused on Abby. "But that's a story for another time. I remembered something this morning when I woke up."

Abby pushed away from the table. "Let me make you some breakfast and then we can talk."

Mrs. Denton grabbed her hand. "I'll eat later. This is important. You never know when God might call me home and you need to know this."

Noah almost laughed at the horrified expression on

Abby's face. "Do you need to go to the hospital? Did those men hurt you more than you admitted last night?"

Abby's voice rose in volume and Mrs. Denton held up a defensive hand. "Pipe down, young lady. I'll probably outlive you all."

Abby looked as if she wanted to argue, but plopped back down in her seat.

"With so much going on last night, I forgot about Sandra Wentworth. She's the local librarian. Your parents pretty much kept to themselves, but I remember your mother loved to read and she visited the library a few times while they were here. Anyway, one day I saw your mama and Sandra riding in a car together. It was strange, because your parents were always together, with the boy, when they were here. They seldom went out to eat and took most of their meals here at the B and B."

Noah's sixth sense kicked in. "What did you think when you saw them together in the car?"

Mrs. Denton smiled. "I thought it was nice that Mary Beauchamp had a new friend. You might want to talk to Sandra and see what she has to say."

"Thank you," Abby said, then looked at him. "Noah, Mrs. Denton can't be left alone, not after what happened last night."

At least he had this covered. "Sheriff Hoyt isn't taking any chances. He's sending someone over to stay until this situation is resolved."

"He better not send that nosy Patty Hatfield over here. That woman—"

The doorbell rang and interrupted Mrs. Denton's tirade. Noah jumped to his feet and removed himself from the line of fire. "I'll get it."

Checking the holster at the back of his jeans, he peered through the peephole. A little old lady glared back at him, so close to the tiny glass he could almost count her wrinkles.

He opened the door and she sniffed. "Took you long enough." Without even saying hello, she marched past him as if she owned the place. Noah was afraid of World War Three breaking out because he had a sneaky feeling this was, indeed, Mrs. Hatfield.

Sparks were already flying between the two adversaries when he entered the kitchen. He almost laughed at the startled expression on Abby's face. He motioned her to follow him and she quickly scuttled out of the room.

"Ethan's deputy is watching out for them since I'm leaving the premises. He's in his patrol car outside. The sheriff just called a neighbor to be inside with Mrs. Denton since she has a slight head injury. He wanted someone with her at all times. Let's go pay Sandra Wentworth a visit."

Abby nodded and they grabbed their coats. Bates brought up the rear.

They left her dog in the car when they arrived at the library. The building was old, filled with endless shelves of books. The air had a musty odor, but Abby loved it. There were a few computers perched on one desk.

As they approached a pretty young woman at the front desk, Noah took the lead.

"Ma'am, we're looking for Sandra Wentworth."

The perky girl, who Abby guessed was somewhere in her early twenties, pointed toward an old staircase in the middle of the room. "Sure thing. Go up the stairs, first door on the right."

Side by side they climbed the wooden steps and Noah knocked on the door.

"Come in," a firm voice called.

Noah opened the door and they entered an office that could have been featured in a historical painting. Everything was antique—tables, chairs, pictures. A woman who looked to be in her late fifties rose from behind a wooden desk with a beautiful patina. There were a few wrinkles around her smiling eyes, but she had beautiful skin. Her blond hair was streaked with a few strands of silver.

"Hello. Susie buzzed me and said you were coming up." She held out a hand, and Noah clasped it and shook. Abby followed suit, but when Sandra Wentworth faced Abby head-on, the woman gasped and turned an alarming shade of white. Abby held on to her hand. "Mrs. Wentworth, are you alright? Noah, fetch a glass of water."

The head librarian took a deep breath and some color returned. She pulled her hand away. "I—I'm fine. Please, have a seat."

Abby watched her carefully, but she seemed to steady herself.

"You're sure you're okay?"

Mrs. Wentworth's lips trembled. "Yes. Well, no, maybe not." She stared at Abby. "You just, well, you look like someone I once knew."

Mrs. Wentworth straightened a pen on her desk, and when she looked back up, a mask of wariness had fallen over her face. In a crisp tone, she said, "Why don't you tell me who you are and why you're here?"

Noah started to speak, but Abby had suddenly had enough. She was at the end of her rope and she wanted answers. "I'll tell you why we're here. Someone has broken into my house several times. I've been shot at. My car has been run off the road, and Noah and I barely escaped the explosion that destroyed my grandmother's house. And that's after someone roughed up my grandmother and put her in the hospital. Mrs. Denton told us you were friends with my mother—Mary Beauchamp—and we need to know what happened all those years ago when they died in a car crash."

Abby snapped her mouth shut, immediately feeling contrite as a stricken expression fell across Mrs. Wentworth's face.

Ashamed and embarrassed, Abby lifted a hand, then let it drop back into her lap. "I'm sorry. It's just that my life has spiraled out of control and I don't know how to fix it. Please, let me start over. My name is Abby Mayfield and this is Noah Galloway. He's the sheriff in a Texas town called Blessing. I teach piano and I'm a choir director." Abby took a deep breath. "Mrs. Wentworth, someone is trying to kill me and I don't have a clue who would do such a thing."

Abby held her breath as the librarian studied them a moment. "I'd like to see some identification, please."

Both of them pulled out their driver's licenses, and Noah added his sheriff's ID, then they passed them over. She put on a pair of reading glasses and studied them in detail. Finally, she handed them back and propped both elbows on her desk. "Driver's licenses can be forged, but I believe you because you're the spitting image of your mother."

Abby's heart raced. Finally! "So you knew her? You knew my mama?"

Noah injected a question. "Why the caution, Mrs. Wentworth?"

"Please, call me Sandra. *Mrs. Wentworth* is a mouthful."

They shared a stilted laugh, but Abby was on pins and needles. What did Sandra know?

"And call us Abby and Noah," Abby responded in kind.

Sandra nodded and leaned back in her chair. "Are you sure someone is trying to kill you?"

Noah answered for Abby. "No doubt whatsoever."

Sandra gave a jerky nod. "I'll tell you what I know, which, I'll warn you, is very little. Your mother was extremely secretive."

Her heart lodged in her throat, Abby nodded. "Anything you share is much appreciated."

"Your mother visited the library the one time they came to Jackson and the cutest boy accompanied her. I asked if the child was her son. She got the strangest look on her face, almost fearful, and peered over her shoulder, as if afraid someone was watching her. I asked if anything was wrong, and she relaxed and laughed. She said they were babysitting for a relative so the parents could take a long-deserved break. I thought maybe I had misread her. We talked for quite a while and had a lot in common, a love of books being one of them, but the last time she came by during their visit…"

Abby found herself leaning forward in her chair. "The last time?"

Sandra lifted eyes full of remorse. "The last time I saw your mother alive, the only way I can describe her attitude was one of fear mixed with excitement. She came to say goodbye, said they'd never return to Jackson. I was disturbed, to say the least. She warned me not to let anyone in Jackson know we had close acquaintance, and if anyone came to town asking questions about them, to deny I knew her, even if it was the police. She said it was too dangerous. Not to trust anyone."

An eerie, creepy feeling stole over Abby and she turned to Noah. "That's the same thing the man said last night. Don't trust anyone."

Noah kept his eyes trained on Sandra. "What about the boy? Was he with her?"

Sandra shook her head. "He wasn't with her that last time she stopped by the library."

She looked at Noah, long and hard. "They didn't have an accident, did they?"

"No, Mrs. Wentworth. We now believe they were forced off the road."

Abby worried for the woman when her face went white again, but Sandra held herself together. "I honored Mary's request. I've never told a soul, until you two, that we were acquainted."

Noah nodded. "Probably wise. Was there anything else?"

Sandra shook her head, a sad look in her eyes. "No, but, Abby, I'm sorry. I wish I could have done something to prevent such a horrible tragedy."

A tear in her eye, Abby stood and Noah followed suit. "It sounds to me like you were a good friend when my mama needed one. Thank you for being open with us."

Sandra stood, rounded the desk and hugged Abby.

"Please be careful. I'll be praying for your safety and that you find the answers you're looking for."

Abby hugged her back, and she and Noah were silent, lost in their own thoughts, as they left the library. When they stepped outside, the first thing Abby heard was Bates. She jerked her gaze to the car where the dog was doing his best to squeeze out of the window they'd left cracked open. At her side, Noah stiffened, grabbed her arm and pulled her into a nosedive behind the rear of the car.

As her shoulder took the brunt of the fall, Abby heard a ping similar to the one at the church. Someone was shooting at them.

TWENTY

His gun already in his hand, Noah scrambled to a crouched position and, with his back to the bumper, made sure Abby was out of the line of fire. She sat on the ground, hugging the back of the vehicle.

Her wide, startled eyes made him want to crush something, or someone. Her cross-body purse was still in position. "You have your cell phone in there?"

She nodded.

"Call 911 and tell them to notify Sheriff Hoyt. After you've done that, go to the other side of the car and crawl inside with Bates. Stay there until you hear sirens."

Noah was impressed when she took a quick breath and pulled herself together. "Where are you going?"

Her courage strengthened his resolve. He was tired of being on the defensive. It was time to get some answers. "I'm going hunting."

He sounded hard and cold, but that's how he felt. He turned and took a quick look around the bumper of the car. All clear as far as he could tell. Without looking back, he took off after the shooter.

As he hustled around the opposite side of the library

from where he thought the shots had been fired, his mind became a whirlwind of activity. He grimaced as he rounded the building, but for the first time in a long time, he said a quick prayer for safety. He had a sneaking suspicion that God had given him something besides Dylan to live for. He had to get his head back in the game. The people after Abby were playing for keeps, and they'd be happy to get rid of Noah, making it easier to get close to Abby, because nobody could, or would, protect her like he would.

Crouched low, with both hands on the gun in front of him, he looked up and checked the roofline as he ran along beside the old brick wall of the library. The building was only two stories high and the bullet had come from ground level, but that didn't mean there wasn't a second shooter. Two people had visited Mrs. Denton.

He took a quick look around the back corner of the building and jerked back as another bullet chipped off a piece of brick. The bullet came from the woods behind the library. Too close for comfort. The perpetrators were getting bolder. He needed to catch one of them for interrogation purposes. They didn't have enough clues to go on and things were escalating. This was his chance. He shouldn't go after them without backup, but he wanted Abby safe.

He took another quick glance around the corner. Nobody shot at him, and he was getting ready to take off toward the woods when a vicious bark filled the air.

Noah immediately switched gears and raced back to the car, castigating himself all the way. What if a second person had backtracked and gone after Abby? He'd never forgive himself if something happened to her. He heard sirens blaring and Sheriff Hoyt brought his patrol car to a shuddering halt, jumping out with his weapon drawn as Noah rounded the corner of the building. Hoyt canvassed the area with his own gun held in front of him, checking all around before concluding it was safe.

Hoyt lowered his weapon and they both approached the car. His heart in his throat, Noah allowed himself to breathe a sigh of relief when Abby threw the back door open and both woman and dog scrambled out of the vehicle. She made a beeline toward him. He released an *oomph* when she rocketed into his chest and wrapped her arms around his waist.

His body sagged in relief. She was okay. He held her tight for a few seconds before pulling back, distancing himself.

Sheriff Hoyt cleared his throat. "I suggest we take it to the station so y'all can tell me what happened," he drawled. "The shooter, or shooters, are still at large."

In less than ten minutes, Noah followed Abby through the police station doors. He couldn't believe he'd allowed whoever was after Abby to get the drop on him. All the more reason to distance himself from his attraction to her. He had to keep his head in the game and stay vigilant. Her life was at stake.

Hoyt sat behind his desk, and Abby took a seat next to Noah. Noah gave the sheriff a quick but accurate account of the shooting.

Before Hoyt had a chance to ask any questions, his deputy came careening into the room, almost stumbling in his haste.

"Sheriff," he exclaimed. "You gotta come outside right now."

Sheriff Hoyt sighed, much like Noah did around Cooper, and Noah hid a smile.

"What is it, Peter?"

Noah could almost see the sparks of excitement bouncing off the deputy.

"It's Ned. He's in front of the station. He caught one of the shooters."

Noah's gaze sharpened as he looked at Hoyt. "Who's Ned?"

Hoyt shook his head and grabbed his coat off the back of his chair. "I'll explain later."

Noah and Abby followed him out the door and through the police station. The cold air hit first, but he soon forgot the freezing temperatures when he caught sight of a man trussed up with a heavy rope, sitting on the sidewalk in front of the building. He couldn't speak due to the rag stuffed into his mouth. Not that he wasn't trying.

But the most intriguing aspect of the odd situation was the bear of a man holding the criminal upright by his coat collar. The man was big. Noah estimated him to be well over six and a half feet tall. Hair covered most of his face, and he had piercing green eyes. Eyes that held far more intelligence than his appearance suggested. His clothes consisted of faded jeans and a heavy fleece jacket. Hiking boots covered his feet.

Abby crowded close behind Noah and he almost smiled at her not-so-subtle eavesdropping technique.

"Bear Man," she whispered, nicknaming the man, and Noah choked back a laugh.

Sheriff Hoyt spoke. "Ned, haven't seen you around in a while."

Noah wanted him to get on with it. He prayed the trussed-up man was one of the shooters.

Bear Man—or rather, Ned—grunted. "Been busy." He jerked his prisoner by the collar. "I believe this belongs to you."

After that short announcement, Ned turned on his boot heel and left. Noah watched him disappear into the woods, which led straight up a desolate mountain. Blessing had a few odd people, but this guy was an entity of his own. Noah also noticed his movements as he walked away. Agile and smooth. This was no ordinary mountain man. Noah had a ton of questions about him, but the sheriff motioned Peter over and they started cutting the captive loose as the deputy read him his rights.

As soon as they removed the gag, he spit on the ground and snarled at all of them. "I want to talk to my lawyer. You people around here are nuts."

Noah moved in front of Abby as she took a few steps back. The captive had a New York accent. Had he followed them all the way to Jackson? Had he tried to kill her?

Anger flashed hot and crushed Abby's common sense. By now, Sheriff Hoyt had cuffs on the prisoner. Avoiding Noah's grasping hand, she marched right in front of him and stuck a finger in the man's face.

"I better not find out you had anything to do with hurting my grandmother."

He opened his mouth, no doubt to blast her, but Bates came alongside her and released a fierce growl that would make a grown person wet his pants. The man took a step back and Abby felt like snarling, herself.

Noah grabbed her arm and pulled her away from the guy. Sheriff Hoyt guided the man forward.

"You have to reign in that steel-magnolia thing you have going, Abby," Noah said in a low voice.

She sighed. "I know. It's just that…"

"It's okay. I understand. Maybe we'll get some answers now."

Hope—the first she'd had since this whole mess started—filled her. "Do you think he'll talk?"

Noah took her hand and followed the procession into the station. "I'm sure he'll lawyer up, but we'll do our best." He grinned. "I do know a few interrogation techniques."

Abby breathed a lungful of cold air before entering the station. Hoyt and his prisoner had disappeared. Peter was waiting for Noah. "The sheriff's locking him up. He'll be back in a minute."

Noah nodded and led her to a bench lining the wall. She sat down and he squatted in front of her. "Why don't you get some coffee and stay here while we talk to this guy?"

She wanted to argue, but Noah raised a brow. Somehow, in the short amount of time they'd spent together, he could already interpret her reactions.

"Fine, I'll stay put."

He met Hoyt halfway down the hall. Abby watched as they disappeared into the back of the building.

She drank three cups of horrible, strong coffee, paced, got a snack out of the vending machine, paced some more, went to the ladies' room and kept walking back and forth across the worn-out linoleum. Bates sat on the floor and watched her with alert eyes that missed nothing. When Sheriff Hoyt and Noah came back down the hall, she searched his face. He didn't look pleased, but neither did he look upset. He motioned for her to follow them and they ended up back in Hoyt's office.

The sheriff sat down behind his desk, and Abby and Noah took the seats facing him.

"Well?" she asked.

Hoyt nodded at Noah and Noah explained, "At first he wanted to lawyer up, but I told him a deal might be on the table if he cooperated."

Abby didn't much care for making deals with a hardened criminal, but she kept her mouth shut. This was what Noah had been trained to do.

"He admitted they were trying to kill you. He and his partner have been hiding in the mountains, waiting for an opportunity to strike."

Abby grimaced at hearing the stark truth, but she shored up her courage. "Go on."

Noah grinned. "They almost froze to death. There were two of them, but his partner called it quits after roughing up Mrs. Denton. He went back to New York. The guy we arrested owes some dangerous people a lot of money and he decided to follow through. Unfortunately, his instructions and payments were dropped at a neutral location. He has no idea who hired him."

"Do you believe him?"

"Yes, I do. I've interviewed many people, and remember, we now believe this is high profile. If someone in a position of power is calling the shots, they'll make sure nothing can be traced back to them."

Abby wanted to weep, but she sniffed and regained her equilibrium.

Noah stood and held out a hand to Sheriff Hoyt. "Once again, I appreciate your help."

Hoyt stood and shook his hand. "Anytime. Let me know how everything pans out."

Abby was curious. "It sounds like we're leaving. Where are we going? What about Ned? What's his story?"

"The sheriff and I both agree, since the killers were likely hired in New York, our answers lie there."

Hoyt answered her question about Ned. "Ned showed up about three years ago, bought an entire mountain and built a cabin. He comes into town once a month to buy supplies, but keeps to himself for the most part. He has returned a couple of lost hikers during that time. As long as he doesn't cause trouble, he can do what he wants. It's a free country."

Abby could tell the sheriff wasn't satisfied with the limited amount of information he had on the man, but that was his problem. She had enough of her own.

"It was nice to meet you, Sheriff."

He nodded and they left. The bracing air smacked her in the face as she loaded Bates into the back of the car and climbed into the passenger seat. Noah rounded the front of the vehicle and got behind the wheel.

"What now?" she asked.

Before he could answer, his phone rang. "Simon, you got something for me?"

She couldn't stop the skipped beat of her heart. She was coming to realize hope was a very fragile thing. Noah opened the glove compartment and grabbed a pad and pen.

"Go ahead."

Abby watched as he wrote a number down. It started with the letters *C-A-M* followed by the numbers three-six-six and her heart leaped again.

"Good work, Simon. Yes, I'll buy you a steak dinner when this is over."

Noah laughed as he put the phone away. "That kid is an empty bucket. If he ate six meals a day, he'd still be hungry."

Abby was about to bust. "Noah!"

He grinned and put the car in gear. "We're picking up our luggage and heading back to New York."

TWENTY-ONE

"Noah Galloway, you better share this instant if you know what's good for you." Her tone was teasing, but there was steel behind the request.

He started the engine and put the car in Drive. "Simon researched all the cars with tags starting with C-A-M. The one I just wrote down raised a red flag because it's owned by a corporation."

Invisible, electric energy came off her in waves. "Well, what's the name of the cooperation?"

He hated to burst her bubble, but this was a good, solid lead. "Simon says it's a dummy corporation, but it gives us a good place to start."

She deflated, and he shifted in his seat, facing her after pulling in to Mrs. Denton's bed-and-breakfast parking area and cutting the engine. "Abby, listen to me. This is a great lead. Simon is a whiz at this. We'll track the corporate owner of this tag. It's only a matter of time. They can use shell corporations, but we will find them."

Her eyes were filled with such faith it made him want to conquer the world.

"I trust you, Noah. We'll find them. Let's load up

and say goodbye to Mrs. Denton. I'll make flight plans while you pack."

Noah felt bad for Abby, even though she insisted she wasn't tired. Her drooping shoulders and the faint crescent moons under her eyes said otherwise.

After saying their goodbyes to Mrs. Denton, and what seemed like a long flight to New York, they checked into a different hotel this time and grabbed a bite to eat before trekking back to the FBI offices.

They had crisscrossed the country several times, and he was feeling the effects, too. Noah had tried to talk her into taking a nap, but she said she was sick and tired of this mess. She wanted her life back, and the only way to do that was to find answers.

He agreed, so they kept moving.

Everyone was waiting in Director Henry Wilson's office when they arrived. After a short greeting period, they took seats.

Wilson started the meeting. "I hear you saw a little action in Jackson Hole."

Noah nodded. "Yes, sir, but we handled it."

"I'm having the prisoner transferred to our jurisdiction. Sheriff Hoyt was very helpful."

"He's a good man."

Abby half listened as drowsiness threatened to overtake her, but the numbers Noah had written down while they were in the car in Jackson Hole kept running through her mind. CAM366. It nagged at her.

Someone shook her arm. "Abby, you okay?"

It was Noah and he sounded concerned. She forced a smile. "I'm fine, but…"

"But what?"

"Those letters and numbers? The ones on the license tag?"

"What about them?"

"They... What if...?"

Exasperation replaced his concern. "What if they what?"

And it came to her like an answered prayer from God. "Give me the phone."

Everyone in the room sent Noah pitying glances.

"Abby—"

She sat straight up, electrified energy pumping through her now. "The phone. Give it to me."

Noah looked at her askance but started digging his cell phone out of his pocket.

Now she became exasperated. "No. Not that one. I need a landline."

Director Wilson grabbed the cordless phone off his desk and handed it to her. "Here you go."

She knew everyone thought she had lost it, but she didn't care. She stared at the numbers on the handset, trying different letter combinations. "The numbers three-six-six could equal *D-O-N*," she mumbled under her breath.

"Abby, what are you talking about?" Noah's words were laced with worry, but she ignored him. She was on to something. She could feel it.

"Simon, do you have your laptop with you?" she asked, terrified she might be wrong, but praying she was right.

Simon reached down beside his chair and grinned when he lifted his computer. "Never go anywhere without it."

"Good, please type in *C-A-M-D-O-N*."

"Abby—"

"Wait," she told Noah. "Just wait." She focused on Simon as he typed in the word.

He looked up and grinned. "How did you figure it out?"

She grinned back. "The keypad on the phone. *D* is the number three, *O* and *N* are the number six. *C-A-M-three-six-six*. Camdon. I tried different combinations, but this one jumped out at me."

"Please, if someone would fill me in, I would appreciate it," Director Wilson demanded more than asked.

Simon turned his computer around so everyone could see the screen. "I ran the original plate and it's owned by a shell corporation. Your combination spells *Camdon*, which could possibly stand for Camdon International. It's a huge corporation based right here in New York, and the owner's heir died recently."

The room erupted into chaos with everyone talking at once. Wilson raised a hand. "One person at a time, people."

Abby's heart palpitated. This had to be the information they needed to solve the mystery surrounding her. She didn't think she could take much more. *Dear Lord, please let this be a clue that will lead us to the truth.*

Noah stared at her, his eyes full of surprise and approval. "How did you come up with that?"

Abby grinned. "God gave it to me."

He nodded slowly and her heart gave a giant leap. Maybe all this had happened so Noah could find his way back to God. If that were true, it would be worth every dangerous moment she'd lived through.

Everyone in the room laughed and Abby looked at Director Wilson. "What did you say?"

His eyes danced. "I said I ought to hire you. You'd make a good code solver for the FBI."

Totally humbled, Abby flushed at the praise. "Thank you, but I've already got a job as a choir director and we've yet to prove the tag belongs to Camdon International."

Wilson started issuing commands. "Simon—"

Simon popped out of his chair, laptop in hand and headed for the door. "I'll get Franny on it right away, sir."

Abby girded her courage and took a deep breath. Avoiding eye contact with Noah, she boldly made her statement. "Sir? Director Wilson?"

He turned sharply. "Yes?"

Abby squirmed in her seat and cleared her throat. "If the plate does belong to Camdon International, I would like to offer my services as bait, if need be."

Noah's entire body stiffened in the chair beside her, but she was determined. She wanted this to end.

"Sir." Noah jumped in before his boss could speak, "As you well know, it's FBI policy never to use a civilian as bait."

Director Wilson's eyes crinkled when he smiled at Abby. "Ms. Mayfield, I appreciate the offer. It's very brave of you, but Galloway's correct in saying we would never place a civilian in the line of fire."

All of a sudden, fatigue weighed down on her and she yawned.

Noah caught the movement and stood. "We're heading back to the hotel. Call if you need us."

Everyone in the room mumbled a goodbye and they were on their way. In the car, Noah roused her after reaching the parking enclosure at the hotel. "Abby.

We're here. Let's get some rest. They'll call if anything happens."

She nodded sleepily and he guided her into the elevator and to her room. After locking the dead bolt behind him, he moved to the connecting door. "This door is unlocked. Yell if you need me, but we should be safe. We're on an upper floor and there are no balconies."

She waited until the door closed. Once again, she fell to bed fully clothed. She heard Bates drinking out of the toilet and reminded herself to put out his water bowl as soon as she awakened. After drinking his fill, he climbed in beside her, his warm body making her feel secure.

In a deep slumber, Abby swatted at her ear. At first she thought it was the fur from Bates's ear tickling her. He always slept with his head next to hers.

She reached over to snuggle next to him, but a deep, low whisper penetrated her sleep.

"Your dog's not here and you need to wake up. Now!"

She recognized that voice and her eyes popped open. She was wide awake now. She tried to yell for Noah, but the man placed a hand over her mouth.

"Listen." There was urgency in his voice. "They're coming after you and we have to get out of here. They'll kill us both. Can I lift my hand? Promise you won't scream?"

Abby weighed her options. If the guy wanted to kill her, he could have done so while she was asleep. She nodded in the affirmative and he slowly lifted his hand.

"Where's my dog? Where's Bates?" was her first question.

He pointed toward the bathroom. "He was drinking

water out of the toilet when I slipped in. I brought a rib bone just in case, threw it inside as a treat and closed the door before he could get out. I think he remembered me from your grandmother's house and that's why he isn't barking his head off."

She scrambled out of bed and threw her robe on before flying to the bathroom. Opening the door, she breathed a sigh of relief and knelt beside her protector and best friend. He was happily gnawing on the bone.

"Some guard dog you are," she said, and chuckled at the red sauce on his whiskers.

Looking over her shoulder, she shot a questioning glance at the man who had saved Noah from the fire at her grandmother's house. "How did you get in here?"

"I waited in the hall. Things are getting hot for the killers and I knew they'd make a move soon. Abby, they're powerful and loaded with money. A hotel employee opened your dead bolt while you were asleep. That's how I got in, and I'm sure the employee was paid to do so. You have to hurry because they'll be here soon. We have to go."

As unobtrusively as possible, she cast a glance toward Noah's door. It was unlocked. She gauged the distance between herself and the door. She could make a run for it or she could yell. The man must have realized her intent. He crossed the room in a flash and knelt beside her. She peered into a face so similar to her own, her heart ached. "Are you my brother?"

Deep sorrow filled his eyes. "I'll answer all your questions later, but you have to trust me. We have to leave now."

"But Noah can help us."

A shuttered expression covered his face. "Stay

with him or leave with me. It's your choice. This thing reaches high places, and I'm positive there are paid informants within the FBI. Maybe your Noah isn't one of them, but his coworkers or boss might be. Abby, they'll kill him if they get the chance."

And those words prompted her into action. She'd never do anything that would put Noah at risk. She stood and faced the man head-on. "How do I know I can trust you?"

Indecision flitted across his face until he appeared to come to a decision. "My name is Sam Camdon. I'm your brother."

Abby closed her eyes in prayer. When she opened them, she nodded firmly. "I'll go with you, but I'm leaving a note for Noah, so he'll know what's going on." She turned to Bates. She didn't want Noah or her dog killed. "Bates, you stay here, baby, and stay quiet."

She got to her feet. With no idea what situations they might face, she decided to leave Bates in the bathroom. "I'll leave Bates here. Noah will take care of him."

"Fine, but hurry. We're running out of time."

Abby rushed over to the desk by the window. Her hands shook as she gathered pen and paper. Just as she was finishing writing the note, the lock on the door rattled and was quickly jimmied. Two burly men stepped in, guns drawn, and closed the door behind them. Her brother must have forgotten to reset the dead bolt.

Abby opened her mouth to yell, but the barrel of the gun swinging in her direction had her snapping her mouth shut.

"Scream and I'll kill you both. Now, walk nice and slowly toward the door. One wrong move and you're both dead."

TWENTY-TWO

Noah awoke to a raucous noise coming from Abby's room. He heard barking, snarling and growling. It sounded like the Malinois was repeatedly hurling himself against a wall. Fear for Abby threatened to immobilize him, but he scrambled out of bed and grabbed his gun off the nightstand. He took a deep breath, centering himself, and placed a hand on the doorknob. He was ready to spring into action.

He threw the door open, took a two-hand hold on the Glock and visually swept the room. Frantic, he checked the bathroom and found Bates, but Abby was nowhere to be seen. The distraught dog followed him from the bathroom to the hall door. It swung open at his touch.

His heart felt as if it was going to beat out of his chest as he sat on the end of the bed. He had failed Abby. Was she alive? The thought almost brought him to his knees. Noah closed his eyes, and for the first time since Dylan's mother died, he fully opened his heart. "God, I beg You." He raised his voice. "Please let Abby be alive. Show me where to find her."

He had prayed for Sonya to live, but she had died, anyway. Would God listen this time?

A cold nose nudged his hand and he looked down. "Bates, what happened? How did they get past you?"

The dog's soulful eyes reflected heartbreak and abashment, much the way Noah felt, but then the dog tugged at his pants leg.

"What is it, boy?" He stood and Bates raced over to the desk sitting in front of the window. A pad and pen lay side by side and his insides froze when he read the message.

Noah, the blond guy is my brother, and he's here. His name is Sam Camdon. He wants me to leave with him. I wanted to wake you, but he said these people will kill you, and I believe him. I left Bates in the bathroom because I was afraid whoever wants me dead might kill him if they catch up with us. It appears they paid a hotel employee to unlock my dead bolt. Noah—

A jagged line started at the last word and ended at the bottom of the page. They had her. They'd stolen her right out from under his nose. A fierce surge of protectiveness raced through him. He looked at the dog. "Let's go find Abby."

The dog stood by the door, his muscular body quivering, ready to roll.

"Let me get dressed and we're outta here."

As he stepped into his room, his cell, sitting on the nightstand, rang. He put it on speakerphone while throwing on his clothes. "Not now, Simon. They have her. They have Abby."

"Then you need to know this. Abby was right. After

sifting through numerous shell corporations, the car tag belongs to Camdon International."

Noah had no idea where they'd taken Abby and her brother, so he decided to go to the top of the company. "Who's in charge of Camdon International?" He heard Simon typing at warp speed.

"By the way, the blond guy in the police sketch is Sam Camdon. From what I can ascertain, he tried to fake his death."

Impatience made Noah snap, "I need to know who's in charge of Camdon International."

Simon ignored his outburst. "The old man's name is Lincoln Camdon. I have to give it to him, he built the company from scratch."

"Give me the address for the New York headquarters."

Simon rattled off the address and Noah memorized it as he and Bates ran out the door and into the hallway. "Tell Alex to meet me there."

"You got it."

A chill racked Abby's body as she and Sam were shoved into a small, cold room. The door clanged shut behind them and she raced back to it and rattled the knob.

"That won't do any good. Even if you get the door open, I'm sure there are guards posted outside." He sounded resigned to his fate.

Abby whirled around and got her first good look at her brother. His short, mussed blond hair and brown eyes reminded her so much of her mother she wanted to cry, but she wouldn't, because they were going to escape. The mere thought of dying brought a fierce surge of love in her heart for Noah. *Why now, Lord, when I might not make it out of this alive?* She had just fallen in love and discovered she had a brother. She took a deep, fierce breath. She refused to die. She had too much to live for.

She marched over to Sam and pointed a finger in his face. "Do you believe in God?"

Confusion spread over his face. "What?"

"I asked if you believe in God. It's a simple question."

He shrugged his shoulders. "I believe in a supreme being. Why?"

Abby rolled her eyes. She should have been terrified out of her mind, given the circumstances, but God was giving her strength. It flowed through her entire being like a strong, roaring waterfall. "Because believing in God is everything, and if you want to get out of this alive, you better start praying."

A hint of hope lit his eyes.

"Now, I want answers, and I mean everything. The whole story."

Sam's lips curved upward. "You're a bossy little thing."

"I'm a choir director and a piano teacher. Of course I'm bossy. Start at the beginning. I have to know everything if we're going to get out of this mess."

"Yes, ma'am." His grin faded. "Before you were born, our parents had a son. Me."

Abby drew in a sharp breath, even though the proof sat right in front of her.

"Our grandfather, Lincoln Camdon, and our father never got along. Lincoln is a tyrant of the worst sort. He wanted his son to follow in his footsteps, but our dad was averse to dealing in the shady side of business. Not that Lincoln ever crossed the line far enough to alert the Feds, but he did unsavory things to get what he wanted. From what my nanny explained to me when I was old enough to understand, when our mother was pregnant with you, the old man claimed me as his heir since his own son failed to fall in line."

Abby sat down next to him on the only bare cot in the room. "That's horrible."

"Yeah, well, it gets worse. Dear old Grandpa put several things in motion to make it look like our mother was going insane. He threatened to have her institutionalized if they didn't agree to take the new baby and leave me with him. Said he'd sue for custody of both children if they didn't agree."

Righteous indignation and a big dose of fury infused Abby and she shot off the cot. "The man's a monster."

"It gets worse. Through the years, I've pieced together what happened. My nanny told me part of it when I was young, and I gathered other pieces here and there. The way I understand it, our parents changed their names and went into hiding when you were a baby, hoping to get me back one day and have a secure location already in place where Lincoln couldn't find us, but unbeknownst to them, Lincoln hired a private investigator to follow them from the time they left.

"My nanny slipped me out three or four different times to see our parents. You were never there. I don't know why. Maybe they were afraid it would confuse you. I was ten years old when my nanny took me to Jackson Hole. Our parents told me they were taking me away with them, and I was so happy."

Abby's heart broke with every word he uttered. That one old man could cause such havoc was appalling.

"They made it sound like an adventure. I assume

they thought they had outsmarted whoever had been following them. I was to go ahead with my nanny, and they would follow us later in their car, just in case someone had tailed the nanny to Jackson. They had decided on a destination, I'm not sure where, but about an hour after we left, two of Lincoln's bodyguards—thugs, really—pulled in front of our car and forced us to stop."

His eyes had a faraway look, but refocused on Abby. "They took the nanny and me back to New York and my nanny was dismissed. I didn't know until years later—Lincoln told me himself—that the men who stayed to watch our parents tried to get them to stop on the road, but they sped up and lost control of their car. They both died in the crash."

Abby slid over and wrapped her arms around her brother. "I'm so sorry for everything that happened to you."

He hugged her back, then pulled away and shrugged, as if it wasn't important, but it was. It was very important.

Abby processed everything he said, then asked, "But why did you fake your death if he wanted you to follow in his footsteps?"

Sam started pacing the room. "I wanted out. I wanted to live my own life, free of the greed and manipulation of the family."

Abby had to know something important before they went any further. "Did you have a happy childhood? Was he good to you?"

His lips tightened. "I did what I was told because he used you to blackmail me."

Shock rendered her speechless for a second. "What do you mean?"

"As a child, he told me something bad would happen to you—my only sister—if I didn't fall in line."

Deep sorrow filled her and Abby lowered her head. Two cold hands encased hers and she looked at her brother.

"Abby, you're my sister, and I loved you from afar. I grew up with everything money could buy. It wasn't so bad. If I was good, every week the old man would show me pictures he had taken of you and mom and dad before they were killed. I didn't want anything to happen to you. At first, I started following you, gathering the courage to introduce myself to you, and I knew something was very wrong when I spotted Julie and Walter in Blessing. I stayed in the background, trying to figure out what was going on. You saw me on that embankment after you were forced off the road. I had followed you to Mocksville and stayed well behind the vehicle that forced you off the road. I pulled onto a dirt road and hid my car, then made my way to the crash site. I had to be sure you were okay.

"I promised myself that I'd introduce myself to you and we would be the family we were meant to be."

"That God meant us to be," she whispered. "And we will have that chance," she said with firm resolve. "I have Noah, and now I have you. Nobody is going to take that away from me. Tell me about the scumbags who are willing to commit murder for money."

Noah and Alex flashed their identifications after entering the Camdon International building, with Bates accompanying them. After discovering that Lincoln Camdon was, indeed, in the country and in his office, Alex grabbed Noah's arm before entering the elevator of the mammoth building. "Let me handle this. You're running too hot and you're out of your jurisdiction."

Noah jerked his arm loose and stepped into the elevator, jabbing the button that would take them to the top floor. "Abby could be murdered at any minute. Don't talk to me about running hot."

Noah didn't miss the look of pity in Alex's eyes. His old partner already thought she was gone, but Noah refused to believe that. God wouldn't take love from him a second time. And he realized with startling clarity that he did love Abby. All crazy steel magnolia mixed with kindness and compassion and a host of wonderful attributes that he didn't have time to list right now. He was ready and willing to take a chance, hoping God would allow them more time together than he had with Noah and Sonya. With renewed resolve he exited the elevator, hoping with every fiber of his being that the perpetrators hadn't already killed Abby and her brother. That they preferred to make it look like an accident to throw off suspicion of murder, and that would give him some time.

A formidable-looking secretary rounded her desk and came running after them as Noah and Alex headed for the only massive double doors on the floor.

"You can't go in there!"

He ignored her and flung the doors open. Marching straight to the huge wooden desk, his gaze bore into the stately man sitting there, talking on the phone.

"Get off the phone. Now!"

The guy wore an expensive suit, and well-trimmed silver hair gave him a distinguished appearance. His eyebrows rose as he took in Noah and Alex. "I'll call you back," he said into the phone and hung up. He peered behind them. "Nancy, that will be all."

Lincoln Camdon's calmness only stirred Noah's anger.

"Security called and said you were on your way up. Can I offer you gentlemen something to drink?"

Noah gripped the edge of the desk with both hands and leaned forward. "What you can do is tell me where Abby Mayfield is, and who's trying to kill her and why."

Either Camdon was a consummate actor, or he didn't have a clue, and if he didn't know where Abby was... Noah refused to go there. He would find her. Alive.

"I don't know what you're talking about." His words didn't match the worried expression on his face.

Noah growled and Bates mimicked him. Camdon shifted in his seat—the only sign of nervousness Noah could see. He had to get through to him. But how? And then it came to him.

"Your grandson, Sam Camdon, is alive."

Lincoln Camdon's face went parchment white and his lips trembled, but he held it together. "What proof do you have?"

"A note Abby left right before she was abducted. Now, I'll ask again, who wants Abby and her brother dead? Who's in line to inherit when you die if both of your grandchildren are gone?"

With a shaky hand, the older man pulled open a desk drawer and opened a bottle of pills. He popped one into his mouth and swallowed. He straightened his tie and squared his shoulders, as if this was a board meeting. Noah wanted to strangle the answers out of him.

"I have cancer. They've given me three months to

live." Camdon raised eyes filled with regret. "I've done many things of which I'm not proud, and I'd like to see my grandchildren again before I die. Abby and Sam's two cousins inherit if there are no other living relatives."

Noah's patience was nearing an end. "Names?"

"Julie and Walter Camdon. My deceased brother's children."

Information ricocheted through Noah's brain and he connected the dots aloud. "Joanne Ferguson and Walter Fleming." He stared at Camdon. "They came to Blessing, Texas, and joined the choir. Abby's the choir director at the church." He was so close now, Noah could almost taste it. "Where would they take Abby and Sam?"

Camdon looked as if he was about to expire on the spot, but the lines on his forehead smoothed out. "His pet project. Walter's pet project. He's been working on something, but wouldn't tell me what it is. He wanted it to be a surprise."

Noah stood up straight. "Walter works for the company?"

Camdon also stood and rounded the desk. "Not after this. I know the warehouse he's using for the project. Let's go."

Noah didn't argue.

Abby's muscles tightened in readiness when the key turned in the lock. She nodded at Sam, who was hiding behind the door. It was a long shot, but it was the only plan she could come up with. The door swung open and Abby shook her head. "Why am I not surprised?"

Joanne Ferguson sashayed into the room. "Yes, it's

me, and if your brother doesn't want you to die this minute, I suggest he move from behind the door."

Sam left his hiding place and came to stand beside her. Walter Fleming followed Joanne into the room, a gun in his hand.

"Hello, cousins," Sam drawled.

"These are the greedy cousins you were telling me about?"

"Now, now, my dear. You're supposed to be a sweet little choir director. Let's not go around slinging mud."

Anger grabbed Abby by the throat. She gritted her teeth and balled her fists. "You hurt my grandmother." It wasn't a question.

"By the way, my name is Julie, not Joanne. And that old bat? She had guts, I'll give her that, but Walter was able to handle her."

Abby saw red and flew at Julie with hands raised and claws extended. She tackled her and they both went sprawling onto the filthy floor. Abby got in a few licks before one of the brutes standing outside the room lifted her off the woman. She struggled, but he had an iron grip.

Julie rolled over and wiped blood off her face. Abby was glad to see a long scratch marring that beautiful, deceitful, murdering face.

Walter helped Julie to her feet and she whipped the gun from his hand. Her face twisted in fury as she pointed the weapon at Abby. "I'll kill you for that," she screeched, but Walter ripped the gun from her hands. She tried to grab it back, but he pushed her away.

"We stick to the plan. It has to look like an accident."

Shoving her hair back, Julie smoothed the lines in her face. "It's too late for that, dear, stupid brother.

After everything that's happened, the cops know who we are now."

"True, but the police have no proof that we killed them. We need to do it somewhere else. A place that's not connected to us. So what if we joined a choir in Blessing, Texas. That doesn't prove we killed them."

She sneered at her cousin. "Maybe you have a few brain cells after all. Fine. Let's get on with it. The sooner these two are dead the better."

TWENTY-THREE

Fear and a sense of urgency made Noah want to storm the warehouse. There was a car parked in front of the building, and Noah's gut told him they were inside.

His heart raced at the idea of Julie and Walter Camdon killing Abby, but Alex's words of wisdom and caution prevailed.

They had called in backup and the building was surrounded by hidden FBI agents. Noah was crouched behind a large bush near the front door, Bates at his side. He gave a thumbs-up to Alex. Lincoln Camdon was to make a call to Julie and request an emergency meeting. Hopefully it would bring them out of the building.

Alex returned a thumbs-up from where he was hiding in the tree line. The call had been made and the die was cast. *God, please let Abby be alive.*

The door creaked open. Julie Camdon strolled out first and glanced over her shoulder. "Let's move it. I want to get this over with."

Bates stood up on all fours, the fur raised on the back of his neck. Noah grabbed his collar. "Hold, boy." Everything had to be timed perfectly. Noah waited until everyone was out and the door closed behind them. Julie and Walter Camdon had two thugs in tow. The one bringing up the rear had a strong hold on Abby's arm. She was struggling and it infuriated him.

But she was alive! Abby was still alive!

He released the dog's collar. No command was necessary. The dog silently circled around to the back of the group as they stepped out of the building, then Bates lunged and sank his teeth into the guy's arm. Abby stumbled free and fell to the pavement. Noah burst from the shrubbery and yelled, "Drop your weapons."

The other thug dropped his gun as soon as he turned and saw his partner writhing on the ground, suffering Bates's attention.

Weapons drawn, FBI agents surrounded the group.

Everyone threw their hands in the air except for one. Julie Camdon casually reached into her purse, pulled out a gun, whipped around and pointed it at Abby.

Abby was on her knees, trying to push herself off the ground. He'd never get to her in time. He watched, as if in slow motion, the gun rise into the air. Julie's finger pressed the trigger.

"No!" he yelled and took a giant leap forward, but he was too late. Something flew past him and the sound of a shot rang in his ears. Time was suspended as he hit the ground and rolled to his feet. His heart in his throat, Noah raced toward Abby, who was curled up in a ball on the ground. He wrapped his arms around her and his voice shook. "Abby, are you okay? Talk to me. Say something, please."

The chaos around him faded into the background as she uncurled her body and looked up at him. Tears filled her eyes and she clasped the front of his shirt.

"I—I'm okay." After a second, she pulled back and twisted her head around in a frantic motion. "Sam! Where's Sam?"

"I'm right here, brave sister of mine." Sam squatted down close to them. "I'd never have believed it if I hadn't seen it with my own two eyes. The old man had a heart after all."

Abby grabbed his hand and squeezed. "I'm so glad you're okay. I just found you, and now we have a lifetime to get to know one another. What do you mean the old man had a heart after all?"

Sam moved to the side and Noah saw Lincoln Camdon lying a few feet away. He had insisted on accompanying them to the warehouse. The ambulance attendants had arrived and were working hard to revive him. He'd been the blur Noah had seen right before he jumped forward. The old man had taken a bullet for Abby.

Noah kissed Abby on the forehead. "It's your grandfather, sweetheart. He saved your life."

Tears flowed freely down her cheeks and Noah wanted to sweep her away from this horror.

"My grandfather?" she whispered.

Sam grimaced. "Julie's dead. One of the agents shot her at the same time she fired on Abby."

Abby tried to regain her feet and Noah helped her up. "Noah, I have to see him. My grandfather. I have to talk to him."

He wanted to wrap Abby in his arms and take her away from this nightmare, but the pleading look in her eyes had him moving her forward. He shoved through the attendants working on Camdon and took a step back as she knelt by the old man's side and lifted his hand.

Several minutes later, Camdon was pronounced dead and Abby got to her feet. She moved into Noah's open arms and hugged him tight. Pulling back, she peered into his eyes. "I thanked him for saving my life, and told him how to get to heaven, that there was still time, if he wanted to. I know the whole story now. He treated my parents abominably, but he didn't hurt Grammy. Julie and Walter did that." She glanced at the covered gurney that was carrying Julie away. "She hurt my grandmother, and I'll have to work on forgiving her, but now she'll never have a chance to ask for forgiveness."

Noah's heart melted at her words—the mercy she showed toward others. Lincoln Camdon had told him the whole sorry tale on the way to the warehouse. Noah held Abby in his arms, aching for her loss, but proud of the generosity she had shown others. This woman was meant for him and he sensed God's blessing.

"Abby." She looked into his eyes. "I'm in love with you, for as long as God allows us to be together. Please say you'll marry me."

"Noah—"

He placed a finger on her lips. She tried to speak again and he hushed her. "I love you with all my heart and I know Dylan will love you, too."

"Noah—"

"Don't say anything now. Just think about—"

Grabbing him by his shirtfront, she kissed him smack on the lips, pulled back and grinned. "If you'd let me get a word in edgewise, I'd give you my answer.

I love you, too. With all of my heart. And the answer
is yes. Yes! Yes!"

Noah picked her up and whirled her around, his
heart filled with joy. God really did have a knack for
bringing good things out of ashes.

EPILOGUE

Six months later

Abby placed a hand over the butterflies in her stomach and smiled nervously at the five most important people in her life and Bates. They stood outside the huge doors guarding the inner sanctum of Camdon International. They were on the top floor of a thirty-story building located in the heart of New York City.

"Do I look okay?"

A lot had happened over the last six months. Her grandfather and Julie were dead, and Walter Camdon would spend a long time in jail. She visited him every week, trying to help in any way she could. He still hated her, but she prayed for him daily. Noah and his father were finally communicating, and he had allowed his dad to visit Dylan. He also promised to get in touch with his half sisters.

When the FBI interrogated Walter, he admitted that he thought the truth was so buried it would never come to light, even though he'd left the three pictures that could possibly lead to his family, to throw everyone off the scent and provide a distraction from their real purpose, which was to remove Abby so they could inherit the Camdon fortune. Walter admitted that they thought Sam was dead, and found out about Abby when they bribed someone to get a copy of the will. They discovered that Abby was next in line to inherit before Julie and Walter.

Noah gave her a peck on the cheek. "Don't forget, deep down, buried under all that Southern charm, lives a steel magnolia, Mrs. Galloway."

The butterflies settled down. "I love hearing you call me that—not," she added, "a steel magnolia, but your wife."

Abby reached over and hugged her grandmother. "Thank you for coming, and thank you for moving to Blessing."

Grammy hugged her back and swiped a tear from her cheek. "I'm just glad to be alive and kicking 'cause I got a new grandson and great-grandson to pester."

Abby squatted in front of Dylan and gave him a hug. He hugged her fiercely, then ducked his head in embarrassment. "I love you, Dylan."

"I love you, too. Mom," he added while studying his feet.

Her heart filled to bursting with happiness and love, Abby held out a hand and her brother took it. "You ready to face the wolves?"

His lips curled in a grin. "You take the lead."

After touring the numerous personal and corporate holdings, Abby and Sam had decided to sell off the posh, expensive houses, cars, etcetera, and had agreed that Sam would handle the business. Abby already had several important jobs: wife, mother, choir director and piano teacher. She and Noah, along with

Dylan and Grammy, would reside in Blessing. Sam would visit often.

Gripping the door handle, Abby realized everything had come full circle. She whispered, "Mom, Dad, I hope you're watching. I love you."

She and her brother opened the imposing double doors simultaneously. Abby marched to the head of the long, intimidating table, Sam at her side. She stifled a laugh as the overpaid department heads of the massive corporation stiffened in their seats when Bates circled the table and got a good sniff of each person. With all eyes on her, she gave the room of well-tailored suits her sweetest smile, then released the steel magnolia.

"Good morning, ladies and gentlemen. There's going to be a few changes now that my brother and I are in charge of Camdon International…"

After the meeting, Abby melted into Noah's arms.

"We were listening at the door. You and Sam did great in there."

Abby smiled when Bates let out a happy bark and Dylan laughed, then she stared deeply into Noah's eyes. "I'm glad Sam is handling the company. Did you know they have interests in everything from vacuum cleaners to technology? My grandfather had his hands in many pies. What's it called? Diversification. Noah, we have to get back to Blessing."

He kissed her forehead. "What's the hurry? We could spend a few days in New York, go out to dinner and relax for a change."

She grinned. "I have a church to rebuild and a new piano to buy."

He kissed her on the lips, right there in front of everyone, before turning her loose and facing their small group. "Okay, people, time to go home."

She waved goodbye to Sam and he disappeared back inside the conference room. She turned, took a deep breath, grinned and followed her new family down the hall and out of the building, her heart bursting with love and excitement for their new lifelong journey together.

* * * * *

SPECIAL EXCERPT FROM

Love Inspired.
SUSPENSE

A K-9 cop must keep his childhood friend alive when she finds herself in the crosshairs of a drug-smuggling operation.

Read on for a sneak preview of
Act of Valor *by Dana Mentink,*
the next exciting installment in the
True Blue K-9 Unit *miniseries, available in May 2019*
from Love Inspired Suspense.

Officer Zach Jameson surveyed the throng of people congregated around the ticket counter at LaGuardia Airport. Most ignored Zach and K-9 partner, Eddie, and that suited him just fine. Two months earlier he would have greeted people with a smile, or at least a polite nod while he and Eddie did their work of scanning for potential drug smugglers. These days he struggled to keep his mind on his duty while the ever-present darkness nibbled at the edges of his soul.

Eddie plopped himself on Zach's boot. He stroked the dog's ears, trying to clear away the fog that had descended the moment he heard of his brother's death.

Zach hadn't had so much as a whiff of suspicion that his brother was in danger. His brain knew he should talk to somebody, somebody like Violet Griffin, his friend from childhood who'd reached out so many times, but his heart would not let him pass through the dark curtain.

"Just get to work," he muttered to himself as his phone rang. He checked the number.

Violet.

He considered ignoring it, but Violet didn't ever call unless she needed help, and she rarely needed anyone. Strong enough to run a ticket counter at LaGuardia and have enough energy left over to help out at Griffin's, her family's diner. She could handle belligerent customers in both arenas and bake the best apple pie he'd ever had the privilege to chow down.

It almost made him smile as he accepted the call.

"Someone's after me, Zach."

Panic rippled through their connection. Panic, from a woman who was tough as they came. "Who? Where are you?"

Her breath was shallow as if she was running.

"I'm trying to get to the break room. I can lock myself in, but I don't… I can't…" There was a clatter.

"Violet?" he shouted.

But there was no answer.

Don't miss
Act of Valor *by Dana Mentink,*
available May 2019 wherever
Love Inspired® Suspense *books and ebooks are sold.*

www.LoveInspired.com

LISEXP0419

WE HOPE YOU
ENJOYED THIS

LOVE
INSPIRED®
SUSPENSE
BOOK.

Discover more **heart-pounding**

romances of **danger** and **faith** from the

Love Inspired Suspense series.

Be sure to look for all six Love Inspired

Suspense books every month.

Love Inspired® SUSPENSE

www.LoveInspired.com

SPECIAL EXCERPT FROM

When a guide-dog trainer becomes a target of a
dangerous crime ring, a K-9 cop and his loyal
partner will work together to keep her safe.

Read on for a sneak preview of
Blind Trust by Laura Scott,
the next exciting installment in the
True Blue K-9 Unit miniseries, available
June 2019 from Love Inspired Suspense.

Eva Kendall slowed her pace as she approached the
training facility where she worked training guide dogs.

Using her key, she entered the training center, thinking
about the male chocolate Lab named Cocoa that she would
work with this morning. Cocoa was a ten-week-old puppy
born to Stella, a gift from the Czech Republic to the NYC
K-9 Command Unit located in Queens. Most of Stella's
pups were being trained as police dogs, but not Cocoa.
In less than a month after basic puppy training, Cocoa
would be able to go home with Eva to be fostered during
his initial first-year training to become a full-fledged guide
dog. Once that year passed, guide dogs like Cocoa would
return to the center to train with their new owners.

A few steps into the building, Eva frowned at the loud
thumps interspersed between a cacophony of barking. The
raucous noise from the various canines contained a level
of panic and fear rather than excitement.

Concerned, she moved quickly through the dimly lit training center to the back hallway, where the kennels were located. Normally she was the first one in every morning, but maybe one of the other trainers had gotten an early start.

Rounding the corner, she paused in the doorway when she saw a tall, heavyset stranger scooping Cocoa out of his kennel. Panic squeezed her chest. "Hey! What are you doing?"

The ferocious barking increased in volume, echoing off the walls and ceiling. The stranger must have heard her. He turned to look at her, then roughly tucked Cocoa under his arm like a football.

"No! Stop!" Panicked, Eva charged toward the man, desperately wishing she had a weapon of some sort.

"Get out of my way," he said in a guttural voice.

"No. Put that puppy down right now!" Eva stopped and stood her ground.

"Last chance," he taunted, coming closer.

Don't miss
Blind Trust *by Laura Scott,*
available June 2019 wherever
Love Inspired® Suspense books and ebooks are sold.

www.LoveInspired.com

Love Inspired®

Inspirational Romance to Warm Your Heart and Soul

Join our social communities to connect with other readers who share your love!

Sign up for the Love Inspired newsletter at **www.LoveInspired.com** to be the first to find out about upcoming titles, special promotions and exclusive content.

CONNECT WITH US AT:

Facebook.com/groups/HarlequinConnection

 Facebook.com/LoveInspiredBooks

 Twitter.com/LoveInspiredBks

LISOCIAL2018

Earn points on your purchase of new Harlequin books from participating retailers.

Turn your points into **FREE BOOKS** of your choice!

Join for FREE today at
www.HarlequinMyRewards.com.

Harlequin My Rewards is a free program (no fees) without any commitments or obligations.

MYR18